HEART
BREAKER

Also by Robert Ferrigno

THE HORSE LATITUDES

THE CHESHIRE MOON

DEAD MAN'S DANCE

DEAD SILENT

HEART
BREAKER

Robert Ferrigno

WARNER
VISION
BOOKS

A Time Warner Company

WARNER BOOKS EDITION

Copyright © 1999 by Robert Ferrigno

Warner Vision is a registered trademark of Warner Books, Inc.

Cover art directed by Diane Luger
Cover design by Janet Perr
Photos from Photonica

This Warner Books edition is published in arrangement with Random House, Inc.

Warner Books, Inc.
1271 Avenue of the Americas
New York, NY 10020

Visit our Web site at
www.twbookmark.com

 A Time Warner Company

Printed in the United States of America

First Paperback Printing: November 2000

10 9 8 7 6 5 4 3 2 1

To my old friend, William Ungerman,
and my new son, Luc

Acknowledgments

My thanks to Doug Stumpf for his insight and humor, and to James in Corpus Christi for the recipe for shrimp à la Jaime. My agent, Mary Evans, is a tenacious and creative advocate, and I am grateful for her efforts on my behalf. My deepest appreciation to my editor, Sonny Mehta.

HEART BREAKER

Prologue

—

"You got a conscience, Valentine, that's your problem."

"I don't have any problems," said Val.

Junior snorted, but kept his face pressed against the telescope mounted on the patio railing of his penthouse. "A conscience can weigh a man down. If his friends aren't careful, it can drag them under with him."

"I don't have any friends, either."

"You done hurt my feelings," said Junior, looking over at him. "Here I called you over to ask a favor and now you tell me you got no friends. What am I to think?"

Val let the request linger. Junior always had a favor to ask, and that was fine—Val did favors for a living. He was a free agent brokering information to all comers, a wiseass with heavy nerve and heavy connections. Still, there was something about the call from Junior this morning, something in his voice . . . a coy eagerness, that was unsettling. Val had almost begged off, but Junior was smart. Excuses would have just made him more suspicious.

"Check out the scope," invited Junior. "We got teenage

tuna catching rays at four o'clock. Zoom in and see if she's a true blonde."

"I believe you." From the waterfront penthouse Val could see girls in bikinis walking along the beach, waves lapping at their toes. Boys played Frisbee, making diving catches, showing off. Overhead, a small plane towed a pink banner advertising one-dollar Jello-O shots at a local titty bar. "I heard you had to dump your strip clubs. How does a man take a loss selling sex and booze to horny drunks?"

"I made money on that deal," said Junior.

"The Indians made money selling Manhattan, too."

Junior spit a brown stream of Copenhagen off the balcony. They stood next to each other, hands on the railing, watching the tobacco juice fall through the air, until it smacked onto the white sand, just missing a tourist lugging a Disney World beach umbrella. "I still got a favor to ask you. Most people, I say I need a little help, they's eager to get on my good side."

Val turned his face into the sun so that his expression was unreadable. His nose was prominent, and his long black hair, combed straight back, gleamed in the sunlight like the wing of a crow. "Yeah, but I've *seen* your good side, Junior."

Junior chuckled, his eyes cold as granite. He was a paunchy cracker in his early forties, with a pocked face, hair like a sunbleached mop, and a nose perpetually peeling.

Most of the good ol' boys who originally ran the drug trade in Florida had been killed off or scared off when the South Americans moved in. Not Junior. The Cali cartel tortured informers with chain saws; Junior threw a barbecue, sent the blackened head to the magpie's family in a Baskin-Robbins cake box. The Cubans introduced Mac-10 drivebys; Junior responded with a truck bomb that leveled Diego Ortiz' mansion on Key Biscayne, killing Ortiz, his wife and children, five servants, and eight bodyguards.

Junior glanced toward the door to the penthouse. "Valentine, es un hombre divertido, verdad, Armando?"

Staring at Val from the doorway was Junior's bodyguard, resplendent in a white sailor suit with gold buttons and epaulets—a slender sociopath from the Medellín slums with a mouth like a Kewpie doll, his hair a nest of braids tied with gold, blue, and red ribbons, the colors of the Colombian flag. He was what the South Americans called a dead boy, an utterly loyal assassin, devoid of compassion or desire. Armando had committed his first contract killing at the age of ten, put a bullet through the ear canal of a priest who refused to hear the confession of an unrepentant drug lord. He was almost nineteen now. He still fingered the priest's rosary beads when he went to mass.

"Armando don't like you, Valentine," said Junior.

"*There's* a blow to my self-image," said Val, wondering what Junior really wanted.

"What do you think of my new place?" said Junior, casting his arms wide. "The estate was nice, but how can you defend all that acreage? I was going broke feeding those fucking Dobermans." He ambled back to the telescope. "Penthouse is better. Private elevator goes direct to a private garage."

Val spotted a van at the far end of the beach, a blue and white custom rig out there all alone. It was Steffano's van. He slowly looked away, a bad taste rising in his throat. "I read yesterday that a tube of acne cream used by Kurt Cobain sold at auction for over a thousand dollars."

Junior unconsciously touched his own cratered cheeks.

"I don't know if it was Clearasil or Oxy-5, but—"

"What's your point?"

Val shrugged. "Kurt Cobain treasured his privacy too—now he's dead and people are selling off the contents of his medicine chest. Maybe if something happens to you, Armando will have a yard sale, too. Wonder what your toothbrush would go for? Or your Maalox?"

Junior stared at him. "That ain't funny."

Val watched the van out of the corner of his eyes. Something was wrong.

Junior placed a hand on Val's shoulder, enveloping the two of them in a fog of Canoe aftershave. "I still need that favor." He showed Val his brown-stained teeth. "I got a funeral I want you to go to, boy."

The balcony was bathed in sunlight, but Val felt as though he had stepped into a pool of ice water. Armando was quick, too quick, but if it came down to it, Val was going to find time to throw Junior over the balcony and onto the concrete seawall below. Like the poet said, Don't go gentle, take somebody to hell with you.

"Don't get your bowels in an uproar," said Junior, grinning. "It's my mama's funeral I'm talking about, not yours. I want you to stand in for me. Take my place. Maybe say a few words at the boneyard. Funeral's in Leesburg, about a two-hour drive outside of Atlanta—"

"You're not going to your mother's funeral?"

"Never been to a funeral, and I don't intend to start off with my mama." Junior sucked back snot. "Besides, I got business here to attend to."

Val watched the tourist struggling over the soft sand toward the water, dragging the Disney World umbrella. A gust of wind opened the umbrella and sent it tumbling down the beach, Donald and Mickey and Goofy turning end over end in the bright sunshine. He didn't believe Junior's story, and he still wanted to know what Steffano was doing parked over there.

"It's funny," said Junior, staring off into the blue distance. "Here I am with a better view than God, and my mama died without ever seeing the ocean. I tried. I even sent a private plane to pick her up, but she wouldn't have it. Said she was born in Leesburg and that was good enough for her." His jaws worked as he stood there, hands on the balcony. "Couple years ago I bought her a new Caddie, pink one with all the trimmings, like Elvis done for his mama. No go. She kept it out in the backyard, letting the weeds grow past the white sidewalls, and never drove it, not once. Said she didn't want folks to think she was uppity, but I think it was something else." He turned to Val. "You believe in the idea of 'dirty money'?"

"Absolutely."

"Absolutely?" Junior was amused, at first anyway. "You picked a damn funny way of making a living then, boy."

Val held Junior's attention, allowing the glare off the sand to start Junior's eyes watering.

Junior blinked. "Fuck it," he said, wiping his eyes. "What do you say, Valentine? You going to the funeral for me? Georgia's real pretty this time a year."

"Why don't you send Armando?" Val glanced at the boy. "He could stop off at Disney World on the way back, buy some mouse ears to go with that little sailor suit of his."

Armando glared at him. His fingers twitched slightly.

Junior laughed and spit over the side. "They ain't never seen anybody like Armando in Leesburg, and they ain't in a hurry to start." He bent over the telescope, slowly swiveling it across the beach toward the van. "I trust Armando with my life, but let's be honest, he looks like a fruit with those hairbraids and painted nails. Shoot, he shows up at my mama's funeral, he's gonna have to kill two or three of my uncles before the service. No, I need *you*, Valentine."

"You still haven't told me why."

Junior scowled. "I got a cousin, Nestor. Me and him grew up together, shared a fold-out sleeper couch in the living room, but we never got along. Little piss-ant used to count the beans on my plate to make sure I didn't get more than him. Well, now I need Nestor's help. I want you to talk to him, Valentine—you got the gift of gab and them eyes a yours don't miss a thing. Talk to him, Val. He'll be at the funeral, that's certain. Nestor dearly loved my mama."

"I don't think so."

"You got family, Valentine?"

"You know I don't."

"That's right." Junior nodded. "No Mama, no Papa, no kin at all. No hostages, huh?" He cleared his lower lip with his tongue. "Just a man who walked out of a cool mist one morning and started making things happen. I remember hearing about this crazy-ass swamp rat, who was wheelin 'n' dealin, moving fast, ready for anything."

"You sound like you're in love, Junior."

Junior snorted. "You're a charmer, Valentine, but my heart belongs to Vanna. You keep your Kathy Lee and Mary Hart, I'd pork Vanna White from now to kingdom come and never complain." He spit over the side, looking at Val. "Fuck it. You going to Georgia for me or not?"

Val wanted to get out of there, call Steffano, and tell him to drive away. *Now*. "I don't like funerals either, Junior. I look at the casket, smell the stink of those lilies, and worry I could catch something."

"Yeah, there is that." A trickle of brown spittle ran down Junior's chin. He wiped it off with the back of his hand. "Maybe I'll just wire a candygram to the wake. Nestor likes them cashew chews." He shrugged. "Sending you to the funeral might have been a bad idea anyway. Your attitude's all wrong. All this bullshit talk about Disney World and zit cream. . . . Nestor ain't as patient as me."

"It's getting late—"

"What's your hurry?" Junior leaned into the telescope, sighting down the beach, fine-tuning the image. "Something here I want you to see."

Val felt an ache in his stomach, like falling out of a tree and having the wind knocked out of you. Nothing to do but fight off the panic and try to keep breathing.

Junior waved Val over. "Check it out."

Val peered through the eyepiece, saw a close-up of the rear window of the van, with Steffano's face, bruised purple, pressed against the glass. The focus was so sharp that Val could see the terror in his eyes. He glanced at Junior. "What's up with Steffano?"

"He's a cop," said Junior, "part of some special state task force. I had the Jackson brothers bring him round for a consult. They been at it for a while now."

"A cop?" Val shook his head. "I don't see it."

"I didn't believe it at first either," Junior said.

"Are you sure?"

"Ain't nothing certain," said Junior. "Sure enough, though, I hate taking chances—you know that—I prefer my fishing when it's done in a barrel."

"Yeah, and maybe toss in an M-80 so you don't have to bother baiting a hook."

"An M-80, that's a good one." Junior smiled. "I like that." He snapped his fingers. "Armando, binoculars, por favor."

Val saw Steffano's head pulled back, then slammed forward into the window, spiderwebbing the glass. "If you're right about Steffano, you're going to bring down some heat. Cops tend to frown on one of their own getting—"

"Not if they think he's gone bad," said Junior, watching the van through the binoculars. "Internal Affairs is going to find a couple of pounds of coke and twenty thousand cash in his crib. Steffano ain't gonna get his name on a plaque at the academy."

Val's mouth was dry. "You should recheck your information. Steffano has good credentials—"

"You want to vouch for him?" Junior asked.

"I worked with him plenty of times," said Val. "I trust him as much as I trust anyone."

"That don't really answer the question, does it?"

Val had no weapon. Armando patted down everyone who entered the penthouse for guns or wires. He glanced toward Armando poised in the doorway—the deadboy utterly immobile, waiting. "Steffano found that deserted airstrip outside Ocala. Remember? We all made money off of Steffano. He deserves—"

"He deserves everything he gets," said Junior.

Steffano's face was jammed against the rear window, his mouth moving. Val was glad he couldn't read lips. "Who gave up Steffano?" he said, still looking through the telescope. "Maybe you should consider the source. We all make enemies, Junior. I'd hate to see you made a fool of by someone who wanted to take over Steffano's action." His head being pulled slowly back, Steffano was screaming now—a pantomime of pain. Blood poured from his nostrils as he struggled.

"Look at that boy holler," said Junior, his eyes fitted to the binoculars. "You just know he's making that van echo. Must be like a funhouse on Halloween."

"I have an interest in keeping Steffano alive—"

"Sure as shit sounds like it," Junior said.

"I'm working with him on something up north. If he's a cop I want to know it, but I don't think you should ruin a sweet deal for me unless you're sure."

"When I was in seventh grade," said Junior, not taking his eyes off the van, "me and Nestor would sit on a hill overlooking this drive-in and watch the skinflicks. No sound, just the night and all that soft pink . . . um umm, good. The silence made the movies even . . . sexier somehow. Why do you think that is, Valentine?"

"Call the Jackson brothers," Val said. "Make them stop. I need this deal up north to happen, Junior. I'll make it worth your—" Blood splashed across the rear window of the van; red streamers trickled down the glass.

"Shucks. Show's over and done." Junior exhaled slowly. "Damn. I told them Jackson boys to take their time, but you know how they are." He turned to Val. "What was you saying, Valentine?"

Val stepped away from the telescope.

"You're upset. I can see it," Junior said. "See, there's that conscience of yours acting up again. I don't know how you stand that thing in your head, all the time *yappa-yappa*." He pulled a cell-phone out of his pocket, flipped it open. "Howdy." Val hadn't even heard it buzz. Junior looked at Val as he listened, one finger massaging his gums. It seemed like it took forever. "Okey-dokey," he said finally, snapping the phone shut. "Steffano admitted he was po-lice, but he said he was working alone. The boys asked him over and over and *then* some, but your name never came up."

Val knew Junior still had doubts about him—a man in his position couldn't afford not to—but Val felt only the sun on his back. "You sound surprised, Junior."

"A little, but hey, I'm happy you're no cop. You crack me up." Junior peeled a tiny patch of skin off his blistered nose. "I got to tell you, though, Armando is plain heartbroke you ain't got a badge somewhere. I can't figure out why he's taken such a hate on you."

Val couldn't think of anything clever to say; he felt numb.

Junior rocked on his heels. "You don't look so good, Valentine. You're not going to cry or nothing, are you?"

"Yeah, boo-hoo, motherfucker."

Junior laughed. "See, that's what I mean. You crack me up, boy." He checked his watch. "*Jeopardy* is on in eleven minutes. You want to stick around? It's Tournament of Champions week."

Val looked past Junior, staring right at the van. "Some other time."

Chapter One

The early bird gets the worm, my *ass*. Val watched the apartment manager's fat yellow tomcat creep through the weeds toward a bird pecking away at something in the dirt. He had just started up the stairs when he sensed movement out of the corner of his eye. He whirled, reaching for the pistol under his T-shirt and thumbing off the safety.

Val slipped the pistol back into his waistband, smiling at himself. If there had been anyone there to see him drawing down on a cat he might have been embarrassed, but it was five A.M. and he was all alone. Paranoia was an old habit—like his grandmother said, better to have good reflexes than good credit. People got killed when they least expected it. They drove their cars into a bridge abutment while tuning in a radio station. They slipped in the shower and broke their necks. Sometimes they awakened from a sound sleep, eyes wide, staring into death.

That's how the Jackson brothers had surprised Steffano, the two of them dragging him out of bed by his hair while he cursed them, told them they were in *big* fucking trouble. The day after watching Steffano die, Val had ambled into the Jacksons' favorite Cuban restaurant, sat down and shared a plate of black beans and shredded chicken with the two of them, buying them pitcher after pitcher of Carte Blanca, listening as Tommy Jackson bragged on how they had pulled Steffano from a wet dream into a nightmare, his brother Troy laughing so hard he sloshed beer down the front of his overalls. Val had laughed along with them, ladling on the hot sauce, his mouth on fire, his eyes cold.

It had been almost eight months since Steffano had been murdered, almost that long since Val had fled the scene, flying out of Miami International under a different name, short-hopping all over the country before landing in L.A. He had been one step ahead of Junior that night. Heart attack or a straight razor, it didn't matter. People needed to pay attention to the signs—there were always signs posted, warning signals, but most people just didn't notice them. Steffano should have known better. Val saw ghosts in the steam from his coffee; he saw phantoms in the rain. He didn't miss a thing. Not anymore.

The small brown bird looked up, then went back to whatever it was peck-peck-pecking at. Wise up, birdie, before it's too late. The dew on the grass glistened like pearls as the cat bellied forward. The scene looked like a commercial for air freshener, but Val knew the killing ground when he saw it.

Val had seen bird carcasses on the manager's doormat, and late one night he had stepped on tiny bones on the stairway, heard them crunch underfoot. If Val could fly, he'd eat on the wing, he'd float high above the earth drinking raindrops and never touch down. If he could fly.

Val heard a noise at the top of the stairs, saw a woman round the corner and start down the steps toward him, a scuba tank slung over her shoulder, mask and fins in one hand. She was so intent on watching her footing that she didn't see him yet. It was Kyle from #301, wearing cut-offs and a black wet-vest, her dark hair pulled back from her face. Val had spotted her when he moved into the apartment complex last month—a pretty, lanky brunette with a deep tan and a kickass walk, like she knew right where she was going. She lived in the apartment down the hall from him, but they had never met. He had looked up #301 on the row of mailboxes though. At first he thought Kyle was a man's name, that maybe she lived with a boyfriend, but the manager had cackled at the idea and said, "*That* one scares the men off." The manager didn't know what she was talking about.

Last evening he had seen Kyle and her neighbor, Brenda, sitting out on Kyle's patio, exhausted from their regular run on the beach. They sat with their bare feet propped on the wrought-iron railing, sweat rolling down their arms as they tilted back beers. He had stared at them for a long time, listening to their throaty laughter, thinking, keep Niagara Falls and the Mona Lisa and even the sunset off Key West, keep them all, this was as beautiful as it got.

The cat inched closer to the bird, back flattened, whiskers fanned. Val grabbed a rolled-up advertising circular from the steps, hurled it into the grass, sending the bird and cat scattering. The bird settled into a stunted palm tree and gazed at Val, its head cocked. You're welcome, thought Val.

"Nice throw," said Kyle, looking down at him. "You're ready for your own paper route."

"I've got the arm," said Val, "but I couldn't handle the responsibility." She didn't react. "My name is Val Duran. I live here too," he said, trying to reassure her.

"Congratulations." She didn't look like she needed reassurance. "I'm Kyle Abbott. I've seen you around."

"I've seen you around, too."

"I'll have to tell my friend Brenda that I finally met you," said Kyle, the air tank perfectly balanced on her shoulder, as she took in his long hair, jeans, and gory Cycle Zombies III T-shirt. There was an alertness about her that attracted him and at the same time made him uneasy. "Brenda has all kinds of ideas about you because you come and go at all hours and always keep your blinds pulled. She's got this thing for bad boys."

"Brenda is going to be disappointed."

Kyle fought back a smile. "First she thought you were in a band—loud, fast rules, that's Brenda's motto, but she never saw you with an instrument, and your apartment stays pretty quiet, so she gave up on that one. Then she thought maybe you were a dealer, but you never have any visitors. . . ."

The zipper on Kyle's wet-vest was half-down. She was tan as far as Val could see. "What was *your* guess?"

"What makes you think I had a guess?" said Kyle. Val hesitated and she smiled again, her light brown eyes crinkling. "Brenda thinks you're cute."

Val was too smart to ask her what she thought. He was tall and wiry but "cute" had never come up. He had his maternal grandmother's flat Seminole cheekbones and smooth dark skin, a sharp contrast to his deep-set blue eyes. It gave him an exotic look. Even in south Florida, where he was born and raised, people had asked him where he was from. The Colombians recognized him as a mestizo, a mixed-breed—they did business with him, but they didn't trust those blue eyes. Smart people, those Colombians.

Kyle reached out with her free hand, gently touched

the scar just above his left ear where the hair didn't grow. "That's a mean one. I bet there's a story behind it."

Val's skin was hot where she had touched him. She was curious, but it wasn't going to do her any good. They stayed on the landing, facing each other, the two of them awkward now. The apartments around them were silent, filled with heavy sleepers waiting for an alarm clock to detonate their rest, but Val and Kyle were alone on the steps, caught at first light.

In the distance Val could hear the surf pounding against the shore, the waves driven by a southwest swell. The Pacific off southern California was colder than the warm waters of the Gulf Stream, less forgiving, but it was an ocean, deep enough to hide anything in. It would do. Kyle shifted the air-tank to her other shoulder. Val moved aside to give her room to pass, but she stayed where she was. He was glad. "Good day to go diving," he offered.

"Do you dive?"

"It's been a while."

Val waited for her to invite him to dive with her sometime, to tell him she knew where he could rent some equipment, but instead Kyle turned toward the rising sun, half-closed her eyes, her face a mask of beaten gold. She was older than he had first thought. From a distance she was early twenties, but up close he could see a network of wrinkles at the corners of her eyes and laugh-lines around her mouth. Early to mid-thirties was his guess. It looked fine on her. Val had some of those wrinkles himself. Some of those same laugh-lines, too.

The landlady's tomcat hissed at Val, baring its teeth as it slunk past the bottom of the stairs.

"I don't blame him," said Kyle, as the cat disappeared around the corner of the building. "You shouldn't have interrupted him before. That sparrow was his breakfast. Cats kill birds; that's what they're supposed to do."

"Not this morning," said Val. "Survival of the fittest is fine in the abstract, but I looked at that mangy cat and just decided, screw the prime directive, I'm helping out Tweetie."

"The prime directive?" She was amused. "Like from *Star Trek*?" An airhorn blared in the distance, the sound of an early morning trucker hurrying to beat the traffic. Kyle kept her eyes on Val. "Your naïve faith in the value of intervention . . . it's sweet, but futile."

"Don't make this into anything important," he said. "I just threw a newspaper, that's all."

"You threw a newspaper to save a bird from being eaten"—Kyle was enjoying herself—"but what about the worms and grubs that the sparrow eats? Who's going to save them? Don't they count?"

"Not to me. I'm not a Buddhist—Richard Gere and the Dalai Lama can sweep ants off the sidewalk, but bugs are just bugs to me."

"So life and death is one big popularity contest to you?" she teased. They had moved closer without being aware of it. "There are creatures you like and creatures you don't like. The ones you like are worth saving; the ones you don't—"

"I *like* cats. I just don't like that particular cat."

"I see," said Kyle. "You have your preferences, but they're not necessarily species-specific."

"Species-specific? I think I'm in over my head here."

"Oh, I doubt that."

The sun was warmer now. At least he assumed it was the sun. "Are you some kind of scientist? You talk like a PBS special."

"I know I tend to lecture—it's an occupational hazard." Kyle held up her face mask and flippers. "I'm a marine biologist."

"Can you get me Shamu's autograph?"

"I don't approve of aquatic parks," said Kyle. "Orca doing tricks for handouts, seals dressed in top hats—it's disgusting."

Val put his hands up. "There's no tuna in my cupboard. You can check."

"I take my work seriously," Kyle admitted. "Too seriously, according to some people. You prefer a sparrow to a domesticated tomcat. I prefer gray whales to just about anything else. They're truly magnificent, Val. You look into their eyes, and they look back into *you*. Our preferences for sparrows or whales is irrelevant though," she said wistfully. "Nature is amoral—speed and cunning, camouflage and adaptability, tooth and claw, that's all that counts."

"Mother Nature loves a winner," Val agreed. He was so close to her that he could see the sun-bleached down at the edge of her jawline. "Me, I put my money on a long shot every time." He nodded at the bird watching them from the palm tree. "Maybe Tweetie there will wise up now that I've given him a second chance. Maybe he'll get faster . . . stay more alert . . . maybe he'll carry a stun gun next time."

"Maybe he'll get eaten as soon as you leave."

Val laughed along with her. She was right of course. They both knew it.

The sky was streaked with purple and orange. Brushfires had been burning east of Los Angeles for the last week, driven by the Santa Ana coming off the Mojave. Thousands of acres of scrub were going up in greasy flames, the fire fed by the hot desert wind that sent ashes

as far as the Pacific. Fat white flakes floated down between Val and Kyle like confetti from a parade somewhere.
He wondered what she was thinking, then glanced around,
suddenly aware of how quiet it was, how vulnerable they
were standing out on the stairs, just a shot away, a kiss
away . . . ashes, ashes all fall down.

Kyle checked her black diving watch. "I have to go."

"Can I help you with that tank?"

She pretended to swoon, then nudged him aside with
a hip-check, grinning. "Thanks, Val, but when I can't manage my own gear, I'll take up embroidery."

Their bare arms brushed. Maybe it was just the warmth
of her skin, but he felt the strangest sensation . . . an intimacy with her that was totally unexpected.

Kyle looked at him funny, as though she had felt it,
too. "See you later."

Val watched her continue down the stairs, her dark
ponytail bobbing along the back of her neck with every
step. He watched her until she had almost reached her
Chevy Suburban, when she turned around and looked right
at him, as though she knew he would still be there. They
stared at each other, neither of them moving, waiting for
something to happen, an excuse to turn away. She finally
waved and he waved back, then hurried up the stairs to
his apartment.

Val was tired, but he stayed awake for almost an hour
thinking about Kyle, seeing her face looking up at him
from the bottom of the steps. He fell asleep still not sure
what was so exceptional about her. He just knew there
was something.

Chapter Two

In retrospect, Charles Abbott III—"call me Kilo, babe"—should have hit on the blonde with the wall-to-wall tits. It would have been a slam dunk; the blonde had been eyeing him for the last half hour while she pretended to listen to the executive doofus standing beside her in the hairplugs and crocodile loafers. Kilo didn't blame her. In a four-star hotel bar full of business cards and best behavior, Kilo was cool, calm, and casual: arms draped across the back of his regular booth, sunglasses pushed back on his head, his deep tan stark against his immaculate tennis whites. He was sitting with his legs splayed, showing off his muscular thighs. Kilo was so fine he could hardly stand himself.

Three sorority girls sat around him getting sloshed on Kilo's champagne, regaling him with talk of rush weekend, Daddy's latest mistress, and bands he had never heard of. The coeds were juicy, but tonight he wasn't in the mood for college girls. Just as Kilo was ready to wave the blonde over, the redhead walked into the bar and that was that. Like Judge Judy said, "Case closed."

It wasn't just that the redhead was a knockout. The Four Seasons lounge on a Friday night was always filled with talent: frisky flight attendants out of Orange County airport, lady lawyers with prim courtroom suits and nasty French underwear, surgically enhanced divorcées with fat settlements and too much time on their hands. Kilo spent most weekends at the Four Seasons, surrounded by pheromones and soft opportunity.

The redhead was something else. There was an edgy glamour to her, a sleek amorality to that kitten face, the wild mane of red hair framing her milky skin. Heads turned as she glided slowly to the bar, and Felipe, the bartender who had seen everything, was suddenly falling all over himself. The redhead sipped her martini, one fingernail idly tapping the crystal rim as she checked out the room, taking her time. When their eyes met, he smiled and she smiled back. One predator to another, he told himself as he rose to join her, feeling himself pulled as though on strings.

SLAP! Kilo barely felt the blow, but he heard it clearly. It sounded like the crack of a whip. A sharp chemical smell tore at his nostrils, and he jerked awake, found himself looking into the abyss. No . . . it was a pair of cool green eyes, bright green eyes, sharp as glass. Kilo blinked, still groggy, and saw the redhead leaning over him with a crushed amyl nitrate ampule in her hand. He took in her long legs, her rounded breasts overflowing the pale green cocktail dress—trouble never looked so good. Kilo smiled and she slapped him again. He felt it this time, tasted blood in his mouth.

"Whoa, bitch." He raised himself up on one elbow, tried to anyway, but he was posied out on the ornately carved canopy bed of the John Wayne Suite, lying nude on the blue striped sheets, his arms and legs tied to the bedposts. John Wayne in full cowpoke regalia stared down at him from a larger-than-life oil painting on the wall, a coiled lariat in his hand, floppy hat pushed back. "Trouble, pilgrim?" the Duke seemed to be asking.

Kilo remembered nuzzling the redhead over drinks, remembered her saying something about selling real estate—he had joked that he would like her professional opinion of his suite as he led her to the elevator. He remembered feeling dizzy as Jackie undressed him, the two of them flopping onto the bed, Kilo giggling, pretending to struggle as she tied him down, so aroused he could hardly breathe. That was all he remembered though. The rest was a blank. He looked up at her now. "Love the mondo-bondo action, babe," he said, wiggling his fingers and toes. "I can't wait until it's my turn."

"You don't get a turn," Jackie said, her green eyes glittering.

Kilo smiled, not liking that answer. "You don't know what you're missing." He tested his bonds, pulled at them, but she had tied him down tightly with the curtain cords. His head hurt worse than any hangover he had ever had.

Jackie ran her hands down her hips, her white net gloves making a sound like static against the short dress.

Kilo gave her one of his patented you-and-me-kid looks, the cool smirk that had launched a thousand blowjobs. "I knew that we were going to connect that moment you walked into the bar—every woman in the room hated you because you were so much better than they were." He gazed into her eyes. "That's when I knew you and I were going to spend the night together. We're two of a kind."

She cocked her head, examining him. "I bet that line of crap works most of the time. Women must eat you up."

Kilo preened. "Usually they come back for seconds."

Jackie reached into the ice bucket near the bed and tugged out an open bottle of Dom Perignon. Chipped ice fell like spilled diamonds onto the carpet.

Kilo made room as she sat down on the bed beside him. He had ordered a couple of bottles of Dom P before he went downstairs this evening, but he didn't remember uncorking one. He was going to have to ease off the hard-partying. Like Gwen said, "You're twenty-eight years old, Charles. Your father and I can't support you forever. He may think you're just going through a phase, but I'm sick of your laziness." Yeah, and fuck you, too, Gwen. You're not *my* mother. Still, there was something about the way this night had gone, the wooziness in the elevator, the blackout. . . . Kilo had never blacked out in his life. "I know it's silly, and hey, I'd be the last one to make wild accusations, but you didn't drop a Roofie into my drink, did you? Maybe a little GBH?"

Jackie watched him with those hard shiny eyes.

"That would be a real waste because I'm a creative guy and downers just slow me down." Kilo smiled. "You want to do a few rails of coke, I'll show you what I can do. I'm the McDonald's of Love, ten billion satisfied customers."

Jackie tipped the champagne bottle to her mouth and drank deeply, her throat stretched back, sucking it down.

Kilo licked his lips, glanced around for something, anything. The room was filled with dark, carved wood furniture, more cowpoke regalia, the top-floor suite, quiet and well insulated. Through the open curtains he could see freeway lights in the distance, headlights blinking in the haze. Everyone was rushing to their dreary little homes, TVs blaring, kids squalling. Kilo would sooner set his hair on fire than live like that. Okay, buckle down, Kilo. Crank up the charm. He smiled.

Jackie drained her glass. She shook the champagne bottle, holding her thumb over the opening, then shoved it under Kilo's right nostril, sending a gush of cold champagne exploding into his sinuses.

Choking, Kilo cried out in agony and twisted away from her, tears running down his face.

Jackie licked foam off the neck of the bottle, then touched Kilo's red nose and watched him flinch.

Kilo coughed up sour champagne.

"That's called the Tijuana douche," Jackie informed him. "I learned it from a boyfriend I had once, a Mexican *federale* . . . Roberto." She lowered her eyelids, savoring the memory. "God was he something."

Kilo felt as if his lungs were filled with shards of ice. It hurt to breathe.

"Roberto's specialty was interrogating hard-core suspects," said Jackie, reapplying her lipstick, "tough guys who spit on the floor and refused to talk, desperadoes who could take a punch better than Mike Tyson." She checked her reflection in the mirror. "That's when they called in Roberto. He didn't use champagne, of course, but Roberto said give him a six-pack of Pepsi and he could make the pope renounce Christ."

"I don't understand—"

"The TJ douche clears out the cobwebs, you have to admit." Jackie tossed her head, her dark red curls tickling her bare shoulders. "And Kilo, right now, more than ever, you need a clear mind."

Kilo shivered—the cold was horribly amplified along

his nerve ends. It felt as if his teeth had shattered at the gumline. He was afraid to touch them with his tongue, afraid he would find only stumps.

"You don't look so good," said Jackie, wiping his face with the edge of the sheet. "Take a deep breath, that will help. That's it. In and out." She waited until his breathing had leveled off, then shoved the bottle under his left nostril and gave him another blast.

Kilo screamed, the sound echoing inside his skull. He thrashed against the pillows; his hands were curled into claws.

Jackie watched him flop on the sheets, waiting until his convulsions had subsided, then she smoothed his damp hair. "I guess I didn't really need to do that again. Roberto said I never knew when to stop. Not that he was complaining."

Kilo tried to speak, but all that came out was the sound of his teeth chattering.

Jackie circled the lip of the champagne bottle with a finger; her face was lit with the inner light of a sweet dream. "The first time I saw Roberto he was crossing a busy street in Tijuana in a pair of ostrich-skin cowboy boots, stopping traffic with his stare. I said to myself, 'Girl, you *have* to try some of that.'" She licked her lips. "Roberto was a total surprise—an animal in public but such a shy boy in the bedroom, always turning out the lights before he undressed, asking permission to smoke afterward."

"What . . . what do you want?" Drops of champagne hung from Kilo's nose, burning the inflamed membranes.

Jackie looked at him. "Why, I want it all," she said, as though it should have been obvious. "Every last bit of it."

Kilo shivered.

"I watched you downstairs," Jackie said, toying with his nipples. "I usually pick men with a wedding ring. . . . Married types don't run to the cops, they just report their wallet missing. You were different. I saw you buying drinks for every pretty girl in the bar—you in your Wimbledon whites and that winner's smile—and I knew you were a major payday." She pinched one of his nipples so hard he cried out. She leaned close and whispered into his ear, her breath warm against him. "So here we are, lying around in a six-hundred-dollar-a-night suite with room-service champagne—what I want to know, Mr. Charles Abbott III, is where's your break-the-bank plastic?"

Kilo's head was pounding so loudly he could hardly hear her.

"You don't check into a place like this without serious plastic," said Jackie, emptying Kilo's wallet onto the bed, "but there's no Platinum AMEX in here. No Visa Gold. Not even an ATM card. Just thirty-seven dollars in cash, an expired California driver's license, and *this*—" she flicked the Shell gas credit card with a fingernail, then slowly ran the sharp edge along his chest. "It's not even in your name," she said, scraping a heart into his hairless chest as he squirmed. "Is this your daddy's card? Did he give it to you, or did you rip him off?"

Kilo couldn't stop his teeth from chattering.

"Does your mommy pack you a lunch, too?" asked Jackie. "Does she fill your Thermos with hot soup and give you milk money?"

"I . . . I don't have any credit cards," Kilo said. "I *don't*. My father . . . my father has an account with this hotel."

Jackie stared at him. "So you're just some daddy's boy wasting my Friday night?"

"We . . . we don't have to waste it," Kilo said, dredging up his charm.

Jackie gently dabbed with the sheet at the champagne dripping from his nose, watching him wince. "I misjudged you. Congratulations. That doesn't happen very often."

"I guess we both got fooled." One good thing about always getting in trouble was that Kilo had learned how to deal with it. He had learned to plead ignorance, to blame someone else, to run for the door and not look back. Kilo could talk his way out of anything. It was a gift. "No hard feelings."

"Poor Kilo," she said softly. "I'm a *very* bad loser."

The room was too quiet. Kilo disliked silence. He worried about the things that grew there, the conclusions people came to, the decisions they made. He needed sound and motion to operate, to work his magic.

Kilo nodded at his bound wrists. "Untie me. Don't worry—I won't call security." He winked at her. "I like a girl who takes the initiative."

"I bet you do." Jackie slid off the bed and picked up a bright red apple from the overflowing fruit bowl on the dresser. She took a big bite, the crunching sound cleaving the silence. "I bet you like a woman on top, riding you. That way she does all the work."

Kilo felt himself getting an erection. He was amazing—he had to admit it.

Jackie noted his erection, but her expression didn't change.

"Untie me, Jackie." Kilo grinned. "Untie me and we'll have such a good time you won't care about credit cards or anything else."

"You told me in the bar that you had a Ferrari parked in the hotel garage. I hope for your sake that you do." Jackie flung aside the half-eaten apple and picked up a cluster of large purple grapes. "Dekker hates being disappointed."

Kilo swallowed. "Who's Dekker?"

"Let's just say he's a man with a *profound* anger-management problem." Jackie threw a grape at Kilo, which bounced off his flat belly. "I've seen Dekker turn somebody's face to steak tartare just for looking at me." She tossed another grape, this time hitting Kilo on the penis. "Wow. I don't know what Dekker is going to think about that big ol' thing."

Kilo heard someone at the door to the outer room of the suite. Frantic now, he pulled at his bonds. An entry card slid into the door lock.

"Gosh, I wouldn't want to be you right now," said Jackie.

Kilo bucked and twisted on the bed, his eyes darting toward the door as someone fumbled with the handle.

Jackie leaned over him and kissed him. "Have you ever heard the phrase, 'A stranger is just a friend you haven't met'?" Kilo stared up at her, still feeling her kiss on his lips. "Well," she said, as the door swung open, "they weren't talking about Dekker."

Chapter Three

A VW van cut in front of Val's battered pickup and immediately slowed. He hit the brakes, his tires squealing, and stopped inches from the van's "Visualize World Peace" bumper sticker. Not likely, asshole. Val had thought he was lucky to get off work before dark, but the southbound 405 freeway was a vast six-lane traffic jam, thousands of engines idling in the sunset, heat and hydrocarbons shimmering in the dead air. Saturday night was on hold. Not that he had any plans.

Val tapped a number on his cell-phone. The back of his neck was damp with sweat. A new Lexus sat on the shoulder, its hood up, radiator boiling out clouds of white steam as the driver, a silver-haired gentleman in a gray pinstripe, pounded on the steering wheel like it was a tom-tom, beating out a message of rage and frustration. As he crept forward, Val watched the man in his rearview mirror. The man's sunflower-yellow pocket square matched his Lexus perfectly.

"Amy Huckebee here." It was evening in Miami, but

Amy answered the phone as though she were still at the office.

"I wasn't sure you were home."

"Val?" Mild surprise but no warmth in her voice. Well, that was understandable. Amy Huckebee was Junior's primary banker, a money-laundering genius with a sense of humor as narrow as her hips. Their first two dates had been punctuated with her asking Val what was so funny. There hadn't been a third date. He had asked—she was potentially too useful not to cultivate—but she had declined, saying she preferred men who were slightly less interesting. It was the nicest kiss-off he had ever gotten, and he had been surprised to find himself disappointed by her rejection. "I understood that you had left town," said Amy. "Are you back?"

"No, I'm still on vacation."

"Is that what you call it?" Val imagined Amy sitting alone in her snow-white living room, with her legs neatly crossed, calculating the opening exchange rate of the deutsche mark Monday morning.

Val watched a white Mercedes convertible creep past. The two teenagers inside were passing a pipe back and forth, their heads bobbing to the base beat of their CD player.

"What can I do for you, Val?"

Val took off his sunglasses and wiped his face. "I'm worried about you."

"Indeed? I've heard several scenarios regarding your sudden departure." Amy paused, and Val could hear the hiss of her gold lighter, the faint crackle as she lit one of her British cigarettes. "But all of them suggest that you should be more concerned with your *own* welfare than mine."

"I know you manage a lot of Junior's money. That's a dangerous job—"

"Junior? Are you referring to Mr. Mayfield?"

"Knock it off." A rusted shopping cart lay overturned by the side of the road, one of its wheels missing. Val thought of abandoned shells on the beach and hermit crabs scuttling across the sand. "Look, Amy, I'm trying to warn you. Have you ever considered what would happen if Junior even *suspected* that you're skimming his accounts—"

"It would be a violation of professional ethics to discuss my clients with you," Amy said. Her voice sounded brittle now but controlled; she always assumed that she was being recorded. "I can assure you, however, that all my dealings with Mr. Mayfield have been in full accord with my fiduciary—"

"I know that and you know that, but the only thing that matters here is what *Junior* thinks. You heard what happened to Steffano?"

"Steffano?" Amy exhaled, and Val imagined the smoke streaming from her nostrils in that high-rise condo with the grid of arranged furniture. "I don't recognize that name."

"You wouldn't recognize Steffano either," said Val, fighting back his anger. "Junior had suspicions about Steffano. . . . That was enough." He listened to her smoke, neither of them speaking. She kept her condo at a frosty sixty-five degrees, but she would be feeling warmer now.

"Let me save us both some time, shall I?" Amy said. "I am aware that you and Mr. Mayfield have had certain business . . . difficulties, and while I don't know the exact nature of your disagreement, I understand it was quite vitriolic. Now, you're trying to deprive Mr. Mayfield of my services. I should be flattered. You must consider me very valuable to Mr. Mayfield to justify this ploy of yours, but I'm afraid it's—"

"Amy?"

"Yes?"

Val spoke slowly now. "This was a courtesy call, Amy. I can make other calls. Not to Junior, not directly, but word will filter back to him. Junior may not be suspicious of you now, but when I'm through he will be."

She was silent now, calculating.

"Junior will never even know the information came from me."

"I . . . I don't believe you would do that," Amy said.

"Risk assessment—that's one of your specialties, isn't it? Junior bragged about you all the time. I guess now we'll see how good you really are."

"This isn't fair, Val—"

"I can't lose," said Val. "You can disappear on your own or wait for Armando to pay you a visit. Either way Junior is denied your expertise."

A news helicopter thumped over the freeway in the direction of the tie-up. Two weeks ago the #10 freeway had come to a complete stop for hours while a man in a Mustang convertible held a gun to his head. The news copters had broadcast the story live, with the man speaking to the home viewers over his cell-phone, his dog sitting patiently beside him in the passenger seat. After a while he had gotten out, emptied a can of gasoline over himself and his dog, and held up a cigarette lighter. The phone lines of every local radio talk show lit up with callers demanding that SWAT take the man out.

"Val, please—"

"How much money are you managing for him, Amy? Twenty million? Thirty?"

She didn't answer.

Val whistled. "That much? That's enough to get you lost—money you could move with a few clicks of a keyboard, untraceable, just blips on a computer screen, skipping around the globe at the speed of light, from the Caymans to Luxembourg to Aruba—"

"Not the Caymans, you *ass,*" Amy hissed, "the transfer codes are porous and the undersecretary is a partner of Junior's." She was even quicker to adapt than he had imagined. She probably had her own shell corporation established somewhere, just in case this day ever came.

"Make your decision soon, Amy, or I'm going to make it for you." Val clicked off the connection before she could speak. A beige Honda Accord edged in front of a jacked-up 4x4. Val smiled as horns blared.

A couple of hours later Val was in the downstairs laundry room of his apartment building, folding clothes, trying to decide if he would really have set Amy up to be killed. The metal buttons of his jeans clanked rhythmically against the inside of the dryer while he grappled with the swampy morality of the question. It was people like Amy who allowed people like Junior to stay in business—men and women with lizard briefcases and understated jewelry, Ivy League bankers who wouldn't dream of cheating at squash, Rolls-Royce salesmen with proper British accents who accepted payment for a new Silver Cloud in cash. Val still hadn't decided when he heard voices coming down the hallway—Kyle and someone else, the two of them laughing, whooping it up.

"Here he is, just like you said." Brenda stood in the doorway of the laundry room, hands on her hips.

"Lucky guess," said Kyle, walking past her into the

room. She wore baggy orange lifeguard shorts, huaraches, and a light blue Cousteau Society polo shirt, her hair in the same thick ponytail as when they met on the stairway this morning.

"You *never* guess, girlfriend, and you're always right." Brenda draped herself over one of the washers and looked up at Val. "Who would have thought that the mystery man himself would be down here on a Saturday night?" She was short and busty with a shag haircut, her mouth a silvery slash outlined with black pencil. Tonight she wore retro silver lamé hiphuggers and a matching tube top that played peekaboo with her belly button. A fine button too. Push it and you could start World War III. She rocked on her towering high heels. It must be like walking on ice picks.

Kyle scooped up his heart-patterned boxers from the pile of warm clothes on top of the dryer. "I like the valentines. What do you think, Brenda?" she said, tossing them over.

Brenda snagged the boxers in midair. "Ummmm," she said, rubbing the warm fabric against her cheek. She pitched them back to Kyle.

"Not every man can get away with underwear like this, Val," said Kyle, smoothing the boxers flat on the table. "You must have a great deal of self-confidence."

"Less and less all the time."

"I find that hard to believe," Kyle said.

"So do I," said Brenda, pushing out her lower lip. She was about twenty-three, and the pout was truly devastating, but he was about ten years past being affected by it. "I'm going to a party tonight at the warehouse in Long Beach." She dropped her head and looked up at him through her long lashes. "I thought if you asked me nicely, I might let you come."

Val glanced at Kyle, who was busy organizing his socks.

"What's the matter," asked Brenda, "don't you like it when a woman makes the first move?"

"I'm an old-fashioned guy."

"That's my favorite flavor," said Brenda.

"Are you going to the party, too?" he asked Kyle.

"I guess that answers my question. Don't bother," Brenda said, huffing, as Val started to apologize. "You haven't hurt my feelings—don't give yourself that much credit." She kissed Kyle on the cheek. "He's all yours."

"Was that an official tag," Val asked Kyle, "or is she going to run back into the ring in a minute and hit me with a folding chair?"

As she picked through his clothes, Kyle smiled and folded and stacked the tangle of jeans and promotional T-shirts from movies no one ever heard of. Val didn't like anyone touching his things; he guarded his privacy . . . but he didn't tell her to stop. "I didn't mean to insult your friend," he said.

"Brenda is a big girl."

"Very mature too. She stuck her tongue out at me as she was leaving." Val could see a long scar on the inside of Kyle's thigh, white against her tan, disappearing into the leg of her orange shorts.

"I told Brenda I didn't think the two of you would hit it off," said Kyle, "but when she heard about you saving the bird this morning, she got all gooey."

"I went back there this morning—" One of the washers went into its spin cycle and began thumping loudly.

Val waited until it had stopped. "I went back to where I saw the cat stalking the bird—"

Kyle threw a sock at him. "Let it *go*, Val."

"The manager's tomcat is fat and so lazy that he hardly cleans himself. Even a dumb bird should have sensed him coming, but this cat leaves trophies twitching all over the building. I kept asking myself—how does he do it?"

Kyle was interested now.

"I checked where the bird was pecking and found corn kernels in the grass," said Val. "I picked up the corn and smelled it. Somebody had soaked it in bourbon." He leaned over the dryer toward her. "Fifty bucks says it's the same generic brand the manager drinks."

A wisp of black hair had come loose from Kyle's ponytail and hung down one side of her face. She made no attempt to brush it aside, just stared at him. "You'd make a good biologist—you've got a healthy curiosity, strong observational skills, and a basic distrust of human nature." She shook out a Ninja Chicks on Mars! T-shirt, raised an eyebrow at the image of a hyperdeveloped woman in a black Ninja cloak being threatened by a tentacled alien. "I don't think I saw this one."

"Powerful film. Two thumbs up, *way* up."

Though it wasn't that funny, Kyle laughed, then stopped herself in the middle, looking quizzically at his shoes. "Did you cut yourself?"

"No."

"It looks like blood."

"It's not blood."

"I've *seen* blood." Kyle didn't step back, not with her body anyway. "That's what it looks like."

"It's fake blood," said Val.

"You've got *fake* blood all over your shoes?"

It was too late now for anything but the truth, not the whole truth, just a slice cut thin as cheesecake. Val pointed at the T-shirt. "I worked on Ninja Chicks for a week, that's how I got the shirt. The alien was a toy the director bought at Target and filmed in close-up. It worked pretty good, but the batteries kept running down. That set was a smooth operation compared to the one I'm on now. The prop guy is a sophomore at U.S.C., a sloppy kid who flings stage blood everywhere and thinks it's artistic."

"You're an actor?" Kyle looked like she wasn't sure whether to believe him.

"Technical advisor, strictly off-camera. I work on ultra low-budget action films—what they call run-and-gun flicks."

"Like John Woo movies?"

"I wish," said Val. "I work out action sequences, make sure the star knows how to hold a Mac-11 when he's playing tough, and anything else I . . ." He looked closely at her. "You like John Woo?"

"How do you get a job like that? I would think there would be a lot of competition."

"Right place, right time—you don't need to be an expert to work in the movies. I was in the military for a few years, and I used to live next door to a cop. Most days I'm just faking my way through." Val shrugged, winced.

"What's wrong?"

"I was blocking out a fight scene today with a Mickey Rourke wannabee who was trying to impress the makeup girl." The laundry room was too small for this conversation, located at the end of the corridor with only one door in and out—a question would bounce off the concrete block walls until it hit something.

"It still sounds like interesting work to me," said Kyle.

"Let's go outside and get some fresh air," he said. "I'll come back for my clothes later. Unless, of course, you also have a party to go to."

"Not tonight."

They walked down the hall, pushed open the side door, and stepped out into the dark—the security lights behind the building had burned out and not been replaced. Val could hear two or three different TV shows coming from the nearby apartments, the laugh track from one overlapping with the squealing tires and gunshots of another. If you paid too close attention, you got dizzy.

Kyle looked up as they strolled along the alley. "First clear night we've had in a week. The wind must have shifted."

Val followed her gaze. The sky was a vast dome strewn with stars, the spilled milk of the Milky Way. "You told Brenda that I would be in the laundry room. How did you know that?"

"Maybe I saw you go down there."

"No one saw me go down there."

"You notice things like that too—who sees you, who doesn't? The same way you questioned whether the manager's cat was up to lord-of-the-jungle status?"

"I like to keep my mind active."

"So do I," said Kyle. "It's Saturday night. Nobody in this apartment building is going to waste a Saturday night doing laundry, nobody but you. That way you're guaranteed your privacy." She smiled. "*That's* how I knew you would be down there."

"I better be careful around you."

"Too late, Val."

They were walking closer now. The alley here was bordered by a chain-link fence on one side. The palm trees overhead rustled loudly, as tree rats fought or mated in the dry fronds, tearing at each other. Love in the wild kingdom.

"You're not from around here, are you?" said Kyle. "You have a faint Southern accent, and that slicked-back hair of yours . . . it's a very interesting look. Not a California look."

"Should I apologize?"

"Don't be so sensitive. I *like* your look. I'm so sick of pretty men . . ."

"Gee, thanks."

Kyle took his hand and kept right on walking, neither of them missing a step. Val felt a faint shock the instant they touched, the same warm sensation he had experienced on the stairs. Her hand was strong and lightly callused, rough from long hours in saltwater. He wasn't complaining. He didn't like soft, dainty women who covered their mouths when they laughed and worried about smudging their lipstick with a kiss. Their hands swung slowly as they walked.

"Does this mean we're going steady?" Val asked.

"I'll let you know," said Kyle. "My mother is having a small birthday party next Saturday. Dinner and drinks. Would you like to come as my guest?"

"This seems to be my night for being invited to parties."

"You would have had a good time at Brenda's party," said Kyle. "The one I'm inviting you to isn't going to be anything like that."

"I'm flattered, but . . ."

"I have a . . . difficult time being around my family," said Kyle. "I thought it might help if I had someone with me. If *you* were with me," she corrected herself.

"Next Saturday?"

"I'm not making a move on you, Val. You don't have to worry about that."

"I'm not worried."

"It's nothing personal. I get ahead of myself sometimes and I regret it when I do."

"Going slow is fine with me."

Kyle threw back her head, trying to hide her pleasure. "It's such a clear night," she said, slowly scanning the heavens. "So many stars . . ."

"My grandmother would see a sky like this, and she'd say that it looked like God had dropped stars across the night and not bothered to pick up after himself." Val smiled at the memory of her, then glanced at Kyle, who was watching him. "My grandmother believes in God, but she doesn't give him much credit."

Chapter Four

Kilo craned his neck as he listened to the footsteps whisper across the carpet.

Jackie sat on the bed beside him. "You look like all the country club boys I ever dated—boys with clear skin and straight teeth, trust fund babies who got a new Porsche when they graduated from high school, and fucked their girlfriends in fancy hotel rooms full of promises."

"I never made promises," said Kilo, still trying to see past her, "and I gave my girlfriend her graduation fuck in a Gulfstream II, thirty thousand feet over Catalina . . ." His voice trailed off as he caught sight of Dekker.

"He's awake?" The man standing beside the bed was a sullen brute with a bad haircut and a black Armani topcoat. Four thousand dollars' worth of cashmere, and he still looked like someone who swung a sledgehammer in a slaughterhouse.

"I'm glad you're here," said Jackie. "Kilo was bucking so hard I was afraid he was going to bust loose."

"You were afraid?" Dekker said. "That would be a first."

"You wouldn't believe the awful things this boy said to me," Jackie said, caressing Kilo's cheek. "Just a flood of pure filth."

Dekker nudged the empty champagne bottle on the floor with his shoe. "A flood?"

Kilo saw the tips of Dekker's ears redden. "That... that's not true."

"A gusher," Jackie assured Dekker.

Dekker smoothed the lapels of his topcoat as he stared at Kilo's nakedness. "You should have written the words down, Jackie. Maybe I could learn something."

Jackie laughed, her joy blooming in the room like a poisonous flower.

Dekker scowled at the heart she had scratched into Kilo's chest. "Move away from him and cover him up with the sheet."

Jackie ignored him. "Where are my manners?" she purred. "Darryl, let me introduce Charles Abbott III."

"M-my friends call me Kilo."

"Kilo, this is Darryl Dekker, former master sergeant in the army reserves."

Kilo licked his lips. "Semper fi, man."

"That's the marines, *shithead.*"

"Dekker is a war hero," said Jackie. "He won a Silver Star in Desert Storm. Remember that one? He's got a letter from George Bush in his wallet."

Kilo looked at Jackie, not sure if she was serious.

"Dekker drove a tank into Kuwait City, right through the minefields," said Jackie. "He didn't let anything stop him. Rockets red glare, burning oil wells—"

"There ain't no Ferrari, Jackie," said Dekker. "I checked out his valet-parking stub. He's driving a five-year-old Fiat convertible with a cracked windshield. So much for our big score." He opened the French doors to the balcony, and the buzz of distant traffic filled the room. "What *happened*, Jackie? I thought you could always tell the winners from the losers."

"You think you could do any better?" said Jackie, getting off the bed. "What were you doing when I met you, Dekker? You were a bill collector in *Bakersfield*."

Dekker turned his back on them. Tugging at the curtain cords around his wrists, the cords cutting into his skin, Kilo tried to sit up.

" 'This one smells like serious money,' " said Dekker, gazing out at the ribbon of headlights unspooling across the darkness. "That's what you told me."

"You were a thug on commission when I met you," Jackie said, raising her voice, "an errand boy, scaring shoe salesmen out of their past-due big-screens and jet skis—"

"You called *me*," said Dekker, still looking out at the night. "You disappeared for almost a year, then phoned me up in the middle of the night saying baby I *need* you." The overcoat billowed in the cool breeze, flapping around him. "I was almost over you, too. I hardly thought of you more than once or twice an hour."

Kilo jerked against his restraints now, grunting with the effort, not caring if Dekker heard him.

"I *did* need you, Dekker," said Jackie, her voice softer now. "I was tired of window shopping, tired of waiting for the good stuff to go on sale, and the good stuff *never* goes on sale. I figured between the two of us . . ." She shook her head. "It's not your fault—"

"No, of course not," said Dekker.

Jackie massaged Dekker's massive shoulders. "Don't be such a baby," she chided, digging into the buttery cashmere. "We haven't met *anybody* yet who wanted to hold out on you. It's just that there's only so much I can do with credit cards. Even that attorney with his corporate account needed clearance for a cash withdrawal. These suits, they're not like us—they need permission for everything." She glanced at Kilo. "That's why I picked cutie-pie tonight—he looked off-leash and twenty-four-carat guaranteed."

Dekker turned. "That wasn't all you saw in him. You weren't just seeing dollar signs."

Kilo fell back onto the sheets, exhausted, his bound wrists circled with rope burns.

"You can't blame me," said Jackie. "Look at him, Darryl. He's a total hottie."

"Maybe I'll break his jaw," said Dekker. "Then he won't be so distracting."

"A broken jaw?" said Jackie. "Is that the extent of your outrage, Darryl?"

Dekker was confused.

Jackie walked slowly over to the bed and looked down at Kilo with those cold green eyes. "I want you to go the route on him, Darryl."

"W-what?" said Kilo.

"I want you to go all the way this time, Darryl." Jackie saw the hesitation on Dekker's face. "A man spills a drink on my shoes and you punch him so hard you rupture his spleen. Kilo steals our time, insults me in the process, and you stand around—"

"That's not what happened," said Kilo, flailing against the cords. "Jackie? Consenting adults, right? *Jackie!*"

"Go the route?" Dekker joined her beside the bed. "That's a little extreme, isn't it?"

Jackie ran her fingers through Kilo's soft wavy hair, luxuriating in the feel, then pulled it hard, making him cry out. "Did you really think you were going to skate on this one?"

Kilo swallowed. "If it makes you feel better," he said, eyes darting back and forth between them, "I apologize—"

"I'll bust him up if you want," said Dekker. "I'd enjoy that, but—"

Jackie slapped Dekker. "He was going to *fuck* me, Darryl." She slapped him again. He took it, unflinching. "He was going to fuck me and dump me." She jabbed a fingernail into Kilo's chest, right into the heart scratched into his skin, and he jerked. "Would you have let me order room service in the morning if I was extra good? Maybe let me stuff the complimentary shampoo into my purse?"

Kilo was so scared he could hardly breathe, but he managed a smile. Like Chuck said, breeding always showed. "With your style, Jackie, I'd have let you put one of the terrycloth robes on my bill."

Jackie tapped her teeth with her tongue. "You really *are* something special. Maybe I should have told Dekker to wait another hour before interrupting us."

"That's enough, Jackie." Dekker loomed over the bed. "Say goodnight, buddy."

"You're sure you can handle the job?" said Jackie. "I wouldn't want you to have to check in with a V.A. shrink afterward, telling him you're having flashbacks—"

Dekker looked at Kilo. "You know, I used to be a mellow guy."

"You were always a badass," Jackie said. "I heard all kinds of ugly stories about you."

"I had a temper," said Dekker, "but I had a good heart."

"I-I can see that," said Kilo.

Dekker sat down on the edge of the bed, the mattress

sagging under his weight. "Something happened to me out in the desert," he confided to Kilo. "Maybe I got bit by some weird sandbug, or got a whiff of Saddam's nerve gas, but I get headaches all the time now and ringing in my ears, and . . . what did the doctors call that other thing?"

"Post-traumatic impotence," said Jackie.

Dekker nodded. "Yeah, that was it." His eyes were dull gray stones. He wrapped his hands around Kilo's head.

"Hey!" Kilo cried.

"Darryl can bend a quarter with his bare hands," said Jackie. "I've seen him do it."

"I believe you," Kilo said, struggling.

Dekker lightly placed his thumbs under the base of Kilo's nose and leaned in close. "First I'm going to crack your nose, then drive it back *just* short of your brain. Wait until you hear the sound that makes."

"Please," said Kilo, "please don't."

"Don't rush it, Darryl," said Jackie. "Checkout isn't until noon."

"You're *really* going to do this?" gasped Kilo, trying to think. There had to be a way out. There always was for him.

"I've been trying to sell real estate for the last few weeks," said Jackie. "You know, do the Jane Doe, legit citizen thing. I was even ready to pay my taxes if I had to. . . ." She shook her head. "I haven't sold a thing. All I do is chauffeur smug bastards around to properties they have no intention of buying. *I'm* getting plenty of offers, though—Hawaii, San Francisco, a nooner in their fancy office. . . ." She checked her manicure. "I'm just sick of being ripped off by guys like you, Kilo. That's what it comes down to."

Dekker loosely held Kilo's face in his hands. "Cotton," he crooned, "the fabric of our lives. . . ." He grinned. "I love *that* commercial. Makes me cry every time I hear it."

Jackie laughed. "Dekker, don't you go blaming sandbugs or poison gas. You *always* had a screw loose."

Kilo thrashed around, managed to pull away from Dekker for an instant.

Amused, Dekker let him be. "Look at your pretty boy now, Jackie, squirming around like a little mouse."

They were really going to kill him. For *nothing*. Dekker was going to crush his skull just because Jackie told him to. Amazing. Kilo drifted in a sea of talkers, idle charmers, and well-tended dropouts who passed their days at the yacht club, spinning grand gossamer plans. Nothing ever happened, of course; no one did anything. But Jackie and Dekker . . . they were going to do what they said they would, Kilo had no doubt about that. He felt a shiver run through his body, a mixture of fear and excitement. He sensed an opportunity here. He just had to survive the next five minutes.

Jackie raised herself up on one elbow. "What's so funny, Kilo?"

"*Everything.*" Kilo was laughing now. "I've been waiting . . ." Champagne trickled from his nose. "I've been waiting my whole life to meet someone like you, Jackie, and when I finally do . . . you're going to kill me."

Jackie watched him.

"What's even funnier . . . I'm the answer to your prayers too, Jackie, but you can't see it." Kilo tried to sit up. "You told Dekker I smelled like money. You were *right.*"

Dekker reached for Kilo, but Jackie waved him off.

"You were right, Jackie," Kilo insisted.

"I'd like to believe you," said Jackie, "but you can't even fill up the Fiat without help."

"You're damned right I need help," said Kilo, jerking at the curtain cords around his wrist, tired of being staked out, helpless. "So *help* me. You want the combination to the vault? You tired of waiting for the door to the money bin to swing open?" His eyes were locked on hers. "Well, so am I. Help me, and you help yourself at the same time."

Jackie stared at him. "Okay, I'm listening."

"Untie me. I'm not talking until you untie me," said Kilo.

Jackie smiled. "Say 'please.'"

"Please."

"Untie him," said Jackie.

"No," said Dekker.

"Are you afraid of him, Darryl?"

Dekker shut his mouth, then snapped the cords with one jerk of his hands. He was beaten now, his broad head drooped among the elephantine folds of his coat.

Kilo slowly sat up, gingerly rubbed his wrists. The sheet fell away, but he made no move to cover himself. He picked up one of the purple grapes that Jackie had thrown at him before and popped it into his mouth.

"Showtime, Kilo," Jackie said quietly. "Now."

Kilo spit the grape out onto the carpet. "Sour." He looked at Jackie, shrugged. "So how much would you charge to kill my stepmother?"

Chapter Five

Kyle kept her eyes on the road, face lit by the green glow from the dashboard as she guided the lumbering white Suburban through the night. The Suburban smelled of the sea, with wetsuits and swim fins in the back, sand ground into the carpet, a starfish dangling from the rearview. Kyle's black hair curled around her bare shoulders. In the dim light she looked like a mermaid caught between the ocean and dry land.

Val flicked the starfish, sent it spinning, a compass searching for true north. He couldn't take his eyes off Kyle. She was wearing a dress tonight, a simple off-white thing that showed off her tan and probably cost a bundle. It kept riding up her great legs, and she kept pushing it down. "You should wear a dress more often," he said innocently.

"You should shut up."

"You're welcome."

The Suburban wound its way up the hills above Laguna Beach, fishtailing around the curves, engine rumbling, headlights barely illuminating the narrow road. Atop the highest hill was the exclusive Aegean Heights colony, its bright lights winking through the mist like a faraway Christmas.

Val leaned his head out the open window and took in the lush landscape—Southern California was a desert, but you would never know it from here. He squinted as they approached the faux-Grecian columns and classical statuary that flanked the entrance to the colony. Maybe he should have worn a toga. "You grew up here?"

"My mother and Chuck bought the place about twenty years ago, right after they got married," Kyle said. "I moved out as soon as I was able."

The roads through the Heights were narrow, with no street markers or addresses. The colony used to have a guard shack and gates at the entrance, but the homeowners association had lost a court case a couple of years ago, and they weren't about to make it easier for tourists. Kyle made a hard left and pulled up to a barred gate in the middle of a high hedge. She picked up a remote control from the floorboard and turned it over and over in her hand, trying to decide.

"Val?" Kyle kissed him, lingering for a moment. "Thanks for coming with me."

He could still feel the warmth of her lips. He wished they were on their way someplace else, just the two of them, but she clicked the remote and the gate swung open. They drove up the cobblestone driveway, stopping in front of what looked like an Italian villa, with bleached terracotta walls and curved windows, the front door a wooden slab studded with black iron discs.

A sleekly handsome man lounged in the doorway, a martini in his hand, watching them get out. A purple orchid pinned to his lapel, he looked as comfortable in his black tuxedo as if he were wearing pajamas. He waved with his fingers.

"That's my stepbrother," said Kyle.

"Is he a florist?"

"God, I'm glad I brought you," said Kyle, getting out of the car. "I'll have to tell that one to Mother."

Kilo looked down his nose at Val and his blue suit. "I see stepsister brought an off-the-rack Prince Charming to the ball." He tried to kiss Kyle, but she put a hand against his chest and held him at bay.

"Charles," a man called from inside, "is that your sister?"

"Yes, Daddy," said Kilo, still eyeing Val. "She's brought a gentleman caller, too." He finished the martini and tossed the glass into the shrubbery.

"Splendid!" A boozy, older man joined Kilo on the front porch. He held out his arms to Kyle and embraced her, then quickly let her go. "It's good to see you, Kyle. You look smashing."

"You're looking pretty good yourself, Chuck."

"I'm a wreck and you know it." Mr. Abbott was tall and stooped, with a high, intelligent forehead. Remnants of Kilo's delicate features were still evident on his face, but there was an air of defeat about him that showed in his slack mouth, his hunched posture. Even his tuxedo seemed limp and lifeless on him. He extended his hand to Val. "I'm Chuck Abbott, Kyle's stepfather." He shook hands vigorously, with the determined grip of a man in failing health who remembered the importance of a strong handshake.

"Val Duran."

"Glad you could join us, Val," said Mr. Abbott. "You've met my son?"

"Yes, I have."

Mr. Abbott was no longer paying attention—he was grimacing at Kyle's car in the driveway. "Still driving that old ugly thing, I see. You should learn to budget your money more effectively—Kilo tells me he's looking into a new . . . something or other. Perhaps he could recommend you to his dealer."

"Why don't we go inside, Chuck?"

"Yes, let's go in," said Mr. Abbott, ushering them inside. "Your mother hates to be kept waiting. I can't wait for you to meet Charles's date. Lovely girl and smart, too. I think you're going to like her."

A fire crackled in the hearth of the spacious living room. Two elegantly dressed women were sitting on a love seat facing the flames, their legs crossed at the knee. One was a gaunt older woman holding a tumbler of Scotch. The skin of her face stretched too tightly across her cheekbones. She was still lovely, but there were bitter creases etched around her mouth. The other woman was younger. She sat on the edge of the love seat wearing a low-cut aquamarine sheath. Her red hair was incandescent in the firelight.

"Gwendolyn," Mr. Abbott called, "look who's here."

"Happy birthday, Mother," said Kyle, bending down to kiss her.

"Good evening, Kyle." Mrs. Abbott accepted the kiss, then took a long drink from her glass. "So nice of you to honor us with your presence."

Mr. Abbott handed Val and Kyle martinis before making introductions. Mrs. Abbott tinkled the ice in her glass as she coolly appraised Val. The redhead was Kilo's date, Jackie Hendricks, a beauty with milk-white complexion and dirty eyes that lingered on Val as she offered her hand.

Kilo must have seen her. He jerked the orchid from his lapel and tossed it into the fireplace. Val watched the purple flower curl in the flames and wished he and Kyle were someplace else.

"Your mother gave me the full tour," Jackie said to Kyle. "Tennis courts, swimming pool, all those bedrooms." She fussed with her hair, not so much to rearrange herself as to stroke the nape of her own neck. "Gwen was kind enough to allow me to peek into your room. What an amazing place. You had your own private world in there."

"*Private* is the operant word," Kyle said.

"I was expecting racks of Italian shoes and party dresses," said Jackie, ignoring the edge in Kyle's voice, "but there wasn't a bit of fluff or prettiness, just books and plaques, and your *closet*, I never saw so many—"

"Kyle was a National Merit scholar," Mrs. Abbott said.

Jackie watched Val. "I'm sure that comes in handy."

"I guess Kyle has told you all about her research, Val," said Mr. Abbott. "She's a real authority on killer whales. Anything you want to know—"

"Gray whales," Kyle corrected him.

"Yes, well, one whale is the same as another, I suppose." Mr. Abbott, standing there in his sad tuxedo, raised his glass to his wife. "A toast to the birthday girl," he said. His voice was full of forced bonhomie, as he urged them all to stand up.

Val touched glasses with Kyle. His attention was drawn to three photographs arranged on the mantel—Kilo in tennis whites holding a huge silver trophy overhead, Kyle serious in her cap and gown, and in the center a large photo of a younger Mr. and Mrs. Abbott reclining in a gondola in Venice.

"That's Gwendolyn and I on our honeymoon," Mr. Abbott said, going over to the mantel. His voice trickled away as he stared at the photograph. He and his wife were cheek to cheek in the gondola, bathed in a golden light, the two of them floating in a lost world, ancient and unreachable now.

"We've had a ban on leaf blowers in the Heights for as long as I can remember," groused Mr. Abbott, holding his knife and fork backward, Continental-style, over his veal chop. "*Long* before Los Angeles and Malibu, though you wouldn't know it from reading the *Times*."

"I didn't know that, Chuck," Jackie said. "That's real interesting."

"You never heard *our* Mexicans complaining," said Mr. Abbott. "They just got out their rakes and brooms and went to work. The rest of us carried on with our business in peace and quiet."

Val glanced at Kyle.

"Just *once* I would like to see the Heights get proper credit," said Mr. Abbott.

"You look familiar, Val." Mrs. Abbott tapped the edge of her glass with a fingernail, repeating the same note over and over. "I *know* I've seen you before. Do you work at the Exxon station at PCH and Main?"

"I applied there, Mrs. Abbott," said Val, "but my test scores weren't high enough."

Mr. Abbott laughed too loudly. "Kyle's brought a live one this time, darling," he said, sawing at his chop. "You've got your work cut out for you."

This time? Val shifted in his seat. The rosewood dining-room table overflowed with candelabra, gilt-edged china, and more utensils than Val had ever seen. Mr. and Mrs. Abbott sat at opposite ends, with him and Kyle on one side, Kilo and Jackie facing them on the other. Val felt out of place here. His dark angular features seemed too primitive for this urbane setting: his nose too big, his hair too long. Even his hands stood out. The Abbotts' hands on the white linen table-cloth were smooth and soft; his own were strong and veiny. As if she had read his mind, Kyle reached over, took his hand, and gave it a squeeze. Her grip was as strong as his. This might be her family home, but she didn't belong here either.

"Do you play tennis, Val?" Mr. Abbott nodded toward the two backyard tennis courts visible through the window. "Don't go up against Kilo—my son will humiliate you," he beamed. "The boy is a champion—second place in the Junior Nationals, 1986."

"He's probably a bowler, Daddy," said Kilo, munching on baby asparagus, "plays in a *league* and wears a lime-green polyester shirt with his name stitched across the pocket."

"Kilo is producing a tennis tournament in a few weeks," said Mr. Abbott, leaning forward slightly in his eagerness. "He's doing everything himself. It's quite an undertaking—some sort of movie star affair from what I understand." He glanced at his wife. "Kilo has been working his connections—"

"I'm not limiting the tournament to just movie stars," said Kilo, shifting slightly in his chair. "Celebrities, that's a much more . . . post-millennium concept."

"How is your post-millennium tournament progressing?" Mrs. Abbott asked. "I haven't heard you speak of it in days."

"What kind of work are *you* in, Val?" said Mr. Abbott.

Val felt Kyle brush his leg with her knee. "I work in the technical side of the film business."

"Is that why you wear your hair slicked back?" said Mrs. Abbott. "Do you play some sort of . . . character?"

"He said he was a *technician,* not an actor, Gwen," said Kilo. "He could be the apprentice plumber on the *Love Boat* for all we know."

"Kilo's in the film business, too," Mr. Abbott bubbled. "He's what they call a 'hyphenate.' That's the right term, isn't it, Kilo? Writer slash actor. He's writing a movie . . . some kind of detective thing, isn't it, Kilo?"

"It's a science-fiction thing now," said Kilo, leaning back in his chair. "Special effects is all Hollywood wants."

Kyle laughed at him and Kilo's face reddened.

"Kyle and Charles . . . they've always fought," Mr. Abbott confided to Val, "quite publicly too, no regard for who else is present. It's healthy, I suppose. . . ." He dabbed his lips with the corner of his napkin.

"What I really need is my own production company," said Kilo. "I've told you that, Daddy."

"Hmmm." Mr. Abbott avoided his wife's gaze.

"Johnny Depp has his own production company," said Kilo. "That's what you need to get attention in Hollywood. Matt Damon has his company. So does Brendan Frasier."

Mr. Abbott looked around the table. "Who *are* these people?"

"Matt Damon was in the asteroid movie," Jackie said helpfully, "and Brendan Frasier . . . he was George of the Jungle."

"See, Daddy?" Kilo played with one of the candles nearest him and made the flame flicker.

Mr. Abbott nodded. "I can understand how a production company might be helpful—" He caught sight of his wife. "This isn't really the appropriate time to discuss this, Kilo, but I'll certainly consider the matter."

Kilo pinched out the candle. "Yeah, right."

"I think working in movies must be *so* interesting," Jackie offered.

"Sometimes," said Val.

"Oh, you're just being modest." Jackie's face was framed by a mass of coppery curls. Heat a new penny over a flame until Abe Lincoln smoldered, and that was the color of Jackie's hair. "I bet you know lots of famous people."

"Fishing for clients, are we?" Mrs. Abbott said coolly.

"Jackie's in real estate," Mr. Abbott explained. "She's working for Harlan Clark."

"Harlan said Jackie was the first person he ever made a sales associate without roots in the community," Kilo bragged. "Jackie can sell anything."

"I'm certain she can." The lines around Mrs. Abbott's mouth deepened. "Did Kilo tell you how he got that foolish nickname of his, Jackie? No? Charles was arrested a few years ago with a kilogram of marijuana in his car. Over two *pounds* of that—"

"Maui Gold, Gwen," said Kilo. "Best pot in the world—five hundred dollars an ounce."

"Thank you, Charles, I defer to your narcotics expertise." Mrs. Abbott toyed with her pearls. "Kilo was originally charged with felony trafficking, but his father spent a great deal of money on an attorney who convinced the district attorney that the kilo of marijuana—or whatever you call it—was strictly for personal use, and thus a misdemeanor. Charles received six months' probation and a permanent nickname."

"The kid was primed for the Davis Cup," blustered

Mr. Abbott, "a felony would have ruined any endorsements or—"

They were interrupted by the cook, a stolid Hispanic woman, who brought in a chocolate cake dotted with candles and placed it in front of Mrs. Abbott.

"Make a wish!" called Mr. Abbott.

Mrs. Abbott blew out the candles too quickly to have wished for anything. She cut the first slice, gave it to her husband, then allowed the cook to serve the rest of them before she retreated to the kitchen.

Mr. Abbott pulled out a small jewelry box from his tuxedo jacket and set it before his wife. "Happy birthday, darling."

Mrs. Abbott cautiously opened the box and stared at the huge diamond earrings gleaming against the dark velvet. "Oh, *my*."

"They once belonged to Ginger Rogers," said Mr. Abbott. "There was an auction at Christie's. . . . I hope you like them."

Hands trembling, Mrs. Abbott replaced her pearl earrings with the pear-shaped diamond ones, modeling them for her husband.

"My God, Gwen," said Mr. Abbott, his face rosy.

"You look lovely, Mother," said Kyle.

"I helped pick them out," said Kilo. "Honest."

Mrs. Abbott ignored him, slowly unrolling the parchment that Kyle had handed her. It looked like a page from a textbook, filled with as many numbers as words. Her eyes teared as she read.

"What is it, dear?" asked Mr. Abbott.

"Kyle has given me my very own star," said Mrs. Abbott, her voice hushed. She held up the parchment. There was a celestial map in one corner, one star colored gold.

"One of my astronomy professors spent last quarter at the Lick Observatory cataloguing stars," said Kyle. "Dr. Murray offered to let me name one after you. I'm *so* glad you—"

"My own star," said Mrs. Abbott.

"We can take a drive to the observatory next month," said Kyle. "It's a Class M star near the Greater Magellanic Cloud."

"I would like that very much," said Mrs. Abbott.

"Your own star," said Jackie. "That is just so . . . sweet."

Mrs. Abbott stared at Val. "I *know* where I've seen you. It's been bothering me since we were introduced. You were on *Jeopardy* yesterday, Valentine something or other. You were wearing that same blue suit."

"Mother, are you tipsy?" asked Kyle.

"Alex, I'll take 'U.S. Presidents' for twenty dollars," Val intoned.

Mrs. Abbott clapped her hands, delighted. For an instant she was young and beautiful again. She looked like Kyle.

"Valentine?" Kyle leaned toward Val. "*That's* what the hearts underwear was all about."

"I beg your pardon?" said Mr. Abbott.

"Your young man bet everything he had in Final Jeopardy," Mrs. Abbott said to Kyle, pleased. "Every dollar. I've always said that boldness is the only quality worth having in a man, but I didn't think you were listening, Kyle."

Kyle draped her arm around the back of Val's chair. "I was listening, Mother."

Jackie watched the two of them.

"You told Alex Trebek you were a pest control specialist," said Mrs. Abbott. "I remember because Alex said that you were the first pest control specialist to appear as a contestant." She looked at him dubiously. "Is that in addition to your film work?"

"No, I'm retired from pest control," said Val.

"See, Daddy," said Kilo, "I told you he had a shirt with his name on it somewhere."

Val smiled, imagining Junior's expression when he saw the show. Junior taped every episode of *Jeopardy*. Half the dope dealers in south Florida were glued to the tube every afternoon, making bets, yelling at the contestants. Junior once shot out a forty-seven-inch Mitsubishi over a missed answer.

"Did you win, Val?" asked Kyle.

"He most certainly did not," Mrs. Abbott said. "Although he *should* have."

Junior had probably already assigned someone to follow up on his appearance—a local with connections at the phone company and DMV, someone who could find out who on the *Jeopardy* crew had a big mortgage and a small paycheck. Val used a P.O. box and an answering service. He had covered his tracks well but not so well that he couldn't be found. Not if someone knew where to start looking.

Mrs. Abbott wagged her fork at Val. "That was the most foolish wager I have ever seen, young man." She glanced at Kyle. "He had the high score going into Final Jeopardy—no one could have caught him. Instead he bets everything, over nine thousand dollars, on 'Classical Opera.' Boldness is an attribute I have great respect for, but being foolhardy, that is something else. Opera was clearly a category Valentine knew nothing about."

"That hurts, Mrs. Abbott," said Val. "I saw *Evita* at the Cineplex."

"The Final Jeopardy answer was 'She had a deadly kiss for Rome's chief of police,'" Mrs. Abbott said to Kyle.

"Who was Madame Butterfly?" blurted Kilo.

"Who was Tosca?" said Kyle.

"Where were you when I needed you?" Val said to Kyle.

Kyle's eyes were so warm that Val felt like taking off his jacket.

"Look, Jackie," said Kilo, "can't you feel the electricity in the room?"

"If you didn't know the answer, Valentine, then you could have taken a *sensible* guess," said Mrs. Abbott. "Instead you wrote, 'Who was Junior Mayfield?'" She was laughing along with him, unable to help herself. "Junior Mayfield—that sounds like the name of a stock-car racer or a . . . sausage salesman."

Junior had put out a contract on him, spread the news that Val had rolled over to the task force. Just being alive was an affront to Junior. To flaunt his name on television, that was an insult that *had* to be punished. Junior was safe in his penthouse, protected from his enemies and the law—as long as he stayed in south Florida.

Kyle sat so close to Val that he could smell her faint perfume with every breath he took. He looked at her and cursed his bad timing. Like his grandmother said, sometimes he was too smart for his own good.

Chapter Six

"Como estás, Junior?"

Junior freeze-framed the VCR, spoke to the speakerphone on the black marble coffee table in front of him, the table strewn with broken bluecrab shells and splintered claws. "Está bien, Fernando," he said lightly. "What do you want?" He already knew.

"Why you home on Saturday night?" asked Fernando.

A tiny piece of crabmeat hung from Junior's upper right canine. He sucked it out, making plenty of noise. "I'm busy," he said, his eyes fastened on the TV screen.

"Ah, *busy*," said Fernando. "Same like you and Armando was busy last week when Gordo and his vatos got scrambled?"

"Who?"

"I never liked Gordo myself," said Frenando, "but somebody left a real mess on his boat. I heard the first cop on the scene blew his dinner all over his shoes." He brayed into the receiver. "If you was a real Southern gentleman, Junior, you send that cop a couple McDonald's coupons, buy him a happy meal to replace the one he lost."

Junior tossed the wooden mallet onto the coffee table, sending crabshells flying onto the carpet. He licked his fingers; his chin was shiny with grease.

"I'm having a few peoples over Monday to watch some private videos," said Fernando. "Be some good time, Junior—imported women and my private stash. You should come. I got a tape of an ol' friend of yours on *Jeopardy*, but maybe you already seen it?"

Junior stared at Val freeze-framed on the big-screen TV, Val caught in mid-sentence as he put his answer in the form of a question to Alex Trebek. He had that grin on his face the whole show, looking right out at Junior. "Yeah, I heard something about it. I heard a dead man was a contestant."

Fernando laughed. "Somebody better tell Valentine, man. He don' look like he *know* he's dead."

Junior inched the video forward, frame by frame. Valentine's grin was gone now, and his face was contorted by the steady digital progression. It looked as if he was screaming. "I'll tell him myself, Fernando," Junior said, breaking the connection.

"I am sorry, Junior," Armando said.

Immobile, Armando stood near the door, wearing purple trousers and a new white leather jacket criss-crossed with zippers, his hair decked out with those silly-ass bows. Junior picked up the wooden mallet. There was Val, hanging out with Alex Trebek, probably going to Alex's dressing room after the show and swapping stories. Junior was stuck here with Armando, who was getting weirder by the minute. Junior half-expected the kid to show up some morning dressed in an Easter Bunny outfit.

"I should have killed Valentine," said Armando.

Junior hefted the mallet. It was heavier than it looked,

an auto body-shop hammer for beating out big dents, the head weighted with lead. "I was the one stopped you that day."

"I should have killed him."

"Yeah, I guess you're going to have to double-up on mass," said Junior. Armando didn't smile; he didn't respond at all. Judas Priest, the kid had no fucking sense of humor. Junior hadn't had a good laugh since Val disappeared. Heck, if the joke hadn't been on him, Junior would have gotten a kick out of Val going on national TV just to fuck with an old pal's head. Val's face stared back at him from the screen. Junior must have watched the tape ten or fifteen times already, unable to stop himself. Gently he tapped the hammer against the side of his head. It hurt, but he did it anyway.

Junior *still* didn't know if Val was a cop. His contact inside the Miami drug task force had told him they were getting inside information from someone close to Junior. It had cost Junior over a half-million dollars to pin the badge on Steffano. That should have ended it, but a couple of weeks later Junior got word that Bernard Sanford, the state's attorney in charge of the task force, was getting fresh information. It had to be coming from Val. Junior had sat on his sunroof all morning watching the bikinis and drinking spiked cherry Kool-Aid. Then he did the unthinkable. He arranged a meeting with Sanford.

They met at a traveling carnival set up in a K-Mart parking lot. It was crowded and noisy, too raucous for a microphone to pick up their conversation. There was supposed to be just him and Sanford at the meet, but Junior spotted at least a dozen agents shadowing them, talking into their lapels. No wonder these task force jerkoffs needed informers and deep-cover boys to make their cases for them.

"Climb aboard, Bernard." Junior shoved aside a fat girl with no front teeth, tapped the white-and-gold striped horse on the merry-go-round. "Come on. I reserved the white gelding for you."

Sanford didn't like it, but he awkwardly hoisted himself up onto the horse. "I compliment you on your timing, Mr. Mayfield. I'm in the process of drawing up a series of multi-count indictments, and your name is quite prominent."

"Let's not get ahead of ourselves." Junior grinned as the fat girl bumped into Sanford, smearing his pants with her chocolate ice cream cone. The music blared as the merry-go-round started to spin, picking up speed. The state's attorney bobbed up and down, hanging on to the horse's neck with both hands, while Junior stood beside him. Armando was behind them, riding a fucking swan.

The meeting with Sanford had been a risk, but when you got right down to it, he and the state's attorney were brokers, pure and simple. Junior had even better information to trade than Val. He and Sanford had come to a mutually beneficial arrangement. Junior's operation was bigger than ever now; his enemies were targeted by the task force. Bernard's budget had increased twenty percent, and last month the vice president himself had flown down to congratulate Sanford for his prosecutorial success.

Sanford had refused to confirm or deny that Val was really a cop, or if he had just gotten scared and decided to roll over. Sanford said he had made inquiries, but even *he* hadn't been able to get a definitive answer. Maybe that was true. South Florida was layered with hustlers, shadow players, and informers, DEA and FBI and ATF, double and triple agents working so far under cover they might as well be stone traffickers because they were never going to see the honest light of day again.

Junior could understand Val having connections with the law. Shoot—a dealer needed insurance, and Junior himself had found that the best heroin, the only real purecut, came from federal agents in business for themselves. Val going to the task force was one thing—maybe he hoped to take over Junior's sources after Sanford unsealed his indictments—but Val actually being police, that was a hard one. If that was true, Junior couldn't trust his instincts, and if Junior couldn't trust his instincts, he was dead.

"Do you want to go out?" asked Armando.

Junior idly picked through the crab remnants on the coffee table. One time Val had taken him into the Miami Dolphins locker room after a playoff game. Dan Marino himself had shaken Junior's hand and given him a pair of his shoulderpads. There were some things that money couldn't buy, and Valentine always seemed to know how to get them.

"We could go to jai alai," said Armando. "You like jai alai."

Junior liked going to jai alai with Val. No matter who Junior bet on, Val always bet against him. Nobody else dared do that. Junior wiped the back of his hand across his lips, then on his shirt. Ancient history. He grabbed the encrypted security phone and punched in Sanford's private number. The state's attorney was a skinny prick with a red bow tie and round rimless glasses, but he did business. That was all that mattered. Sanford picked up on the second ring. "It's me," said Junior.

"I don't appreciate being called at home," said Sanford.

"I'm using the security phone."

"That's not the point."

"The point is Valentine was on TV yesterday. He was on fucking *Jeopardy,* Bernard."

"I beg your pardon?"

"*Jeopardy,*" said Junior. "That's *my* show."

"You own a television show?"

"The people I deal with know that *Jeopardy* is my show," Junior barked. "They see Val shooting the breeze with Mr. Alex Trebek, and it makes me look like a joke. Next thing you know there's a line of South Americans stretched around the block waiting to park their dicks up my ass."

"Indeed."

"Indeed? Look, Bernard—I end up stuffed inside a fifty-gallon oil drum, we *both* lose. Val's out in California, somewhere around L.A. I know that much. I got my own people looking for him, but you government boys got ways of finding—"

"Junior, I am *not* about to use the power of my office to aid you in the commission of a homicide."

"You like playing Eliot Ness though, don't you? You like that well enough. Picture in the paper and interviews with six-o'clock-news pussy, that's nice, isn't it?"

"I would advise you not to overestimate your value—"

"Are you protecting him?" Junior demanded.

"We've already dealt with that question—"

"You ain't dealt with nothing, you college prick."

"Junior, I've warned you before about the use of profanity."

"Valentine got something on you, too? Is that it?"

"Our mutual acquaintance enjoys neither the protection nor the interest of the task force."

"What the fuck does that—?" Junior heard a dial tone.

"Junior?" Armando stood there, as frozen as Valentine's TV self—only Armando's eyes moved, alert to every sound and sensation. It was like he hoarded his energy, kept it tight and focused, exploding into action only when he needed to. "Junior, if you want, I can go to Wolfie's and pick you up the special hot fudge sundae."

"I'm getting fat as a hog, Armando."

Junior remembered airboating with Val across the Everglades at seventy miles an hour, eating baby back ribs and tossing them over the side, Junior shooting gators with an Uzi. The sweet life. If Val had stayed lost, Junior might have let him live, but Val had persisted. Anonymous calls tipped the local cops to Junior's secret airstrips and warehouses. Someone had even gotten word to Kiki Mendoza about Junior's cooperation with the state's attorney. Junior had to hand over a surplus Chinese submarine full of coke to the task force to silence that rumor. The bust made all the papers. Sanford, in flak jacket and mirror shades, promised to end the "scourge of narcotics and the vipers who prey upon the innocent." It was a good speech, and besides, Junior had a second sub in operation anyway.

Bam! Junior smacked the mallet onto the coffee table, scattering crabshells. "I thought Val was my friend." *Bam!* The tabletop rang. "I blame myself, Armando. That sumbitch *truly* amused me, so I cut him more slack than I should have. I'm too good-natured—that's my problem." Junior wasn't a man to hold a grudge. He had more important things to think about than Val—out of sight, out of mind. Until last Friday. *Bam! Bam! Bam! Bam!* Junior beat on the table, spraying crab juice and bits of shell in all directions. He beat on the marble until he was exhausted and his hand ached from the vibration.

"We will find him, Junior. When we do, I will amuse you too."

Breathing hard, Junior picked up a splintered blue claw. His hair was plastered to his face. He sucked out the last remnant of sweet flesh. "Fuckin' A," he said, chewing with his mouth open.

Chapter Seven

$\mathbf{V}$al held on to the roof of the Suburban, bracing himself as Kyle raced down the winding road from the Abbotts' estate. His head banged against the side window as they slewed onto the gravel shoulder, pebbles splattering against the flimsy guardrail. Kyle had kicked off her high heels and was driving barefoot, downshifting smoothly on the hairpin turns. Its engine screaming in protest, the Suburban drifted across the yellow line, and Kyle gunned it, cutting off the corner of the blind curve before returning to her proper lane. Val's head banged the window again. "When I drive, I like to stay in my own lane."

"Adaptability is the highest virtue," said Kyle, not taking her eyes off the road. "Staying between the lines is fine on a straightaway, but not here. There's no traffic. I can take advantage of *both* lanes for maximum speed. Applied Physics 301."

"I like this new side of you," said Val, swaying against her as the Suburban skidded toward the edge. "Kyle Abbott, daredevil, thrill seeker, violator of law and order."

"I'm no daredevil," said Kyle, above the sound of the tires squealing, "I know every inch of this road."

"You're a reckless woman. No telling what will happen to me if I hang around you."

"You look like you can take care of yourself," said Kyle, winding out the gears. "I know I'm speeding, but I just want to put as much distance between me and that house as possible."

"Your family didn't seem so bad."

"I thought you were a better liar than that."

"I'm out of practice," said Val.

"My mother liked you."

"Is that good?"

"Unprecedented." Kyle's right knee was resting comfortably against his left now. The vibration of the big engine moved through them in tandem. In the flash of oncoming headlights, Val could see the fine hairs along her nape gleaming. "What about your stepfather?" he asked, imagining brushing those soft hairs with his lips. "Did Chuck like me?"

"Hungry for approval, are we?"

"Desperate."

"I like that in a man," said Kyle. "Chuck liked you well enough, but he likes everybody well enough. My mother is the one you have to worry about."

"Beautiful woman."

"Yes." Kyle's jaw tensed. "You meant my mother, right?"

"Who else? Jackie? No, I was talking about your mother. She's lovely. I see where you get it."

Kyle stared straight ahead, pleased, as they passed through the marble pillars at the entrance to Aegean Heights. Pacific Coast Highway was almost deserted this late at night, flanked by nail-care parlors and cheap motels, closed surf shops, and bars with their doors wide open. Val stretched out in his seat, the clean ocean air whipping past. It felt like no one could ever catch them. Searchlights swept the sky in the distance—a Planet Hollywood opening or a midnight sale-athon at Westminster Mall. Maybe it was an air raid, a rogue B-2 pilot flashbacking to Vietnam, readying his nuclear payload for the streets of Little Saigon.

"What did you think of Jackie and Kilo?" Kyle said, interrupting his reverie. "You haven't said anything about *them.*"

Val shrugged. "A perfect couple."

"Perfect couple of what?" They both laughed. "You should have seen your face when Kilo told you I had been married twice before," said Kyle. "You looked as if you had been slapped."

"I *was* surprised. Two marriages . . . it's out of character, at least from what I know about you. You seem so sure-footed. It's hard to imagine you making a couple of bad marriages."

"A few minutes ago you said I was a reckless woman. Now I'm serious and dull. Make up your mind." Accelerating, Kyle ran a red light. "And they weren't bad marriages, either. They just didn't last."

"What were your husbands like?"

"You make it sound like a convention," Kyle said tightly. "There were only two."

"So what were these *two* guys like? I'm interested."

It took her a while to answer. "Mack ran a charter boat out of Cabo San Lucas. My mother was appalled, but I was eighteen. I knew everything. Mack made a great cup of coffee and could read the ocean better than anyone I ever met. He's the one who got me interested in gray whales. We were married almost six months. David was a geology professor at the university. He had an international reputation and a great body, but every conversation was a seminar on geoplastic rock formations. He even managed to make sex boring." Her laugh was so warm that Val was jealous. "That one lasted almost a year. I learned my lesson." She nudged Val. "What about you?"

"I'm saving myself for the right woman."

"Let me know if you find one," said Kyle. "I've just about given up on men."

"You could have fooled me."

"What does that mean?"

"I don't think you've given up. I think you're just careful," Val said, a little high from all the alcohol, feeling way too good. "That first evening in the laundry room, Brenda didn't really want to invite me to a party, did she?"

"Of course she did."

"You put her up to it."

"She thought you were sexy. I told you that."

"Yeah, and I believed it at first—who wouldn't?—but the more I thought about it, the encounter in the laundry room just seemed too convenient. I think her invitation was a kind of test you were running on me. An experiment."

"Do you have a license for that ego, mister?"

Val smiled. "Brenda is very attractive, and I've always appreciated a woman who can carry off silver lamé hiphuggers, but she and I . . . we're not each other's type. Maybe you needed to make sure of that."

"And you and I *are* each other's type?"

"I hope so," said Val. "I think you do too."

"That's a charming scenario," said Kyle, her eyes still

on the highway. "It makes me out to be manipulative, crafty, and devious. If you and I truly are the same type"— she glanced at him, then back at the road—"what does that make you?"

Val stared at her. Most people, when confronted like that, would have sputtered and stumbled, whether it was true or not, but Kyle admitted nothing, just turned his words back on him.

"*What?*" said Kyle. "I can hear you thinking."

"I feel like a tourist at the beach on the first day of vacation," said Val. "Here I am edging out into the ocean, one step at a time, the water knee-high, waist-high, chest-high, and suddenly the bottom drops off and I'm in over my head. That's the way I feel when I talk with you— like I'm one step away from going under."

"That's one of the nicest things anyone has ever said to me." Kyle veered onto the shoulder of PCH, the Suburban bumping, throwing up gravel as it churned along a narrow rutted road posted "No Trespassing." They were in an unpopulated bit of coast just north of Laguna, with high bluffs overlooking the ocean. Where the road abruptly ended in a small cul-de-sac, Kyle turned off the ignition, coasted down, and parked. "The beach down there is called the Grottos. It's one of my very favorite spots. I used to come here to escape all the time when I was a kid. Not many people know about it. A few surfers and locals, that's all."

Val followed her to the edge of the cliff, carefully sat down beside her, next to the tilted, "Danger Unstable Ground" sign. Her party dress was dirty, but she didn't seem to notice, leaning back, feet dangling in space. Stunted eucalyptus trees overhung the bluff, their twisted branches creaking in the wind. Val could see a small cove cut into the cliff-face below, a white sand beach gleaming in the moonlight. There were boulders in the water; with waves breaking over them in a swirl of foam.

"What is it?" said Kyle. "You look like you're a million miles away."

"Not quite that far."

"I've told you about my husbands," said Kyle. "I've shown you my family in their natural habitat, in their awful masticating splendor. If I can let my guard down, so can you."

"You haven't let your guard down."

Kyle looked toward the ocean, not responding.

A footpath wound down to the beach from the cul-de-sac—Val could hear a faint hum from the freeway, but it might as well have been crickets calling. "The cove down there reminds me of a place I used to go with my first real girlfriend," he said at last. "Same white sand beach, same sense of isolation. 'No Trespassing,' just like here." He ran his hand over the tough dry grass on the bluff. Even the grass felt the same. "The Margaret Mac-Neil Wildlife State Preserve, that's what it was called. We used to park her car about four miles away and hike in before sunrise so we wouldn't be spotted. They arrested you if you got caught."

"I bet you never got caught."

"The preserve was beautiful—ficus trees and royal palms, sea grape bushes and all kinds of birds. Sometimes we would see this other young couple down the sand from us, but we never spoke, just nodded and kept our distance." The tide was coming in, rushing across the breakwater toward the beach. Out of the corner of his eye, he could see Kyle watching him. "This must have gone on for a couple of years, then one day—we hadn't seen them for months—one day the other couple showed up and they had a baby with them. They seemed so happy lying on their blanket, legs tangled, laughing. My girlfriend and I didn't talk about it, but we *knew* . . . we knew we weren't going to go back there anymore." He tugged at the grass, pulled a clump up, and tossed it over the edge. "We loved each other, we really did, but we weren't going to have babies together. We broke up not long after." He shrugged. "That's my story."

Kyle kissed him. "One of them."

Val kissed her back, but she slid her face away from him, left them cheek to cheek. He didn't push it. They stayed there overlooking the cove, watching the waves.

"I wasn't totally honest with you before about my marriages," Kyle said quietly. "The divorces—they weren't really so . . . painless."

"I didn't think they were."

"You thought I was lying?"

"Just protecting yourself."

Kyle nodded. The breeze whipped sand around them, but she ignored it. "Mack . . . the charter boat captain—he was a good sailor but a nasty drunk, and when he wasn't at sea, he was drunk." She looked at Val. "Mack used to say that I threw my education and my family in his face, that I thought I was better than he was. We had been married about three months before he slapped me. He said it was long overdue. I had never been hit before. Never. Mack was sorry, of course—he cried. Real tears too. I actually told him it was my fault for provoking him." She shook her head. "I apologized to him. Can you believe that?"

"You wouldn't apologize to him today. That's what counts."

Kyle stared at the waves crashing on the beach. "The second time it happened, Mack hit me harder. I drove into Cabo and got a hotel room for a week. He sent me flowers every day. The third time . . . the *last* time it happened"—Kyle chewed her lower lip—"we had a little house just above the bay, cute little place too. I was cleaning an eight-pound snapper he had caught that day while Mack sat with his feet propped up on my books, working his way through a bottle of tequila. Before I knew what was happening, he had staggered over to the sink, reached in, and rubbed a handful of guts in my face. He said rich girls needed to learn to enjoy getting dirty. I told him to go fuck himself, and he punched me, split my lip. I fought back this time, but it just made him madder. He grabbed me, bent back my little finger, wanting me to admit that he was just as smart as I was."

Val put his arm around her and felt her trembling.

"I told him he was smarter than me," said Kyle, "stronger, *better.* I begged him, but it didn't matter. He broke my finger, then he started to choke me, telling me he was going to give me a real education." She was sobbing, trying to hold it back. "I stabbed him."

Val rocked her in his arms.

"I grabbed the boning knife off the counter and drove it into his chest," she said, not looking at him. "It was awful, blood all over the floor. I kept slipping in it, afraid I would fall. He was a strong man, and he kept coming and I . . . I kept stabbing him."

"It wasn't your fault, Kyle. You were only protecting yourself."

"I wish the Mexican authorities had seen it that way," said Kyle. "Mack was very well liked. He used to take the local big shots out on his boat, no charge, cervezas all around. I was arrested. I don't know what would have happened if it hadn't been for Chuck and my mother. I couldn't wait to move out of their house, but as soon as I got in trouble . . ." She tossed a rock over the edge, listened as it bounced its way down the steep slope. "The two of them flew in, hired a good Mexican attorney, and started shoveling out money. All charges were dropped. The Baja police force got a new cruiser, a red Camaro with a CD player and gold wheel covers, and I got a quickie divorce."

"You *survived*. That's all that matters."

"Mack must have written me twenty or thirty letters from the hospital, but I never answered. About a year later, his boat went down in a storm. They never found the body." Kyle looked at him. "I should never have married him. My mother warned me; even Chuck knew better. But I went ahead with it anyway. I was going to show them."

Val smoothed her hair. "Don't blame yourself—" There was a beeping. "I have to get that," Val apologized as he reached into his hip pocket. "My grandmother is the only one with my number. . . . It could be important." He flipped open the cell-phone. "Hi, Gramma, everything okay? No, I was awake. Are you all right? I was awake, Grace. I'm with a friend. That's right, Grace, a lady friend." He looked at Kyle. "Grace says you should be careful." Kyle smiled as Val listened. "That sounds good, I'd like that. I'll pick you up at two o'clock. Okay, one o'clock. Yes, ma'am, see you tomorrow. Love you." He snapped the phone shut.

Kyle stood up and brushed off her dress. They barely spoke on the drive back, filled up with each other's secrets, intoxicated by the intimacy. Words might spoil it. He walked her to the door. The two of them stood there, her key still in the lock, waiting. Val leaned toward her and lightly kissed her ears. She cocked her head, allowing him to caress her neck with his lips. "Can I come in?" he asked.

Kyle pushed open her door. "Not tonight. I told you, I can't make any more mistakes."

"I don't want you to." Val watched the pulse in the hollow of her throat. "How about tomorrow? We could go to the beach."

"I thought you had to take your grandmother shopping."

Val felt himself flush. "I forgot."

"It's not your fault. I've clouded your mind with my feminine wiles," said Kyle. "I have to work tomorrow anyway. I'll be running statistics at the university all day."

"We could go out tomorrow night."

"About the laundry room. . . . I didn't set you up, not exactly. I was just taking advantage of the situation." Kyle smiled, closing the door on him.

Val stood there looking at the door, hoping she would change her mind, then he gave up and headed to his apartment. Going slow wasn't so bad. He preferred it actually. Not that he had a whole lot of experience with going slow. Maybe that was why he had made so many mistakes himself.

Val jerked upright in bed, the room in darkness, fully awake now, already reaching for the 9mm Glock—he kept the gun at hip level so that he didn't have to search for it. A man could die in the time it took to fumble under his pillow—even the Tooth Fairy was armed and dangerous these days. Val rolled out of bed, listening so hard his head hurt.

No sound, nothing extraneous anyway. Wind in the

palm trees, the dry rustle of dead fronds outside the window, and traffic in the distance. Even before dawn the freeways buzzed with ambition. It made him homesick for the sultry indolence of Miami, cruising down A1A, windows rolled down so he could smell the oleander blooming along the median. He swiveled toward the front door, the windows, but there were just the faint familiar sounds of the building: water running through pipes, a sharp cough from the apartment below.

Val felt sweat on his forehead. It was warm in the room, but he slept without air conditioning, slept with the windows wide open—an air-conditioned bedroom was a cool, comfortable deathtrap. Even in Miami, Val had slept on the sheets instead of under them, skin glistening with the moist tropical air. If Steffano had turned off his air conditioner, he might be alive today. He might have heard the Jackson brothers outside his house, but he was always a heavy sleeper, even when they were kids.

The hot Miami nights had helped to kill Steffano, but Val still longed to go home. Florida was steamy and ripe, trees drooping with oranges and mangos, the night thick with frogs and mosquitoes. Los Angeles was a fast-lane asphalt desert, baking the brain, hardening the heart. All the sprinklers and irrigation canals wouldn't change that. Nothing grew in L.A. without help, and what sprouted between the cracks of the concrete was stunted and deformed. L.A. was a refuge, a temporary refuge, but it would never be home.

Val pulled on a pair of shorts and slipped out the door. Clouds slid over the moon as he passed Kyle's apartment. He shouldn't have gone out with her tonight. He should have short-circuited things when he had the chance. It was almost too late now. They had touched. Voices in the street brought him to the top of the stairs, then down the steps, taking them two at a time. A block away three young guys walked toward the beach kicking around a Hacky Sack. Val waited until they had disappeared before backing off the 9mm. It took a little longer for his heart to stop racing.

Val walked back up the stairs, happy against all reason, smelling salt from the sea, pretending it was the Atlantic and wondering if he would ever see it again. His bare feet made no sound on the concrete. He had grown up barefoot. The soles of his feet were so thick he couldn't feel the hot pavement underfoot, so tough he could dance on stones.

If Val wasn't careful, he was going to get Kyle hurt. When Junior came after someone, he liked starting on their family and friends—"the soft, sweet parts," he called it. Val hadn't thought that anyone knew his grandmother even existed, but Junior had found her anyway. Given time, Junior would find Kyle, too. Val was going to have to disappear before that happened. He wished she had invited him in. It would have been a bad idea, but he would have gone in, closed the door behind them, and to hell with Junior and Armando and everything else.

Chapter Eight

Kilo should have worn socks to the swapmeet. And gotten a typhoid shot. He edged away from the family of Cambodians that swirled around him, their silver teeth chattering, the women's long embroidered skirts sending a warm breeze licking across his bare ankles. He had opted for a royal blue, bubble-pattern Versace shirt, blue rayon trousers with the cuffs loosely rolled, and buttery yellow loafers. Socks would have ruined the whole look, but he should have worn them anyway. If he had known where Jackie was taking him, he would have worn hip waders. "Can we leave *now*?"

"Don't be such a baby," Jackie said.

Kilo watched her flipping through a rack of gauzy lingerie, her eyes hidden behind large dark glasses, her red hair tucked under a pink kerchief. Her plain white slacks were perfect with the pale pink top and the understated makeup. He wondered who she was copying.

"We shouldn't be here," warned Dekker. "Not *together*."

"A couple of fraidy cats," said Jackie, fingering a

wispy yellow slip. "You couldn't ask for a more anonymous place for us to shop."

"Kilo's not anonymous," said Dekker. "That shirt is loud enough to wake the dead."

"The gorilla in a black Member's Only windbreaker is giving fashion pronouncements," said Kilo. "I'd rather have Ray Charles pick my wardrobe than you, Dekker."

"Keep it up, motherfucker," said Dekker.

"Darryl, get me an orange juice," said Jackie, still going through the lingerie while the attendant kept watch from over the pages of *Soap Opera Digest*.

"Why don't you send Kilo?"

"Because I asked you, Darryl."

"Get me one too!" Kilo called. He turned toward Jackie. "He's not going to get me anything, you wait and see."

Jackie held up a lavender peignoir to the attendant, a sun-blasted woman with a mustard stain on the front of her paisley dress. "How much?"

Kilo didn't hear the price, but Jackie snorted and walked away. He trailed after her, dodging a blond teenage girl with open-pit acne and an *I am the god of FUCK!* Marilyn Manson T-shirt.

The Big Value Swapmeet was set up on the twenty-acre parking lot of a former aerospace plant. Here it was, barely ten A.M., and the asphalt swarmed with trailer trash and coupon clippers, Orange County lumpen searching for generic tennis shoes and ten-pack underwear, cheap stereos and green pigskin sofas, small appliances that fried cheese and pureed baby food from table scraps. Kilo had no idea what he could possibly have done to deserve being here. He preferred places with a high cover charge, a dress code, a membership fee, *something* to keep the poor and ugly where they belonged, with their noses pressed up against the glass.

Jackie leaned over a table stacked with rows of ceramic Buddhas, picked one up, and rubbed its belly. "You want to make a wish too, Kilo?"

A fat 'n' happy couple brushed past him in matching denim cut-offs, their doughy knees dimpling. "I wish I wasn't here," said Kilo.

"You call this a mango?" Val's grandmother backed the produce manager up against the organic broccoli, waving the unripe mango in his face as she chomped down on her cigar. "Skin is loose, pulp is hard, and it don't have any smell at all. This pitiful thing don't deserve to be called a mango."

The manager stared at the thin, unlit crook in her mouth.

"Come on, Grace," said Val.

"I still don't know why we couldn't go to the farmer's market," she grumbled, pushing the shopping cart. She was a proud old woman with lively eyes, skin the color of Georgia pecans, and white hair hanging loose past her shoulders.

"The farmer's market is closed for health code violations," Val said for the fourth time.

"I could smoke at the farmer's market," Grace muttered.

"Farmer's market is open-air. California has a law against smoking indoors."

"You didn't used to care so damned much about the law."

Val put a hand on her shoulder. "Grace, I still don't care much about it."

"Larry's Cornucopia," said Grace, picking through a pyramid of tangerines, her blue-veined hands trembling slightly. "Who do they think they're fooling?" She nicked a tangerine with the edge of her yellowed thumbnail, sniffed, then dropped it into her basket. "No Dixie Belle grits, no pole beans, no field okra. . . . You keep your damned California and get me back to Florida." She stopped, seeing that she had hurt him. "The house you got me is real nice, Valentine—big refrigerator that makes ice cubes and a shower that gives you a massage. I'm not complaining."

"I'm sorry I got you into this, Grace."

The cigar swiveled to the other side of her mouth. "I was getting tired of that old shack of mine anyway. Roof leaked, and it needed new mosquito netting."

Grace had lived in that clapboard house in the Everglades for almost fifty years, out there with the gators and the blue herons and the warm breeze off the Gulf. She missed her soft kerosene-lantern light and her cast-iron bed that had come all the way from Atlanta, missed sitting on the back porch drinking Southern Comfort and watching the fish jump. Their hurried flight across country had left her no time to pack, no time to adjust to leaving everything behind. He had found her a small place on the edge of the Bolsa Chica wetlands in Huntington Beach, hoping that it would feel like home. He might as well have taken her to Mars.

Grace's eyes lit up. She shuffled over to a small display of small mottled-yellow fruit, scooped up a handful, gently kneading them. "Key limes. I haven't seen these since we left Miami."

His mouth already watering, Val separated the edges of a plastic bag for her.

"I'm going to make you the best Key lime pie you ever had," said Grace, shoving limes into the bag, buying more than she could possibly use. "Just the way you like it, not too sweet. You remember how Steffano loved my Key lime pie? Too polite to ask for seconds. . . . It's okay if we talk about him, isn't it? I think about him, that's all."

"So do I." Val smiled. "He used to be scared of you. Did you know that?"

"You told him I was a witch. That's why he was scared of me."

"I thought you *were* a witch, Grace."

She was silent now, surrounded by the sharp smell of the limes. "I know you feel bad about running away from that Junior, but running away from death is nothing to be ashamed of. That's the good sense you were born with. Seminoles was the only native people who *never* signed a peace treaty with the white man, *never* believed their promises. We fought as long as we could, then we run off just like you did, retreating into the Everglades where the white man was afraid to follow. No Trail of Tears for us, boy. Seminoles lived high on catfish and froglegs. You did right to get us out of there."

"I'll get you back home someday, Grace—that's a promise."

Grace loaded the bag of limes in her cart. She tossed her head, sending her braids tumbling. She was almost eighty but still such a girl. When he was a kid, he'd get up early and find her dancing by herself in the kitchen, making breakfast with the radio on. "When you coming over to paint my tire gators?"

"Soon."

"You make me gators then don't bother to paint them. . . . What's the sense?"

In Florida, Grace had dozens of used-tire gators set around the border of her house like sentinels, retread tires cut in half and carved into jagged teeth, then painted and positioned into the ground so they appeared to be the gaping jaws of alligators. Val could still see the Jackson brothers creeping toward the gators in the darkness, sawed-offs loose in their grip, the wet ground squishing under their weight. Moon over Miami, just enough light for Val to see what they had in store for her.

Grace pushed her cart toward the seafood counter, one wheel squeaking. "So when was you fixing to tell me about this lady friend of yours?"

"Her name is Kyle." Val pointed to the end of the counter. "The catfish is over there."

"Time you made some babies," said Grace. "You're not getting any younger."

"Little premature there, Grace. Kyle and I . . . we're just getting started."

"You wait too long you're going to be sorry." Grace picked up a ten-inch catfish from a bed of crushed ice and examined its eyes. "This Kyle girl, what's she like?"

"She's smart . . . and I smile a lot when I'm around her. I don't know why." He watched her put down the catfish, pick up another. "She makes me nervous though."

"Well, your Grampa scared the devil out of me the first time I saw him, too." Sliding a finger along the belly, Grace felt the flesh of the catfish. "I was right to be scared." She smiled. "My life would never be the same again and I knew it."

"It's not just that. She's very . . . guarded. Defensive." Val saw her bemused expression. "I *know* what you're thinking, but maybe I don't need a woman like myself, Grace. Maybe I need a more trusting person, someone open and honest—"

Grace laughed in his face. "God never made a woman like that in all his life."

Dekker shoved his way through the crowd of shoppers. "Here's your orange juice."

"Where's Kilo's juice?" asked Jackie.

"Who do I look like—Jeeves the butler?" Dekker glared at her, sweating in the sun. "You're going to push me too far someday."

"Not today though." Jackie took a long swallow of her orange juice, then offered the cup to Dekker, making him drink while she held the cup up to him, making him finish the rest of it. "I want you and Kilo to get along, Darryl. It's important to me."

"You get along with him well enough for the both of us," said Dekker, wiping his mouth.

Kilo stepped over a crushed cone of green cotton candy. "I've been thinking," he said to Jackie in a low voice. "Forget taking care of Gwen in the Newport Cinema parking lot—sometimes Chuck comes along at the last minute. Nail her on the way to her Tuesday night bridge game or coming back from her Guild meeting on Wednesdays. Chuck is *never* with her then." He chewed his lip. "I wouldn't want him to see her . . . you know."

"That's sweet." Jackie ambled along the tables, one hand trailing over the merchandise.

"She doesn't carry a gun, does she?" Dekker asked. "You'd be surprised at all the old biddies pack a little thirty-eight in their purse."

Kilo shook his head.

"She looked like a feisty lady to me," said Dekker. "I was watching her with binoculars when she blew out the candles on her birthday cake."

Kilo glanced at Jackie. "You didn't tell me Dekker was out there."

"Get used to it, cutie-pie," said Dekker. "You *sure* she doesn't carry a gun?"

"Gwen doesn't believe in guns," said Kilo. "She'll have the Mercedes locked though. That's the first thing she does when she gets behind the wheel. You just put a bullet through the window and into her head—"

"I can figure it out," said Dekker.

"Don't forget to take her purse, too—"

"You want to do the job yourself, asshole?"

Jackie walked over to a table of remaindered Halloween masks. She tapped a Scream face with a forefinger, then moved on to Nixon, the Alien, Julia Child, Freddy Krueger. The table featured cheap costumes, well beyond the pull-date for hip, but the Vietnamese teenager running the booth was doing good business, making change while she gnawed on a strip of beef jerky.

"On her way back from her bridge game, Gwen takes the Seaside cutoff," Kilo said to Dekker, still watching Jackie. "There's a four-way stop at Albright . . . lot of underbrush where you could hide. I've seen illegals there some mornings, hanging around looking for work." He grinned. "The usual suspects, huh?"

"That's pretty good," said Dekker, impressed in spite of himself.

"Like I said, I've been thinking about this for a long time."

Jackie picked out a Nixon mask from the table, then Godzilla, then held up another one, inspecting it. Kilo didn't recognize the face at first. It was O.J.'s wife, what's her name . . . Nicole. That had been a hot mask a couple of years ago. Kilo had gone to a club where half the babes were decked out like Nicole. Some even had fake bruises. Jackie put down Nicole, selecting O.J. instead, then reached into her purse.

Kilo caught up with Jackie as she strode toward the parking lot. The O.J. mask stared back at him from a clear plastic bag, Nixon and Godzilla stuffed at the bottom. "What's your hurry, Jackie?"

"Me and Kilo came up with a pretty good plan," Dekker said. "It's a little different than we first talked about, but . . ."

Jackie kept walking. O.J., Godzilla, and Nixon swinging with every step.

"Don't you want to hear my plan?" asked Kilo.

"No." Jackie unlocked the door to her car and got in. "The carjacking is out."

"What's going on?" said Dekker.

"Have you ever been to Del Mar?" asked Jackie.

Dekker shrugged. "I went to the track there once. Kind of a ritzy town."

Jackie handed him the bag of masks. "You're going to do a home invasion at the Abbotts instead. Less chance of being interrupted."

"At my house?" said Kilo. "I don't know if that's—"

"Darryl, I want you to do a trial run in Del Mar," said Jackie. "A couple of weeks ago, I babysat an open house there. Total waste of time, but there was a big place across the street that had the same security fence the Abbotts have."

Dekker stared at the masks in his hand. "When?"

"Get in, Kilo." Jackie started the car. "Gwen and

Chuck are expecting us for lunch—it would be rude to be late."

"When do you want me to go to Del Mar?" asked Dekker.

Jackie looked at him over her sunglasses. "Tonight's the night."

Chapter Nine

Kyle looked around as they walked toward the turquoise house, glass crunching underfoot. Broken streetlights had left the whole block in darkness—she could see a glow from the rear of the turquoise house, half-hidden behind a cinder-block fence topped with razor wire. "Are you *sure* about this?"

"Trust me," said Val.

They were in the middle of Santa Ana, a mix of crumbling apartment buildings and neat homes with well-tended gardens, the walls and fences scrawled with gang graffiti, every window and door barred, every bicycle and lawn chair chained in place. Val's pickup was down the street, parked in front of a bungalow with a statue of Our Lady of Guadalupe set out in the front yard, unfettered and unmarked, a quiet blessing left in peace.

"We couldn't visit your friend in daylight?" said Kyle.

"Oscar designed his backyard to be seen under artificial light."

They had gotten off at an I-5 freeway exit Kyle had never taken before. The billboards were all in Spanish.

Packs of dogs ran free. Val drove with one arm out the window, making rights and lefts, until she was totally lost. This deep into the barrio most of the street signs had been torn down, and there were hardly any numbers on the houses. When she mentioned it, Val smiled and said there were no street markers in Aegean Heights either, and for the same reason. Kyle spent three or four months a year in Baja. She went weeks without hearing English spoken, but the Mexican peninsula, for all its poverty and stark volcanic landscape, seemed less alien, less threatening, than this part of Orange County. She was an outsider here, and Val's loose-limbed demeanor just made it worse.

"You're enjoying this, aren't you?"

"First time I've seen you scared. It's kind of attractive."

"I'm not—" Kyle jerked as a pair of huge homeboys stepped out from the shrubbery flanking the wrought-iron gate, the two men impassive as double-door refrigerators in baggy khakis and high-buttoned Pendletons.

"Valentino!"

"Oscar!"

A short man scampered across the lawn toward them, his black suit flapping. "Es buena gente, vatos," he said to the homeboys. "Valentino es indio blanco." Oscar opened wide the gate, waved Val and Kyle inside. The homeboys resumed their station, folding their massive arms across their chests, their bandannas drooping low on their foreheads.

Pushing back his steel-rimmed glasses, Oscar eyed Kyle. A balding man in his mid-forties with a long nose and a wispy brown goatee, he looked like an intellectual rodent. "Come round back. Don't stand out in the open."

They followed Oscar down the stone path toward the

rear of the house. "Got a present for you." Val reached into his jacket and handed a videocassette to Oscar.

Oscar stared at the scrawled title on the generic cassette box. *"The Mummy Walks at Midnight,"* he squeaked happily. "Nineteen thirty-five. Studio went bankrupt before it could be distributed. I've only *heard* about this film, Valentino. Where did you get it?"

"You're welcome," said Val. "I need to talk with you later, by the way."

"What did you do now, hombre?"

"Not nearly enough." Val saw Kyle staring, trying to take it all in. "It *is* beautiful, isn't it?"

Kyle could only nod. Interspersed among the orange and lemon trees, lit by yellow and blue lights, was . . . a miniature golf course. At least Kyle thought that's what it was. She walked closer to the first hole. A channel of green Astroturf right-angled into a large upright mosaic slab depicting a busty female vampire, her batwings spread over a world globe dripping blood. The hyper-realistic mosaic was a mixture of bottle caps, pulltabs, pennies, seashells, bits of glass and plastic scraps, and thousands of tiny ceramic tiles, all placed so carefully that Kyle could hardly detect the matrix of concrete.

"La Hija Del Diablo!" Oscar nodded at the vampire queen. "Starring Lola Montoya as the Devil's daughter and directed by Umberto Saíz. A truly great film."

Val squinted at the Devil's daughter, admiring the tiny silver beads forming her fangs. "She reminds me of your brother's girlfriend," he said to Kyle.

Kyle laughed. "Stepbrother." She bent down, examining the vampire queen, lightly touched the blood-tiles, each of them a slightly different shade of red. "I went to an exhibit of folk art at the Whitney last year, Oscar. This is so much better than anything there."

"Galleries are decadent," Oscar said over his shoulder, walking toward a metal camp cooler decorated with Batman action figures.

"Those are new." Val pointed at the tiny angels suspended from the jacaranda tree in the center of the yard, dozens of gilt seraphim, rhinestone eyes sparkling. "Oscar told me that he's been working on his backyard for eight years, and it's not complete yet."

Kyle looked over at the rear of the house. Three other homeboys lounged on sagging sofas on the back porch, talking quietly among themselves. Music leaked from inside the house, a mournful guitar ballad. Razor wire and broken bottles topped the cinder-block fence. "Oscar seems to need a lot of protection."

"Oscar has a lot of friends. A lot of enemies, too."

"Is he dealing drugs? Is that why he doesn't show his work?"

"Don't let him hear you say that." Val turned away from the angels. "Oscar is an immigration attorney. The INS doesn't like him because he keeps beating them in court, and the coyotes don't like him because he's cutting into their business." The bug zappers along the fence line crackled. "Coyotes rip off the illegals, rape them, dump them in the desert to die. What Oscar charges his clients doesn't even cover the filing fees."

"Is he running for pope?"

Val smiled. "Not yet. Oscar created a voter registration organization that brings in big bucks from the Brentwood cocktail-party crowd—that takes care of most of the overhead." He waved to Oscar, who walked toward them carrying cherry popsicles. "Next November, he's running for Congress. Lot of new voters, from what I hear."

Oscar passed out the popsicles, then pulled a bottle of mescal out of his suit jacket, unscrewing the top with a practiced flick of his thumb. "To beauty." He saluted Kyle. He took a swallow of the cactus liquor, offered her the bottle, pleased when she accepted. "Come on, chica, I give you a tour and afterward you and Valentino can play a round. Looking is good, but to fully appreciate the course you must play."

They strolled around the golf course, sucking noisily at their popsicles, chasing the fruity sweetness with belts of mescal. The holes themselves were difficult, requiring not only precise shots but an inverted strategy, a willingness to hit the ball in what seemed like the wrong place. Val and Oscar argued the fine points of the horror movies featured, while Kyle studied the mosaics, the glow from the mescal slowly spreading through her body.

They stopped beside the fourteenth hole, *Attack of the Mysterians,* which portrayed a brainy alien lusting after an Earth female as a fire-spouting robot loomed in the background. Oscar told Kyle that the golfball had to be hit directly into the alien's bulging right eye to make it to the green. He had been giving her tips on every hole, saying he didn't want Valentino to take advantage of her. He waved at the mosaic. "These Mysterians," he said to Kyle, slurring his words, "I can't really blame them for coming here for females."

Kyles head felt heavy. It was a strange compliment but well intended.

"My father did tile work for the church in our village," said Oscar, mousy face twitching. "Adam and Eve driven from Eden, the Great Flood, a crucifixion that made even the tax collector weep—my father saved more souls than the priest." He pushed up his glasses and rubbed his eyes. "My father believed in martyrs. Me, I have always preferred monsters."

"I don't believe in monsters," said Kyle.

Dekker slumped in the living room of the house in Del Mar, sobbing, the Nixon mask sticking to him. Furniture was splintered across the carpet, the eggshell-white walls ruined. He could hear the wife making gurgling noises from the master bedroom, but the husband was quiet now. Dekker got to his feet, tugging at the moist latex mask and breathing hard as he slowly peeled it off. The air was cool on his skin. He looked at his reflection in the full-length mirror and saw Jackie's face staring back at him.

"I didn't believe in ghosts or goblins even when I was a kid," said Kyle. "Never needed a night light. Never thought something was under the bed."

"Forgive her, Oscar," said Val, "she had a sheltered upbringing."

"Don't patronize me." Kyle took the mescal from Oscar, finishing the last of it. "Horror movies are fake," she said, her throat on fire. "I'm used to the real thing."

"Oh yes," mocked Oscar, "the white girl knows true horror."

Kyle jabbed a finger at the fifth hole, *Invasion of the Body Snatchers*. A sleeping man was being drained by the greenish pod underneath his bed; pink tendrils from the pod entered his body. The mosaic was so realistic that the tendrils seemed to pulse with life. "That's your idea of horror?"

"That's the *original* version," said Oscar. "The best version." He belched.

Kyle waved Val and Oscar closer. A little dizzy, she was definitely feeling the liquor. She waited until she had their complete attention. "There's a water beetle, *Dytiscus*," she confided, "and the larval form of this beetle has sickle-shaped mandibles, sharp as razors." She curved two fingers of her right hand to show them. "The larvae floats in the water, barely moving, until something tasty, maybe a mosquito wriggler, swims by and then *Dytiscus* . . . strikes." She slammed her two curved fingers into Oscar's arm and he jumped.

Val laughed, then quickly held up his hands as the homeboys got up.

"Those mandibles are not only hooked, they're hollow—as much feeding tubes as jaws," said Kyle. Her voice was low, melodramatic. "While the wriggler thrashes around, *Dytiscus* starts pumping digestive acid up from its stomach, down the mandibles and into the wriggler. The victims of your pod-people are drained while they sleep, but the wriggler is alive. Within minutes its internal organs are dissolving, and *Dytiscus* reverses the process, sucking the—"

"Madre de Dios," said Oscar.

"When *Dytiscus* is done, the wriggler is just an empty bag of skin drifting off in the water." Kyle grinned at Val in triumph. "*That's* a horror show."

Val applauded. "I am *so* glad to be a mammal."

Kyle looked at Val and wished they were alone.

Oscar pulled a couple of putters from a large golf bag and gave them to Val, along with a handful of red-striped range balls. "I will be back soon." He laid a hand on Kyle's shoulder. "Perhaps it is Valentino I should be worried about being taken advantage of."

Feeling the effects of the mescal and the magical quality of Oscar's mosaics, Kyle and Val took their time playing the course, hitting the cooler for more popsicles. The night was humid, and the air thick and tinged with gasoline. Santa Ana was too far inland for the offshore winds to blow away the heat or pollution. Val took off his jacket, dropping it on the grass. Popsicle juice ran down their bare arms, and they licked it off, unable to eat fast enough. Val put his arms around her and kissed her, their mouths tingling with cherry ice.

"Thank you for bringing me here." She sighed.

Val kissed her eyes.

"I feel safe with you," said Kyle. "God, I don't know why I said that."

"Valentino!" Oscar stood on the porch. "I have to leave soon. You still want to talk?"

Val kissed her again. "I'll be right back."

Kyle watched Val go into the house and turned back to the seventh hole, *It Came from Beneath the Sea*. There was a working waterfall and a giant octopus lurking under the cascade of water, one tentacle holding a luxury sailboat. She imagined Kilo onboard. Her laugh was cut off by a beeping from Val's discarded shirt. She looked toward the house. "Val?" None of the homeboys got up to get him. "Val!" The phone kept beeping.

"I figure you want to talk in private," said Oscar, standing in the kitchen. "I don't blame you for keeping secrets from la chica." He clapped Val on the back. "That's one beautiful woman, man. I wouldn't tell her anything about myself either."

"It's not like that."

"If you say so." Oscar opened the tap in the kitchen sink and let the cold water run before filling a glass, draining it and refilling it again. "Too much mescal for a Sunday night." The kitchen was hung with garlands of dried peppers and ropes of garlic. A large pot of beans simmered on the stove. "So, what do you need from me, Valentino?"

Val handed Oscar a photograph that had been taken in Key West of Junior standing beside a hoisted 800-pound blue marlin. His face was sunburnt raw. He had fought the fish for over two hours, finally gave up, and emptied his .45 into the marlin, then dragged him aboard.

"Thas' a nice fish, man, and one ugly fucker standing beside him."

"Hello?" said Kyle.

"Well, howdy there. Who am I talking to?"

"Are you calling for Val? He's not here right now, but I can go get him—"

"That's all right, I'll talk to you. This here's Junior Mayfield. Me and Val is old friends."

Kyle started toward the house. Junior Mayfield . . . the name sounded familiar, but she couldn't remember where she had heard it. "Yes . . . well, I'm Kyle. I'm a friend too."

"Heckfire." Junior chuckled. "I guess that makes you and me friends, too."

"Junior is going to show up soon looking for me," said Val. "He'll check into some swank hotel: the Peninsula, the Bel-Air, the Mondrian, strictly four-star accommodations. You've got people working at every hotel in the city—"

"Cooking, cleaning, making beds, parking cars . . ." Oscar had a sly grin. "I think the gringos are not such good workers. Too lazy." He flicked the photograph. "So why is this Junior looking for you?"

"He wants . . ." Val stopped, hearing a baby start to cry. The sound set off other babies until there were tiny wailing sounds coming from many directions. Val had been inside Oscar's house only a few times, but now, as always, he sensed the house overflowed with humanity—out of sight, out of earshot, but *there*. He imagined rooms within rooms, false walls and false ceilings, basements and sub-basements—the house a vast shelter with new arrivals waiting patiently for a safe departure. Val waited as the crying slowly subdued, the babies hushed and suckled, nursed into silence. He looked at Oscar. "Junior has this idea he wants to kill me."

Oscar tugged at his goatee. "That's all?"

Val thanked Oscar and stepped out of the kitchen door. He saw Kyle coming across the grass, holding out his cell-phone. She looked upset. He hurried toward her and took the phone before she could speak. "Gramma?" No answer. He imagined her stroked out on the carpet or sprawled at the foot of her bed. "Grace, if you can't talk, just tap twice on the receiver and—"

"I've fallen and I can't get up . . ." A voice croaked, then erupted into laughter.

Val wanted to turn his back on Kyle—as though Junior could see through the phone.

"Got your own little hotline to Grandma's house," Junior drawled. "I bet you got that crazy ol' bitch stashed someplace close, so you can run over every time she hears a bump in the night." He spat. "Ain't you going to ask me how I got your number? All the trouble I went to . . . you wouldn't believe what it cost me."

"Val? Is everything okay?" asked Kyle.

"That Kyle . . ." Junior sniffed into the receiver. "Smells like quality pussy. Just the way she says your name, I can tell it's serious between you two. What's your secret?"

"Everything is fine," Val said to Kyle.

"Your grandma would wash your mouth out with pine tar soap if she heard you lie like that," said Junior. "Fernando told me you was on *Jeopardy* last week. Sorry I missed it."

"I hope I didn't get you into trouble."

"Oh, pooh. Nothing I can't handle." Junior spat again. "You wouldn't know where I could find the Jackson brothers, would you? They plumb disappeared. Didn't pack a bag or take a toothbrush either—Tommy Jackson's rottweiler was going nuts from hunger, about chewed through the chain-link fence by the time Animal Control got there."

"Sounds to me like an alien abduction. You should give Scully and Mulder a call."

"Remember when I said you got too much conscience for your own good? Well, I'm not so sure anymore."

Val should hang up. He really should.

"You still there, Valentine? Hey, we're still pals, aren't we?"

"You bet. I wouldn't go to your mama's funeral, but I'll come to *yours*. I'll bring a full bladder too."

Junior laughed, haw-haw-haw. "I miss you, boy. The people I have to deal with, you know what they're like, no sense of humor and that fucker at the state's attorney's office, Christ, oh dear, Sanford is worse than Jamaicans. I miss you, Valentine. You was—"

Val turned off his cell-phone. Kyle watched him. The bug zappers were going full blast on the perimeters of Oscar's shrine to cheesy horror movies. The insects, attracted to the light—moths, mosquitoes, and yellow jackets—were drawn to death by their own desires. Junior knew about Kyle now, knew that she meant something to Val. That was all Junior needed.

"I'm sorry I answered your phone," said Kyle. "I thought it was your grandmother—"

"Don't worry about it." Val smiled. "So what did you and Junior talk about?"

Chapter Ten

"You're dead, fucker," Foster hissed, nudging the left side of Val's face with the barrel of the .44 magnum. It was a ridiculously big gun.

Val stood inside the darkened room and tossed his keys onto the coffee table. Missed.

Foster closed the front door with his boot. "Are you scared?" He jabbed Val's cheek with the barrel of the gun, pushing him farther into the room. "Are you?"

Val felt the metal cold against his skin. "Yes." He could see Foster out of the corner of his eye, a big man in the shadows, light glistening on the tips of his blond crewcut.

"You're scared."

"That's what I said. You should check out the Miracle Ear infomercial on channel 22—put it on your credit card. You'll hear birds chirp again."

"Oh, I hear just fine." Foster pulled back the hammer of the .44, the click resonating. "I heard *that* clear enough."

Val's knees wobbled, but he kept it from spreading. There was something about the sound of a revolver being cocked against your skull. Once you heard it, you never forgot it. That sound did a number on you forever after, and nothing you could do about it.

"You hear that?" said Foster, tiny flecks of spittle dappling Val's neck. "That was the gate to hell being unlocked."

"What do they need to keep hell locked up for?" said Val, taking short quick breaths. "What's there to steal?"

"I heard you was a talker," said Foster, irritated. Val felt the barrel brush his cheek as Foster tried to keep it steady. It was hard to draw down and hold a weapon, particularly a heavy handgun like a .44 magnum. "Well, I never seen a talker yet that didn't lose his water waiting for the hammer to fall."

"'Lose my water'? Who writes your dialogue?" Val inclined his head farther against the barrel, and Foster pulled away a bit, slightly off balance now. It was a reaction, most people weren't even aware of doing it. "Such a nice soft gun," Val yawned, then whipped up his left hand, knocked the revolver aside, then hooked one of Foster's legs and tripped him, twisting Foster's gun-hand, pointing the revolver down at Foster's head. The hammer fell on an empty chamber. "Bang," said Val. The whole movement had taken less than two seconds. Val looked up at the director. "How was that?"

Courtney Lyons, the twenty-three-year-old director of *Rogue Justice,* took a deep drag on her clove cigarette. She sat with one chubby leg slung over the arm of her canvas-back chair, her circa-1967 white canvas Beatle boots bouncing back and forth, John-Paul-George-Ringo smiling as they swooshed through space, moptops forever. Lyons was a short, hardass brunette with a garden-shears haircut and an unfiltered voice that could sandblast graffiti off a concrete overpass. Today she was wearing a demure, scoopneck cashmere sweater, a pukka-shell necklace, and a frilly poodle skirt corroded with burn-holes and droppings from a double-cheese Fatburger lunch. She looked like a preppy who had taken the wrong exit off the cultural freeway and never made it back.

Six months ago Lyons had been directing rock videos on spec and making the buzz at Sundance. Now she had two quickie features on her résumé and was one step closer to accepting a little gold man, thanking her parents and agent, and skanking all the assholes who told her that she couldn't direct. Lyons worked fast and cheap, needing a minimum of setups and retakes, an autocrat with a distinctive visual style. She probably *was* going to get an Oscar someday—then put lipstick on the statuette and stick it in her bathroom so that no one would think she took the honor seriously. She dragged again on her cigarette, considering Val's query.

"You *prick,*" Foster glowered, getting awkwardly to his feet, rubbing his hand. He was a pneumatic bodybuilder who spent more on steroids than acting lessons. "You almost broke my wrist."

"The move has to be done full speed or it doesn't work, Dennis," said Val.

"You try that again I'm going to fuck you up good," Foster threatened.

Val tucked the gun into his belt, waiting for Courtney to decide. The .44 was a special revolver with a plugged muzzle, the sides of the barrel vented. When blanks were fired during actual filming, the flash from the sides would look realistic to the cameras, but the actor would be safe. Val still double-checked the revolver beforehand. Every year one or two actors were killed by their own ignorance or the armorer's ineptitude. "What's the verdict, Courtney? You like the takedown?"

Lyons peered at him through a cumulus of fragrant Indonesian smoke, drumming on the arms of her chair. Yesterday one of the producers had stopped by the shoot and spent a couple of hours watching, arms crossed, occasionally whispering into a mini-tape recorder. Her cigarette popped, a smoldering clove landing on one of the pink poodles embroidered on her skirt. She ignored it. She had ignored the suit yesterday, too, but Val noticed that her black-lacquered nails were bitten ragged today.

"Courtney?"

"I don't think so, Val." The dim overhead lights gleamed off the three gold rings in the right side of Lyons' nose. "Give me something else, and *fast. Tick-tock, tick-tock.*"

Val bit his lip.

Lyons waved the lighting technician in. The two of them talked about the next couple of setups, their heads bent over his notes. Still rubbing his hand, Foster started to walk away. "Stay on your mark, meat puppet!" Lyons barked, not even looking up, and Foster jumped back into place.

"Meat puppet?" Val laughed. "Where's that from, Courtney? Is that the *Outer Limits* episode with Steve McQueen?"

"You're slipping. Meat Puppets was a band I listened to in junior high." Lyons tossed the notes back to the lighting tech. "The takedown was impressive, Val, but it wasn't a signature move."

"Impressive but not a signature move," Val repeated.

"Oddjob slicing off a statue's head with his steel derby in *Goldfinger,* Thelma and Louise laughing as they drive over the cliff—*those* are signature moves." Lyons beckoned to the waiting set designer and he approached, offering the sketches she had demanded he redo. She flipped through them, handed one back and dumped the rest onto the floor. The set designer retreated, still facing her—the Last Empress rides again. "You see, Val," said Lyons, "you know guns and tricks and police procedures, but *I've* seen two films a day, every day, since I was ten years old."

Val looked over to where Kyle stood silently at the back of the set. He couldn't read her eyes, but he knew she was enjoying herself. She had wanted to see what he did for a living and was curious enough to take a Friday off from work, and he had wanted to show her. Maybe he was hoping to impress her, or maybe talking with Grace had gotten to him. He and Kyle didn't have much time left now, and he wanted to make the most of it.

Junior was coming. It had been two weeks since Val's appearance on *Jeopardy* had aired, almost two weeks since Junior had called him at Oscar's golf course and gotten Kyle. It had taken some tap-dancing to keep the truth from her.

"How much money do you owe this . . . Junior?" Kyle had asked.

"Too much." The jacaranda tree overhanging Oscar's backyard swayed in the breeze, its purple blossoms drifting down among the mosaic monsters. *"You didn't tell Junior your full name, you're certain of that?"*

"Junior was your bookie?" Kyle sounded dubious.

Val nodded. "The Dolphins had a bad year, and I followed them right into the toilet. The last game of the season I doubled up—Dolphins blew a two-touchdown lead in the last quarter and that was that." They were seated *on a bench beside the seventeenth hole,* Yog, Beast from Beyond Time. *"You didn't tell Junior where we live, even indirectly?"*

Kyle shook her head. *"Maybe you should offer to pay Junior off in installments."*

"That's a good idea. I'll have to run that past him."

Val should have left after the phone call, moved out so Kyle wasn't put in danger, but he didn't. Any day now Val was going to have to abandon his apartment. He was going to have to stop seeing Kyle. Maybe stop breathing, too, while he was at it.

"Realistic simply isn't *realistic,* Val." Lyons snapped her fingers, and her assistant placed a freshly lit cigarette between her lips. She puffed away, still maintaining eye contact with him. "Not realistic enough for the big screen. We have higher standards here than out there in the world."

"You have no idea how disappointing it was the first time I saw a real car accident," said Dalton, the screenwriter. A lumpy man sitting cross-legged on the floor, he was poised over his laptop. "The accident happened on La Cienega, right in front of me, but there was only my one angle and the sound of the windshield shattering. . . . It just didn't play right."

Val wasn't listening. A few days after his *Jeopardy* appearance, Val had gotten a couple of messages on his pager. Mr. Hedelston from accounting said he wanted to Fedex Val his prizes, but Val had given the producers only a post office box. They needed a street address. Right. "Mr. Hedelston" didn't worry him, but Junior talking to Kyle that night at the miniature golf course—that had unnerved him. Val had focused on Oscar's angels floating serenely through the branches of the jacaranda tree as Junior went on about how much he liked talking with Kyle, asking what her favorite kind of candy was so he could send her a two-pound box.

People made mistakes when they panicked. They forgot to cover their tracks. They hurried through an airport where every porter had their photograph memorized. They applied for new utilities under an old name. That's what Junior wanted. Better for Val to stay put, to make sure he had a safe place to land before he jumped. Val was fooling himself—he stayed because he didn't want to leave Kyle. It was a lousy reason. He had seen men killed because they were locked into a certain woman, a certain man. He had seen Chester Marx get killed because he had a weakness for the butterscotch milk-shakes at Jane's Café. The things you cared about were dangerous, but not caring about anything was even more dangerous.

"My problem with your blocking, Val, is that it's too . . . obvious," said Lyons. "No snap-crackle-pop. No Trix are for kids. It just lies there in the bowl. I mean, here we have Jack Dread surprised walking into his apartment late one night"—her hands drew pictures in the air— "Foster puts a gun to his head. . . . That's another thing, Val, does it *have* to be a gun? Why can't Jack Dread be threatened by something a little more . . . exotic? Maybe a Filipino butterfly knife or a blowtorch—"

"How about a crossbow?" said Val.

Lyons brightened. "A crossbow. . . . Yes. A crossbow is *very* cool."

"Maybe one with a laser sight and a heat-seeking arrowhead like the Green Arrow used?"

"I see." Lyons pursed her lips. "It's too bad you're not paid to make jokes, Val. You could probably do better than your day rate here."

"I don't want to argue with you, Courtney—"

"You *couldn't* argue with me, Val. Comprendo?"

"Comprendo? What's next, Courtney, 'Saddle up, we're burnin' daylight, buckeroos!'" Even Lyons had to smile. "Look, the takedown I demonstrated *works*," he said, using the brief opportunity his sense of humor invariably gave him, "but if you don't want to—"

"What about"—Lyons steepled her fingers—"what if, instead of Jack Dread knocking Foster's gun away, what if Jack put his hand in between the hammer and the ... the rest of the gun, whatever you call it."

Val could see Kyle covering her mouth, trying not to laugh. It felt like they were co-conspirators.

"I thought the way Val disarmed Foster was just fine, Courtney," John Delaney purred, stepping forward. His handsome face seemed to strain to maintain his trademark good humor. "Very direct. Decisive."

"Thanks for your *input*, John," said Lyons, "but the studio seems to think I know what I'm doing."

"Of course they do, darling." Delaney ran a hand through his thick brown locks. An aging soap opera star recently outed by a supermarket tabloid—*"The Soap Idol and the Boy Toy!"*—he was attempting to resurrect his career with an action film, portraying Jack Dread, ruthless undercover cop, sensitive single parent. "Still, why not give Val a listen? He may have something to add to the mix." He showed her his good side. "I hate to make a fuss, but I can't afford to appear farcical on the screen, darling." He looked at Val. "Show me that takedown move again, would you? It's going to take some practice, but I'm sure with your help I can fake my way through."

"No problem, John," said Val.

"Run through it on your own time, boys," Lyons

snapped, "I need Val to block out the fight scene in the warehouse." She checked her call sheet, then clapped her hands. "Biker hardcore!" Four burly walk-ons in leather pants and mesh T-shirts shuffled onto the soundstage. "Let's *go,* Val, chop-chop!"

Delaney raised an eyebrow at Val. "Chop-chop?"

"Chop-chop, John."

Chapter Eleven

"I *am* sorry my wife couldn't join us, Jackie," Mr. Abbott apologized yet again, raising his voice to be heard as the private jet taxied down the runway of Orange County Airport. The setting sun turned the surrounding glass office towers ablaze, but the interior of the Gulfstream III was an oasis of blue—cool blue carpet and walls, blue-veined marble bathroom, and a hostess wearing a blue Lagerfeld knockoff. "Gwen *wanted* to celebrate your first home sale, but she doesn't really appreciate Las Vegas."

"It was a spur of the moment idea, but I *was* a little disappointed, Chuck," said Jackie, mimicking his concern. Her nylons rustled as she crossed her long legs. The sound was a rough caress to Kilo and drew his attention, held him there. She sat beside him, wearing an off-white kid leather suit that highlighted her milky skin and smoldering red hair. "You and your wife have been so kind to me that I was hoping to share my good fortune with you. Perhaps my next sale—"

"Absolutely," Mr. Abbott assured her. "I'm sure Gwen won't want to miss that."

Kilo felt himself pushed gently back into the plush leather seat as the plane picked up speed. His eyes were still on Jackie. There was a radiant wickedness to her, a cruelty as consuming and impersonal as a forest fire—Kilo saw flames in her eyes and longed to throw himself in. This afternoon when the limo came for them, Jackie had gotten in first, her skirt riding up. Kilo tried not to stare, but she had noticed and whispered that she had two tiny freckles at the very top of her right thigh, two freckles set in the hollow of her hip. She had kissed him lightly and said that maybe tonight she would let him see them. He didn't believe her, he really didn't, but he had thought of little else on the drive to the airport except those two freckles. As the plane screamed down the runway, Kilo clasped his hands behind his head. Let the games begin.

"I hope you don't mind my taking care of the transportation, Jackie," said Mr. Abbott. "I appreciate your offer to buy tickets, but I have an account with Avjet Executive Charters."

Should have gone with the Gulfstream IV, thought Kilo. Probably worried about Gwen eyeballing the account, complaining that he spent too much on his son and not enough on her daughter. Next trip it would be the Gulfstream V. They could fly to Australia nonstop on the G-V . . . if there was anything in Australia he wanted to see, which there wasn't.

"A girl could get used to having a jet on call, Chuck," said Jackie, her teeth flashing. "I feel like Liv Tyler on my way to a premiere."

Mr. Abbott blinked, not recognizing the name, then settled back in his seat. Even for an overnight to Vegas he wore a charcoal three-piece Savile Row suit, the knot in his rep tie perfectly dimpled. Mr. Abbott had often lectured Kilo on the importance of keeping up appearances, of holding the line against a rising tide of the sloppy and the crass. Kilo was sleek in a steel-blue Hugo Boss two button that shimmered like sharkskin. The plane lifted off, rising steeply over the rows of office buildings, and Mr. Abbott kissed his wedding ring for luck. He noticed Jackie watching him and blushed.

"I think that is *so* sweet," said Jackie.

"I always do that on takeoff and landing," Mr. Abbott admitted as the hostess approached with champagne. "It's a silly superstition, but I can't help it."

"Now I know where your son gets his romantic streak." Jackie reached over, patted him on the arm, and Mr. Abbott beamed, smiling so hard it looked as if he was going to blow his left ventricle.

Kilo knew just how the Chuckster felt. He had spent most of his life lying in the orchard of good and evil . . . or was it the garden? Whatever, he had spent twenty-seven years lounging in the soft grass, waiting for a golden apple to drop into his lap, and it kept landing just out of reach. Not that Kilo *bothered* to reach for the apple—what was he, the fucking shortstop for the Angels, some wetback from the Dominican Republic diving for a hard grounder? No thanks, Pancho. Three weeks ago Kilo had been trussed out on the bed at the Four Seasons, ready for love or a reasonable facsimile and seeing Jackie coming at him with a bottle of Dom P. Now he was flying high, about to cash in his genetic jackpot. Rocking back and forth, Kilo basked in his own glory.

Jackie was different today too—more like the way she had been the first night he met her, giddy, urging him forward into her fantasy. All of that coquettishness had ended the moment Dekker walked into the suite at the Four Seasons. After that it was threats and plans, and even when they were alone, Jackie had rebuffed him. Oh, she had played the loving-girlfriend game around Gwen and Chuck, but she had resisted even his smoothest moves, warding him off, saying she could never be sure if Dekker was watching them. Today though she was looser, freed from Dekker's watching eyes, more demonstrative, ready for anything. Well, Kilo was ready too. Maybe that's what was turning Jackie on.

Kilo grabbed the champagne from the hostess, popped the cork, and filled their flutes. He filled one for the hostess too, a slim Asian girl, who batted her lashes as she accepted the drink. She looked vaguely familiar, and Kilo wondered if he had ever boned her at the hotel.

"I want to thank you, Jackie," said Mr. Abbott. "You too, Kilo."

"What are you thanking me for, Daddy? I didn't do anything."

"It's just so nice to see you so happy," said Mr. Abbott, "so determined. I haven't seen you like this for a very long time. I wanted to tell you, that's all."

Looking into his father's watery eyes, Kilo felt a tightness in his chest. The Chuckster was a good dad, handing over a pony on Kilo's sixth birthday—what ever happened to that stinky thing?—skiing in Gstaad, surfing in Fiji, tennis lessons from a USLTA champion. Yeah, every time Kilo needed anything, Chuck had been there with his checkbook. Love was a beautiful thing.

The plane roared across the desert. The pocked terrain rushed beneath them as they headed toward the neon promised land. Kilo felt his heart pounding with anticipation. His whole life was going to change. It was a change for the better, but he felt a twinge of regret.

*Hibiscus bushes had been planted along the iron se-
curity fence—red flowers tickled Dekker's face as he
pressed his face against the bars, watching Mrs. Abbott
read in the living room. The Mexican cook had left about
a half hour ago. Her husband picked her up at the front
gate in an immaculate, classic T-bird.*

*Dekker had crouched in this exact spot a few weeks
ago, peering through the bars as Mrs. Abbott blew out the
candles on her birthday cake. He had watched Jackie hold
hands with Kilo under the table, seen the flirty way she
inclined her head when she talked to the stepsister's date.
There was something about the hawk-faced guy that had
bothered Dekker. He had kept his distance from Jackie,
that wasn't it. Dekker didn't like his wary posture, the way
he turned around and looked out the windows, looked right
at Dekker as though he could see in the dark.*

*Clouds rolled in off the ocean and blotted out the
stars. There were no streetlights in the Aegean Heights
colony. The residents trusted their fences and the armed-
response signs dotting their lawns. Bad decision. Most
rent-a-cops had crumbs on their neckties, and fences were
good only for keeping out Girl Scouts selling cookies and
Bible thumpers selling heaven. Someone like Dekker could
always get in. Restless, Mrs. Abbott walked around her
living room with a drink in her hand, pulling books from
shelves, replacing them. Maybe she sensed what was coming.*

"Kilo told me you're a blackjack expert," Jackie said,
holding her champagne between thumb and forefinger.
"I'm impressed, Chuck."

"Well, I always had an aptitude for mathematics," Mr.
Abbott said shyly, plucking at the crease in his trousers,

"not that I ever really used it. Still, I did win thirty-eight thousand dollars at the Nugget on our last trip, almost enough to cover Kilo's losses. We had a good time, didn't we, son?"

"Yeah great, Daddy," said Kilo, distracted, thinking about Dekker, worried that something was going to go wrong. California didn't have the gas chamber anymore, but they had lethal injection. Kilo saw himself strapped on a gurney with a doctor slipping an IV into his arm. He stared out the large, oval window of the Gulfstream, wishing that he could take everything back. Even if the plan went smoothly, there was no reason to think that Jackie and Dekker wouldn't turn on him—they were greedy and untrustworthy. Dekker at least was predictable, but Jackie . . . every time he thought he had her figured, she fooled him. Last night the two of them had hit the clubs in L.A. There was a moment under the lights at Silicone, seeing the way all the other men looked at her, there was a moment that Kilo wished he and Jackie could have met some other way, without Dekker, without plans. Kilo studied his reflection in the window, taking some small comfort in his good bone structure.

Dekker tested the dried Super glue on his fingertips. He had no fingerprints anymore, no identity. Jackie had called him two o'clock this afternoon and given him the go-ahead—two rings at the Starbucks payphone. He had almost spilled his mocha.

Dekker braced his feet against one of the vertical bars of the fence, grabbed the one next to it, pulling with his hands, pushing with both feet, muscles bulging as he strained, veins in his neck standing out. Breathing hard now, he stopped, gasping from the perfume of the sur-

rounding flowers. The bars were bent but not enough. He tightened his grip. He could hear Jackie's voice in his head, urging him on, and Dekker cried out, sagging, exhausted. The fence gaped wide. Dekker imagined himself and Jackie taking a long drive up the California coast afterward, heading for Big Sur in a convertible, top down, her red hair streaming in the night, her telling him to drive faster, faster, faster. Dekker eased through the fence and headed toward the house, moving quickly now. He felt an emptiness inside himself, a vast howling where his heart should be.

"Jackie was telling me about the plans you two have been making," Mr. Abbott said to Kilo. "I have to say I couldn't agree more."

"Yeah?"

"There's still plenty of money to be made in Orange County real estate," said Mr. Abbott as the plane began its descent over Las Vegas. "I don't have an eye for value myself, but I'm sure Jackie does." He smiled at Kilo. "God, I look at the two of you, and I see Gwen and myself twenty years ago."

Kilo didn't know what his father was talking about.

"I told Jackie if you and she find suitable income properties, I'll be happy to discuss with your stepmother the idea of giving you an advance on your inheritance," Mr. Abbott said. "I know in the past Gwen's been very . . . conservative with your allowance, but I see this as an investment. An investment in you, Kilo, an investment in our family."

Kilo looked at Jackie.

"I never knew you had an interest in business," Mr. Abbott said to him. "I never could even balance my checkbook, but I think this real estate partnership is a very healthy sign of maturity." He winked at Jackie. "Do I have you to thank for this, my dear?"

Jackie sipped her drink. "You don't give him enough credit, Chuck." She looked right at Kilo. "Your little boy is full of surprises."

Mr. Abbott started toward the front of the plane. As he slipped into the galley, Jackie dropped her hand in Kilo's lap, casually traced the outline of his penis with her fingernail. Kilo could hardly breathe, unable to move for fear she would stop.

Dekker moved across the Abbotts' sculptured grounds, a shadow among the shadows, the topiary animals blind in the darkness. Some of the things Jackie asked him to do made him sick. But he did them just the same. He hadn't been with her since they went to the swap-meet. She said it was too dangerous for them to see each other until it was all over. That hadn't stopped Dekker from keeping an eye on her. He had watched her and Kilo play tennis and watched them shop for clothes. He wondered what Jackie was doing right now. He wondered if she was thinking of him.

The Gulfstream came in low over the strip, Kilo staring out the window. The huge black pyramid of the Luxor was floodlit and menacing, even set among the McDonald's arches and Kentucky Fried Chicken giant oscillating buckets. Kilo could see the golden lion in front of the MGM Grand and the New York, New York roller coaster. People on the roller coaster were holding their hands high as they plunged down a steep slope. Kilo could almost hear them shriek.

When he was fourteen, Gwen and Chuck had taken him to Magic Mountain. His father was scared of thrill rides—he said it was doctor's orders—so Gwen and Kilo had done every ride in the park, from the Hammer to the Depth Charge, even Thunder Road, the two of them holding hands, yelling so loudly they were hoarse by lunch. It was the best time the two of them had ever had together. Kilo checked his watch, wondering whether Dekker was through yet.

If Dekker screwed up, Kilo was going to cooperate with the cops, maybe hire Johnnie Cochran to handle his defense. Johnnie could probably plea-bargain the charges down to probation or house arrest. Kilo would insist that Brad Pitt play him in the major motion picture, and if they filmed some scenes on the tennis court, he wanted to play the part of his own opponent. He still had an awesome backhand. He just needed to concentrate on his game. House arrest would be an opportunity to focus. In six months he could be ready for the circuit again. He and Jackie could blame everything on Dekker. Kilo had Johnnie Cochran on his side, and there wasn't a jury in the world that would convict Jackie. She could get away with anything.

"Should we tell your father, Kilo?" Jackie piped up.

Kilo jerked.

"Is it a surprise?" said Mr. Abbott. "Oh, do tell me, *please*."

"Of course it's a surprise, silly," said Jackie. "I think we should tell him, Kilo."

Kilo stared at Jackie. What was she up to now?

Jackie took Mr. Abbott's hand. "Kilo and I just decided"—she smiled, unable to contain herself—"Kilo and I . . . we're getting married."

"Married?" said Mr. Abbott.

"Married?" said Kilo.

"You don't mean tonight?" said Mr. Abbott.

"I know it's sudden," said Jackie. "Kilo and I *had* planned on waiting, but this just feels right."

"The idea of you and Kilo getting married without Gwen being present, without Kyle . . ." Mr. Abbott shook his head. "It just doesn't seem proper."

"Daddy's got a point," said Kilo.

"We're in love, Chuck, that's the most proper thing there is." Jackie dabbed at her eyes. "Chuck, you kiss your ring on takeoff. Well, I'm superstitious too, and tonight's the night—it really is. When we get back, you can throw a big reception and invite as many people as you want. Please say you understand."

Maybe Chuck understood, but Kilo didn't. Getting married wasn't part of the plan. Not the one he knew about and not the one Dekker knew about either. Kilo was sure of it.

"Please, Chuck, please say we have your blessing," Jackie implored.

"Gwen and I eloped too," said Mr. Abbott, misty-eyed. "We had chartered a three-masted schooner to take us to Acapulco, and on the way we decided to have the captain marry us. Kilo and Kyle were furious when we told them. They both thought we were rushing ahead, not acting our ages. Remember, Kilo?" He offered Jackie his handkerchief. "I'm certain Gwen will understand—there is a certain romance to just going forward no matter what, ignoring all doubts and obstacles."

"Yes, there is," said Jackie.

"Congratulations," Mr. Abbott said, brushing her cheek

with his lips. "Congratulations to the *both* of you, Kilo, you devil," he said, pumping Kilo's hand.

"Oh, he is, Chuck," said Jackie, "he truly is."

Kilo felt the plane tilt as it continued its approach to the landing field. The lights through the windows appeared to spin out of control. The enormous, grinning neon clown at the entrance to Circus Circus looked like he was falling over. The whole world had shifted, and Kilo couldn't tell what was up or down anymore.

Chapter Twelve

Val and Kyle stepped out the back door of the warehouse-soundstage, blinking in the late afternoon sun. Trash littered the alley, yellowed newspapers tumbled past. There weren't many amenities in the industrial district, but the rents were cheap, the freeway close, and there were always plenty of toothless-and-tattooed extras eager to make some fast cash. They separated. Kyle went to pick up fish tacos from the stand around the corner, and Val to buy a six-pack of Inca Cola from the Korean grocer. He had wanted them to go together, but the director had called for only a half-hour break. Kyle had given him a dirty look at the implication that she might need him along for protection. They met back at the cluster of stunted trees outside the soundstage. Val checked the grass under the trees for syringes, then spread his leather jacket on the ground.

"Always the gentleman," said Kyle, dragging over a large piece of cardboard for both of them to sit on. She took the open bottle he passed her, finished half the sweet Mexican soft drink in one long swallow, and handed him a fish taco. The paper bag was transparent with grease.

She took a bite of another taco. "Good," she pronounced, licking guacamole off the corner of her mouth.

Still chewing, Val wiped her face with his napkin, then wiped his own.

Kyle washed down her first taco with the rest of her cola. The rich brown foam coated her upper lip. Val loved watching her eat. He enjoyed the pleasure she took in it. She wasn't worried about looking dainty or pretending she didn't have an appetite. "What?" she said, noticing him watching her. "They're small," she said defensively, taking another taco out of the bag. "Besides, seeing you play the tough guy made me hungry."

"Yeah?"

"Yeah."

"I was afraid you'd be bored," said Val.

"Sure you were."

Val crunched into one of the dull green jalapeños, felt fire in his mouth. He took another bite, sweat rimming his forehead.

Kyle reached over and picked up one of the jalapeños. "I enjoyed seeing how a movie is made, but I'm still curious how you learned all those things." She chewed the hot pepper thoughtfully. "Bolo knives and kick fights and how to get away from somebody holding a gun to your head. They don't teach that in school."

"It was an extra-credit course," said Val, breathing around the flames singeing his lips.

Kyle handed him another cola. "I'm serious."

Not really hungry, Val busied himself with another taco. "When I was a kid, my best friend . . . Steffano, he just *knew* he was going to be a cop when he grew up. He was a skinny kid, Adam's apple as big as a cue ball, way too honest for his own good. I used to steal magazines for

him from the mini-mart: *True Detective, Thrilling Crime.*
He would read them cover to cover, never even bending
a page, then return them to the store." Val smiled. "He
used to say that someday he was going to have to arrest
me."

Kyle watched him as she munched another jalapeño.
It could have been a green grape for all the effect it had
on her.

Val checked the alley. "When Steffano got accepted
into the police academy, you would have thought he had
hit the lottery. He'd come home at night and run through
what he had learned that day. I'd help him practice, whether
it was hand-to-hand combat or time at the gun range or
whatever. I didn't have the discipline or the inclination for
the academy—I ended up bodyguarding. There are a lot
of celebrities in Miami, and even more wannabees, who
like to think they need protection." He shrugged. "Bodyguarding gave me an entrée into the movies. One of my
clients in Miami was an L.A. producer down there scout-
ing locations. He helped me find work when I moved out
here."

"So, *did* Steffano ever have to arrest you?"

Val grinned. "I got away clean."

"I'm not surprised." Kyle finished the last of the
jalapeños. "There's a place in Baja that I go to a couple
times a year. It's just a spot on the map, but the water is
warm and clear and the grays come in close. There's an
old woman in the nearest village that makes incredible
tamales. I've never tasted anything like them. She grows
her own habañeros—they can melt lead." She looked up
at him. "I'm going there in about a month. You'd like it."

"I bet I would."

Kyle picked through a pile of greasy chips. "Lately,

I've been having a . . . sensation that something bad was going to happen to me. An accident maybe or a robbery." She hesitated, playing with the chips. "I think of myself as a rational individual, not easily spooked, but the last few weeks I've been edgy—triple-checking my diving equipment, then checking it again, locking my car as soon as I get behind the wheel . . ." She shook her head. "I actually had to force myself to get the tacos by myself."

"I couldn't tell."

"A couple of weeks ago I got a complete physical, even insisted on an MRI, though there was no indication one was needed." She shook her head. "They didn't find anything wrong with me. I'm never sick, but I still almost had them do a retest."

Val believed in signs and portents, the wind in the willows and the clouds in the sky. They were all trying to tell us something, that's what his grandmother said. He didn't know about that, but he knew it paid to keep your eyes open. Grace said she had seen the Jackson brothers in a dream—that's how she recognized them when they drove past her house that afternoon just before dusk. Val didn't care how Grace did it. All that mattered was that she had trusted her dream and called him, said two men were going to kill her when it got dark.

Kyle bit into one of the chips, tossed it aside. "That first morning, when we bumped elbows on the stairs . . . I felt like you were standing there between me and whatever was out there, *protecting* me." He reached for her, but she shook him off. "I'm not *helpless,* Val. I can take care of myself. It's just . . . I'm scared." She pushed aside the chips, angry, knocking them over onto the grass. "Is that stupid or—"

"It's not stupid."

"You felt it, didn't you?" said Kyle. "That morning on the stairs, when our arms brushed—there was a connection. You felt it too. I saw it in your eyes."

Everyone in L.A. was psychic, from the script girl who wanted to check Val's heartline to the kid bagging groceries at Ralph's, who saw the future foretold in the final figure on the cash register receipt. Most of them got it wrong, but Val believed Kyle. He *had* felt it too, just like she said.

"That's why I came on to you in the laundry room." Kyle blushed. "I was afraid and I . . . I felt safe around you."

Val was looking at her but seeing Steffano's contorted face in the window of the van, his hands on the glass, swimming in blood.

"I shouldn't have said anything," said Kyle. "I've embarrassed both of us."

"This feeling of yours . . . maybe it wasn't so much about you." Val glanced down the alley. "You have this premonition that you're in danger, and you feel a connection with me. What if instead of protecting you, *I'm* the one putting you in danger?" He watched her consider the possibility. He had expected her to be at least momentarily confused by his question, expected her to offer a hurried dismissal, but Kyle was thinking about it.

"*Should* I be scared of you, Val?"

"Not of me."

"The bookie you owe money to . . . Junior . . . is that who you mean?"

"Junior doesn't believe in the concept of innocent bystanders. Maybe you should stay away from me, at least until I settle up with him."

"Would you like that?"

Val didn't answer.

"Neither would I." Kyle waited a few moments for that to sink in.

"I've only got a couple more hours' work here. Maybe we could take PCH back," said Val. "There's a market in Long Beach where we can pick up fresh shrimp and swordfish steaks. If you let me use that hibachi of yours, I'll cook us dinner—"

"Deal."

Chapter Thirteen

"I never had the killer instinct," Mr. Abbott said to Jackie, his voice trailing off.

Jackie waited to hear what was coming next, nervous now for the first time. Through the side windows she could see Kilo approaching from the airport terminal, followed by two men in white jackets carrying armloads of flowers. Mr. Abbott had sent Kilo off as soon as the luggage was loaded, handed him his platinum card, and said a woman should be surrounded by bouquets on her wedding night. Jackie had known it was just another excuse for Mr. Abbott to be alone with her. The driver was merely a phantom behind the smoked glass of the limousine.

She had expected Mr. Abbott to make her an offer, a buyout to call off the wedding and leave—100K and a first-class ticket to New York or London or wherever. Maybe even 200K. She wouldn't accept it. She might be tempted, but she wouldn't accept it. Even if she could have called off Dekker. Two hundred thousand was a lot of money, but Kilo was just an aneurysm away from millions. Dekker would be a problem, but she could deal with him.

"My father, Kilo's grandfather, now *there* was a man with the killer instinct," Mr. Abbott said wistfully. "My father bought half of Orange County for five dollars an acre from illiterate bean farmers in their third year of a drought. Father told me he liked to close a deal at high noon, when the sun was baking the land and not a cloud in the sky." He sighed. The sound filled the limo like air from a child's balloon. "I was a great disappointment to my father."

Kilo and the flowers were closer, but Jackie was cool and in control now. It was Mr. Abbott who was sweating in the air conditioning, hurrying to get out his story.

"I always had a problem taking the advantage," said Mr. Abbott. "I was too much the gentleman and Kilo is the same way. Gwen says I've spoiled him, and I'm afraid she's right. A man needs a bit of the killer instinct to survive. He needs to be willing to go for the jugular." His smile was weak. "I was lucky. I found Gwen, and she had enough strength for both of us."

Jackie felt a faint vibration through the thick carpet of the limo as the engine idled. That warm tingle was the hum of money, insulation from the bumps and raw edges of life. This wasn't the first time Jackie had ridden in a limousine, but it was the first time she sensed that limos and private jets would be her normal mode of transportation. She had entered a new world, grand and perfectly modulated, more lavish and secure than she had ever thought possible. Jackie nodded sympathetically at Mr. Abbott, wondering if Dekker was finished yet with his wife.

"Gwen doesn't like Kilo very much," Mr. Abbott said, lowering his voice. "I hate to admit it, but it's true. I'm sure you've noticed—you're a very bright young woman, Jackie, very forceful, and I think Kilo needs that. Gwen isn't going to be happy with you getting married to Kilo. She'll say it's too quick, and perhaps I agree, but I think if anyone can give Kilo some spine, it's—*Hello,* Kilo," he said as the door of the limo was flung open. "Lovely," Mr. Abbott said, as the two valets carefully laid down their load of flowers. The backseat was suddenly awash in color. He handed them a crisp hundred-dollar bill, and they backed away, thanking him profusely.

Kilo knocked a couple of bouquets onto the floor as he sat beside Jackie. "Any other errands you want to send me on, Daddy?"

"I booked the presidential suite at the Bellagio for you and Jackie while you were gone," said Mr. Abbott. "You'll feel better after you've freshened up." He flipped the intercom switch. "Bellagio's, driver."

Jackie reached over and hit the intercom. "Cruise the strip first, driver. Make a complete circuit." She looked at Mr. Abbott. "I want to check out the wedding chapels. See what strikes my fancy."

"That's a bride's prerogative," Mr. Abbott said genially.

"What's the groom's prerogative?" said Kilo.

"You'll find out," said Jackie, and Mr. Abbott looked away, embarrassed. Kilo smiled. She didn't blame him; she could hardly wait either. The *presidential* suite.

"Miss?" It was the driver on the intercom. "If you intend to get married, you'll need a license. I can swing by the city office now if you like. It's open until midnight."

Dekker sat on his haunches outside the back door to the Abbotts' house, peeking through a window into the kitchen. The night air carried the scent of freshly cut grass and a sharp odor of chlorine from the swimming pool. The kitchen was clean and efficiently laid out—white tile floors and granite counters, rows of copper pots dangling from overhead racks, stainless steel knives stuck point down on a magnetized strip. A heavy cleaver hung by itself. Bring down an ox with that.

He pressed an ear against the window, heard Mrs. Abbott's television in the living room. The security system wasn't on now or his contact with the glass would have set it off. He should begin, but he felt sluggish, his chest filled with sand, Saudi sand, fine as dust, trickling through him like an hourglass.

Dekker was going to have to act soon. Once Mrs. Abbott decided to go upstairs she might prime the response unit, particularly since she was alone now. Most people waited until they were leaving the house or going to bed to activate the unit. Jackie had described the system to him—a Drake VII, motion and noise activated, directly wired into both the police and the security service. That's probably why the Abbotts so rarely turned it on—it was too sensitive. A few false alarms, police cars pulling up out front, sirens blaring in that nice, quiet neighborhood . . . better to just not activate it. Rich people didn't believe in the bogeyman, and if they did, they were certain they could pay him off.

Somebody was going to pay off the bogeyman tonight, but it was going to cost a lot more than money. Dekker's only regret was that it was Mrs. Abbott who was going to pay and not Kilo. Every time he thought of Kilo and Jackie together Dekker wanted to break something. Preferably something that bled.

Heat rose from Las Vegas Boulevard, shimmered in the evening air—curbside Vegas, where distortion *ruled*. The marriage license had taken just a few minutes, thirty-five dollars and ready for love. The sidewalks swarmed with tourists in shorts and Hard Rock Café T-shirts, women in pink curlers with mouths like octopi, dull-eyed fathers bent forward by the weight of their baby backpacks. Bet *they* wished they had pulled out in time. Jackie looked at Kilo, and he shook his head slowly, smiling, as though he knew just what she was thinking. The guy had possibilities.

They passed the Graceland Wedding Chapel—"Ceremonies with the King"—and the drive-up window of the Tunnel of Love. Jackie rejected the Speedway of Love out at the racetrack, and Kilo said no to Liberace's Las Vegas Villa.

A couple of pimply teenage girls stood on the corner in mini-skirts and crop tops, smoking cigarettes and trying to look twenty-five. They glanced over as the white limo pulled up to the traffic light, trying to pretend they weren't impressed. Somebody should have told them to use a good astringent and moisturizer, something with sunscreen and extra collagen. The shorter one was already getting a belly. It was sexy now, but in a few years she'd be buying control-top panty hose and drinking Diet Coke by the case. The taller one had posture and attitude going for her, nice tits too, but she didn't know how to apply makeup and her hair was all wrong. She would cash in her dreams for the first boy with a pompadour and a 4 x 4 on credit. The light changed. Trying to peer in, the two girls leaned closer as the limo slid slowly past. Jackie watched them through the smoked glass.

"You know those two?" said Kilo.

Jackie turned away. She wanted a cigarette, though she hadn't smoked for years.

Dekker saw Mrs. Abbott coming into the kitchen and flattened himself against the side of the house. She came to the door. He could see her looking out into the back-yard through the glass door front. She flipped on a light, illuminating the swimming pool and the tennis court. Dekker could have just torn the heavy door off its hinges and be done with it, but he held back, not sure why. He heard the deadbolt turn and the door opening.

Mrs. Abbott stepped out onto the porch, still holding her drink. She looked out past the swimming pool, shading her eyes from the light with her free hand. "Scat!" Dekker laughed. He couldn't help it. Mrs. Abbott turned toward him and said, "Oh. I thought you were a coyote." Her eyes widened, suddenly aware of her predicament— she ran back inside. She tried to slam the door, but Dekker was right behind her. She splashed her drink in his face, hurled the glass too. Dekker grabbed her by the shoulder, and she screamed.

"Stop!" Jackie said into the intercom. "Pull in here."

The limo slid into the driveway of the Red River Wedding Chapel, gravel crunching under the tires. A neon sign of a John Wayne look-alike in chaps and rawhide vest was astride the chapel like the Colossus of Rhodes, "Let's get hitched, pilgrim!" flashing as America's cowpoke tipped his ten-gallon hat.

Jackie clutched Kilo. "This is perfect!"

Mr. Abbott looked ill.

"When Kilo and I first met," said Jackie. "John Wayne

was right there in the room with us. Remember, Kilo? This is like returning to the scene of the crime."

Kilo craned his head to look up at the neon Duke. "Whoa."

"I see," said Mr. Abott, who didn't.

Dekker was bent over in the living room, his hands braced on his knees, trying to catch his breath. There was a bump on his forehead where Mrs. Abbott had hit him with her whiskey glass, and deep scratches down the side of his neck. Mrs. Abbott lay sprawled across the gold brocade sofa, panting, watching him with those angry eyes of hers.

"Who are you?" she hissed.

Dekker touched his neck and saw blood on his fingers. His heart wasn't in it tonight. That's all there was to it.

"Get out," said Mrs. Abbott, raising herself up on one elbow. "Get out of my house!"

Most people saw Dekker under these circumstances they started crying—the guy at the house in Del Mar had blubbered all over himself, big guy too, kept whining "Why us?" All Mrs. Abbott said was "Get out," and she didn't even say please. What a grand old bird. Dekker straightened up and took a step toward her. "Look, lady, make it easy on the both of us."

"Kilo sent you, didn't he?" spat Mrs. Abbott. That stopped Dekker. "I thought so. He's been so courteous these last couple of weeks, so considerate—'Can I get you a cup of tea, Mother?' Mother." Her mouth twisted. "That craven little shit. I hope you got paid in advance."

Dekker didn't answer. Heck, he agreed with her.

Mrs. Abbott got to her feet. "I intend to look at a pho-

tograph from my honeymoon, so you're just going to have to wait to murder me," she said, limping over to the fireplace. She picked up a photograph from the mantel, a photo of her younger self and a handsome man in a gondola. Mr. Abbott, probably. "Have you ever been in love?" she asked Dekker, still looking at the photo, touching the faces with her fingertips, reading the past like a blind woman.

Dekker moved closer. "Yes, I have."

"I doubt that." Mrs. Abbott kissed the photo. "A man like you. You don't know what love is."

"You're wrong, Mrs. Abbott," said Dekker, closer still.

The John Wayne impersonator pinned an honorary deputy sheriff badge on Kilo's suit and shook his hand. This corpulent pretender with a bad Texas accent, an oversized Stetson, and a nebulae of exploded capillaries across his nose then offered Jackie a "schoolmarm" bonnet. She waved him off, and John Wayne knew better than to press his luck. Mr. Abbott stood off to one side with a pained smile on his face. The limo driver, who had agreed to be a witness, stood solemnly next to Mr. Abbott, his hands clasped in front of him.

The interior of the Red River Chapel was decorated with saddles, coiled lariats and cowboy boots, fake log cabin paneling and knotty pine linoleum—posters from *The Man Who Shot Liberty Valance, Stagecoach, Red River,* and *Rio Bravo* hung on the walls. The song, "Back in the Saddle Again," played softly over the sound system. Jackie and Kilo had bought plain gold bands—"made from authentic 'North to Alaska' nuggets!"—from the chapel's general store.

Jackie wondered if Dekker was through yet. He wasn't

going to like her getting married to Kilo. She smiled, and Kilo grinned back at her, assuming that her smile was meant for him. Husbands were always the last to know what was in a wife's mind. And they weren't even married yet.

"Well, deputy, are you and the little lady ready to get hitched?" John Wayne asked Kilo. "Then let's get to it, buckeroos!"

Mrs. Abbott carefully put the photograph back on the mantel, then grabbed the fireplace poker and smacked Dekker across the head as he came toward her. The blow stunned him for a moment—as much from surprise as anything. She hit him again, this time even harder, flat against one ear. If she had been able to use both hands, she might have really hurt him, but she dropped the poker and ran across the living room. He came after her.

She knocked over an end table and started up the stairs, but he kicked the table aside and stumbled up the stairs behind her. The two of them were clumsy from pain and exertion. As she reached the landing, he grabbed her neck. Her strand of pearls broke, and pearls bounced down the hardwood steps. It sounded like rain.

"Do you, deputy Charles Abbott III, take Miss Jackie Hendricks to be your lawful wedded wife?" asked John Wayne.

Kilo looked at Jackie. "Damn right."

Mr. Abbott sniffled.

"And do you, little lady," said John Wayne, "do you, Jackie Hendricks, take Charles Abbott III to be your lawful wedded husband?"

Jackie saw joy and anticipation in Kilo's face, as well

as a trace of fear. It was more than just bridegroom jitters. Kilo had finally gotten his wish, and now he was realizing that a dream delivered brought risks and burdens that the dreamer never imagined. Get used to it, Kilo, the dream always loses something in translation.

"Little lady?"

Jackie looked at Kilo and smiled. "I do."

Chapter Fourteen

Val chased Kyle up the steps, following her legs as she hit the second-floor landing and kept right on going. He was carrying a twenty-five-pound bag of charcoal briquettes slung over one shoulder and a bag of groceries clutched to his chest.

"Slowpoke," said Kyle, beating him to her door and unlocking it. She took the briquettes from him and walked into the kitchen. "I'll fire up the hibachi. You can start this special recipe you've been bragging about for the past hour."

"No brag. 'Kebobs à la Jaime' is a crowd pleaser."

"I thought this was *your* recipe?"

"I stole it from a guy in south Texas."

Kyle slid open the glass door to the tiny deck. "Your friend Steffano is going to arrest you yet."

Val rooted around in the lower cabinets looking for pots and pans, but there were just cans of soup, jars of asparagus tips and artichoke hearts, and a row of Evian bottles. He tried more cabinets as Kyle poured briquettes onto the hibachi. Val found a single battered iron skillet inside the stove, with rust flakes around the rim. He looked over at her. "You need help."

"There's beer in the refrigerator," Kyle called.

"Right." He popped a couple bottles of Becks, brought her one, then went back to the kitchen and started unpacking the groceries. End-cut bacon, cherry tomatoes, limes, garlic, cilantro, swordfish steaks, fresh shrimp, and a package of bamboo skewers. He cut thick slices of bacon, laid them in the skillet, and adjusted the gas-burner to medium heat. Then he rinsed off the shrimp in the sink, cleaned them under the cold running water, and put them in a ceramic bowl. The bacon was sizzling now, its salty fragrance filling the kitchen. Val was about to ask Kyle if she preferred her shrimp with the head on or headless, then decided to just leave the heads on.

"Smells good in here." Kyle came in from the deck to put her empty bottle in the recycling bin. "You want another beer?"

"Still working on the first one." Val cut a couple of limes in half, squeezed them over the shrimp, then crushed garlic cloves with the flat of his knife and mixed them in with the shrimp. He put the bowl in the refrigerator.

Drinking another beer, Kyle leaned against the counter and watched him work.

The directness of her gaze should have made him self-conscious, but instead her attention established an intimacy between them. She was right there the whole time, right there with him. He unwrapped the swordfish steaks, cut the firm white flesh into cubes, then moved to the stove, still feeling her eyes on him.

"Do you have any other domestic talents?" asked Kyle, as she peeled the label off her beer.

Val smiled and gave the skillet a couple of shakes, sending the bacon popping.

When the executive jet hit an air pocket, Junior bounced half off the leather couch. "Yeehaw!"

Staring straight ahead, Armando was belted into one of the conference chairs, working rosary beads through his fingers, *clickity-clack, clickity-clack.*

"I know you don't like flying," said Junior, "but there weren't no way I was taking the train to L.A. Fuck that Casey Jones routine."

"I am fine, Junior." The beads whipped through Armando's fingers.

Junior watched Armando suffering. The boy was dressed in a racing-green flying suit he had bought at an aviation supply store, a green jumpsuit with Velcro straps and zippers on the arms and legs. "Look, Armando, if it makes you feel any better, the odds of dying in a plane crash are supposed to be about the same as being killed by a runaway horse."

"My cousin was killed by a donkey," Armando said quietly. "It stumbled on a mountain path and fell on him."

Junior laughed. "I got to tell that one to Valentine when we catch up with him."

Val unwrapped the bamboo skewers. To make the kebobs, he alternated cherry tomatoes, bacon, and swordfish. "This afternoon on the set, when Dennis and I were trying out that fight scene . . . you got off on it, didn't you?" The cherry tomato popped on the skewer, and seeds spurted onto the counter.

"I beg your pardon?"

"I just got this feeling from you when I took him

down." Val slid another accordion of bacon down the skewer, working faster now. "Something . . . primitive. Like the heat at a boxing match—"

"Or a cockfight?" Kyle said innocently.

Val smiled. "Something like that."

"You're going to hurt yourself if you're not careful," Kyle said.

Val looked down. He had filled eight skewers, used up all the ingredients, and was now pushing the point of another skewer into his index finger. He quickly squeezed lime juice across the kebobs, drizzled them with a little more bacon grease, then put them into the refrigerator to set.

Kyle kissed him. "I'm going to change." She brushed against him in the small kitchen.

Val watched her go into the bedroom and half-close the door. He heard water running and went out onto the deck to check the hibachi. The coals were almost ready, nearly pure white. The stars were out in the night sky. The sliver of moon was sharp as a scythe—a bad luck moon, according to his grandmother. Never plant a garden or make a baby under a sharp moon she had warned. Nothing good will grow under its feeble glow. He was going to have to talk with Grace about that.

Val went back inside. Through the partially open door he could see Kyle reflected in the bedroom mirror. He looked away, then turned back, watching as she peeled off her blouse and tossed it aside. She stepped away from the mirror, and he was left with the memory of her small breasts cupped by the lacy white half-bra. He turned away and made more noise in the kitchen than he needed to putting the shrimp on skewers. Her breasts had been smooth and brown. She must know a private place to sun-bathe. Maybe someday she would show him where—

"That's better," said Kyle, coming out of her bedroom. She had changed into an off-white tanktop and cutoffs. Her hair was unbraided now, brushed out around her bare shoulders.

"Much better."

She smiled and he smiled back. Suddenly the kitchen seemed even smaller. Val took her in his arms and kissed her, pressing his hands into the small of her back. The two of them were so close that he could feel her heart beating against his chest. Maybe it was his own heart. He couldn't tell anymore. When they slowly disengaged, the feel of her body lingered against his skin, as though they were still embracing.

"I . . . I should do something," she said. "I've got some messages," she said, noticing the red light blinking on her phone answering machine in the living room.

"Chicken." Val watched her walk into the living room. He heard a familiar voice from the answering machine. It was Jackie. Val couldn't make out what she was saying. He started toward the refrigerator.

"You fucking *bitch*!"

Val turned and saw Kyle standing in the living room with her mouth open. "What's wrong?" He walked over to her. "Kyle?"

She didn't answer.

"What is it?"

Her lips pulled thin, Kyle pressed "Rewind" on the answering machine.

Beep. "Hi, Kyle, this is Jackie." She sounded giddy. "Chuck, Kilo, and I are in Las Vegas. You won't believe it, but Kilo and I decided to get married. Talk about short notice! Anyway, sorry you're not home, but we'll have a big party when we get back. I know you and I are going to be friends. I always wanted a sister, Kyle, hope you did too! Bye!"

Kyle picked up the phone, punching in numbers so hard Val thought she was going to break her finger. The phone rang and rang until the Abbotts' answering machine came on the line. "Mother, are you there?" Kyle said to the machine. "Mother, pick up! Mother? Damn." She hung up the phone, looking unsure what to do next.

"Why don't you help me put the skewers on the grill," Val suggested. "There's nothing you can do now but congratulate the blushing bride and groom."

Kyle grimaced. "Sure, let's kill the fatted calf."

Chapter Fifteen

Kyle drove through the open gate, saw three police cars parked in the circular front driveway of the Abbotts' house, and hit the brakes. Tires squealing, the Suburban skidded up behind a brown Ford with a "My Child Made the Tustin Pentecostal Academy Honor Roll!" bumper sticker. An Orange County coroner's van was half-parked on her mother's prize rhododendrons. She was still cursing as a uniformed officer moved toward her car.

"Ms. Abbott?"

She threw open the door before the cop could help her out and walked right past him. Pushing open the front door, she slammed it in his face. She leaned against the wall, her eyes closed. I will not cry, I will not cry, I will not cry. She stayed in the vestibule listening to the house whisper while she regained her composure. Let the house whisper. She wasn't afraid of the whispers. There were plenty of worse things to be afraid of.

Her hair was soggy against her neck, and her gray sweats were still damp and crusted with salt. She had come in from diving early this afternoon. Her apartment still smelled faintly of last night's shrimp dinner with Val. She came in and turned on the shower, listening to her messages as she undressed. She had stopped what she was doing as Kilo's voice, frantic, crackled from the machine. He demanded to know where she was, angry that she was never there when he wanted her. Finally he told her what had happened to Gwen.

Kyle passed Chuck's downstairs office and saw a technician in a white smock carefully brushing fingerprint powder on the walnut desk. She hurried on, hearing voices in the living room. A strobe flashed on the stairway. A photographer was firing away at something, the camera's motor-drive swooshing. Her mother was a stickler for cleanliness and very demanding of the help. But there was a dark stain on the stairs, and halfway up a smear of something on the wall, a handprint ringed by yellow marker. She turned away and looked out the windows, but there was no relief there. Police tape ringed the fenceline, yellow tape flapping in the wind. She thought of the festive pennants at the Tijuana bullfights, the smell of spiced beef in the bright sunshine, and almost threw up. She wished that Val was with her. She had banged on the door to his apartment before she left, calling out his name, but there was no answer.

From the doorway to the living room, Kyle could see Jackie sitting on the love seat. A middle-aged man in a rumpled gray suit sat beside her, taking notes. A drink in his hand, Mr. Abbott slumped in a leather armchair nearby, ice cubes clinking as he tried to hold himself steady. His hair tousled, Kilo hovered over him, dapper in a raw silk sport coat, ready for his close-up. Seeing a metal star drooping from the lapel of the jacket, Kyle was seized by the crazy thought that the police had deputized Kilo, the way that flight attendants passed out plastic wings to children, making them official pilots.

Fingerprint powder dusted all the smooth surfaces, doors and windows, coffee tables, lamps, even the light-switch plates. Her mother would have been furious at the mess, but her mother was gone now. Only her things remained—the carefully chosen furniture and paintings, the medieval tapestry drapes, the photographs, the dark Italian Renaissance chests. Kyle must have made a sound because Mr. Abbott suddenly looked up from his chair, smiled at her, then started to cry.

Kilo eyed her damp clothes and dripping hair. "Glad you could make it, but you didn't have to dress up." He still had his snotty attitude, but his heart wasn't in it. At that moment Kyle almost liked him, glad that Kilo was at least making the attempt to maintain some semblance of normalcy.

Mr. Abbott put down his drink and walked toward her. She embraced him. "How are you doing, Chuck?"

"What am I going to do?" Mr. Abbott reeked of Scotch. His eyes were red-rimmed and bloodshot. "What am I going to do, Kyle?"

"Oh, *Kyle*. God, I am just *so* sorry," said Jackie.

Over Mr. Abbott's shoulder, Kyle saw Jackie curled up on the love seat, her mascara ruined, a pillow clutched to her chest. She wore a white kid skirt and jacket—maybe that was her wedding dress. Kyle saw the thin gold band on her ring finger and had to resist the impulse to tear it off her. The man in the gray suit sat casually beside Jackie, looking down his long nose at Kyle, appraising her, a grisly man wearing cheap black oxfords with white socks.

"Did . . . did you know that Kilo and Jackie got married last night?" Mr. Abbott said to her. His eyes were glassy. "Congratulations are in order, don't you—"

"I know, Chuck."

"Did Gwen tell you?" Mr. Abbott jerked. "No, of course not. Your mother didn't know . . . and now . . . it's too late." He jerked again. "Kilo and Jackie, these two impetuous kids decided to tie the knot last night. Just like that. So romantic. Your mother and I . . . we were the same way once." He sat down and covered his face with his hands.

Kyle reached for him, but Kilo got between them. He patted his father on the back. "You're going to be okay, Daddy. I got some Valium—"

"Miss Abbott?" The man in the gray suit had an absurd soup-bowl haircut, like one of the Three Stooges . . . what was his name? Moe. The head Stooge. Once again she wished Val was with her. "Miss Abbott?"

"Yes?"

"I'm Detective Dillinger, with the O.C. Sheriff's Department," he said laconically, "and I heard all the jokes, so no cracks, okay?" The man had an ugly, inappropriate grin. "Just call me Phil. Everybody does." He inclined his head toward Kyle. Maybe it was an attempt at a bow. "Sorry we have to meet under such unpleasant circumstances."

"Where's my mother, detective?"

"I don't blame you for being upset," said Dillinger. "There's never a good time for a homicide, but this one sure had lousy timing—right in the middle of a happy occasion. At least it was happy for some folks." He glanced at Jackie. "Your sister-in-law said she didn't know how you'd take to her and Kilo getting hitched. I've seen that before, best and worst families, makes no difference. None of us wants to see another place set at the supper table."

"Your sociological theories are of no interest to me," Kyle said.

"I'm just a student of human nature. I don't mean to set myself up as a college man." Dillinger stuck his pinky in his ear and twisted the finger back and forth. "Still, I think one way or the other, crime is all about territory, naked ape stuff like you see in a *National Geographic* special." He extracted his pinky and examined the tip. "Why don't you sit down, Miss Abbott? The room's been dusted and cleared. You won't hurt nothing."

Kyle didn't move. "Where is my mother, detective? Where . . . where is her body?"

Dillinger shrugged. "Your mother's body has already been removed. The M.E. said he wanted to start the autopsy ASAP." He tried that same inappropriate grin. "Usually there's a week-long backup at the coroner's office, but I guess you rich folks in the colony got pull with the front office." He looked around the living room. "Got to say, this here's the nicest crime scene I ever investigated," he said to no one in particular, dragging the toe of his heavy shoe across the carpet. "This fancy rug feels softer than my bed. What's a square foot of this stuff cost, Mr. Abbott?"

Mr. Abbott looked up, startled.

"Never you mind," said Dillinger. "Heck, I guess if I got to ask, I can't afford it."

"You're being very rude, detective," said Kyle.

"I get that a lot," Dillinger said. "Guess I've been on the job too long and seen too many botched drivebys and scalded babies that nobody knows anything about. Inez says if I'm not careful, she's going to enroll me in charm school."

Kyle stepped right up to him. "Perhaps you can tell me exactly what happened to my mother, detective?"

"She's *dead*," Kilo called to her. "I already told you that on the phone, Kyle."

"Quiet, Kilo." Mr. Abbott shushed him, his voice shaking. "Please."

"She doesn't pay attention to anything I say." Kilo pouted. "The only thing that matters to Kyle is Kyle. Well, she's not the only one who's upset."

"I'm aware that my mother was murdered, detective," Kyle said. "I want to know the circumstances. How it happened. Where—"

"I'm still taking statements," said Dillinger, holding up his notebook, as if that settled things. "Not wanting to be insulting to you, miss, but you're going to have to hold your horses—"

"I will show her, Phil." A short stocky woman stood halfway down the stairs. She was wearing a canary yellow dress that emphasized her ripe hips and mahogany complexion. She had pronounced the detective's name "Feel," drawing out the word.

"You sure about that, Inez?" Dillinger asked.

The woman's broad Olmec features were immobile, her face a regal mask devoid of emotion.

"Whatever you say," said Dillinger. "Miss Abbott, this is my partner, Detective Holguin. Inez, this is Miss Abbott."

"Yes," said Holguin, watching Kyle, her dark eyes hooded, the lids covering half the iris. It gave her the impression of being able to see without being seen. "You are Kyle. The educated sibling."

Dillinger guffawed and waved dismissively at Kilo's protests. "You don't argue with Inez, kid, particularly when she's right." He scrunched up his face at Kyle. "When I saw all them science ribbons and certificates in your old bedroom, I expected you to show up wearing Coke-bottle glasses and a lab coat." He eyed her soggy sweats and wet hair, shaking his head. "Instead, you come in looking like one of them lady jocks in the Tampax ads."

"Phil," Holguin said reproachfully.

"I did it again, didn't I? Got no manners at all anymore. I'm sorry, miss," Dillinger said to Kyle. "I just can't help the way my mind works."

"Come, Ms. Abbott," Holguin beckoned. "I will show you where your mother died."

"Don't touch anything," Dillinger warned Kyle.

"I am sure she knows that, Phil," murmured Holguin, turning on her heel.

Kyle followed Holguin up the stairs. The blue paper surgical booties worn over her shoes rustled with every step. Kyle kept waiting for her to apologize for her partner's behavior, maybe say he was overworked and a really good cop, but the detective didn't say anything. At the top of the stairs, Holguin indicated a box of medical supplies, and waited while Kyle slipped on booties. There was another dried smear of blood on the wall, and like the one on the landing, it was circled by a yellow marker.

"That is not your mother's blood," said Holguin. "At least we do not think so. There was hardly a mark on her, certainly no cuts or abrasions. Just some bruising on her arms and her neck, of course." She hesitated. "Your mother probably did not suffer greatly."

"How the hell do you know that?"

Holguin watched her.

"I mean, is that supposed to comfort me, detective? She's still dead, isn't she?"

"Your mother's neck was snapped, Ms. Abbott. It is a quick way to die."

"Thank you . . . for answering me. I can't stand being patronized."

"I can see that."

Kyle nodded. "I need . . . I need to see where it happened. It's not real unless I see it. I know that must sound crazy—"

"My brother was murdered three years ago," said Holguin, walking beside her down the hallway. "His death was not . . . unexpected, yet I still felt compelled to place my hands on the sidewalk where he had fallen. It was the only way I could rest." Holguin's face was smooth and unlined, but she gave the impression of being older than Kyle. "From what we can surmise, your mother was surprised downstairs. The killer came through the fence and broke into the house through the back door—"

"The house has a security system," said Kyle. "It's hooked directly into—"

"Even the best system is of no use when it is not turned on." Holguin stopped and Kyle stopped too. The master bedroom was just around the next corner. "Your mother and the killer struggled downstairs, then your mother must have fled upstairs, with the killer in pursuit. He caught up with her in the bedroom." She betrayed no emotion, but Kyle sensed her sadness. "Your mother must have thought she was safe. It is a very thick door and the lock was thrown, but the killer broke right through." She placed a hand on Kyle's arm. "I want you to prepare yourself for what I am about to show you."

Kyle took a deep breath.

Holguin led her around the corner. The bedroom door was buckled, hanging almost completely out of the frame.

Kyle stared at the damage. She moved closer, hesitated, then looked into the trashed bedroom. The drawers had been emptied, and her mother's clothes lay on the floor. But what drew all her attention was a chalk outline sketched into the carpet. One hand of the outline was stretched out, reaching for something. The body was curled up. Kyle began crying now, in spite of her promises to herself, sobbing so loudly she was afraid Kilo would hear her.

Holguin patted her on the back. "You should be *proud* of your mother, Ms. Abbott," she said, and Kyle's sobs ebbed, as she drew strength from Holguin's certainty. "Your mother must have been very courageous. The blood . . . we think it was from her assailant. We found blood on the fireplace poker, and there was skin under your mother's fingernails. She was a fighter, and Detective Dillinger and I will not let such bravery go to waste. Are *you* courageous too, Ms. Abbott?"

Kyle straightened up and roughly wiped her eyes.

"Good," said Holguin. "If you are satisfied, we can examine your bedroom. You can make an inventory of anything missing while I ask some questions. Can you do that, or do you need to go downstairs?"

"Of course," said Kyle, as they walked toward her old bedroom. "Do you have any idea who might have done this?"

"Not yet."

"Of course," Kyle said bleakly, "it's too soon."

"Yes," said Holguin, "it is early."

"Detective, I apologize for my . . . reaction before. I'm not usually like that."

"You have nothing to apologize for. I have seen the macho ones keel over from seeing a spot of blood on the carpet. I have seen others, like your stepbrother, fight off the giggles. It is nerves. It means nothing. Your stepfather, however . . ." Holguin shook her head. "I think you should notify his doctor. The surviving spouse bears a heavy burden, Ms. Abbott, and sometimes it is too much for even a strong man. Your stepfather—you will pardon me—does not appear to be a strong man."

Kyle nodded.

"Your stepbrother and his wife live here?" Holguin asked.

"Yes, I guess so."

"That is good," said Holguin. "Your father should not be alone at a time like this. This is a time for families to draw closer. You have someone, Ms. Abbott?"

Kyle hesitated, then allowed herself to say it. "Yes, I have someone."

Chapter Sixteen

"Val?" Mr. Abbott stood in the open doorway, a glass of orange juice in his hand. He had missed a few spots shaving. "How . . . good to see you. Kyle isn't here. I don't know where—"

"I know she's not here, Chuck, I came to pay my respects to Mrs. Abbott. I thought Gwen was an extraordinary person. I see a lot of her in Kyle."

Mr. Abbott blinked in the morning light. "How kind of you, Val, how . . . proper. Please come in." His suit drooped and his tie was clumsily knotted, but he managed to walk down the hall without staggering, his carriage strictly erect.

Val had driven over without calling, driven through the open gates, the front door not even locked. People who have experienced a violent crime in their homes often react in one of two extreme ways—either they become paranoid, changing locks, barring windows and doors, or they sink into fatalism, realizing that anyone is vulnerable, ignoring even the most basic precautions.

Kyle had come to his apartment last night, her face

pale, voice flattened of all emotion. It was her fault, she told him, her mother had been murdered and it was all *her* fault. Kyle had a premonition of danger but never warned her mother, so self-centered that she assumed her premonition was all about herself. Val tried to hold her, but she didn't want to be held, and after her initial outburst, she didn't want to talk either. She just didn't want to be alone. They watched TV until she fell asleep on the couch—Val covered her up and went to bed. She was gone when he woke up.

Mr. Abbott sat down on the sofa with both arms braced, guiding himself onto the cushions as though he might shatter. "Shall I have the cook prepare you something? A drink, perhaps?"

Val sat down beside him. "I just wanted to see how you were doing. I know it's only been a day since . . ."

Mr. Abbott kept blinking. "That's very kind of you. At the door, when I said that Kyle wasn't here, I didn't mean to display anger. It's just that I've hardly seen her since . . . the incident. I appreciate your visit, but I just would have preferred that Kyle come with you."

"She needed to work—"

"Sunday morning and Kyle decides to work," Mr. Abbott said coolly.

"She spent all day Friday with me on the set," Val said, "so she needed to make up the time. I know she's planning on coming by later today to help with the arrangements."

"Yes, the *arrangements*." Mr. Abbott gulped his orange juice, a bit of pulp caught at the edge of his mouth. "The funeral home has already called. Very efficient. Of course, they have to be." He licked his lips, missed the bit of pulp. "Jackie offered to pick out something from Gwen's closet . . . a dress for Gwen to wear."

Val laid his hand on Mr. Abbott's shoulder. "I'm sure that's something Kyle would prefer to do herself."

"Yes, I can understand that." Mr. Abbott smoothed his necktie, touched his hair. "I couldn't stay here last night, couldn't even if I had wanted to. The female detective, Inez something, said they wouldn't be finished doing whatever they do until late—she practically ordered me out of my own home. I've never liked police. I've never even gotten so much as a traffic ticket, but they scare me."

"They scare all of us, Chuck. It's good you left last night—"

Mr. Abbott interrupted him. "Jackie and Kilo should be on their honeymoon. Instead, they chose to keep me company at the Four Seasons." He shook his head. "God, we must have talked half the night. I never realized my son had so many ideas." He turned toward the kitchen. "Lupita!"

The cook emerged in the doorway, drying her hands on a towel.

"Another orange juice," said Mr. Abbott, "and this time make it stronger."

The cook didn't move, her round face disapproving.

"Lupita, kindly make me an orange juice that I can *feel*. Val, will you join me?"

"No, thanks."

Lupita nodded, went back into the kitchen. They waited, not speaking until she had returned and given Mr. Abbott a fresh glass.

Mr. Abbott gulped his drink. "Much better, Lupita!" he called. "Lupita usually has the weekend off, Val, but she came by right after mass, said she had lit a candle for Gwen."

"Did the police tell you anything, Chuck? I know it's early—"

Mr. Abbott shook his head. "Those louts asked more questions than they answered. They treated me like an employee." He idly swirled his orange juice, the liquid rising almost to the rim but not spilling over. Practice makes perfect. "Public servants?" he said disdainfully. "I think not."

"Have there been any similar attacks in the Heights recently?"

"The rude detective—Dillinger—asked me to make an inventory of what was missing." Mr. Abbott's voice quavered—he was running down again. "The truth is I couldn't really think straight. What is missing? There is only one thing missing that really matters, just *her*, that's all that matters." He looked at Val. "I'm afraid I'm . . . quite useless."

"I think you're holding up pretty well, Chuck."

"Do you think so?" Mr. Abbott smoothed his hair again, struggled to lift his chin. "Making a proper appearance, it's a small consolation, but a consolation, nonetheless."

"Kyle told me that the break-in was initiated through the back fence. I stopped there on my way up here—someone forced the bars apart."

"Dillinger said that there are small hydraulic jacks that thieves use to break into homes, jacks available at any auto parts store." Mr. Abbott looked at Val. "What is the sense of having a fence if any psychotic can just waltz in off the street and murder one's wife?"

"I don't think it was a jack," said Val, not sure if this

Dillinger was a half-assed investigator or deliberately keeping Mr. Abbott in the dark. "There were no pressure marks on the bars to indicate a jack—"

"Gwen should have gone with us to Las Vegas—I should have insisted." Mr. Abbott stared at the carpet. "Kilo and I *tried* to convince her, but my wife is . . . my wife *was* a very determined woman."

"Chuck?" Val waited until he had Mr. Abbott's attention. "You must have a lot of service people for a home like this," he said gently. "Pool maintenance, lawn care, house cleaners. . . . Did you notice any new faces lately?"

"That's just what the rude detective asked me. New faces, how very succinct. You have a clever mind, Val—my wife appreciated your clever mind." Mr. Abbott looked at him. "There were no new faces in our lives—that's what I told the detectives. None. Except for you, of course. And Jackie."

"Would you mind if I looked around upstairs? Kyle said . . . she said that's where Mrs. Abbott was killed."

Mr. Abbott swirled his drink. "I don't think that would be a good idea."

"Once the police have cleared a crime scene, you're free to walk around," Val said. "Any evidence has already been logged and—"

"I haven't been upstairs since Kilo found her," Mr. Abbott said weakly.

"I'd . . . I'd like to look around your bedroom for something personal, something that belonged to Mrs. Abbott," Val said, thinking fast. "A coin from her purse, a handkerchief, a comb. Something she would have touched."

"Whatever *for?*"

"I'm going to put together a spirit pouch for her," said

Val. "For her coffin." He watched Mr. Abbott breathe through his mouth. "I'll put a keepsake of Mrs. Abbott's in the pouch, and a pinch of sugar and salt to pay the guide, the spirit guide. For Mrs. Abbott to cross over to the other side. My grandmother is a Seminole . . . she says the dead sometimes need help to cross over. Particularly if they've been taken before their time."

"Is your grandmother a . . . voodoo person?" Mr. Abbott had the good breeding to keep the contempt out of his voice, but he couldn't keep it out of his eyes.

"Making a spirit pouch for your wife is a sign of respect," said Val. "I met Gwen only that one evening, but I liked her *very* much."

"She liked you too, Val—she said she found you quite refreshing. And chivalrous. That was the word she used, 'chivalrous.'" Mr. Abbott tugged at his cuffs, bemused. "Strange."

"Well, we had *Jeopardy* in common."

"Yes, you did," said Mr. Abbott, without even a hint of irony. "Gwen said if you had played the game more craftily you might have ended up on the Tournament of Champions."

"I wasn't cut out to be a champion, Chuck."

"Very few of us are." Mr. Abbott rubbed his temples, his fingers white with the effort. "I keep thinking . . . just two days ago we were all together in this room, Kilo filled with lofty ideas and Jackie bubbling over with her first sale. She actually gave me a handful of business cards to pass out to potential clients—Gwen thought it gauche, and it *was* gauche, but I kept them anyway. Jackie is a hard woman to refuse."

"Mr. Abbott? Would you mind—"

"I know, trinkets and sugar to pay the guide to paradise." Mr. Abbott tried to smile. "Ah well, it seems even in death good help is hard to find."

Val stood up. "I won't be long."

Mr. Abbott tried to get up, almost lost his balance. "I'll come with you," he said, recovering. He followed Val to the foot of the stairs and stopped, breathing hard, then forced himself to take the first step. All that breeding evidently counted for something.

One of the banister's oak spindles had been snapped, as though someone rushing up the stairs had reached out for support and it had given way. There was no way Mrs. Abbott would have been strong enough or heavy enough to have caused that.

Mr. Abbott edged away from the bloodstains on one side of the wall as they climbed. "They think it was just one man who did all this—I don't know how they came to that determination." He moved down the hall hesitantly, repeating what the police had told him, what he had overheard the forensic technicians say to each other.

"That's Kyle's old room," said Mr. Abbott, stopping in front of the open door. "She gave the police a brief inventory of what was stolen, but I don't think she cared about any of it. Some jewelry. Kyle came home only between marriages—we always welcomed her back with open arms, but she was never comfortable here. She preferred her studies to her own family. That sounds terrible, but it's true. I love Kyle as though she were my own daughter, but she was never comfortable around the rest of us. Now Kilo is different—Gwen used to say he needed to be tossed out of the nest, but Kilo knows how to enjoy himself, and he was always ready for a party or a vacation. It's impossible to have a bad time around Kilo."

Val did a quick walk-through of Kyle's room, knowing he would give it more attention later. "If Mrs. Abbott fought with her attacker downstairs and then was chased up here . . . the bedrooms must have been ransacked *after* she was killed," he said to Mr. Abbott, following him down the hall. "The killer was either a very cool customer or he had some sense that there was plenty of time."

"I wouldn't know." Mr. Abbott slowed his pace, barely moving now—the master bedroom gaped open, its door splintered, shards of wood in the carpet. "I . . . I'm going to stay out here."

Val eased past him, avoiding the yellow chalk outline as he looked around the room. The dresser drawers had been overturned, the Persian carpet lifted up, the mattress askew. It had been a sloppy, unprofessional search, unsystematic and time-consuming.

"Gwen's jewelry was taken, most of it anyway, although the fool missed some of the pieces with the most sentimental value," Mr. Abbott said. "Gwen kept her treasures wrapped in a stocking in her socks drawer. She was always more astute than I. My coin collection was taken. All of it—a *complete* run of Indian head pennies, Mercury dimes, Buffalo nickels, Morgan silver dollars. I started that collection when I was a boy. I should have kept it in the safety deposit box, but I enjoyed taking it out, looking at them. All that history. I tried to interest Kilo in numismatics, but . . ."

Val picked an earring off the floor, a single pearl earring.

Mr. Abbott stood in the doorway. "Yes, that should buy Gwen's way into paradise or anywhere she desires to go. Take it."

"Thank you."

"Are you through?"

"I'm sorry, Mr. Abbott. I really am."

"Lupita is having her cousins come by to clean the whole house, scrub it down, top to bottom," Mr. Abbott said. "Maybe I'll feel stronger when the house is back to the way it was." He shook his head, looked away. "The way it was." He smoothed his jacket. "Kilo said he and Jackie will stay with me here for a few weeks, but I hope they stay longer. I'm moving in to one of the guest bedrooms downstairs so they'll have plenty of privacy. Newlyweds need privacy."

"You don't have to keep me company, Chuck."

"I used to be considered good company," muttered Mr. Abbott. "Chuckie Abbott might not be the sharpest knife in the drawer, but he's damn good company, that's what they used to say."

"I'm just going to look around a little bit if you don't mind."

"I was born to wealth and privilege, that's my problem," Mr. Abbott said. "I was a spoiled child, insulated from the roughness of life, to my great and lasting detriment." His eyes were watery, but there was an angry, imperious edge to his voice now. "Gwen thought I had spoiled Kilo, too, thought I had ruined him with my indulgence, but she was wrong—people underestimate Kilo because he's talented and good-looking and doesn't suffer fools gladly, but let me tell you, this horrible thing . . . this killing, it's brought out the *best* in him."

Val didn't respond.

"This is Kilo's room," said Mr. Abbott. "Look at the mess. There wasn't much to steal, but the bastard made up for it by destroying what was left."

Val waited until Mr. Abbott had disappeared down the stairs before entering Kilo's room. Metal tennis racquets had been beaten shapeless against the headboard of the bed; the dresser had been overturned and clothes strewn everywhere. A gold-plated loving cup lay covered with broken glass, one side caved in—it looked as if the killer had thrown the trophy into the full-length mirror.

Val walked back into Kyle's room, still thinking about the personal attack on Kilo's room—in contrast, Kyle's room was barely touched. Her closets had been searched, clothes and boxes pushed aside, but there was no wanton destruction. He riffled through the stacks of glass mounting-boxes, stacks of them, carefully indexed—beetles, spiders, wasps, butterflies, locusts, moths, grasshoppers, thousands of them. Maybe the killer had been disgusted by all the bugs and got out of there as soon as he could.

The walls of Kyle's bedroom were lined with framed awards from various national honor societies and a photo of a younger Kyle receiving a plaque from a beaming President Ronald Reagan. She had the intellect and the discipline to accumulate this vast range of insects, had spent years of painstaking work on the collection, but she had left it all behind when her interests turned to marine biology, to orcas and dolphins and gray whales. Mr. Abbott couldn't let his childhood collection go, but Kyle had moved on and never looked back.

Val walked away from the closet, too, trying to imagine Kyle growing up in that room, looking out over the swimming pool, hearing Kilo smacking a tennis ball for hours on end with his private coach. Had there ever been stuffed animals in Kyle's room, pictures of long-haired teen rock stars? He wondered what she must have thought about in bed, surrounded by her catalogue of pinned insects. He didn't mind live bugs—he had grown up with red ants and scorpions, flying cockroaches and clouds of mosquitoes. Florida state disease-control trucks had regularly rumbled through his neighborhood laying down thick white clouds of DDT when the skeeters got too bad—he and Steffano had ridden their bicycles behind the truck, playing in the fog, pretending they were fighter pilots lost in the clouds. Live bugs were one thing. Dead ones gave him the creeps. Well, as Kyle had said the first time they met, he was no scientist.

Val could hear the shower running in the guest bedroom as he descended the stairs. He looked around the living room, saw clear into the kitchen where Lupita was wiping down the countertops, the sound of her radio filtering through the house, a mournful country-and-western song. Last night Kyle had cried out, half-awake—"I'm sorry, Mama," she had said, "I'm so sorry." He had tried to comfort her, had told her it wasn't her fault, but she was already sound asleep.

Premonitions were ambiguous and untrustworthy. In Miami, Val had premonitions about him and Steffano all the time, terrible visions of running through fields of fire, hair smoldering—a lot of good that had done them. Kyle had a vision of danger, but even *now* it was impossible to tell if that premonition foretold her mother's murder or her own. Junior was coming. That was the only thing Val was certain of.

"Mr. Abbott?" Val rapped on the door to the guest room. "I'm going to leave—Kyle will be here as soon as she can." He waited for an answer, but there was only the sound of the running water. A small pile of business cards lay on a table in the entryway—he stopped on his way out the door, picked one up and tucked it into his pocket.

Chapter Seventeen

Jackie was talking to her office, hand on her hip, when Dekker walked through the front door. It felt like a chip of ice running down her back. "I'll get back to you, Barry," she said, clicked off the phone. "You surprised me, Darryl."

"Yeah, well you surprised me, too." Dekker closed the door behind him. "How much is this joint?"

The sun shone through the huge windows overlooking the Pacific. The house was a four-bedroom contemporary set high on the bluffs overlooking Laguna Beach, with a tiny kitchen, a cracked fireplace from the last earthquake, and a 180-degree unobstructed view of the water. "Two-point-six million." She smiled. "Are you interested?"

Dekker walked around the room in his black Armani topcoat, hands in his pockets, the collar turned up. A bandage covered one side of his cheek where Mrs. Abbott had hit him with the poker. "Great location, but the appliances are a little outdated. What are the local schools like?"

Jackie checked her watch. "You shouldn't be here."

"Where should I be?" Dekker was a thundercloud filling the sunny room.

Jackie stood her ground. "We have to be careful, Darryl. Did anyone see you coming in here?"

"I'm very careful, don't you remember?"

"Good—"

"You must have a lot on your mind these days if you've forgotten what I'm like."

"Yes, I *do* have a lot—"

"I saw you last night," said Dekker. "You and Kilo went out for dinner at the Yacht Club. Should I tell you what appetizers you ordered?" His face seemed puffier. "I watched you feed him, right off your fork—you pretended to put it in his mouth, then pulled the fork away as he went for it. He finally got a taste though; you gave it to him eventually. After he begged. Kilo was wearing those stupid-looking loafers the color of French's mustard—he had a whole closet full of ugly-ass shoes like that."

"Those loafers are Bottega Venetas, and they're butter cream, not mustard. Eight hundred dollars a pair and soft as rose petals, Darryl."

"Drawers full of silk underwear, stacks of custom shirts and more suits than The Men's Warehouse. I couldn't believe it. You ask me, I killed the wrong member of the Abbott family."

"I didn't ask you."

Marrying Kilo had changed everything; the alteration was so abrupt that it had surprised her. She was one of the anointed ones now, one of the golden ones, by marriage if not by blood. Sunday she had simply mentioned that she needed a special outfit and some other things for the funeral, and Mr. Abbott had handed over his AMEX, not even looking up from his newspaper. She had driven straight to Fashion Island and its collection of exclusive salons, running up charges—Armani, Angiolini, Missoni, Bulgari—slowly at first, escalating rapidly, sending salesgirls scurrying, eager to fetch her pleasure.

"Neither of you saw me at the Yacht Club, but I was there," said Dekker, breathing harder now. "You turn over in your sleep, Jackie, I'm right beside you. You paint your toenails or leave the water running, I know about it."

Jackie reached out, touched the bandage on his cheek and he closed his eyes like a puppy. "Mrs. Abbott hurt you."

"Just a little."

"You let her hurt you. You *wanted* her to."

"Why would I do that? A person would have to be sick to—"

"You're going to ruin everything," said Jackie.

"What about you?"

"It's not all dinners at the Yacht Club," said Jackie. "One minute Kilo feels like Lex Luther, criminal mastermind, the next minute he's blubbering about getting a lethal injection and it's all your fault and my fault, everybody's fault but his own."

"I could fix that."

"What are you really doing here, Darryl?"

"I wasn't just muscle when I met you, Jackie," said Dekker. "I wasn't just some lowlife repo man running down deadbeats—I was a *collector.*" His face reddened. "I was a good liar too, almost as good as you. People would tell me all kinds of things—big guy like me, you wouldn't think so, but I'm an easy guy to talk to."

Jackie laughed. "Yeah, you're a regular Dr. Laura."

"I can be sensitive when I want to be." Dekker's hands were still in his topcoat. He looked out the window at the waves breaking on the beach, the sand lined with towels and sunbathers. "I can be invisible too."

Jackie was tempted to laugh again, but she didn't. Something was going on with him.

"A big man gets noticed," Dekker explained, "but fat people are invisible. The trick is learning how to slump, to dress oversize and lumpy. I could walk down Main Street like the big Kahuna in a pineapple-pattern mumu and shower slippers, and the whole block is going to be busy window-shopping and checking their shoeshine." He faced her, backlit by the sunlit Pacific, his face in shadow, his voice a wisp, the topcoat hanging off his shoulders.

The transformation was amazing. She was used to seeing Dekker as a looming, hostile presence, but he was smaller now, shrinking before her eyes.

"Remember how I found *you* that first time, Jackie? You were so cautious, but I walked right up to your new apartment, a big dumb lug in checked pants carrying a pizza. Once I had my foot in the door, the little red Corvette was going back where it came from. You miss four payments, the dealership loses patience."

"But you didn't repo my Corvette that day, did you?"

"No, I didn't."

"You handed me back my keys and told the finance company you couldn't find me," said Jackie, allowing herself that smile now. "You've got your gifts, Darryl. I've got mine."

"All you saw was my size," said Dekker, "but I'm more than meat."

"I know that. That's why I chose you."

"I love you, *that's* why you chose me. It makes it easy for you."

"Who said I liked things easy?" Jackie aligned the

edges of her paperwork with a rap against the counter, tucking the contracts into her slim leather folder along with the gold-nibbed Mont Blanc. "I'm in a hurry. I've got a townhouse in Dana Point—"

"Did you think I wouldn't find out?" said Dekker. They had both been waiting for him to say it ever since he walked through the front door.

"I was counting on it, Darryl. I thought you would have the sense to understand why I did it and act accordingly."

"You *married* him."

"We had a marriage ceremony. Papers were signed. That's *all.*"

"You married him," Dekker repeated. "I read about it in the paper over breakfast. 'Local Newlyweds Return to Grisly Scene.' I read the article three times. My coffee got cold. The waitress kept coming by, she kept asking me if I wanted anything else and I didn't know what to say to her."

"I did it for you."

Dekker stared at her. "Thank you." His mouth twitched. "Why don't you give me a tour of the house?" he said softly.

Jackie couldn't speak.

"That's what you do, isn't it? Show off the goods, right?"

"Yes . . . that's right." Jackie led him out of the living room. "This is the study," she said waving at a small room. "There's built-in bookcases and a dedicated phone line for—"

"Do you like being married?" asked Dekker, following her into another room. "Did you wear white at the ceremony?"

"You were worried that Kilo was going to screw us," said Jackie, "afraid that after you did your job he was going to jaunt off to Switzerland or Hong Kong and there wouldn't be anything we could do about it. Marrying Kilo was our insurance policy. California is a community property state and Kilo and I didn't sign a pre-nup. You should have seen Mr. Abbott's face." She brightened. "What do you think of the house? There's only a half-bath in this room and the closet is small, but—"

"No Jacuzzi?"

Jackie shook her head.

"What about the master bedroom? You know I'm partial to Jacuzzis."

"I think there's a whirlpool in the master." Jackie could feel her heart beating.

"I'd still like to see it."

Jackie glanced at her watch again.

"Make time, Jackie." Dekker followed her up the stairs and into the master bedroom. Light flooded in through the open curtains, the Pacific spreading out before them—if his eyes had been good enough, he could have seen all the way to Japan.

"It's not what you think," said Jackie.

"What am I thinking, Jackie?"

"Be like that." Jackie shook her head. "Come on out, Kilo," she called.

" 'Mrs. Abbott . . .' " Dekker grimaced. "I just can't get used to it."

Jackie sat down on the king-sized bed, crossed her legs. "I'm Mrs. Charles Abbott III now. Kilo's father wants to buy this place for us as a wedding present—it's not hard to get used to." She turned her head. "Kilo! Get *out* here."

"You're Mrs. Charles Abbott III, good for you," said Dekker. "Where does that leave me?"

Kilo poked his head out of the master bathroom. "That you, Dekker? I thought I heard voices—"

Dekker grabbed him by the collar, dragged him into the room.

Jackie lolled on the bed. "It makes me feel like a movie star lying here looking out at the water. Kilo wanted to give this big old bed a workout, Darryl, but I told him I wasn't that kind of girl."

Kilo tore free from Dekker's grasp, buttons popping onto the carpet.

"I know you're fucking him, Jackie."

"Strictly platonic, dude," Kilo disagreed. "Donny and Marie Osmond."

"I don't like that word, *fucking,* Darryl," said Jackie.

"That word never used to bother you." Dekker sat down beside her on the bed, making the whole side sag. "I shouldn't even be talking with you—I should just kill Kilo."

"What did I do?" said Kilo. "Every time you get bored or frustrated, you start with this 'let's-kill-Kilo' routine. I'm starting to take it personally."

"I should kill him, kill you, kill myself," said Dekker.

"You're so depressing, Darryl," said Kilo. "It's a sunny day, birds are chirping, and my stepmother is getting buried tomorrow. So put on a happy face—look at the three of us—this is like old times at the John Wayne Suite."

"Shut up."

"We *won,* Dekker," said Kilo. "I used to spend the whole afternoon practicing my serve and fantasizing about killing them, Gwen and Chuck both, but I could never figure out how to get away with it. Look at us now. We *did* it."

"What do you mean *we?*" said Dekker.

"Give me a little credit, boys," said Jackie. "There's plenty to go around."

"My apologies, *Mrs.* Abbott," said Kilo, smiling.

"Keep it up, fuckwad," said Dekker.

Jackie smiled. Kilo had been a pleasant surprise, this rich cutie-pie with the clean fingernails and the sweet breath. She had pointed out that there was no reason to kill *both* Gwen and his father, a big inheritance would just invite police attention—besides, Chuck was a walking blank check. It was Mrs. Abbott who was standing between Kilo and Daddy's money. Jackie liked Gwen, but, as she told Kilo, bad things happened to good people all the time. Kilo had actually clapped his hands with glee.

"In a few months, when things calm down, I want to set up my own production company," said Kilo, strutting around the room. "Four or five million dollars should do it. You need to spend money to make money, that's what I always told Chuck." He nodded at Dekker. "I'm going to take care of you, Darryl. I'll put you on the payroll and give you an expense account. You're going to *love* being an executive."

"Listen to him, Jackie," said Dekker. "This is the man you married."

"Don't be such a party pooper." Jackie lay back on the bed, listening to the waves crashing in the distance. "What are you wearing to Gwen's funeral, Kilo? I want to make sure we look good together."

Kilo laughed. "How about something with **bells on**?"

Chapter Eighteen

Serene Harbor was a great place to be buried—fifty-four acres of manicured grounds straddling the hills around Laguna Niguel, no headstones or crypts to disturb the rolling expanse of clipped green grass, just flat bronze plaques. Serene Harbor was another exclusive community, a gated enclave protected from care and woe and beggars shaking dirty Have a Nice Day! cups at pedestrians. Ocean views available.

The breeze carried the overpowering scent of flowers from the bouquets surrounding Mrs. Abbott's white coffin. The Romanesque pavilion where the memorial service was held was open to the air, the marble pillars and cantilevered roof designed to impart a sense of classical calm to the proceedings. Val stood in the front row wearing his only suit, head slightly bowed, sweating, wanting to get into some other clothes.

Kyle stepped to the microphone and cleared her throat, her amplified voice crackling. "My mother didn't like going to funerals," she said, letting her words float across the assembled mourners. There must have been three hundred of them, most of them middle-aged and older, the yacht and tennis club set come to bid farewell to one of their own. "Mother said the speeches were too long, the grass kicked up her allergies, and you couldn't get a good drink." The crowd rippled with laughter.

Val saw tears in her eyes.

"Mother would be very happy that you all came out today to honor her memory. My family and I"—she glanced at Kilo and Mr. Abbott, then to Jackie—"wish to extend our gratitude. Mother was a strong, sensible, compassionate woman who believed in playing by the rules and not complaining about the outcome. Her death . . ." Kyle stopped, tried to speak, took a deep breath. "Her death proves that the world is neither fair nor sensible, but since Mother accepted the world and all its many imperfections, we have no recourse other than to accept her death, too." Kyle stepped down from the dais as Kilo approached her, the two of them air-kissing, before she returned to her place beside Val.

Kilo strode onto the podium in a fine black suit, slim and boyish, his hair cut short on the sides, combed up into a slight pompadour, a black orchid in his lapel. Val had never seen anyone look so good in clothes. A collective sigh went up from the women in the crowd as Kilo stood there, drinking in their expectations, surrounded by white roses.

"It's no secret that Gwen and I had our problems," Kilo began. "She was tough and I never quite lived up to her standards." His handsome face broke into a grin. "To be honest, I wasn't even close." He was serious now, surveying the mourners. A woman in the audience started quietly weeping. "Kyle said that life is not sensible." He nodded to her. "That may be true. I don't pretend to be as intelligent as Kyle, but I do know this—if Gwen's death has any meaning, then maybe it's the fact that her passing has given me the opportunity to be the man she always wanted me to be." He cleared his throat. "I won't let you down, Gwen," he said softly. He patted the white coffin, stepped off the podium and into the arms of Mr. Abbott.

The string quartet started playing some classical thing. Kyle took Val's hand as the mourners slowly made their way past the open coffin. Mrs. Abbott was wearing the two-carat diamond earrings that Mr. Abbott had given her for her birthday and her favorite dress, a simple plum-colored suit that Kyle had picked out, the spirit pouch tucked unobtrusively in a pocket. Everyone said she looked wonderful, but Val considered that a relative term.

Jackie stood beside Mr. Abbott, shaking hands with people she didn't know, accepting their condolences. She was wearing an elegant black dress and a single strand of black pearls that Mr. Abbott had retrieved from their safety deposit box. He had offered the pearls to Kyle first, but she had refused—her mother had never liked those black pearls, that's why they were in the vault.

A scrawny, bald gentleman with yellowed teeth and an enormous gold stick pin walked over to Kyle—he looked like a turkey vulture that had hit the mother lode. "Hell of a thing," he said, blue eyes blazing. "I only hope the bastards who did it appear in my court. I'll get them the hot shot, you can count on that."

"Thank you, judge," said Kyle.

"Your mother was proud of you, young lady." The judge's teeth snapped. "I was her friend for thirty-four years, and she always knew what she was doing. I think you're cut from the same cloth."

Kyle shook his hand and the judge moved off—she took the opportunity to lead Val out of the pavilion and onto a rise of lawn overlooking the crowd. "Thanks for coming," she said. "It seems like I'm always dragging you along to bad times."

"I had a good time at your mother's party," said Val. "I'm grateful that I got the chance to meet her."

Kyle turned her back to the mourners. "Kilo invited us to go out with him and Jackie this evening."

"Are you up for it?"

Kyle looked out over the rolling grounds. "He's trying, but I don't know why—there's nothing in it for him. Chuck is the only one he has to please now, and that's never been hard for Kilo." She shook her head. "Maybe Jackie qualifies as a good influence."

Behind Kyle's back, Val saw a man break away from the crowd and start up the hill toward them. A cop. He was sure of it. "Why don't you give Jackie a chance?" he said, watching the man amble across the grass. "What can it hurt?"

The man had the cop walk, a slow, fatigued swagger, knowing he had the force of authority behind him but too overworked to flaunt himself. A cop could walk into a brick wall and be surprised that the wall didn't step aside. Directors had a similar unhurried gait, even the ones who were over budget and running out of excuses. Directors and cops were part of the pantheon of minor gods, their judgments capricious and final, ruling by force of personality more than anything else. Directors had the advantage of not having to worry about the Bill of Rights or the I.A.B., but then they didn't get to carry a gun or speed through red lights, siren blaring, so it evened out.

"Would you mind, Val?"

"What?"

"Would you mind if we went out with Kilo and Jackie?"

Val watched the cop getting closer. "Sure. Anything you want."

"Don't make promises you can't keep." Kyle slipped her hand in his. "I'm glad we—"

"Miss Abbott?"

Kyle turned.

"Hi, Miss Abbott." The cop wore a gray suit with frayed cuffs and a clip-on tie, his narrow face topped by a Moe Fine haircut. Val had seen that same soup-bowl cut on surfers, an old-fashioned look that suited their baggys and laid-back attitude, but on the cop, the haircut spoke of a kitchen chair surrounded by newspapers, bits of hair drifting down onto the headlines, and trying to save a buck. "Miss Abbott, Inez and me wanted to give our condolences to you and yours." He glanced at Val, then looked back at the pavilion. "You got quite a turnout here. Helps I guess."

"It's not a ball game, detective," Kyle said coolly. "Turnout doesn't affect the outcome."

The man grinned. He had a slack, easygoing mouth and eyes like a shark. "Hey, pal," he said, thrusting a hand out to Val, "I'm Phil Dillinger with the Sheriff's department. No cracks about my name or I'll arrest you and plant a bloody glove in your car. No, seriously, me and my partner, Inez, we're running this case."

"Val Duran."

"Like Roberto Duran, the boxer?" Dillinger threw a lazy punch at Val's jaw. "Hands of stone, that's what they called him. Duran was the last Panamanian middleweight champ—one hell of a puncher, but he didn't have any heart. 'No mas, no mas,' " he parroted. "You're not related to him, are you, Val?"

"Not that I know of."

Dillinger squinted at Val. "You're the boyfriend? The one was at the birthday party." He snapped his fingers. "I heard about you from Kilo. You're some kind of movie-flunky, right?"

"I was at the party," said Val, refusing to rise to the bait. "You've got that right anyway."

"Wasn't that house something?" said Dillinger. "A regular *Lifestyles of the Rich and Famous,* all that expensive stuff just sitting around collecting dust, ivory and gold knick-knacks. I never even seen a grand piano before, not close up, and that dining room table probably took a couple of whole trees to make. If I didn't like my job, I might have been tempted to fill my pockets with what the killer left behind. Heck, why deny it, I considered it anyway—it's not like they would miss it. I bet you got some light-fingered fantasies at the birthday party, pal?" He plucked at Val's suit. "Don't try to tell me you weren't tempted, too, you and me are the two worst-dressed guys at the wake."

Val extricated himself from Dillinger's grasp. It was a standard razzle-dazzle performance, but the cop did it well, switching from crude comments to insults to suggestions of camaraderie in crime. If one tactic didn't trip a suspect up, the sudden changes would. It usually worked too.

Dillinger did a slow 180-degree turn, surveying the expanse of rolling lawn, hands on his hips. "Got to say, Miss Abbott, this here's one nice boneyard." He winked at Val. "The rich come into this life with a silver spoon and go out with a silver spade."

Kyle was fuming.

"Are you making any progress on the case, detective?" said Val.

"Little bit," Dillinger said. "Putting the pieces together one by one." He brightened. It wasn't pretty. "Heck, I guess I should talk to you while I got you here."

"I don't know anything, but go ahead."

"People always say they don't know nothing." Dillinger patted his jacket. "Sometimes they say that because they got something to hide, or they just don't want to get involved." He shoved his hands in his pants pockets, annoyed now. "A guy like you, friend of the family, maybe you really don't know nothing, or maybe you're just being modest."

"I'll do whatever I can to help," said Val. "Mrs. Abbott was a fine lady."

"That's what I hear," Dillinger said absently, patting down his jacket again. "Must have left my notebook in the car. No big deal," he said to Val, "I'll catch you later."

"I can give you my pager number," said Val.

"Oh, I'll find you if I need you," Dillinger assured him, then turned back to the pavilion, watched Jackie shaking hands beside the casket. "That new sister-in-law of yours is a real eye-catcher, Miss Abbott," he said admiringly. "There's something about a redhead . . . they run a little hot, if you get my drift. Yes, ma'am, Kilo is going to have his hands full with her." He looked at Kyle. "Jackie said she called you the day before the homicide and asked you over for a family celebration . . . some real estate deal. Why didn't you go?"

"I was busy," said Kyle. "Val had already invited me to visit his film set."

Dillinger looked at Val. "Was that the only day she could have come to the set?"

Val knew what the detective was up to. Dillinger was trying to set them against each other, get them used to second-guessing their decisions. Soon each would be contradicting the other, separating themselves. "I had cleared her visit with the director for Friday. They don't usually like visitors on the set."

"Jackie didn't give me much notice," said Kyle. "Hardly any notice at all."

Dillinger nodded. "Jackie is one spontaneous girl, from what I understand. One minute it's dinner and drinks and the next she's decided to up and move the party to Vegas. Must be nice. For me a big date is steak'n'lobster night at Sizzler with the missus." He smacked his lips. "Nothing like drawn butter to make a meal, if you ask me." He rocked on his heels. "Miss Abbott, you must have felt real upset when you found out you missed a trip to Vegas."

Val tried to stop her, but it was too late.

"I didn't know they had gone to Las Vegas until we got home from the set that evening," said Kyle. "By then it was too late."

"That's right, you expected them all to be *home*, didn't you?" said Dillinger, nodding. "That's the modern family for you—Daddy and the lovebirds are cruising in Vegas, Mama stays home alone, and big sister, she's off with her new boyfriend. No wonder the country's going down the sewer pipe."

Kyle pushed back her hair. "Now, I understand. Homicide investigation is just a hobby with you—your real expertise is in family dynamics."

"Family?" Dillinger shrugged. "Hey, I don't even send Christmas cards back to West Virginia, but Vegas, that's different. If my ugly uncle Earl invited me to Vegas, I'm *there*—you ask me, Siegfried and Roy are one of the seven wonders of the world. I hear stories about those boys being fruits, but I don't believe it. No fruit could make them tigers toe the mark the way they do."

Val put his hand on Kyle's arm, felt her trembling with rage.

"I'm real sorry about your mama, Miss Abbott," said Dillinger, "but you got to admit, it sure was lucky that Jackie upped and decided on taking that trip to Vegas. Otherwise they might have *all* gotten themselves killed."

"Maybe if they had all been home, the killer would have passed the house by and found someplace less crowded to rob," Val interjected. "If Jackie hadn't moved the party to Vegas, they might all still be alive."

Dillinger turned on Val. "That's one theory, pal, but in my *educated* opinion, if they had all been there, Miss Abbott here would be going to a four-way funeral today. This fella who broke into the house, he's something wild, maybe on some kind of street drug that pumps him up— you ask me, I think he'd have gone through the whole family like shit through a goose." He nodded to Kyle. "Beg pardon, for my language, ma'am. When all's said and done, I'm just a hillbilly with a badge."

Chapter Nineteen

"Isn't this great?" said Kilo.

"A blue marlin clearing the water is great," said Val. "Dirty Eddie's conch chowder is great and so is Kyle's laugh. This is a toilet with a cover charge."

"No, dude, this is the *place*," insisted Kilo, draping an arm around Val's shoulders in a boozy camaraderie. "When you need to get hammered in style, the Hepcat Lounge is the only place to go." He sagged against him. "I don't know about you, but *I needed* to get wasted tonight."

"I hear you." Serene Harbor was lush and beautiful, the day was clear, but there was no such thing as a happy funeral. Getting wasted wasn't such a bad idea—Val wished he could afford to let his guard down.

On stage a pretty young woman in a thrift-store cocktail dress throttled the microphone, belting out a truly awful karaoke rendition of "Smells Like Teen Spirit," slurring the words, damp curls plastered to her cheeks. If Kurt Cobain weren't already dead, this would have killed him.

The Hepcat Lounge was a trendy dive, a post-rave

outpost located in a dingy, converted garage in Long Beach. "Everyone is a star" was evidently the theme. To prove the point, the main room featured free-range karaoke and amateur porn videos running continuously on the monitors chained to the ceiling. The chairs in the lounge were mismatched, the drinks watered, and the cocktail servers inept—the Hepcat would be totally happening for another six months, then get written up in *L.A.* magazine and become an Afghani restaurant.

Kilo grabbed Val's arm. "You're coming to my tennis tournament, aren't you?"

Val looked around for Kyle and Jackie. Even two women as wary and independent as they were had to go to the ladies' room as a team.

"I've been working on this fucking thing for months, but until Gwen . . ." Kilo shook his head. "Until Gwen was killed, the Orange Coast Celebrity Tennis Shootout was going nowhere. My only two stars for the weekend were the guy who plays the grand piano at Fashion Island and the KTTP weekend weather girl." He grinned. "Now my phone is ringing. I have the new *Baywatch* hunk, *confirmed*, an L.A. Laker, *confirmed*, and one of the *Friends* . . . well, that's a definite *maybe*."

"Wow."

"I'm doing it for Gwen, that's what made the difference," said Kilo. "It's now the Gwendolyn Abbott Memorial Celebrity Tournament, with all profits going to some stupid charity." He peered at Val in the dim light. "Look at us, Val, you and me sitting here like the two caballeros—what's funny is that I didn't even like you when I first met you. It's true. I looked at you across the dining room table, and all I was thinking was here's another one of Kyle's dipshit dates hoping to make it to dessert."

"I was thinking about you, too, Kilo."

Kilo brightened. "Really?" He pulled the bottle of champagne from the ice bucket. Women at nearby tables smiled at them through the blue tobacco haze—even drunk, Kilo attracted female attention. Maybe it was those bedroom eyes and the hundred-dollar haircut, or maybe it was Kilo's bleary confidence, his belief that for him there would always be roses and never a thorn. "I respect you, man. If anybody can handle Kyle, you're the one to do it."

"Your opinion means a lot to me, Kilo."

"Are you serious?"

"No."

Kilo nodded. "I'm cool with that," he said, raising his voice over the screeching onstage. "You and big sister . . . I can see it." He leaned closer. "Dude to dude, Kyle has always scared the hell out of me, even when we were kids. All those bugs of hers lined up, wings pinned back like they're marching off to war. That's pretty weird, you have to admit." He checked out a woman in a fringed, white plastic go-go outfit. "I mean, she never had a doll or anything."

"Not even Brainiac Barbie?"

Kilo refilled Val's glass, spilling champagne. "Kyle is too smart for her own good. Smart women should be smart enough to hide it, but Kyle lets you know right away you're in over your head."

"I hate to tell you this, but you're in over your head with Jackie, too."

"Yeah, I worry about that." Kilo looked across the crowded room, waved to a couple of women in fringed leather go-go outfits. "It's not like I'm stupid. Kyle probably told you I flunked out of USC, but that was a career decision—my classes got in the way of tennis." He spun an ice cube on the table, colored lights reflected on its surface. "Okay. So I crashed and burned my first year on the tour, but I made my move. Like Nike says, 'Just Do It.' Well, I followed the swoosh—I *did* it."

"Sure, that swoosh beckons, you have to follow," said Val, enjoying Kilo's self-centered musings and tennis bum philosophy. Val used to listen to Junior go off like that for hours, coke rapping visions of jet helicopters buzzing the Superbowl, private islands stocked with tigers, and quiet candle-lit dinners with Vanna White. Val had sparred with Junior, shooting down his fantasies even while he was entertained by them. It wasn't Junior's dreams that bothered Val.

The woman onstage finished "Smells Like Teen Spirit" to cheers and whistles, and three sweaty men elbowed her aside for the microphone—Silicon Valley software developers in for a *Star Trek* convention, each wearing Mr. Spock ears and Starfleet communicators on their lapels. The music to Alanis Morissette's "You Oughta Know" blasted out of the sound system. The three Spocks blew the first couple of bars, but after that they were synched, howling out the treacly lyrics in perfect harmony.

"Are you having a good time?" Kilo asked. "Jackie didn't know if you and Kyle would like this place, particularly after the funeral, but I thought, what the heck, how long are we supposed to be in mourning?"

"About five hours, evidently."

"You're kidding, right? Jackie said I should watch out for you."

Val watched the three Spocks perform. "Coming here wasn't such a bad idea—maybe it will take Kyle's mind off her mother for a while."

"I come here all the time—people can be anything they want at the Hepcat." Kilo nodded at a nearby video monitor where a bare-breasted woman was rolling across a water bed. "That's a *guy*. Trust me."

Kyle and Jackie made their way through the tables toward them—Kyle had been withdrawn after her mother's memorial, but tonight she was trying her best to have a good time. She mostly ignored Kilo, which helped, and she and Jackie seemed to have come to some sort of tense accommodation.

As the three Spocks finished their song, arms spread wide, Kilo popped up and gave Jackie a wet kiss. "Showtime." He headed for the stage.

The waitress set down two beers, sloshing suds across the tiny table. "Fifteen dollars."

"I didn't order these," said Dekker. "Alcohol interferes with my medication."

"Two-drink minimum." The waitress held out her hand, took his twenty and left without giving change.

Dekker hunkered into his overcoat, already dizzy from the stink of smoke and sour perfume. He could barely see Jackie and Kilo across the crowded room, but he had a clear view of the monitor suspended directly over their table—a man and woman pumping away so eagerly that their nude bodies kept leaving the camera frame. Dekker had to look away, disgusted, eyes burning, feeling the room collapsing in on him.

Ever since Desert Storm he had been allergic to everything from chocolate to newsprint, with new substances being added all the time. Teams of V.A. doctors had examined him, but all they had done was hand him jars of tranquilizers and told him to buck up. He rubbed his sinuses. Yesterday he had gotten such severe muscle spasms from a liverwurst sandwich that he had to retreat to the bathtub, afraid that the synthetics in the mattress would throw him into cardiac arrest.

Dekker craned his neck, trying to see Jackie, worried that she had spotted him and slipped off with Kilo. Or the *other* one, the hawk-faced bastard with the wiry build. The same guy Jackie had flirted with at Mrs. Abbott's birthday party. Dekker was no psychic, but this guy looked like trouble. Fine. Mr. Trouble meet Mr. Dekker.

The three idiots in the Spock ears finished their song. Dekker imagined taking a flame thrower. . . . Oh, sweet suffering Jesus. He stared at the stage as Kilo posed in the spotlight, music swelling around him.

Elvis's "Suspicious Minds" was one of Val's favorite songs. It still was, even after what Kilo was doing with it. "Interesting pelvic thrust he's got going there," he said to Jackie as a table full of women cheered Kilo on.

"You're next," said Jackie. "I bet you have a good voice."

"Only in the shower."

"That sounded like an invitation for a private performance," said Jackie.

"Val," said Kyle, "would you please get me a mineral water? The waitress seems to be ignoring our table now that Kilo has left us."

Kilo was finishing his encore, "In the Ghetto," as Val made his way back to their table with Kyle's bottled water and Jackie's double gold tequila. He was almost there when he glimpsed a man on the far side of the room, a big man in an overcoat who peered back at him—then the dancers surged and he was lost to view.

Kilo gave a sloppy karate move to the crowd, then jumped off the stage to applause and made his way back to their table. He reached for the champagne, chugged straight from the bottle. "Well, what did you think? It felt like being in Vegas with all those lights on me." He took another swig, looked at Jackie. "Sometimes I wish that Gwen had come with us to Vegas."

"*Sometimes?*" said Kyle.

"You know what I mean," said Kilo.

"I'm tired." Jackie forced a yawn. "Come on, Kilo. It's been a long day for everyone."

"I invited Gwen to come with us," Kilo said, waving the champagne bottle at Kyle. "All she would have had to do was say yes."

"Gwen hated Vegas," snapped Kyle. "You knew that."

Val watched Jackie squirm.

"She just had to get into the fucking limo," said Kilo. "That's all she would have had to do and she'd still be alive."

"Are you blaming *her* for what happened?" said Kyle.

"Kilo didn't mean that," said Jackie. "Kyle, please," she said as Kyle pushed back her chair. "It's late and we're all saying things we're going to regret."

Val got up too, and so did Jackie and Kilo, but Kyle had already stormed off, pushing her way toward the front door. Val tried to pay, but Kilo tossed a handful of bills onto the table. "I still don't know what I said that was so bad," said Kilo, looking from Jackie to Val.

There was a solid knot of people ahead of them as they edged toward the door. No way was Val going to catch up with Kyle now—he hoped she would be waiting for him at the car. The three of them moved slowly forward through the crowd, Val in the front, just a step ahead of Kilo and Jackie. As they inched past the bar, Val saw the television tuned to the news. Footage from Mrs. Abbott's memorial service came on, the white-haired announcer looking suitably solemn, mouthing words lost in the noise of the club.

Val winced, then glanced back, not at the TV, but at Jackie and Kilo's reflection in the mirror behind the bar. It was an old undercover trick, he didn't even know why he did it. The TV showed Kilo speaking in front of the coffin, then panned across the grieving crowd, stopped briefly on Kyle, then lingered on Jackie dabbing at her mascara. In the mirror he saw Kilo and Jackie exchange glances, secure in the darkness. Jackie checked for Val's back, then reassured, went back to watching the TV.

Val took a step forward, his eyes still on the mirror. The TV showed clips of Mrs. Abbott's life—she had spent a lot of time on the golf course and holding a drink at charity events, always in style, always beautiful. The camera returned to the funeral, zoomed in on the garlands of white lilies and weeping well-dressed mourners, and in the mirror Val could see Kilo *grinning,* his expression utterly incongruous with the sadness of the scene. He looked . . . proud of himself. Jackie was more guarded, but he saw her teeth flash as she whispered in Kilo's ear, the two of them pressed so close together now that it was obscene. A waitress edged past Val, bumping him, and when he checked the mirror again, Jackie was watching him in the glass.

Chapter Twenty

Jackie drove out of the Harlan Clark Properties parking lot and roared through a red light—Val waited until she took the freeway on-ramp before he pulled into the lot, sliding into the space she had just vacated. As he started up the walkway, he loosened his tie, slipped on a pair of nonprescription eyeglasses, and deliberately misbuttoned his suit jacket. He had even gotten a haircut.

The receptionist looked up as the door opened, slid the current issue of *Vanity Fair* under the counter. He was a thickset, freshly pressed young man with sandy hair, rosy cheeks, and good posture. Born to be a hall monitor. "May I help you?"

"I sure hope so." Val handed over a freshly printed business card. "I'm Tom Burroughs, assistant compliance officer for the Department of Licensing. Please tell me that"—he fumbled with his day timer—"Please tell me that Jacqueline Hendricks hasn't left for lunch already."

"It's Jacqueline Abbott now," said the receptionist, putting the card on his desk, "and you *just* missed her. Everybody's gone until one-thirty."

"Darn," said Val. "So you're holding down the fort by yourself"—he glanced at the nameplate on the desk, Barry Allendale—"Mr. Allendale?"

The receptionist nodded glumly. "Thanks for the mister."

"I know what you mean," said Val. "I rode the desk at a small office in Redlands a few years ago. One day our top salesman, the Six-Million-Dollar Man himself, knocks over a standing ashtray, sprays sand and butts all over the floor, then he looks at me and says, 'Take care of it, Tomster.'"

"What did you do?" Allendale's pale blue eyes were fragile as china teacups.

Val gave an embarrassed shrug. "What *could* I do?"

"I hear you. What do you want to see Jackie A about?"

"Jackie A? Like Jackie O? That's good."

Allendale blushed. "I came up with that one myself." He leaned forward slightly. "Is there some kind of . . . problem?"

"I really shouldn't talk about it. I could get written up."

"Sure, I understand." Allendale rustled papers on his desk. "I didn't mean to—"

"It's just routine."

Allendale tried to hide his disappointment.

Val didn't blame him. He had watched Jackie talking to the receptionist, and from clear across the street he couldn't miss the arrogant tilt of her head as she lectured him.

"What the heck, we wage slaves have to stick together," said Val. "I'm here to go over Ms. Abbott's paperwork. The head office has me running all over the country doing spot checks of recent hires. I guess they've had complaints about fly-by-nighters running off with escrow funds or—"

"Harlan Clark is not a fly-by-night outfit," Allendale huffed.

"Don't I know it," said Val, "but the bosses are worried that if we don't check everybody we're going to get slapped with a lawsuit for targeting downscale shops." He took in the marble entryway, the blond leather couches in the waiting room, the plush carpet. "This place is as swanky as I've heard. You wouldn't believe some of the boiler rooms—"

The phone interrupted him. "Harlan Clark *Properties*," chirped Allendale. "Mr. Griffin is not in at this time. Would you like to be connected to his pager or his voice-mail? *Thank* you." He punched a button on his phone console, hung up.

"I bet you have agents climbing over each other to get hired on here. Ms. Abbott must have some impressive résumé."

"It's impressive all right," snorted Allendale.

Val feigned confusion.

"She should be back this afternoon—you can see for yourself."

"Ah. She shows well."

"*Great* curb appeal." Allendale pursed his lips. "Mr. Clark hired her himself. The sales manager had promised me the next opening—my present position was supposed to be strictly temporary—but he was overruled. I got my license two months ago," he said bitterly. "Scored in the top ten percent, but that doesn't seem to matter."

"That's just not fair," Val commiserated. "Can she sell?"

"Well, she's already made her first sale," Allendale

admitted, "but there again, she's been given some very good homes right off the bat."

Val glanced at his watch. "I wish I could wait around for her, but I'm on a schedule you wouldn't believe. My supervisor doesn't have any idea what it's like out here, dodging sig alerts and jackknifed tractor-trailers. I blew the engine of my agency car last week, now I'm stuck driving my pickup, but she doesn't care. All she says is, hit the road and make sure you save your receipts. I should put in a receipt for the bottle of Maalox I keep under the seat."

Allendale pulled open a desk drawer, held up the bottle of Maalox that Val had seen him swig from earlier. "Great minds . . ." He replaced the antacid. "At least you get to drive around, make a pit stop when you need to. I don't even get to go out for lunch."

"Hey, do you want me to pick you up something? I remember what it's like."

"No, but thanks—" The phone rang. "Harlan Clark . . . yes sir. I'll take care of it immediately." He punched a button on his console, hung up. "Dickhead," he hissed.

"That's *my* supervisor's name too," said Val. "Look Barry, I could really use a favor."

"What is it, Tom?"

"I just need to take a look at Jackie's application, make sure all her statements and documentation jibe with the state file—"

"I could get fired for showing you that without permission."

"I understand," said Val. "It wouldn't take very long though, and if Jackie hasn't followed procedure to the letter . . . well, I just may have to bounce her file to the Compliance Division. You did say you were next in line for a sales position."

"I . . . I don't know."

"Sure, okay," said Val. "She's probably one of those types who keeps things neat and perfect anyway. I probably wouldn't find any problem—"

"She's a corner cutter," said Allendale. "She wanted me to pretend to be another buyer for a beachfront condo in Laguna so we could bid up the price on her own client. On my one day off, no less."

"That's not really my department. Still, if she's playing fast and loose with one set of rules . . ."

Allendale glanced toward the empty offices behind him. "The sales manager keeps all the files." He bit his lip, unsure. "Did I tell you that I scored in the top ten percent in my real estate exam?"

"You're wasted answering phones, Barry."

"Sir, *please*."

"Just working on my Slushie, miss," said Dekker, watching Val leave the real estate office.

"It's a Slurpie," mumbled the 7-Eleven clerk. She had barely looked up from her marketing textbook when he had paid for his drink—now she was nervous, realizing how long he had been standing, looking out the window.

Dekker had been waiting in the 7-Eleven for Jackie to leave for lunch or to show a house—he had started toward his car when he saw Jackie jam out of the parking lot, then noticed Mr. Trouble driving in from the opposite direction. Mr. Trouble hadn't got enough of Jackie last night at that weird karaoke club. Dekker stepped back into the 7-Eleven and took up his post.

"I told you, *sir*, there's not supposed to be any loitering on the premises. It's not up to me. It's company policy."

"It's too hot outside," said Dekker.

"It's company policy," repeated the clerk.

Dekker sucked at the last of the drink as he watched Mr. Trouble walk toward his pickup truck. He must have intended to show up and surprise Jackie for lunch. Well, the surprise was on *him*—he had missed her.

"Sir, please, I've asked you—"

Dekker tossed his empty cup into the trash, headed toward the door, but there were two cops coming in. Dekker stood aside for them. Never get between a cop and a donut, that was his motto.

"This the one?" said the shorter of the two cops, the other one stationing himself by the door.

The clerk nodded.

"What's the problem officers?" Dekker saw Mr. Trouble starting his pickup.

"He was just leaving, officers," said the clerk. "I got scared. We've been robbed so many—"

"I have to go, officers," said Dekker, careful to maintain a polite demeanor. Mr. Trouble was still trying to start his pickup, grinding away on the piece of junk.

The short cop stared up at Dekker. "May I see some identification, sir?"

"Why?" said Dekker. "I haven't done anything."

"There's an ordinance against loitering, sir," said the short cop, a nasty twerp with a pair of handcuffs tiny as a tie-tack. "How long would you say this gentleman was standing around, miss?" The **other cop** was frozen in position like Quick-Draw McGraw.

"I . . . I'm not sure," said the clerk.

Dekker carefully took his wallet out of his back pocket.

"Please remove your driver's license from the wallet, sir," said the short cop. "Sir?"

"Whatever." Dekker watched the pickup pull out of the parking lot and disappear down the street.

Val chose a computer at the far end of the row, right beside a scrawny teenager with a skateboard tucked under the console, his fingers flying over the keyboard. The copy center charged an hourly rate to use their computers as long as you had your own Internet account, and Val had several, all under different names. He logged on, gave his password, and waited for the system to verify him, listening to the music blasting from the skateboarder's headphones.

Val could still see Kilo's gloating expression as he watched Gwen's funeral on the news last night. He could still see Kilo and Jackie standing behind him, grinding away as the camera panned across the mourners . . . as though they had something to celebrate. Maybe they were just two hustlers in love. Maybe there was more to it than that.

"Password Accepted" flashed onscreen. With Jackie's Social Security number and personal history from her Harlan Clark application, Val tapped into Infosearch. He typed in one of his credit card numbers to pay for the search, then Jackie's name, Social Security number, and most recent address. Within five minutes the printer at the end of the aisle started chattering.

The database went back seven years. She had moved around a lot in that time—Sacramento, San Francisco, San Diego, Fresno. She had never been married. No felony history at all. No arrests, no convictions. Lousy driving record. Five speeding tickets and one non-injury accident in the last four years.

Tsk-tsk. Jackie had lied on her application at Harlan Clark—she wasn't a college graduate, although she did have a valid real estate license. No previous sales recorded, though. She also had a cosmetology license with a Bakersfield address, apartment 441, listed on the application. Bakersfield was a rough town, food stamp country, full of bikers and migrants and hard-ass farmers. He imagined Jackie teasing hair with a rat-tailed comb while her next bleach job sat reading last month's *Cosmopolitan.*

Val noticed the skateboarder standing behind him, reading over his shoulder. "You mind?"

"Infosearch, huh?" the skateboarder said dismissively, pushing his sun-bleached hair out of his face. "That is *so* dick."

"Yeah?"

"You can't get unlisted phone numbers through Infosearch," the skateboarder explained, "can't get beeper numbers or bank account numbers or medical records. Can't get itemized credit card transactions either half the time." He had Val's attention now. "DigDirt.com is a serious base. So is Spy ForU. The trick is to use multiple databases to make sure you don't miss anything. You're kind of a novice at this, huh?"

"I didn't think so until now."

The skateboarder picked something out of his braces. "I ran my English teacher through the bases last month. Bitch has a lien on her house for stiffing a plumber and she gets on my case for ganking my midterm."

"Maybe I *could* use some help."

"Step into my office," said the skateboarder, sweeping his hand toward the next computer cubicle. "My name's J. Edgar. It's not my real name, J. Edgar was—"

"I know who he was."

"Cool." J. Edgar rubbed his thumb and index finger together. "Payment got to be straight up Benjies, strictly C.O.D.—I don't trust plastic."

"I don't have Social Security numbers for some of the people I want you to run for me. Can you run a search without—"

"That's funny." The skateboarder patted Val's hand like a Boy Scout helping a little old lady across a busy intersection. "That is *way* funny."

Chapter Twenty-One

"Is that Tori Spelling?"

"I do not know, Junior," said Armando.

"Sure as shit looked like Tori Spelling," said Junior, rubbernecking behind the wheel of the rented green Range Rover, almost rear-ending the car in front of them.

"*Everyone* here looks like Tori Spelling," said Armando.

At that instant the streetlights along Rodeo Drive winked on, and Junior thought it was a perfect Hollywood moment, twinkle twinkle little stars. He made an abrupt U-turn, horns blaring all around them, gave a middle finger salute to Beverly Hills in general and the blue-haired cunt in the Lexus in particular. "I think Tori went in there." He rolled down the tinted windows, checking out the flashy Western shop across the street. "You see her?"

Armando sat quietly, his eyes hidden behind sunglasses shaped like pink hearts.

The young cowpoke handling valet parking at the Western shop had rhinestones covering his vest and chaps—he flashed in the twilight like a Fourth of July sparkler. Junior tried to see around the valet as he opened the door of a Rolls, helping a middle-aged woman and her ratty little dog out. "Dammit, Armando, do you see Tori Spelling or not?"

Armando looked at Junior over the pink frames. "I see a flabby old woman trying to walk in purple cowboy boots."

Two girls strolled past their car, giggling at Armando. Junior didn't blame them—those Lolita glasses of his were bad enough, but he also wore white bike shorts and a checked half-shirt that showed his belly button. Sometimes Junior thought Armando picked his clothes and accessories for maximum trouble potential, just so he could show off his skills. At least Armando had gotten rid of the nest of pigtails—now his black hair was shaved along both sides, the top left long and swept back. It was like he was wearing a crown on his head.

Junior could understand the wild outfits if Armando was queer, but if Armando had any sexual preferences he kept them to himself. Junior didn't care who fucked who and where they put it—heck, he was no bigot, sex was a transaction, just like everything else. That was one of the reasons he liked Miami—no questions asked, wrap it up and take it home. He had offered Armando hookers, male and female, black, white, yellow, all the flavors, but Armando had always refused. He often watched from a corner of the room while Junior partied with a pro, but that wasn't so much peeping as Armando keeping watch, doing his job. No, the kid was definitely receiving at a different frequency from the rest of the world.

Well, shit, if Tori Spelling was in the Western shop, Junior couldn't see her. He gunned the Range Rover, the evening breeze rippling his baggy pants and white cotton shirt. The Rolex Presidente hung loose around his wrist, the way the Colombians favored, free and easy like an ID bracelet, and truth be told, that chunk of Swiss gold signified Junior's presence more than his fingerprints.

They had arrived late last night, rented the Range Rover, and driven straight to the Chateau Marmont, but just like Mary and Joseph, there was no room at the inn—the bungalow where Belushi speedballed himself to death was taken. Junior settled on a bungalow at the Doheny Grand—it reminded him of the Marmont and he could see the "Hollywood" sign from his sunken bathtub.

Junior took a left off Rodeo, headed down a residential side street lined with palm trees, the houses large, the lawns greener than a golf course. Junior had fun imagining the look on Val's face when they finally got their hands on him. Val was one funny guy—it was going to be interesting to see how long he kept that sense of humor once they went to work on him. Junior still wasn't sure what they were going to do, but it was going to have to be something spectacular, something that would be passed around the south Florida grapevine with a mixture of fear and admiration.

The car phone beeped. Junior let Armando get it.

"It is Martin," said Armando, holding out the phone.

"You talk to him," said Junior, still looking for movie stars.

Armando listened for a few minutes. "Martin says he left three messages, but Val never called back. Martin is going to start contacting people who worked with him in films—perhaps Val gave one of them an address where he—"

"Val's too smart for that," said Junior.

Martin was a local fixer, diligent and well connected.

After Val's appearance on *Jeopardy,* the network affiliate's switchboard got a call from a woman who said she had seen Val on a film set in Santa Barbara and wanted to get in touch with him. The switchboard operator called Martin. After confirming that Val *had* been making the rounds of non-SAG production companies, Martin had called Val's contact number and left a message offering him a five-day shoot.

"Val has a girlfriend, name's Kyle," said Junior. "You tell Martin to find out if he ever brought a woman onto the set. A girlfriend wouldn't be so cautious—she might have introduced herself to the crew or chatted away over the donuts." Junior waited until Armando had relayed his instruction and hung up. "What do you want to do now?"

"I do not care, Junior."

"You got to want to do *something*. We could go to a movie or listen to some music, maybe go to that place with the movie star footprints . . ."

"I have never seen the Pacific Ocean," Armando said hopefully.

"Is that all?" Junior held the map up with one hand, steering with the other. The Range Rover roared down the street as he tromped the accelerator, feeling the rush of power through his flip-flops.

Junior had come a long way from a shotgun shack and a two-hole outhouse in Leesburg, Georgia. Ten years ago he was a low-level Atlanta dealer with a reputation for ruthlessness and always giving a fair count, but Miami was where the money was. He relocated, undercutting the competition in south Florida, outthinking them, punishing anyone who opposed him. He was an artist of brutality, as creative in his own way as his cousin Mildred with her découpage dinner plates. The things he had done . . . shark-fishing with human chum, that was the beginning of his Miami rep. If there really was such a thing as hell, Junior was going to get the penthouse suite, and Armando would sleep on the fold-out bed in the living room.

"What is so funny, Junior?"

"You wouldn't get it."

Junior had millions stashed in overseas bank accounts when he met Valentine. He had a fleet of freighters registered in Panama and a complete run of Batman comic books in mint condition, including Detective #27, the first appearance of Batman. He also had an ulcer, high blood pressure, and migraines so bad he wanted to take an ax to his own skull.

He flew in a yoga expert from India to help him relax, some hairless fuck who tried to tell him that nonviolence was the path to paradise and hamburgers were poison. Junior had shipped Gandhi back on the next flight to New Delhi. After that he tried shiatsu massages, aromatherapy, and a coffee enema—he drank herb tea that tasted like dirt, wore copper bracelets, and one desperate night Junior had actually placed his head against the TV screen as evangelist Benny Hine held out his hands, offering to heal the afflicted. Nothing helped. Then he ran into Val and everything changed.

"Are you thinking of Valentine?"

Junior glanced over at Armando but didn't answer.

He first met Valentine at a party thrown by some Russian mobsters who had rented a house in Hialeah—a real wingding with piles of pharmaceuticals and pepper vodka and stoned blond hookers too young to have pubic hair. The reds were bragging about their access to surplus Migs and Burmese heroin and atom bombs small enough to fit *into a hippie backpack. This one huge Cossack with a shaved head had been making cracks about Armando all night in Russian. Big laughs all around. Junior had ignored it, but he could see Armando getting wound tighter by the minute.*

Around mindnight, the Cosack draped a big arm around Val's shoulders and started bellowing this Donna Summer disco song like his lungs were tearing—Val had smiled, then picked up an ice sculpture of Lenin and smacked the Cossack across the back of the head, the sculpture exploding, ice scattering everywhere. The Cossack slumped forward and fell face-first into a silver tureen of Beluga as guns popped out everywhere—it was fucking great. Junior hated disco, too.

Junior and Valentine had hung out regularly after that—jai alai, the dog track, trips to the Bahamas, bonefishing in the Keys. Val took no shit. He cracked Junior up is what he did, and like the Reader's Digest *always said, laughter was the best medicine. Within a month, Junior's blood pressure was down to 140/80 and his migraines were gone. Armando had never liked Val, but Junior had written it off as just bitterness, because Val had beaten him to the punch with that Cossack.*

Junior listened to Armando's nails tapping against the wood trim of the Range Rover. All along the block, Hispanic women trudged out of the big houses, kerchiefs on their heads, burdened down with shopping bags as they walked down the long driveways. Junior glanced at his watch—seven P.M., quitting time at the plantation. He kneaded his temples—ever since Val made his television appearance, his head had been pounding. "I should have listened to you about Valentine."

"He was never afraid of you," explained Armando. "I knew he could not be right."

"Live and learn, that's what I say." Junior glanced over at Armando's bare midriff. "You want to get a ring for your bellybutton? Be like a souvenir of our trip. Let's make this a *real* vacation."

Val rubbed his eyes, stretched out on his couch. J. Edgar was as good as his brag—the computer printout was almost two hundred pages of itemized credit card bills, college transcripts, insurance claims, civil judgments, property tax filings. Val started reading at the kitchen table, then took his coffee and moved into the living room to get more comfortable. Now he was too comfortable. There was just too much information to take in at one time, too many numbers—technical research had never been his strong suit.

Val had given the skateboarder Jackie's name to run, given him Kilo, too. At the last moment, he had added Kyle's name to the list. He still wasn't sure why, but he had her checked out just the same. It felt like he was cheating on her.

Kyle's file was put aside on the floor beside the couch—he wanted to start with Kilo. The first entry in Kilo's file was a DUI at age fourteen. There was no licence to suspend, but he was given a severe reprimand by the judge. There were numerous disciplinary incidents at two, no, three prep schools. He must have been a good tennis player though—he had a national Junior ranking at one point. Flunked out of both UCLA and Southern Cal, not there long enough to even declare a major. Arrests for public urination, public intoxication, another DUI, seven arrests for possession of a controlled substance, all of them dismissed, and one drug trafficking charge pleaded down to simple possession. Val was rifling through the printout faster now. Three stays at the Betty Ford Clinic, most recently six months ago.

At age twenty-one Kilo received control of a $500,000 trust fund. Val cross-checked his tax records. A Porsche had been purchased the same day Kilo came into his half-million. A Ferrari the day after. He had also invested in a gold mine in Indonesia, the one that made all the papers later because it contained no gold. There were hundreds of cash disbursements, bills for acting lessons, voice lessons, screen tests, and script consultants. Less than a year after Kilo received his trust fund, the Ferrari was repossessed.

Kilo's finances for the last five years were a disaster, page after page of different credit cards, each with their balances months overdue then suddenly paid off by Mr. Abbott. All of them were revoked now. Mrs. Abbott must have put her foot down.

Jackie's credit history was almost as bad as Kilo's, except she just didn't have anyone to bail her out and co-sign for her. She had no bankruptcies, but there were numerous missed payments and late charges on her accounts. Sears had canceled her. Even Target had cut her off. About a year ago she had skipped out on her apartment lease, the same Bakersfield apartment listed on her cosmetology license—the apartment management company had filed for damages. For the last year Jackie had no work history, nothing that necessitated a W-2 form anyway. Now she was working at a prestige office, driving a Mercedes, and married to Charles Abbott III.

Val yawned. He had hoped to find something in their background, something that would have explained their private glee in the Hepcat Lounge—as if they had put one over on the rest of the world. Kilo may have resented Mrs. Abbott, but there was no history of violence in their files, no sudden, desperate need for money. They were just a couple of aimless narcissists who had found each other and fallen in love. Lucky them.

Val reached for Kyle's printout.

A black Buick slowly pulled up alongside of the Range Rover, pacing them, the carload of thugs scrutinizing Junior from the shelter of their hooded sweatshirts. They locked eyes with Armando, catcalled, but Armando just tapped his fingers against the dashboard, a steady, unhurried tattoo. Junior kept one hand on the wheel, clasped a .45 against his leg with the other. The Buick slowly pulled away. Junior laid the .45 back down on the floorboard then noticed that Armando's drumming had shredded the leather dashboard. There goes the fucking deductible.

Junior believed in firepower, but Armando liked the personal touch. Last night the kid had spent hours perched beside a reading lamp in the hotel, carefully shaping these thin blades and epoxying them into place—the lacquered nails of Armando's index and middle fingers were surgical-steel chips sharp enough to shave with, painted pussy-pink to match his real ones.

"Valentine made you laugh," said Armando.

"Y'all still on that?" Junior shrugged. "The fucker's funnier than Carrot Top."

"I do not amuse you?"

Junior had to look twice to make sure that Armando was serious. "Heckfire, Armando, I never even see you smile." Before Armando could respond, Junior saw a flash of blue lights behind him, heard the whoop-whoop of a police siren. There was no shoulder on the freeway, so Junior took the next exit, pulled over in a deserted industrial area, passed a shuttered gas station with broken windows. An auto graveyard ran the whole length of the road, arc lights throwing shadows, flattened cars piled higher than the security fence. Junior pushed the .45 under his seat.

"May I see your license, sir?"

Junior looked up at the Santa Monica cop standing beside the Range Rover, chest thrown out. He looked like the good-looking blond guy on the *Adam-12* reruns. Miami cops looked shabbier than the dopers. Junior pulled out his wallet, removed the license, and handed it over. He smiled. "Hell's bells, I'm in California less than three hours and already I'm in trouble with the law."

The cop checked Junior against the photo on the license. He stared at Armando, taking in that dizzy bellybutton outfit of his, the pink heart-shaped glasses.

"Did I do something wrong, officer?" said Junior.

The cop looked back at him. "You're losing your license plate, Mr. Mayfield."

"Beg pardon?"

"Your license plate," repeated the cop. "The top bolts must have come off. It's hanging by one edge. I couldn't read it. You need to fix it."

"I'll stop at the next gas station," said Junior. "Thanks—"

"This is a rental car, isn't it?" said the cop. "Let me see the paperwork, please."

Junior rooted around in the dash, handed the rental agreement to the cop. "I thought I saw Tori Spelling before. We was on Rodeo Drive. Some real nice shops there."

The cop read through the paperwork like he was studying for a final exam.

"That is a very pretty badge, Mr. Policeman."

The cop stared at Armando. "What did you say?"

"I said your badge, it is very pretty."

"We seen Ellen at a Shell station"—Junior was talking fast—"pumping her own gas too—I guess she hit some hard times after her show got canceled. Armando thought he saw the old guy who played Barnaby Jones, but I think that guy's dead."

"Buddy Ebsen," said the cop, his eyes on Armando.

"Excuse me?" said Junior.

"Buddy Ebsen played Barnaby Jones." The cop watched Armando. "He's still alive."

"I told you he wasn't dead, Armando," said Junior. "Armando here said Barnaby Jones choked to death on a Salisbury steak—he's going to have to read up on his TV trivia," he said to the cop, hearing the faint tapping of Armando's fingernails on the dash.

"How old are you, kid?" the cop asked Armando.

"I am old enough, Mr. Policeman. That is what this man told me."

"Armando, cut the shit," said Junior. "He's nineteen, officer—"

Armando peered over his Lolita shades at the cop. "How old are you, Mr. Big Policeman?"

"Step out of the car, kid. You stay right where you are, Mr. Mayfield, both hands on the wheel where I can see them." The cop glared at Junior as Armando got out and slowly walked around the car.

"God dammit, Armando—"

"I *said* keep your hands on the wheel, Mr. Mayfield." The cop popped the strap on his revolver.

"Anything you say, officer," said Junior, keeping his voice level and nonthreatening. He looked around—the road was deserted, no cars in sight, just the metal carcasses at the auto graveyard stacked to the sky. "We don't need this nonsense, Armando—we got more important things to do."

The cop's hand rested on the butt of the revolver. "Tell me the truth, kid—I won't let him hurt you."

"Thank you, Mr. Policeman," said Armando, right beside the cop now. "I am not scared anymore, not with *you* here." His hands fluttered in the air, his pink fingernails reminding Junior of flamingos taking off. Son-of-a-bitch, the kid was actually smiling. Armando had him a real nice smile too—he should show it off more often.

Kyle had received a B once in advanced physics; that was the low point of her long college career. Like her stepbrother, Kyle had also received $500,000 at age twenty-one, but while Kilo had blown through his money, Kyle had invested hers—she had lived off the trust for the last ten years, used it to pay for her education, travel, and research. The geology professor had even gotten a chunk of it in the divorce. She lived simply, owned her car outright, and paid her rent on time. Credit record was clear.

Her major expense for the last four years had been her research in Baja. She had a long-term lease on beachfront property near where the gray whales birthed and that was expensive, even in Mexico. Along with the boat rentals, equipment, and support personnel, her research added up to over $150,000 a year. She had received an annual National Science Foundation grant that matched her own contribution, but this year—he double-checked her records, the printout spiraling across the couch—this year there was no evidence of such a grant in her bank statement.

Val sat up, flipped quickly through the pages. There was no NSF money because Klye didn't have the matching funds. Her inheritance was almost gone now. She had no savings and her stocks had been liquidated. He had been wrong—her car wasn't paid off, she had used it as collateral six months ago for a loan to pay her tuition. While her prior credit history was perfect, her two credit cards were near their limit. She had been making only the minimum payment for months now.

In the final stages of her research, Kyle was unable to complete her work without a substantial infusion of cash. He remembered the first time he had met Mr. Abbott, the way Chuck had chastised Kyle, telling her she was going to have to learn to budget her money. Val let the printout spool onto the floor, feeling a hollowness in his chest—he couldn't help wondering how much Kyle would inherit from her mother's estate.

T he sun on his back keeping the cold at a distance,
Val floated in the water, hearing no sound save for his
breathing through the snorkel. About twenty-five feet
below, he could see Kyle peering into a crevice in the
rocks, her ponytail trailing behind her in the currents. The
boulders at the edge of the breakwater were covered with
starfish, sea urchins, and anemones—Kyle looked as if she
was stretched out on a living carpet, a magic carpet of undulating reds and pinks, blues and greens and yellows.

*He had awakened on the couch a couple of hours ago,
started going over the printouts again when he recognized
Kyle's footsteps coming down the corridor and shoved the
papers out of sight. She had rushed him as he unlocked
the door, pushing him back into the room and onto the
sofa. "I'm done!" she had said, looking down at him, her
hair wild, eyes wide and bloodshot, past exhaustion. "I
finished all my preliminaries, I just need to continue my
fieldwork in Baja." She shook out her hair, straddling him.
"Help me celebrate. . . ." She bent forward, limber as an*

*otter, held his head in her hands and kissed him. Kyle
laughed. "Come on," she said, disengaging herself from
him. "I want to show you the Grottos in daylight."*

Val watched Kyle lazily poke around on the bottom
now, barely moving her swim fins. They had parked at the
cul-de-sac above the Grottos, then followed the narrow
trail down to the beach. The night of Gwen's party it had
been high tide and most of the rocks were submerged—
it was low tide now, revealing a jumble of enormous stones
extending out into the ocean, a man-made reef built to
slow erosion by the winter storms. Kyle said surfers ruled
during an offshore swell, but most of the time there were
only the waves and the bark of an occasional seal. She was
surrounded by silvery fish now, synchronized schools of
them darting in close then retreating. He watched her long
sinewy legs and didn't blame the fish for being interested.

The Grottos were beautiful, but his suspicions in-
truded, tainting the moment—he wished he had never
started digging into Kyle's background, wished he didn't
know how badly she needed money.

Kyle pulled a spiny sea urchin from its resting place
with her bare hand; avoiding the spines, she brought it
close to her face, then carefully replaced it. Val took a
deep breath, started down toward her—he had been surprised by a Moray eel once while diving off Boca Raton,
a big one shooting out of its hiding place, jaws wide and
teeth like hypodermics. Val still had the scar on his leg,
the Moray's bleached skull left behind on his coffee table
when he fled Miami. Kyle pulled another sea urchin off
the rocks, headed up with a gentle kick of her flippers,
meeting him halfway, the two of them rising in tandem.

They broke the surface together, gasping for breath.

Kyle pushed her mask onto her forehead and so did he—they rocked in the offshore swell, water glistening on her face. She was so happy it hurt to look at her. They treaded water with slow steady kicks, their knees brushing. She unsheathed her knife, made a delicate incision on the underside of the sea urchin, then reached inside the body cavity with her little finger and scooped out a smear of orange eggs. Her eyes sparkled as she slid her finger into his mouth, surprising him—he hesitated, then sucked the roe off. The eggs were cool and salty, pungent and female as the sea itself.

"Ummmm."

"I thought you'd like that," said Kyle. "Not everyone does."

"It *is* a little coldblooded."

"This from the man who serves shrimp with the heads on." A wave caught her and she laughed, blew spray, then scooped another taste for herself. She licked her lips, then rinsed the husk in the water before letting it sink, dispersing the residue of eggs.

The two of them bobbed along in that salty soup of life and death, giving in to pure sensation, mindless and content. He didn't want to speak ever again, just stay like this—talking was going to ruin everything. A screeching directly overhead shattered the stillness, two gulls fighting over a fish one had captured, batting at each other with their wings. One finally broke away, the fish grasped in its beak, while the other screamed in frustration.

"Are you sure you have to spend the next six months in Baja?" asked Val.

"That's how long it takes. I told you that."

"I know, I know." He could feel her against him, their warm thighs intertwined. "It's just that six months . . ."

She touched his face, traced his lips with a fingertip. "I'm going to miss you, too."

Val put his arms around her. The sun was hot against his neck as they floated in the cool water. She kissed him and he tasted urchin roe, felt her tongue deep in his mouth. "What are you doing?" he asked.

"Counting your teeth."

"Making sure I'm a good investment?"

"A girl has to look out for herself," said Kyle, beads of moisture strung along her lashes like opals. She ran a hand down his spine. Slid her hand under his suit. "You have a strong back."

"That's not my back."

"No, it's not."

"For a girl who likes to go slow, you're kind of picking up speed here."

"Hush." They were belly to belly now, adrift in the long moment.

"I am a little surprised at you leaving the country at a time like this," he said.

"That's sweet, but Baja isn't that far away." Kyle nestled against him. "If you want . . . you could hop a plane and be there in an hour."

"No, it's not that—"

"I wish you would, Val. I hate leaving you now. We're just getting started."

"It just seems like a bad time to leave—you must have a lot of work to do right now, settling your mother's estate and everything."

Kyle pulled away from him slightly.

"I mean . . . there must be plenty of loose ends that require your signature."

"You're just trying to keep me here." Kyle smiled. "Selfish bastard." She wrapped herself around him, and they sank slowly under the waves, kissing until they both ran out of air and had to kick their way back to the surface. She was breathing hard. "Why *don't* you come to Baja with me? It's so primitive there, you're just going to love it—I have a camp on this little beach about sixty miles north of Cabo San Lucas, nothing much, just some tents and boats and a generator that works only half the time, but it's on a private bay with the bluest water you've ever seen." She bit his ear. "We can watch the whales mate—maybe we'll pick up some pointers."

"Sounds great."

She looked hurt. "I didn't mean to push. I thought you'd be happy."

The sun was low on the horizon, the sunset turning the water around them to flame. "This base camp on the private beach—it must be expensive to maintain . . . but I guess you can afford it now."

"What does that mean?"

"Your inheritance . . . that changes everything, doesn't it?"

Kyle stared at him. "I don't believe you said that."

"It's nice to be rich . . . that's all I'm saying."

Kyle's eyes flashed. "Money . . . is *that* what you're interested in?"

"That's not what I meant—"

Kyle shook her head. "I'm sorry to disappoint you, but I'm almost broke and I'm not going to inherit anything. No stocks, no bonds, no real estate. Maybe you should be dating *Chuck*; he's the one with all the assets—what little my mother owned goes to him."

Val felt his mouth opening and closing like a fish out of water. He had suspected her of wanting her mother dead. She had just accused him of being a fortune hunter. He could try to explain to her that they were both wrong, but he didn't think it would help.

Kyle looked as sad as she was angry. "You should have inquired about my prospects sooner, Val, you wouldn't have wasted all that charm of yours on a lost cause." She turned and started swimming toward shore, her powerful kick spraying him.

"Kyle! I didn't mean . . . Kyle!" Val pulled down his mask and snorkel, started after her. Through the clear green waters Val saw the rocks stacked below, thousands of tons of them limned with algae. At low tide, Kyle said, high school kids squeezed into the caves below the piled boulders, smoked dope in the candlelit mossy grottos, boomboxes cranked, the latest sounds bouncing off the smooth stones. He extended his stroke, slowly closing the distance between them.

The water was shallower now—a solitary white basketball shoe resting on the bottom, surrounded by waving blue anemones, the laces still tied in a bow. He slowed for a moment, wondering what had become of the other shoe, afraid that if he dove down to retrieve that lone hightop he would find a human foot inside, picked clean of flesh, just a collection of small knobby bones scattered across the insole. He brushed her ankle with his outstretched hand, but she kept swimming, and he was afraid that he had ruined things between them. He never could leave well enough alone.

She beat him to the beach.

"Please, Kyle!" He stumbled, lost his footing on the soft sand. "Please wait . . ."

She stopped and he hurried beside her, but she barely noticed him, looking instead to where they had left their blanket and cooler. Val saw Detective Dillinger lounging on the blanket, feet crossed at the ankles, toasting them with one of their own beers.

Chapter Twenty-Three

Dillinger sat on their blanket, waving as Val and Kyle splashed out of the shallows. He had taken his shoes off. There was a hole in one of his white socks—it went well with the soupbowl haircut. Detective Holguin stood in the shadow of the cliff wearing a crisp, burnt orange suit, ready for the office, ready for court. Kyle had pointed her out at the funeral. Holguin had been hovering around Mr. Abbott, nodding sympathetically, letting him talk. Dillinger was the lightning rod of the team, crude and accusatory, but Holguin was more dangerous—it was probably only when Holguin recited the Miranda rights that a suspect would realize he was under arrest.

"What are they doing here?" said Kyle, as gulls wheeled overhead, screaming at them.

"Gosh, you two make a nice couple," said Dillinger.

Kyle tossed her mask and fins near the blanket, spraying Dillinger with sand, then wrapped a towel around her shoulders. Val took a bottle of mineral water out of the cooler, passed it to Kyle, but she didn't take it.

Dillinger brushed sand off his pants, noting the rejection. "Trouble in paradise, pal? What happened—you use the wrong fork with your shrimp cocktail?" He tossed the empty beer can aside. "Hope you don't mind me helping myself to a cold one—it's hard to pass up imported beer."

"Do you have some news for me?" asked Kyle.

Dillinger pulled a pack of unfiltered Camels from his jacket, shook one out, and lit it with a practiced flick of his Zippo.

Holguin stepped into the sunlight. "I'm Inez Holguin, Mr. Duran." She shook hands with Val, dark eyes appraising him, her grip firm. "Your neighbor, Brenda, told us where the two of you were, Mr. Duran. This is a fine spot for a picnic. So secluded—"

"Fine spot, but it's posted, Inez." Dillinger blew smoke through his nostrils. "That means 'No Trespassing,' Miss Abbott. Maybe you figured the signs don't apply to you."

"Do you have something to report?" asked Kyle. "Is that why you're here?"

Dillinger picked a fleck of tobacco off his teeth. "We don't report to you, Miss Abbott."

"Kyle," Holguin said gently, "there was a very aggressive home invasion in Del Mar two weeks ago. . . . We think it might be connected with your mother's murder."

Kyle wrapped the towel more tightly around herself, shivering now.

"This Del Mar house was on a corner lot, just like your folks' home," said Dillinger. "Place had an iron security fence, too, not that it did the couple who lived there any good either."

Val watched Dillinger and Holguin bat their information back and forth—two detectives didn't spend Friday afternoon tracking down a victim's family just to give them an update.

"Did the people . . . the people in Del Mar . . . did they give you a description of the person who broke in?" asked Kyle.

Holguin sighed. "I am afraid not—the husband was dead at the scene, and the wife . . . she has a broken neck, very much like your mother's injury, although this woman survived. She was in a coma until yesterday and is still very unstable."

Dillinger stood up, flipped his lit cigarette onto the sand. "She told the Del Mar detective working the case that Nixon did it—lady must have been a Democrat."

"The Del Mar police found a Richard Nixon mask at the scene," explained Holguin.

"That's a start, isn't it?" said Kyle. "If you find out who broke into the house—"

"Have you ever been to Del Mar, Mr. Duran?" Holguin said lightly. "It's a small town but quite nice. I understand you recently moved to the area."

Val pulled on his T-shirt. "You sound like a tour guide, detective."

Holguin smiled.

"You've been to La Jolla, though, haven't you?" Dillinger said. Holguin grimaced, but he kept on talking. "That's where they were shooting the movie, right?"

"Inez, what's going on?" said Kyle.

"Old man Abbott said you worked in the movies," Dillinger said to Val. "Me and Inez must have called every production company in L.A. You're not a union man, which don't surprise me. We also found out that about a month ago you worked in La Jolla on some stupid horror movie."

"The check bounced," said Val. "Did the production company tell you that?"

"What does this have to do with my mother's murder?" said Kyle.

"La Jolla is next door to Del Mar," said Val.

"*Right* next door," said Dillinger, his eyes the color of anthracite.

"Mr. and Mrs. Carlyle—the unfortunate couple in Del Mar—often went to La Jolla for lunch," said Holguin, her voice downy as the seagull feathers tumbling across the sand. "We are investigating whether either of them was there when Val was shooting his movie. I understand the production drew quite a crowd of locals."

"You think *Val* is involved?" said Kyle.

Holguin smoothed the lapels of her crisp orange suit. "No . . . no I don't really think so, but . . . we must consider all possibilities." She nodded to Val. "I am sure you understand, Mr. Duran."

"That's ridiculous," said Kyle. "I *know* him, Inez."

"We are often surprised by those we think we know," Holguin said wearily, "and those we love the most, we know the least." She shook her head, laid her hand on Kyle's shoulder. "I know what it is like to be the daughter with different dreams, the one who chooses her own way—I too have had difficulties with my family. Kyle, you have known Mr. Duran only a few weeks . . . perhaps with your mother dead, it is time to draw closer to those you truly know."

"Getting cozy with Chuck and Kilo isn't something I'm interested in," said Kyle.

"All that money at stake," said Dillinger, "I sure as shit would be interested."

"*Phil,*" chided Holgun.

"If the rich folks in the Heights want kid-glove treatment, they should set up their *own* police department," said Dillinger, "instead of contracting with us uneducated pukes in the Sheriff's department."

"Kyle, I apologize for this unpleasantness," said Holguin.

"Mr. Abbott said that you thought a hydraulic jack had been used to spread the bars of the fence," said Val. "I took a look around the house and grounds—"

"Helping us out, huh?" Dillinger sneered. "I bet you got a 'Support Your Local Police' bumper sticker on your car just in case you get popped for speeding."

"A jack would leave clear pressure marks on the fence, but I didn't see any," said Val. "I think whoever went through the Abbott's fence used his bare hands."

"Hear that, Inez?" said Dillinger. "The security company said it would take Mighty Joe Young to do it barehanded, but if you two agree, I guess that settles it."

"It is not necessary to patronize Mr. Duran," said Holguin, watching him. "He is a man of experience."

Val tensed at the phrase, and he saw Holguin note that, too. "Were there any marks on the fence in Del Mar?" he said, pressing on.

"I am afraid we are not currently releasing that information," said Holguin.

"Heck, Inez, we can tell him," said Dillinger. "There wasn't any pressure marks on the Del Mar fence. None at the Abbotts' neither. That's another reason we know the two crimes are connected—it's what we professionals call police science."

Val ignored the sarcasm, pleased with the information. If the Del Mar home invasion was linked with the Abbotts', that meant Kyle wasn't involved. Neither was Kilo.

"Kyle, perhaps you and I could go for a stroll," said Holguin. "We will leave the boys to argue over who is king of the hill."

"I don't think that's a good idea." Val bit his tongue, but it was too late.

"Thank you, Inez, I'd *love* to."

Val watched them start down the beach. Even with her shorter legs, Holguin kept up with Kyle's long stride. Within the next two minutes Holguin would start asking questions, doing it so elliptically that they wouldn't even seem like questions.

Dillinger rubbed his five o'clock shadow, the sound like sandpaper. "I shouldn't have given you such a hard time in front of your girlfriend. I apologize, pal—I was just putting on a show for Inez. Actually, I'm kind of impressed with you."

"Golly gee, thanks."

"No, really." The setting sun illuminated every pore on Dillinger's face. "You had a nice thing going with those two-bit movies, I got to give you credit—all the starstruck lookie-loos inviting you over for cocktails and a swim in the pool, don't bother bringing your bathing suit either. Yeah, everybody wants to rub up against that Hollywood heat. You scout the prospects, inventory the goods, then a few days later, Mighty Joe Young comes in to do the dirty work."

"Is this some more of that police science you were telling me about?"

"The Abbotts, though," Dillinger continued, testy now, "if you don't mind a little constructive criticism, you took a chance there—you were connected to them. Sloppy work on your part, but I guess Miss Abbott was too good to pass up." He leaned toward Val, winked. "She ain't got no money of her own, buddy, I hate to disappoint you."

Val could see Kyle and Holguin round the edge of the cove—in a moment they were going to be out of sight.

"Looks like those two really hit it off." Dillinger smiled. "Wonder what they're talking about?" He hunched his shoulders against the wind-blown sand. "Inez wants answers she gets them, simple as that. I been working with her for three years, and I still don't know how she does it." He shook his head. "She don't even have to *ask*."

"I know you're just . . . I know you're doing your job," Val said carefully, "but I hope you and your partner are working some other avenues too. Mrs. Abbott deserves that."

"There you go again, trying to help me out." Dillinger's neck flushed. "You must think I'm just a dumb cop can't think for himself."

"I didn't have anything to do with Mrs. Abbott's murder. That's all I'm saying."

"That's what you're saying all right." Dillinger reached into his suit jacket, brought out a worn billfold and pointed to a photo of a sullen teenager in a football uniform. "This here's Donny." He tapped a photo of a skinny girl with braces and Dillinger's eyes. "This is my little Desiree. I wanted you to know that I'm a family man with a mortgage, not some rookie out to save the world. I see them slinging crack on the corner or walking down the street with a TV set on their shoulder . . . I roll on by." He stared at Val. "I got only homicide on my mind."

"I can see that."

Dillinger slipped the billfold back into his jacket. "We lifted plenty of prints at the Abbotts' house—most of them quickly cleared—but there was a partial on the mantelpiece, a right thumb print, that really gave us fits. We finally got a hit from the FBI database, but the Bureau clammed up, referred us to a state task force in Miami. The task force didn't want to tell us anything either. Took them two days to even fax us your photo."

Val felt an ache in his stomach—it was as if he had gotten the wind knocked out of him.

"You told me your name was Duran, but the utilities for your apartment are registered to J. V. Dagget, and now I find out your real name is Raybaugh. Valentine Raybaugh. *Valentine?*" Dillinger raised an eyebrow. "Your mama and daddy must have been drunk when they stuck you with that one. And you *kept* it?"

"Who did you talk to at the task force?"

Dillinger shrugged. "This state's attorney, some guy with a voice squeaks like a clarinet. He's been calling every day, wanting to know if we've brought you in yet."

"His name is Sanford," said Val. "He keeps a flak jacket in his office to impress the secretaries, but he gives an order and cops jump. I better start packing my Miami clothes."

"You're in California now—Miami is going to have to get in line."

"Don't let Sanford hear you say that," said Val. "I've seen him tell a homicide detective to fetch his morning coffee, then send him back when the cop forgot his three sugars. I bet he squeezed you and Holguin dry."

"If anybody is being squeezed, it's this Sanford," bristled Dillinger. "He wants you bad and that's all Inez needed to hear—she kept hanging up on him until he lost the attitude and played nice. Inez, she's going to be chief of detectives someday. Sanford finally told us you used to be some deep-cover cowboy. He made you sound like serious business, but I figure you were just the best liar at the academy."

"I was never at the academy."

Dillinger whistled softly. "I heard they allow that sometimes. You must have been some special case. Or *thought* you were. That's the problem with you cowboys— you're stuck in the middle of no man's land without a compass, no right, no wrong, and scumbags as far as the eye can see. No wonder you lose your way."

"I know right where I am, Phil."

Dillinger shook his head. "You ever hear of the Jackson brothers, smart guy? I guess they disappeared, and Sanford wants to talk to you about it. *That's* where you are."

"Then do your duty, officer."

Dillinger ignored the challenge. "You got to be a little crooked to work undercover, that's what I always heard. Smoke a little weed, do a little blow, toss around money like it's dirt—you need to act like trash to hold your cover, that's what you tell yourself. When did you start to enjoy it, Valentine? That's what you undercover boys really got to worry about—you wake up some morning and forget who you really are, find all you got left of yourself is that wiseass grin. It must have been fun while it lasted."

"Yeah, Phil, sometimes it was." It didn't matter what Val admitted to; if Dillinger had enough to arrest him, he wouldn't have spent so much time talking. It was a stupid mistake—Dillinger had lost all leverage now.

There was a beep-beep and Dillinger checked the pager on his belt. "Is that me or you?"

Val stared at his watch. "JUNIOR L.A. OSCAR."

"That's a pretty neat toy," said Dillinger, trying to see.

Val should have felt more than he did. Junior was

here—it was what he had been waiting for. He should have felt happy or scared or excited, but he didn't feel a thing.

"Don't look so glum, chum—me and Inez aren't going to let you get shipped off to Florida," said Dillinger. "We got plans for you. Of course, getting arrested *is* probably going to put a crimp between you and Miss Abbott. I seen jailhouse romances work, but most likely you should kiss that one good-bye."

Val watched Kyle and Inez approach, walking arm in arm like old friends.

"Before we heard about the Del Mar break-in, I was looking at Miss Abbott for setting up her mama's murder," said Dillinger. "Family first, that's my motto. Inez, she liked Kilo for the deed and that made some sense, but Kyle . . . I don't know, a brainy woman always sets me on edge."

Val waved at Kyle. "You learn to like it, Phil."

Chapter Twenty-Four

Val watched the detectives trek up the narrow trail as Kyle pulled her blue sweats on over her bathing suit. "How are you doing?" She didn't answer. "I know I've screwed up here. All I can do is tell you how sorry—"

"Sorry about counting my mother's money for me?" Kyle pushed back her sleeves as though she was ready to throw a punch. "Or sorry for lying to me since the day we met?"

"It's not like that."

"I'm not usually open with strangers, but there was something about you that made me trust you. Pretty stupid, huh?"

"Would you give me a chance to explain?"

"I shouldn't be so hard on myself for being fooled; you're a trained professional. You lie for a living." Kyle's eyes were fiery as the sunset. "It's just *embarrassing* to spend so much time with a person, to have . . . thoughts about that person, and then find out . . . I had to find out from Inez who you really were."

"Inez has no idea who I really am."

"Who are you then? Tell me." Kyle waited, but Val couldn't bring himself to answer. "That's what I thought. Inez said that you were an undercover police officer—"

"Not exactly."

"Not exactly?"

"It's complicated."

"Tell me who you are." Kyle stepped toward him. "It's your last chance with me, I swear to God it is."

Val's mouth was dry. There were dark clouds on the horizon, storm clouds lit by the sunset, but clouds meant nothing. The Miami sky was draped in peaceful, white cumulus clouds while Steffano was being murdered, clouds soft as cotton balls and not nearly enough of them to staunch the bleeding.

"Good-bye, Val."

"Wait! Wait. I . . . I was never a cop, not one that Dillinger or Holguin would recognize, but I was . . . connected to law enforcement. South Florida is a different world. There are so many layers of cops and robbers flip-flopping from one side to the other, and everybody deals, Kyle, *everybody*. I had a friend, Steffano, who was an undercover cop working for a drug task force, the latest and greatest, the one that was finally going to win the war." Val was talking faster now, feeling the sadness growing in his throat. "Steffano needed backup he could trust, someone off the books who couldn't be traced back to the department—that was me. He was my friend and I was supposed to protect him, but I . . . I didn't do my job."

Kyle watched him. "He's dead?"

Val nodded.

"Junior . . . your *bookie* . . . did he kill your friend?"

"Junior is a major trafficker—the last of the cracker mafia who used to run the Florida dope trade. After he had Steffano killed, I went to a state's attorney named Bernard Sanford, told him I was ready to testify. Sanford was going to indict Junior, but Junior made him a better offer."

"So now you're here."

"I'm here and so is Junior."

"In California?"

"In L.A." The wind whipped sand across the beach. "I'm sorry I lied to you."

Kyle didn't respond.

"I wish I could say I was doing it for your own good, but if I really had your best interests at heart, I would never have gotten involved with you. I would have walked right past you on the steps that first morning. It was just . . . you just looked so fine standing there, geared up and ready to hit the beach. You got to me. I couldn't stop thinking about you. I still can't."

Kyle watched him, then suddenly bent down, shook out the blanket, then gathered their gear, tucked them out of sight against the cliff face. "Put on your sneakers," she said, pulling on a pair of aqua socks, belting on a fanny pack.

"What's going on?"

She walked out onto the slabs of granite piled deep along the shore, moving lightly across them. Halfway to where the waves crashed onto the forward edge of the breakwater, she stopped, got down on one knee, and disappeared. When Val reached the spot, he saw her standing in semi-darkness, looking up at him through a narrow opening in the rock. She beckoned.

Val thought of Junior sitting beside a hotel swimming pool, smoking a Havana and talking too loudly. He could call Oscar for the location and be there in a couple of hours, catch Junior and Armando watching reruns of *Andy of Mayberry,* Junior yukking it up at Barney. He could get it over with one way or the other.

"Val?"

Junior was going to have to wait. Val slid down the rocks and landed beside Kyle, banging his elbow. There wasn't much room, but it wasn't so bad—he could look up and still see the sky.

"This way." Kyle edged into an irregular crevice that he hadn't noticed. "This way, Val. You either trust me or you don't."

Val scooted after her, his shoulders brushing the sides of the fissure, the rock smooth from the action of the waves, speckled with barnacles. After about thirty feet the passage sloped down, then opened up into a space big enough to stand up in. The walls were still warm from the sun, the rocks overhead jumbled together so that light slanted into the room from several angles, giving just enough illumination to see Kyle's face.

"The surfers call this the Playhouse," said Kyle, her voice echoing.

Val didn't like that echo, and he didn't like the Playhouse either. There was a couple of inches of water seeping through the rocks below. Crushed beer cans rolled back and forth in the eddies; chicken bones lay in a soggy KFC box. The damp walls were covered with murals and intricate graffiti: surfers riding tsunami-sized waves, a great white shark taking a bong-hit, devils in tophats and mermaids lassoing swimmers, all of them dotted with tiny atolls of coral. Wine bottle candelabras were stuck high in the rocks, melted wax frozen into red and yellow and blue stalagmites. Crabs scuttled for cover as Val walked over, trying to read the smudged names written in magic marker on one wall—T-Boy, Amber, Squid, Rambo, Drake. He looked at Kyle. "Are we supposed to add our names to the list?"

"I hope not. That's a partial list of people who've drowned in the Grottos. It's easy to make a mistake down here—kids forget to check the tide chart, or they get lost or too stoned to find their way out." Kyle brushed her hair back. "Last month they found a couple in a room at the edge of the breakwater called the Church. They must have been making love when the tide came in."

Val stared at the nicknames on the wall and tried to imagine the young faces that went with them.

"They call it the Church because someone inset pieces of colored glass on one whole wall—it's a beautiful room, but it floods *fast*," said Kyle. "By the time the couple realized they were in trouble, the entrance was under water. There are a lot of passages out of the room, but only one of them leads anywhere." She shook her head. "Search and rescue found their bodies jammed in a dead-end passage, naked, their fingers raw from clawing at the rocks."

The Playhouse seemed smaller now, the walls closing in. "You ready to go back?"

"You should see your face," Kyle took out a small flashlight from her fanny pack and snapped it on. Standing upright, she edged between two rocks, slowly disappearing. "Come on," she said, her voice muffled by the tons of stone.

Val looked back toward the exit. He tried counting his heartbeats, but he couldn't keep it. He had to follow her. Otherwise it was time to go back to the beach by himself, go back and keep right on going. He knew that much about Kyle.

The passage kept getting smaller, forcing him onto his

hands and knees, following the sound of her breathing and the intermittent glow of her flashlight, as they twisted through the cramped darkness. The sound of the sea crashed around them, deep and resonant through the breakwater. "I really hate this," he called.

"Didn't you ever want to be Indiana Jones?"

"No." Val crawled forward on his belly, slithering through cool stone, eyes burning, afraid to take a deep breath, afraid that there wouldn't be room for his chest to expand. He missed the sun and the fresh air and being able to stretch out and not touch anything. He clamped his teeth shut on his fear, inched forward and banged his head on an outcropping of rock. "Kyle?" A light flashed on him, and he saw that the passage was deeply fractured here, several seams opening up through the rock.

"Roll over," said Kyle. "You have to go forward on your back."

"There's another passage to my right," said Val, teeth chattering. He didn't want to roll over, didn't want to feel the weight of the rocks against his face. If he did that, he was going to start screaming, and once he started screaming . . . He focused on the beam from her flashlight. "This other route—it looks like there's more room that way—"

"That one narrows down to nothing. I almost got stuck in there once. Just roll over."

Yeah, roll over and play dead. The light from her flashlight seemed dimmer now. He rolled over on his back, just like she told him to, pushing himself forward with his heels. Coral scraped against his cheek, and he sensed that the passageway was sloping upward, the warm air smelling like the inside of a conch shell. He kept pushing himself forward now in the darkness, faster, his clothes soaked with sweat, afraid to stop, afraid to think of where he was.

He was stuck where he was—stuck in a stone cocoon with his arms stretched straight ahead, his shoulders wedged tight. "Kyle?" No answer. He tried to back out, but his feet kept slipping. "Kyle?" No screaming allowed, Val. Do *not* scream. He tried again to back out. Managed maybe a millimeter. "Kyle!" A light shone in his eyes. He wasn't crying; he was just blinded.

"I was wondering what happened to you."

He could see Kyle's face was about ten feet ahead of him. She must have turned around somewhere ahead. "I'm stuck."

Kyle considered it. "You're bigger than I am. I've never taken anyone else here." She wriggled toward him, flashlight playing over the rocks. "Drop your right shoulder."

"I'm *trying*."

"Stop, you're making it worse. Relax. Take a breath. Let it out. That's better. Good." She moved closer, shone the light overhead so that her face was illuminated. "Look at me. Keep breathing. Relax. You're too tense—that's why you're stuck. There's plenty of room for you. Keep your eyes on me, Val. I'm not leaving. We're above the tideline here, so there's no hurry. Just keep breathing. Good." She grabbed his arms and slowly pulled him free, gave him a quick kiss and then began backing up, pushing herself nimbly with hands and knees, leading him to the next room.

Val popped out of the tunnel, landed on the floor. He saw Kyle watching from a ledge a few feet above the floor, her face directly in a pillar of golden light. Val got slowly to his feet, looked around. Unlike the Playhouse, this small, dimly lit room was warm and dry. "Is there another way out of here?" he said softly, not wanting to have his voice bounce back at him. "I don't think I can handle going back that way."

Kyle nodded. "There's another route. It's more indirect but not as tight a fit."

"I'll take it."

Kyle continued to stare at him. The room was dimly lit, tiny shafts of light from the fading sunset piercing the mosaic of boulders overhead. "I've wanted to bring you here from the moment I saw you trying to save that sparrow from the cat. I knew it was futile, but I was glad you made the effort." Her hair glowed with the last of the sun. "I was *so* attracted to you."

"I could tell."

"You had no idea."

Val smiled. "I had hopes. A man who joins lost causes has to have hope."

"I had hopes too." Kyle flicked a butane lighter, lit a candle on an outcropping of rock, then another and another and another. The flickering lights danced across the walls, making the realistic images painted there appear to be moving. The room was a single 360-degree mural of the ocean depths, a panoply of sea life in deep blues and greens—hammerheads and dolphins and yellowtails, graceful anemones, octopi and seals. Dominating the scene was a depiction of a gray whale birthing a calf in a plume of blood.

Val stood in the center of the room, trying to take it all in. "You did this?"

Kyle nodded. She made room for him as he scrambled up beside her on the ledge. "We're high on the breakwater, just below the surface, so it almost never gets flooded." There was an Oriental carpet covering the ledge, the faded wool stiff but better than the rock. She took his hand, placed it on the boulder overhead. "*Feel*. The sun hits these slabs directly—it stays warm and dry in here almost all night." She put her arms around him, brought his face next to hers. He kissed her and she laughed. "That was nice, but I wanted to show you *this*," she said, pointing upward. Through a large crack in the rock Val could see the twilight sky burning with stars. "Our own skylight," she said.

Val could hear the rush of water below. "You *do* know about the tides and—"

She kissed him, her tongue warm in his mouth, and he kissed her back, the two of them surrounded by stone and an endless sea. "I wasn't sure you were really going to follow me here. Are you scared?"

"*Very.*"

"Is there anything I can do?"

He smiled back at her. "God, I hope so."

She tugged off her sweatshirt, then her pants, folded them into a pillow, averting her eyes as she peeled away her bathing suit. She lay down and pulled him to her, kissed him so gently that he was the one who felt naked. "I forgive you for lying to me." Her eyes filled with tears. "I have waited for you so long . . . you have no idea."

"Yes, I do," he said, breathing his certainty into her.

He was aware of his hands taking off his clothes, Kyle helping him, the two of them carefully embracing on the carpet, as though afraid that a too-sudden contact would detonate them. He took a sharp breath as he felt her skin against him, feeling himself sweat from the heat of her. She laid her hand against the back of his neck, drew him to her, her tongue tickling him. His hand slid down her side, cupped her buttocks and she sighed, and the sound whispered off the surrounding rocks. He kissed her bare throat, licked his way to her breasts, and she arched against him as he tugged at one of her nipples, tasting salt as it stiffened in his mouth.

She grabbed his hair, pulled him up to her, kissed him as she encircled his penis with her hand—his groan bounced off the rocks. He saw her smile, felt her twisting under him as he slowly entered her—she cried out, one leg pressed against the small of his back, her eyes wild in the candlelight. There were no lies between them now, no past, no future, only this moment. Kyle shuddered, head thrown back, her throat white as frost under that patch of stars.

Chapter Twenty-Five

"Maid service!" Carmen rapped sharply on the door of Villa #9, waited a few moments. "Maid!" She listened, then slid her key-card into the slot, opened the door. "Señor?" No response. She beckoned to Val, ushered him inside, and closed the door after him before he could even thank her.

Val listened to the faint sound of Carmen's linen cart clattering along the tiled sidewalk. The villa was well insulated, cushioned from the heat and noise. The living room was large, with a gas fireplace, two sofas, and a big-screen TV. The heavy drapes had been pulled open, bright sunlight filtering through the inner curtains—he could see out, but no one could see in. That's the way Junior liked it. That's the way Val liked it too.

He made a quick check of the villa, anxious now, wanting Junior to show up so they could get it over with. It was a plush two-bedroom suite with king-sized beds, Italian marble sinks and tubs, gold faucets, a full bar, and four televisions besides the big screen. Val found a stainless-steel .45 automatic under a pillow in the master bedroom and a

.38 taped under the toilet tank lid. He took the gun from under the pillow, checked to make sure it was loaded, and left the .38 where it was. There were no guns or knives in Armando's bedroom, but someone had scratched crosses into every bar of soap in his bathroom. Thinking of Kyle's long fingers and clear manicure, Val picked up a bottle of hot pink nail polish on Armando's nightstand, then replaced it.

It had been dark when the two of them had finally crawled out of the Grottos yesterday, banged-up and sore from rolling around the rocks. A true Hallmark card first-time experience. They had spent the night together in her apartment, luxuriating in the cool sheets, making love, dozing, making love again, barely talking—Kyle seemed to need words even less than he did. They stayed together through the morning, Kyle lounging around in an oversized T-shirt, her hair still wet from the shower, while Val cooked pancakes and eggs, the two of them ravenous, wolfing down their portions, stealing bacon from each other's plates. He didn't call Oscar until his third cup of coffee, putting it off as long as he could. Oscar asked if he needed any special help—Val thanked him anyway, went back to sit beside Kyle in the breakfast nook. The sky was overcast. She said it was a good day to stay inside, her hand resting comfortably on his leg. Val had actually considered it.

Val moved around the bungalow, opening drawers and closets, riffling through Junior's *Hot Rod* magazines in the living room. Through a side window he saw Carmen pushing her laundry cart down the walkway, saw her glance at the bungalow, then hurry on. Val was already stepping back into the master bedroom when he heard Junior's voice booming outside.

Junior opened the front door, laughing. A woman answered, her voice lazy and flat.

Val hadn't expected Junior to have company. Another woman spoke up as Val ducked into the closet, the slatted door making a faint sound as he slid it back along the track. He eased inside among the clothes, careful not to make the hangers squeak—Junior's loud shirts reeked of Canoe.

Junior sauntered into the bedroom, flipped on the stereo—Jimmy Buffett crooned over the speakers and Junior sang along. "Changes in latitudes, changes in attitudes." He had a good voice—Junior had sung in the church choir back in Georgia until he was fourteen and discovered crystal meth.

Val pressed himself deeper into the closet, watching Junior through the slats. The .45 felt heavy and awkward in his hand. Ugly gun. Excessive.

"Come here, Vanna!" Junior walked past the closet, one arm around a big-eyed blonde wearing a skin-tight glittery sheath. She *did* look a little like Vanna White.

The other woman followed them in. She was a brunette in a white lab coat, her oversized glasses falling down her nose—a look-alike Scully from *The X-Files*.

"Join the party, Armando," said Junior, busily laying out mounds of cocaine on the glass coffee table, Vanna beside him. "Have some fun."

Armando glided into Junior's bedroom, did a quick survey, his narrow adolescent face creased with distaste. He wore a purple Speedo and an unbuttoned white gauzy shirt that billowed behind him as he walked. There was a new gold ring in his naval, and he had cut off his braids, his hair cropped short along the sides of his narrow skull. Val missed the braids—Armando looked too much like a rodent now, one of those voracious little beasts that ate twice their body weight every day.

"Suit yourself," Junior said to Armando, bending over to snort up a hill of cocaine through a plastic straw as the kid headed back into the living room. Scully knelt in front of the coffee table, her glasses sliding down her nose as she started in.

"What's wrong with the kid?" asked Vanna, ladling the cocaine up to her nostrils with a long fingernail. "He's sweet but creepy."

"I'm just a country boy—I give up trying to figure out Armando a long time ago." Junior sighed as she unzipped him. "I been in love with you since I was fifteen. I used to sit there in front of the TV and practice buying a vowel from you."

Vanna giggled.

Through the slats in the closet door, Val could see Armando in the living room, stationed beside the front window, occasionally glancing into the master bedroom. Junior sang along with the stereo, his voice muffled by the woman's flesh—it sounded as if he was under water. Val imagined Junior sinking slowly into a pool of darkness, and that made him think of the Jackson brothers. It had been eight months, and the memory was still so fresh his chest hurt.

Grace had spotted them driving slowly past her house late that afternoon, two hard-looking men in a new Firebird. No way they belonged way out there in the Glades. Val got there forty minutes after she called him, almost blew his engine in his haste, parking behind her house, hidden from the road. He knew Troy and Tommy Jackson would wait until dark—they would park out of sight, but they wouldn't want to walk too far.

Val lay in the high weeds along the road, waited out there with the snakes and clouds of mosquitoes until after midnight before they coasted up onto the shoulder, lights off. They got out of the Firebird laughing softly, shotguns at the ready. Troy carried a five-gallon can of gasoline, complaining that he always had to carry the gas and it made his clothes stink to high heaven.

Val wiped the sweat off his palms, passing the .45 from hand to hand as Junior grunted away with the two hookers. He had tried to do the right thing after Steffano was killed, sidling up to Bernard Sanford at his daughter's ballet recital. He had offered the state's attorney everything he had on Junior—names, dates, stash spots, air strips, complete confirmation of everything Steffano had put in his reports. He even promised to testify in open court if needed.

"You want to come up for air, do you?" said Sanford, his eyes on the stage where four little girls in yellow tutus stumbled around to classical music. "Feeling chicken-hearted, are we, Val?"

Val held himself back. "Junior had Steffano killed."

"Fortunes of war." Sanford smiled as the four girls twirled on tiptoe, arms stretched overhead. "Look on the bright side. Now you're beyond suspicion—that was the brilliance of having you in place as a backup. I don't wish to brag, but—"

"Don't brag."

Sanford blinked. "I don't like your tone."

"Pick up the Jackson brothers and offer them a deal. Maybe they'll roll over on Junior. If not, I'll give a deposition and you can start the indictments."

"I don't think we're at that point yet," said Sanford, plucking at his floppy bow tie as he watched his daughter dance. *"Indictments need to be orchestrated for maximum—"*

"I'm done, Bernard."

"Brava!" Banging his hands together louder than anyone else in the audience, Sanford clapped as the four girls bowed onstage. *"Brava!"* He looked at Val as the applause petered out, his mouth a tight circle.

In the end, Junior had made Sanford a better offer. Val shouldn't have been surprised. Sanford had clerked for a Supreme Court judge, but the law was just a chess game to him, a high abstraction devoid of justice. Junior was playing a different game entirely. He had grown up scratching for pennies, been given Goodwill clothing without the goodwill, too smart to accept a life of poverty, too impatient for pie-in-the-sky sermons. Junior was a monster, but Val understood him better than he understood Sanford.

"Y'all come back now," Junior said to the hookers, ushering them out the front door. He ambled back into the living room, plopped himself down in the overstuffed chair, and picked up the TV remote.

Armando walked into the bedroom and Val froze as the kid rechecked the bathroom, the windows, then slowly walked toward the closet. Val held his breath as Armando stood there, eyes narrowed.

Val slammed the gun through the thin, wooden slats of the door, drove the heavy butt of the .45 into Armando's face. He flung open the door, clubbed Armando again, stepping over him as he fell. In the living room, Junior struggled to get up from the easy chair—Val jammed the gun in his mouth, thumbed back the hammer, and Junior put up his hands, trying to talk around the gun pressed against his soft palate. Val shoved the .45 even farther into Junior's mouth, making him gag, arms flailing, then jerked it out, pressed the gun just above his eyes. A string of spit hung off the barrel, curled across Junior's freckled nose. "Welcome to L.A., Junior."

Junior coughed, hacking away, the .45 bouncing against his forehead.

"So how do you like California so far?"

"You can keep it." Junior spit blood onto the carpet, and more dribbled down his chin. "I keep getting lost, and there's no coconuts on the palm trees." He wiped his mouth with the back of his hand, glanced toward the bedroom, and saw Armando still crumpled on the floor. "How . . . how did you know I was here?"

Val kept the pistol pointed at the red indentation he had made in Junior's forehead. Junior felt around in his mouth. "You broke my tooth," he said, flicking a chunk of yellow enamel at Val. "They got names for guys who hide out in closets watching other folks fuck."

"Is that what you were doing? Fucking? I thought you were passing a kidney stone."

"That Vanna White, she was something, wasn't she? I been waiting all my life to get a piece of that."

"You're still waiting. That wasn't Vanna—that was an amazing simulation."

Junior spit out another piece of tooth. "She was close enough for me." He nodded at the gun aimed at him. "That .45's got a hair-trigger. I'm just telling you for your own good. You look a little nervous, that's all." His eyes darted to where Armando lay, then back to Val. "You sure have given me a world of trouble—Amy Huckebee run off with fifty-seven million dollars of my money. You put her up to that, didn't you? I can't see her doing that on her own. Fifty-seven million. . . . I guess we're even now."

Val smiled.

"I hope you're not contemplating violence," Junior blustered. "This New Age fatman on Oprah says negative thoughts are toxic. I know you're still peeved about what happened to Steffano, but it ain't worth giving yourself cancer."

"Oh, I'm far beyond peeved."

"I'd feel better if you put that thing down while we—"

Val kicked him in the right knee, Junior's bad knee, the one that had gotten wrecked playing high school football. "How do you feel now?" he asked as Junior howled. Before Junior could answer, he kicked him in the knee again.

"Goddamn son of a bitch!" Junior rocked back and forth, nursing his leg. "This sadistic shit, this ain't like you, Val."

"I've been taking lessons."

Junior licked his lips. "I don't want to die here. There's no reason for that to happen."

"I had lunch with the Jackson brothers a few days after they killed Steffano—did you know that?"

Junior bared his tobacco-stained teeth. "Look at my knee. I'm going to need a cortisone shot just to—"

"One day the Jackson brothers were ready to kill me, the next we all sat around buying beers for each other and talking about going deep-sea fishing."

"That's the way it should be," said Junior. "Let bygones be—"

"They told me that Steffano wouldn't shut up in the van—he tried jokes and money, even told them about a rib joint he discovered in Liberty City, best hot links he ever tasted, that's what he told Tommy Jackson. Steffano even offered to tune up Troy's *new* Firebird—he said it sounded like a coffee grinder. Tommy thought that was pretty funny, but Troy wasn't amused."

"That Troy, he loved that car," said Junior, gingerly trying to straighten his knee, sweating now. "What did you do with them boys anyway?"

Val saw Armando brace himself against the floor, his eyes still closed.

"Everglades are shriveling from the drought," Junior rattled on. "Couple of tourists spotted Troy's Firebird in a dried-up lagoon, roof-deep in black mud. Police dredged the whole area, but they didn't find a speck of them two boys, just a couple of Mosbergs and Troy's porkpie hat. Remember that porkpie? He got it on our trip to Bimini, bought it for two dollars from that colored gal with the glass eye. Troy said it was his lucky hat." He laughed. "Maybe he should ask for his two dollars back."

Val swung the pistol, caught Armando across the bridge of the nose as he sprang up. Junior leaned forward, that was all. Val kicked him in the knee anyway.

Junior writhed on the chair, cursing. "No!" he barked as Armando tried to stand, blood pouring from his nose. "Dammit, Armando, stay *down*."

Val picked up a heavy crystal ashtray and bounced it off Armando's head. He fell hard and didn't move.

Junior leaned forward, trying to get a good look at Armando. "He's . . . he's still breathing, ain't he?"

There was blood on Val's shirt . . . but it didn't come from Armando. He dabbed at the bloody fabric, not believing it at first. The shirt had been slashed, his belly neatly sliced just above the navel. He hadn't seen a knife in Armando's hand, didn't even think the kid had touched him. He wiped his hands on his pants. It wasn't a deep cut, but it hurt.

Junior stared at Val. "Jesus, what happened to you? You're leaking all over."

"How's your knee?"

Junior tried to spit on the carpet, but his mouth was dry and it landed in his lap. "You ain't going to kill me. That dance you done with the Jackson boys was one thing, but shoot an unarmed man . . . I don't think so." He swallowed. "I . . . I know you, Valentine—you ain't got murder in your heart."

"Then why are your hands shaking?"

Junior tried a grin. "Well . . . ain't nothing certain in this bitch of a life."

"It's nice to see you scared, Junior. Nice to see you on the other end for a change."

"I been scared before. I been scared plenty of times. Lots worse times than this."

"This is *now*, though," Val said quietly. He watched the sunburn drain from Junior's face until it looked like he was wearing a soft waxy mask—only Junior's eyes remained alert and alive. "Maybe you should go back home," Val said finally.

Junior blinked.

"I don't need to kill you, Junior," said Val. It sounded like he was talking to himself. "There was a time when I thought I did. . . . I thought it would make me feel better, that it would somehow balance out for what you did to Steffano." He shook his head. "It won't."

"That . . . that's right."

Val smiled. "Besides, you'll be dead soon one way or the other—you know I'm right. It's over between us, Junior. Go on home, you don't belong here."

"I . . . I don't like it here anyway." Junior sat back, wiped the sweat from his face with a pillow. "First you want me out here, now you don't." His eyes narrowed on Val. "You didn't come here today to kill me, did you? No, you came here to prove something to me . . . prove that you could take out Armando and—"

"I don't care about you. I came here because I wanted to prove something to myself. Fly away home, Junior. The next time I see you, I *will* kill you."

Junior shook his head. "I never will understand what got into you. We had some good times, then you went and spoiled everything. You gone deaf? We had fun, didn't we? Otherwise, what was the point? Tell me, what was the fucking point?"

Val still didn't answer.

Chapter Twenty-Six

Val could feel blood seeping through the bandage and into the waistband of his pants as he walked toward his apartment. He had taken a long and circuitous route home from the Doheny Grand, stopping once to throw Junior's .45 off the Santa Monica pier, stopping again to buy bandages and antiseptic, taping himself up in the parking lot of a Fast Rite Drugs. The wound wasn't deep, but it bothered him that Armando had gotten so close. Nothing had gone the way he thought it would.

Val had parked a few blocks from his apartment, just in case he had been followed. He moved quickly now as he got closer, a folded newspaper wrapped around his own 9mm, his finger resting along the trigger guard. He was startled to spot Jackie walking down the stairs, deep in thought, one hand grazing the banister. The newspaper fluttered toward his feet as he tucked the pistol into his waistband, winced, then moved it into the small of his back and covered it with his tattered shirt. He stepped out into the dim light.

Jackie stopped in mid-step, not recognizing him for a

moment, then smiled. The night seemed colder. "Is Kyle with you?"

"No." Val met her at the bottom of the steps. "She's not home?"

"I forgot, you and Kyle are neighbors. When I saw you . . . I just assumed you were together." Jackie looked at him. "Your shirt is torn. There's blood—"

"We were shooting a film tonight—I was climbing over a barbed-wire fence and caught myself. It's nothing."

"That's the biggest Band-Aid I've ever seen."

"What did you want to see Kyle about?"

"I didn't realize you were in such a risky area of the movie business. Kilo says Hollywood stars are too important to climb their own fences or drive their own cars or do anything strenuous—he says the studios hire gofers to do everything but wipe the stars' asses." She moistened her lips. "I can't see you wiping anyone's ass."

"That's the producer's job."

"Is that a joke?"

"It's a gofer's joke." Val took a step around her. "I'll tell Kyle that you came by."

Jackie blocked his path. "I already left her a note. This is really fortunate, our running into each other. I need your help."

"Is something wrong with Mr. Abbott?"

"It's far beyond Chuck. Can we go someplace more . . . appropriate and have this conversation?"

Val hesitated. "My place is a mess."

Jackie looked at him. "Don't worry, I won't tell." Like Kyle, she wasn't afraid to stare directly into a man's eyes, but there was a hooded quality to Jackie's gaze. She looked into *you*, but you weren't able to look back into her. "I bet you're a *real* meat-eater," she said, watching him with those green eyes.

"What does *that* mean?"

"Rare steak and beer from the bottle." Jackie shook out her coppery mane. "Domestic beer and a Porterhouse that bleeds. That's how I see you." Jackie absently caressed her neck. "I know a spot in Long Beach that serves strictly aged beef, cut thick and tender. I'd like to see you put those strong teeth of yours to that."

"Interesting line," said Val. "Somehow I can't imagine you using that one on Kilo."

"I didn't use that one on Kilo," Jackie said, her fingers dipping lower, stroking the base of her throat. "I brought out the heavy artillery for him."

"I guess it worked. You bagged and tagged him."

"What's the matter, Val? Don't you believe in love at first sight?"

"Is that what it was? Love?"

"Of course." Jackie offered him her hand, the same hand that had been stroking the pulse in her throat. "Well, shall we go eat? You look like you could use a steak—it will help you get your strength back. With a woman like Kyle, you need all the strength you can get."

Val agreed with her about that, but he wasn't going to let Jackie know it. He suddenly felt a warmth at the back of his neck, as though someone was watching them. He turned around but didn't see anything. He was too jumpy.

"Well?" said Jackie.

"I'm not hungry."

"Are you worried about Kyle?" said Jackie, her eyes bright. "Kilo said she was jealous, but a man like you must be used to that. I won't get you in trouble. Promise."

Val laughed. He didn't know what else to do.

"I'm not here for myself, Val, I need to talk with you," said Jackie, annoyed. "I would have thought you were concerned about Kyle."

"I *am* concerned about—"

"Then quit acting like a ten-year-old and invite me up to your apartment," she said. "We can have our conversation and then I'll leave."

All that was missing was for Jackie to stamp her feet. Still, he did want to know what she was doing here. "This way," he said, starting up the steps, not looking back. He was going to regret this. He already did. Neither of them spoke until Val unlocked his door.

"You live right down the hall from Kyle, how *convenient*," said Jackie as she slipped past him, her hair brushing his cheek. "I bet you two have worn a groove in the hallway. I'm glad Kyle has found someone like you. Particularly with all that's happened." She looked around the room. "Why your place isn't a mess at all. My feelings are a little hurt."

"Run them under the cold-water tap."

Jackie smiled. "Most men fall over themselves being nice to me."

Val indicated the couch. "Can I get you anything?"

"That's better." Jackie sat on the couch, fluffed back her hair, still not answering, making him wait.

Val sat down in a chair, facing her. If she wanted something, she could get it herself.

Jackie fanned herself with her hand. "It's warm in here. Don't you have air conditioning?"

"It's broken."

"They have people who fix broken air-conditioners."

Her upper lip was damp. "They drive panel trucks and wear jeans."

"You said you wanted to talk about Kyle. Why don't you start?"

Jackie wiped her lip. "This isn't going well, is it?" She recrossed her legs. "I'm sorry for my poor manners. I . . . I was hoping we could be friends."

"I . . . I bet you were," said Val, mimicking the catch in her voice.

Jackie smiled. It was one he hadn't seen before, the little girl with her slip showing, not knowing how cute she looked. "I'm usually a much better flirt. I do hope I'm not losing my appeal."

"Your appeal is still intact."

"I was worried that getting married had thrown me off-stride," said Jackie. "That can happen you know."

"Diminished flirt appeal—that would be a terrible price to pay for . . . what did you call it? Love at first sight?"

"You're very clever," Jackie said. "I enjoy talking with you."

"You said you were here because of Kyle."

"Yes, that's right." Jackie sat back. "Kilo and I have been calling Kyle for the past couple of days, leaving messages. No answer. We've invited her to dinner, to breakfast, to go for a swim. *Anything.* No response from her, not even the courtesy of a refusal. Kilo said to forget about it, but I can't." She played with a strand of her hair, twisting it back and forth. "I know she and Kilo have had . . . problems, but things are different now. Chuck is falling apart. Kilo has been playing nursemaid since the murder—the two of them are probably in the game room right now, playing eight ball for a quarter a point. We're *supposed* to be on our honeymoon. . . ." She looked at Val. "That must sound selfish to you. I just thought . . . I was hoping that Kyle could sit with the family tomorrow at the tennis match. It would mean a lot to Chuck."

"I'll tell her, but you know Kyle—she does what she wants."

"Yes, I know Kyle." Jackie massaged her cuticles. "This is my chance to be part of a family again. It may not be much of a family to her, but it's *my* family now, too. I know Kyle and I got off on the wrong foot, but I came here tonight to make one last effort to talk with her, to let her know I'm no threat to her."

"Inviting me out to dinner might not have been the best way to do that."

"Kyle wasn't here," said Jackie, as though that explained everything.

"Kyle's not too approachable at this point," said Val. "Her mother's murder . . . well, she's still trying to recover her balance."

"My father was killed by a hit-and-run driver when I was eleven . . ." Jackie looked away. "There was no insurance, no money . . . there was plenty of blame though. My mother and I nearly drowned in it."

Val resisted the impulse to sit beside her on the couch.

"I'm a tough cookie, I know that, but I've had to be." Jackie tried to hold her hands steady. "I got a second chance when I married Kilo, a second family, and I *won't* let it be destroyed too. Not without a fight." Her mascara ran down her smooth white cheeks. "There's no way to bring Mrs. Abbott back. There was no way to bring back my father, but we have to go on. We have to make this terrible thing bring us closer *together,* not drive us apart."

"Kyle is a tough cookie too. Give her some time."

"I want her to give *me* a chance," said Jackie. "Not just me either—I'd like her to give Kilo a fresh chance, too. I know the way he comes off to people, but he's not like that. These last few days he's really had to dig deep inside himself. You would hardly recognize him, Val."

"I'm sure that's true." Val hoped he sounded sincere.

"I don't blame you for not believing me," said Jackie. "Kilo was an asshole at the birthday party, and he made an even bigger fool of himself at the karaoke lounge."

Val didn't contradict her.

"God, I must look a mess." Jackie fumbled in her purse, dabbed at her eyes with a tissue. "Talk to Kyle when you see her, maybe she'll listen to you. It's obvious she's taken with you." She touched the tissue to her nose. "I told Kyle I wanted her to think of me as a sister, and I meant it." She smiled weakly. "I'm not so bad once you get to know me."

"I'm sure."

Jackie stood up and Val stood up too. "Thanks for letting me talk. It's meant a lot to me." She looked around for a mirror, but there wasn't one. "You're coming to the tennis match tomorrow, aren't you? Kilo invited you—"

"Of course, I'll be there."

"Maybe we could go out afterward, *all* of us, Chuck too—like a real family." Jackie kissed him on the cheek, opened the door. "Kilo has worked so hard on setting up this tennis tournament." She stood in the doorway, the security light from across the hall turning her hair incandescent. "I think he's really going to surprise everyone."

Dekker watched Jackie walk down the steps of the apartment building and wished he was dead. He didn't know who was the bigger fool, him or Kilo. Dekker had watched her go upstairs with the hawk-faced guy, the one who had stopped by her office a few days ago. The name on his mailbox said Valentine Duran, but he would always be Mr. Trouble to Dekker.

Dekker had followed Jackie over to the apartments, had sat scrunched down in the front seat of his car as the two of them jabbered away at the bottom of the steps. When they had walked upstairs, Dekker had started crying, angry at himself for giving in to his emotions, weeping uncontrollably, steaming up the windows of his car. Jackie hadn't stayed long with Mr. Trouble, not more than ten or fifteen minutes. It was a good thing too, otherwise Dekker might not have been able to restrain himself. There was a limit.

Chapter Twenty-Seven

"Mind if I sit here, Mack?"

A beefy man in desert-pattern cammies stood in the aisle of the bleachers, a stolid nurse holding on to one of his arms. Val had watched them making their way up to the very top of the grandstand, pausing twice so that the big man could catch his breath. The man had looked familiar, but Val couldn't place him.

"Sure." Val moved over. They had the whole row to themselves. The nearest spectators were six or seven rows down.

"Thanks," said the big man, settling himself down on the aisle next to Val, the heavy wood planks groaning. He had unhealthy mottled skin and close-cropped hair the color of steel wool. "I need to stake out the end spot in case I have to leave suddenly."

"Is this it, Sergeant Dekker?" asked the nurse, exasperated. Sweat stained the edge of her white cap. "Are you absolutely sure that we've *finally* found where you want to sit?"

"Thanks, nurse, I'm going to be just fine here with

this commanding view of the terrain and this gentleman here to keep me company."

"Glad to hear it." The nurse handed Dekker a liter bottle of Evian with a "Gwendolyn Abbott Memorial Pro-Am" sticker on the side.

Val saw Jackie far below making regular passes along the grandstand in a long, wispy white dress, showing off her trim ankles, a floppy Panama hat protecting her features. He still didn't know what she had really wanted last night. It had been past midnight when Kyle got home. She had shrugged off Jackie's visit, insisting on rebandaging his wound while he told her about Junior and Armando, her fingers gently pressing him back onto the sheets, kissing his gauze-wrapped belly, promising him that she'd be careful. He had awakened next to her this morning and wished they could spend the day in bed.

Dekker pointed to the nurse moving briskly down the steps. "She don't understand why I like sitting way up high, but I guess you do."

Val let Dekker drone on, remembering the feel of Kyle against him this morning, the way she had closed her eyes as he kissed her shoulder blades, caressing her strong back. She had asked him if Junior and Armando would go back to Miami now, asked if they had been scared off. Val had caressed her hips instead of answering, not wanting to lie to her. She had let it go, not pressuring him for reassurance—maybe she already knew the answer.

"Most folks head for the good seats where everybody else wants to sit," said Dekker. "All those bodies pressed together like anchovies in a can. Me, I like to secure my perimeter and still have somebody to talk to."

Val wondered how long he was going to have to stay

here before he could excuse himself. "I'm not much of a talker."

"Fuck you then, Mack," said Dekker, turning away. "I ain't asking for any favors."

Val appreciated Dekker's hostility, his wounded pride. There was entirely too much make-it-a-great-day rah-rah crap in L.A., like it was one vast pep club. He took a closer look at Dekker's uniform, noted the perfectly rolled sleeves, but it was the single medal on his chest that drew his attention—half the vets at the tournament sported good-conduct fruit salad, but Dekker was the only one he had seen wearing a Silver Star. No wonder the nurse had taken Dekker wherever he wanted. "Are you an in-patient at the V.A. hospital?"

"Off and on," said Dekker, "but I came here under my own power today."

They were at the top of the grandstand overlooking center court of the Orange County Racquet and Yacht Club. It was a beautiful Saturday afternoon, wisps of clouds drifting across the turquoise sky, so clear you could see Catalina. White-suited waiters ferried frozen daiquiris and fresh raspberries to the beautiful people in the prime seats, while the hoi polloi clustered on the surrounding bleachers sucking down donated Snapple. There were scores of kids in wheelchairs and braces, disabled veterans with bad haircuts and a dozen different styles of camouflage fatigues, retarded adults in happy-face "I'm a winner!" T-shirts, all of them wandering around the edges of the dozen clay courts.

Kilo's brainstorm was a hit—at the last minute converting his celebrity/amateur tennis tournament into a fundraiser for OC United, Mrs. Abbott's favorite charity. Mr. Abbott had underwritten all costs, and Mrs. Abbott's well-publicized murder had guaranteed media coverage, but, still, you had to give Kilo credit. A former Miss California and the current host of the top-rated L.A. television morning show were announcing the matches, and two state senators and a former governor had already stopped by to shake Mr. Abbott's hand and offer condolences while the cameras snapped away.

Dekker stared at a row of men on gurneys watching one of the matches, each one attended by a candy striper with a sun umbrella. "Looks like they cleaned out the long-term-care ward—those guys are going to get sick with all the rich food the girls are spooning into them."

Kyle walked over to center court and sat in one of the luxury boxes with Mr. Abbott, Kilo, and Jackie. She looked around, finally spotted Val, and waved. He waved back.

"This Mrs. Abbott, she must have been quite a lady," said Dekker.

"She was."

"You sound like you knew her."

"I met her only once, but she was something," said Val. "Have we ever met before?"

Dekker smiled. "If we had, you'd remember."

Val laughed along with him, not sure why.

Dekker took in Val's jeans and striped rugby shirt. "All these rich folks in their frilly white outfits, showing off the fact that they don't get down in the mud with the rest of us." His face darkened under the clear blue sky. "I read a book in high school about a guy stokes the furnace of a luxury liner—this guy does all the work keeping the boat moving, but the passengers treat him like he's got the mange."

"I remember that one . . . I think it's called *The Hairy Ape*. I liked it too, but it's got a sad ending."

"Tell me about it." Dekker tapped Val's thick wrists. "Looks like you're a working man yourself—here we are, a couple of hairy apes enjoying the sunshine with the rich folks. Well, they'll put us back below decks soon enough." He cracked the seal on the water bottle, offered it to Val. "Come on, I hate to drink alone."

Val drank, handed it back. It was nice up here with the steady *thwok* of tennis balls making music, the crowd spread out like an open fan. He wished Mrs. Abbott was here to see it. "I noticed your Silver Star, Sarge. You receive that in Nam?"

"I look that old?" said Dekker.

"At least."

"An honest man—how did you ever survive this long?" Dekker shifted in his seat, stifled a groan. He shook out four pills from a prescription bottle, chewed them noisily, washed them down with a swig of water. "The star is a souvenir of George Bush's Desert Follies." He smacked his lips. "I'm no hero, if that's what you're thinking."

"Yeah, they used to give Silver Stars away in MREs. Right next to the chocolate pudding."

"Tapioca." Dekker smiled. It was a scary smile, full of crooked teeth and pain, but there was a real man behind that grin. "What's your name, Mack?"

"Val."

"I'm Darryl." They shook hands, Val's hand lost in the bigger man's grip. "You sound like you did time in uniform, Val."

"Marines," said Val. "I spent half my tour doing house-to-house searches in Lebanon."

Dekker looked out across the lush grounds of the Racquet and Yacht Club. "House-to-house is some rough duty. I rode an M-1 in Desert Storm. Nice machine that Abrahms; not much headroom, but it packed a punch." He lowered his voice so that Val had to lean closer. "We were one of the first units to enter Kuwait City. Now *there* was a shit-hole—yellow scorpions crawling over the faces of dead kids, the sky so black with smoke you needed headlights at noon. Total confusion. Our first night operation we got into a firefight with another allied unit and took a round right through the turret. Let me tell you, Val, friendly fire *ain't* really—"

The crowd cheered and Dekker stopped. Kilo had stepped onto center court and was taking a bow to all four corners. He was the only player wearing gold terrycloth wristbands with his tennis whites. Kilo's opponent was one of the lifeguards from *Baywatch*. It was hard to tell who was getting the most applause, but Kilo acted like it was obvious to him.

"You don't get a Silver Star from getting hit by friendly fire, Darryl."

"You're persistent, aren't you?" said Dekker. "Most people can't keep a thought in their head, but you—"

" 'Conspicuous gallantry,' that's the bare minimum," said Val.

"Something like that." Dekker drank from his water bottle, but his mouth wasn't working so well and water dribbled down one side of his mouth, turning the collar of his cammies a deeper brown. "The Abrahms went up like a torch, 120mm cannon shells exploding, smoke and screaming everywhere. . . . One of the hatches was melted shut, but I squeezed out the other one. I thought about running away, but. . . ." He stared at the tennis court, lis-tening to the sound of the tennis balls being smacked around. "I pulled Garrett out first, then went back and got Paulson." His face twitched in the sun, and Val could see a fine network of scars where the skin grafts had woven together. "I went back again for Sarris, but. . . ."

"I'm sorry."

"Garrett and Paulson are still holding down a bed at Walter Reed. I'm not so sure they're grateful for what I done."

"I'm glad you made it back."

"Me too," Dekker said. "Otherwise I wouldn't be at this here feelgood gangfuck of vets and Jerry's kids."

"Kilo is just trying to do some good."

"Kilo?"

"The hunk in the far court, the one with the gold wristbands," said Val. "He organized the tournament. Mrs. Abbott was his stepmother."

"Who's that redhead he was sitting next to before? She some movie star?"

"She's Kilo's wife. Her name is Jackie."

"Man, some guys have all the luck," said Dekker. "*Jackie,* huh? You sound like you know her."

"Just a little bit."

"A bit? Exactly what piece do you know?"

Val turned to Dekker. It was a weird joke.

"Do you know her elbow?" asked Dekker, his puffy face grinning. "Her knee? Hey, Val, can I have the part you don't want?"

"You got me wrong, sergeant."

"It's 'sergeant' now?"

"I should get going."

"Sure, Val. I should too." Dekker started to stand, groaned. "Oh, *man.*"

"Can I help you?" Val put his hand on Dekker's shoulder. He had expected him to be soft, but the man was solid. "Are you okay?"

"I better get to my car," said Dekker, breathing heavily. "I've got more meds there. Can you just walk me there, marine? I hate to ask the nurses. If I fall, it's going to take two or three of them to get me on my feet."

"No problem."

They walked down the stairs together. Val's hand was on Dekker's shoulder, feeling the big man's fatigue and pain with every leaden step. The people in the lower seats gave them plenty of room. A nurse approached them at the bottom of the stairs, but Dekker waved her away. "My pal here is taking care of me just fine, nursie," he said and Val could only shrug helplessly at the woman.

"Where are you parked?" Val asked.

"Not too far," said Dekker. "I don't like to use the handicapped spaces. Save them for the guys who really need them—that's my motto. You start using those spots you can't stop yourself. Next thing you know you're pissing in a bag because it's too far to walk to the bathroom. Am I talking too much?"

"No."

"We're almost there," said Dekker, his voice tiny. "Just stick with me, okay?"

"Lean on me, Darryl."

"I do that I'm going to kill you," said Dekker.

Val struggled on with him, feeling the big man settling around him, growing heavier with each step. They were both soaked with sweat. He kept looking around to see if there was a wheelchair available, but the outer edges of the parking lot were empty. A cheer went up from the crowd.

"Your buddy Kilo must have won," puffed Dekker.

Val was too tired to correct him.

"Right down here," said Dekker. "We're almost there."

"That's what you said five minutes ago."

"This time I mean it."

There was a long sustained round of applause, and Val could hear the announcer's muffled voice over the PA system. He turned around and saw people slowly streaming out of the club grounds onto the far side of the parking lot. Policemen were getting out of their cars, coffee cups in hand, to direct traffic.

"Here we are." Dekker sounded happy. No happier than Val to finally be there.

Val saw a new, powder blue Cadillac, an odd car for Dekker. . . . "I *know* where I've seen you," he started, remembering the man he had glimpsed in the karaoke club. Before he could say anything more, Dekker grabbed him by the back of the neck and threw him into the side of the Caddy. The sound echoed in Val's head as he slumped slowly to the ground. He tried to stand, but his legs were wobbly.

"Little late, pal," said Dekker.

Val fought, but Dekker slammed him into the car again. This time he didn't even hear the impact. Dekker's laughter was the only thing he heard.

Chapter Twenty-Eight

"Wake up, marine." Dekker shook him. "Wake *up!* You're going to be dead a long time."

Val opened his eyes, head throbbing, but he couldn't focus. He was turning toward the sound of Dekker's voice when something heavy and metallic smacked against his ear. He groaned, tried to rub his head, but his hands were taped behind his back, his ankles taped together, too.

"You should be careful," said Dekker, tucking Val's 9mm into his cammie jacket. "This thing might have gone off and hurt somebody."

Val must have been out for a while because it was late afternoon now, the light less intense. He was stuffed into the passenger side footwell of the Cadillac, his head and shoulders below window-level. Everything hurt. He tried to swallow, but his throat was dry, almost choking on his own fear. He knew where Dekker was taking him.

"Comfy?" asked Dekker. "Anything I can do to make your stay with us more comfortable? Adjust the picture on your television? Maybe an extra mint on your pillow? You name it, I'll—"

"Did you come in from Miami or is Junior using local talent? I didn't see you at the Doheny Grand. . . ." Val tried to sit up.

Dekker shoved him back down without even bothering to take his eyes off the road. He pulled a couple of prescription bottles from his cammies, twisted them open, and upended them into his mouth, chewing noisily, pushing half-bitten red and blue tablets back into his maw as they fell out onto his lips. He held up one of the bottles to Val. "Pain pill?"

Val shook his head. That hurt too.

Dekker gave the bottle a shake, the pills rattled. "Make you feel better, marine, guaranteed. Look at me, ain't I the picture of health?"

"No, thanks."

"What a trooper." Dekker's nose started to bleed. "Damn." He smeared his cheek with a swipe of his hand, then pulled Kleenex from a box beside him and stuffed his nose with tissue, tufts of yellow tissue curling out of his nostrils.

Val wanted to laugh at Dekker's noseplugs, but he knew that would hurt too. He wondered if he could somehow slip his foot over to the gas pedal, floor it, and get them into an accident, a fender bender, a flaming rollover even. Junior and Armando would be waiting for him at the end of the ride. Val tried to move his legs—there was no room to maneuver, but he kept at it. Anything was better than meeting those two trussed up and helpless.

"Settle down," said Dekker. "We're almost there."

"That Silver Star of yours was a nice touch—I let my guard down when I saw that. Did you get it at a hock shop?"

"You want me to break something on you? Pick a

bone, any bone, because there are some things I take seriously."

Val believed him. "Gallantry under fire, Darryl, that says something about you, something no one can take away, no matter what happened before or since. A man who deserved a Silver Star can do better than Junior. You've got to have more respect for yourself than that."

Dekker turned on the air conditioner. No, it must have been the heater—Val felt a blast of warm air against his legs. The tissue dangling from Dekker's nose fluttered in the warm breeze. The big man was shivering now. Val could see the setting sun beating down through the dark tinted glass. It was at least ninety degrees inside the car, and Dekker had the heater turned up full blast.

"Summer cold? I always pick up something when I fly." Val was still trying to find out if Dekker had come out with Junior. If he was an L.A. pickup rather than a Miami import, there was a chance that he might be reachable.

"The army used depleted uranium to make the shells we fired in Saudi," Dekker said. "DU, that's some dense stuff, punches right through an M-1's armor—it's toxic though. They didn't tell us that. This one colonel in charge of radiation safety said it was an oversight. That's what he called it, an oversight. Not that it would have mattered if the army *had* told us. What were we supposed to do?" His mouth twitched. "Doc at the V.A. last month wanted to do another liver biopsy on me, but I passed." He drove faster, then slowed down, as though running a traffic signal. "I don't like needles. Besides, it's too late anyway."

"Never too late," said Val.

"It's too late for me." Dekker put on his turn signal, made his move. A horn blared. "Too late for *you*."

Val kept working at the metallic tape balled around his wrists, trying not to move his shoulders so as to give it away. The tape was strong, but there was some flex to it—he was making progress.

"I bet you're surprised to find yourself stuck down there, and a big, dumb lug like me sitting here with my hand on the wheel," said Dekker, teeth chattering now. "Reversal of fortune, huh? Maybe you're not as smart as you think you are."

"I'm not even as smart as *you* think I am, sarge."

"Humility." Dekker smiled. "I like that. Humility goes a long way with me."

"Exactly how far would that be?"

"Not as far as you need, Mack."

Dekker's hands were shaking on the wheel as he leaned forward, staring through the windshield. "Un-fucking-believable. They're actually going back to the Laguna house. Throwing it right into my face." He patted his pockets again, came up empty. "Fine. There's all kinds of pain killers. . . ." He smiled to himself, like he had made a joke.

"Junior's going to Laguna?"

Dekker tore the bloody twists of tissue from his nose, hurled them onto Val's chest. They slowly uncoiled in warm air from the heating vent. The engine labored as they started up a steep hill, the automatic transmission shifting back and forth, trying to find the right gear.

Val felt the car moving down a winding street, sensed them slowing down. Through the window he glimpsed high hedges and fences. They were in a residential area now. Any minute now Dekker was going to pull into the driveway of a nondescript rented house, the garage door would close, and that would be that. The final *Jeopardy* answer would be "Please Don't." He hoped he would have as much courage as Steffano. He liked to think that he would spit in Junior's eye, but you never knew what you were going to do when you stared into your nightmare. No reflection there. No heroes either. Eight or nine years ago Dekker had been risking his life to pull his buddies out of a burning tank. Today he was dragging Val off to be murdered.

Dekker turned off the heater, switched on the air conditioner. "I'm roasting," he complained, wiping his brow. "I can't tell if it's hot or cold anymore. My thermostat is shot—ain't that a bitch?"

"You're never going to collect from Junior," said Val. "I don't care if you're being paid in cash or product, you're going to end up next to me."

Dekker shook his head. "I don't get it. His driver's license says 'Charles Abbott III,' his daddy calls him Charles, Jackie calls him Kilo, and *you* call him Junior. How many names does that asshole have?"

Val didn't answer. There was no reason for Dekker to lie to him now. If he wasn't working for Junior, what was Val doing taped up like a mummy?

"There they go," muttered Dekker. "Well, you and I will just cruise around for a little while, give them time to get down to it. Knowing Jackie, it won't take long."

"You know Jackie?" said Val.

"We *all* know Jackie, don't we?" Dekker cuffed him across the face, made his head ring. "Don't we?" Dekker hit him again, staring at Val, his pupils dilated so wide Val couldn't tell what color his eyes were. "I *saw* her come by your apartment last night—that was the last straw. I bet Kilo didn't know anything about that, did he?"

"Darryl, you're wrong—"

"Is there anybody on this planet who *isn't* fucking her? Other than me, of course, but then I don't count, do I?"

"Darryl—"

Dekker cuffed him. "You're lucky I didn't pay you a private visit last night after she left. I wanted to, but I held off. Who says I'm short-tempered?" He smacked Val again. "Who says I can't wait for dessert?"

Val tried to butt Dekker under the jaw with the top of his head, but he couldn't get any leverage and almost blacked out from the pain.

"You are one relentless gung-ho *motherfucker*," said Dekker. "I like that."

"Untie me," Val gasped. "I'll show you what I can do."

"I'm tempted."

"Don't be tempted, Darryl, *do* it."

Darryl nodded. "You're okay in my book. It's not much of a book, but your name has got a check mark next to it." He went back to driving, one hand on the wheel, the other draped over the back of the passenger seat, just two buddies out for a leisurely spin. "You want to hear some music, Val? What kind of music do you like?"

Val tried to think, but his head hurt so badly. "Did Jackie send you after me?"

Dekker punched buttons on the stereo. "Me, I feel like a little country."

"Did Jackie send you?"

Dekker fiddled with the bass controls. "I love country music. Booze, broads, and betrayal, sad songs for a sad afternoon."

"You're a pathetic fuck, you know that?" said Val. "I'd love to get a shot at you, one on one, Dekker. I'll play you a sad song."

"I bet you would too," said Dekker, amused. He found a country station, cranked it up, the singer wailing away all twang and bathos. It actually sounded pretty good, but Val was in no position to really appreciate it. He was too busy working on the tape around his wrists, his shoulders cramping from the awkward position.

They drove around for six or seven songs, an engine-additive commercial, and a pitch for heating oil futures. Dekker rocked back and forth, singing along to the music, his nose bleeding. The two of them were a mess. Val had almost managed to pull free when Dekker drove onto gravel, slammed on the brakes. The big man threw open the door and moved around to Val's side, almost dislocating his shoulder when he pulled him out. "You're going to love this," said Dekker.

Val's bound feet scraped along the ground as Dekker carried him by the scruff of the neck. The Cadillac had pulled onto a residential construction site—Val could see the Pacific through the skeleton of two-by-fours that rose from a concrete slab as he was dragged along. They were on one of the high hills around Laguna. The slab was one of the many homesites being rebuilt after the earthquake last year. There was no one around, not a kid on a bike or a jogger running hills, but Val yelled anyway. Dekker clapped a hand over his mouth and carried him into the overgrown bushes of the large house next door, one that the earthquake had missed.

"I know every inch of this ridge," said Dekker. "I scouted the terrain, just in case. Jackie is a creature of habit—she finds someplace she likes, she comes back to it. She's not like that with men, though," he said, crushing Val's face in his big hands. "With men Jackie likes the Kellogg's Variety Pack." The big man dragged Val around the house and down a narrow walkway, stumbling in his eagerness. "Here we are, right on schedule." He shoved Val's face against a picture window. "Ain't that a pretty sight?"

Val couldn't see a thing; his face was pressed flat against the glass.

"What do you think, marine? You want to join the party?"

Val felt himself hoisted effortlessly above Dekker's head. He was airborne for a moment, actually flying, then there was pain and the sound of breaking glass.

Chapter Twenty-Nine

Jackie threw her head back on the bed as Kilo nuzzled her breasts, his lips brushing her nipples. He had such a light touch. She liked watching him kiss his way along her body, connecting her beauty marks, kissing down her breasts, across her taut belly, down to that single, sandalwood-colored spot on the hollow of her inner thigh. She rolled her head across the pillow, groaning as he entered her with the tip of his tongue.

The tennis tournament had been a total, complete, and utter success. Three television stations had sent camera crews, and the society reporter for the *Orange County Times* had spent a half hour interviewing her, the photographer shooting about a zillion pictures. She had also gotten eight exclusive residential listings, each one booking for over three million dollars. Real estate was easy once you had the right connections, and Jackie was better connected now than she had ever dreamed of. Kilo had even won his match with what's-his-name from *Baywatch*, although Jackie heard that what's-his-name had a muscle pull. Not that Kilo cared—you would have thought he had won Wimbledon the way he flung his racquet into the air, not even trying to catch it. Oh yeah, over two million dollars had been pledged for that charity, too.

She arched her back, getting a good view of Kilo between her legs. Mrs. Elvira Bargeen had come up to Jackie at the end of the tournament and offered to put her name up for consideration into the Gold Coast Guild—that old scarecrow had to be wearing at least a five-carat rock on her finger. Stone, she corrected herself, a five carat stone. Jackie moaned as Kilo kissed her—she felt him smile. The Gold Coast Guild! Pavarotti had been scheduled for their grand ball last year, that's what Jackie had heard. Then he hurt his voice and Julio Iglesias had filled in. There, Kilo. Right there. The Gold Coast Guild . . . There. Her head rolled back and forth across the pillow. *There.*

Kilo had wanted to go home with Chuck and keep him company, maybe give Daddy a chance to show his appreciation, but Jackie had insisted that they go back to the house in Laguna for a private party instead.

Jackie shuddered, clawed at Kilo's head, tearing at his hair as he brought her off again and again. She lay limp among the sheets, momentarily exhausted as he slowly kissed his way up her body, tickling her with his eyelashes. Kilo was good. Very good. Handsome, rich, and a great fuck. Kilo was astride her now. He wiped his mouth as he looked her in the eyes, then reached under her, positioned her hips. She smiled and threw her arms around his neck—

The picture window exploded in a rain of glass.

"Earthquake!" Kilo scrambled off the bed, hands over his head, knocking over the nightstand, sending the lamp and her purse onto the floor.

Jackie sat up. Dekker? She saw him stand up, nonchalantly brush himself off, blood streaming down his face, wearing that ridiculous brown camouflage uniform. She was looking for her purse when she realized that there was someone else in the room, curled up on the carpet, moaning. Val? What was *he* doing here?

"Whoa!" Kilo stood at the foot of the bed, a naked traffic cop holding up his hand like that was going to stop Dekker. "Whoa!"

"What do you think you're doing?" said Dekker.

"I . . . I don't know." Kilo put down his hand.

Jackie spotted her purse alongside of the bed, surrounded by shards of glass and her wispy underwear.

"We're going to have to get somebody in here to clean up this mess," Kilo said to Dekker, avoiding the glass, not making any effort to cover himself. "I didn't even hear you knock."

"You were pretty busy," Dekker said gently.

Kilo had a self-satisfied smile. Jackie tried to get his attention, but he was still a little loopy from the sex. "We were celebrating—"

"Celebrating what?" Pieces of glass were embedded in Dekker's skull, flashing in the light. "Your little ping-pong match?"

"Tennis match," Kilo corrected him. He pointed a toe at Val, who was face-down on the carpet. "What's he doing here?"

"So you win a tennis game and think you're entitled to throw a fuck into Jackie?" said Dekker. "Is that the way you figure it?"

"Get over it, dude," said Kilo. "We're *married.*"

Dekker lightly slapped him. "I'm going to have to wash your mouth out for that, Kilo."

Kilo looked over at her. "Jackie?"

"I'm okay," she said.

"Not you, *me*," said Kilo, rubbing his cheek. "Call him off."

"Yeah, call me off, Jackie."

"What are you doing here, Darryl?" said Jackie. "What's *Val* doing here?"

"You didn't think I knew about *him*, did you?" said Dekker. "You made so many mistakes about me I can't even keep track of them all."

"Get dressed, Kilo," said Jackie.

"Have you stopped taking your medication?" Kilo asked Dekker. "You can have some of mine if you want."

"I don't need your medication," said Dekker. "I got my own—I earned my meds, too. I didn't just call up my daddy's doctor and say gimme."

"Kilo, get *dressed*," said Jackie.

"That makes you a better person than me?" Kilo laughed. "You *earned* your meds?" He strutted around the room. "I put on a major tennis tournament today—I thought of it, I planned it, I *did* it. Me. From now on Kilo's calls are going to be returned. From now on Kilo's credit is pure platinum. Turn on the TV—CNN is running a clip of me jumping over the net. I look like a snow leopard— that's what the producer said."

Dekker got down on one knee beside the bed as though he was going to propose to her. "Was it worth it, Jackie? That's all I want to know."

"Turn on the TV, Dekker," burbled Kilo. "I bet I get a call from Leno in the next twenty-four hours. 'The Jaw,' that's what people in the business call him."

Jackie sat on the edge of the bed, her purse so close she could almost touch it with her outstretched foot.

"You know why I'm here, don't you?" said Dekker.

The tone of his voice woke Kilo up. He looked around at the destroyed room, scared now, looking for someplace to run.

"You should have seen yourself today, Jackie," said Dekker. "You looked . . . so beautiful. You fit right in with all those society ladies." He held out his hands to her—he must have slashed himself on the window because he was bleeding all over. "You're rich and Kilo's on CNN, but what about me? You don't need me anymore, and I can't allow that, Jackie. That's not what I fought for."

Out of the corner of her eye Jackie could see Kilo going for his tennis racquet. She was surprised he didn't make a rush for the door—he must be *totally* crazy in love with her.

"Tell me," said Dekker, "what am I supposed to do now, Jackie?"

She leaned forward, cradled Dekker's head in her hands. "Look at Val rolling around on the floor, trying to get up. Why don't you do something about *him*? That would be a start."

"Don't worry, Jackie," said Dekker. He got up, advancing on Kilo. "I'm going to do something about everybody."

"Get back!" Kilo waved his tennis racquet at Dekker, swinging wildly, the air whooshing with his phantom serve. "Back!"

Dekker laughed. "Fore!"

Jackie slid off the bed and grabbed her purse.

Kilo smacked Dekker in the head with the edge of his magnesium-alloy racquet, split the skin, but Dekker seemed oblivious of his injury. Kilo bounced on the balls of his feet, still waving the racquet.

Jackie fumbled in her purse, pulled out the revolver

and aimed it at Dekker, closing her eyes as she fired. The room echoed. Dekker lifted Kilo up by the neck as Jackie fired again, this time trying to keep her eyes open. She heard Kilo grunt. "Don't you hurt him, Darryl!" she ordered. The gun in her hand was shaking as if it was alive.

Dekker stared at the gun. He looked more disappointed than scared.

"Put him down!" said Jackie.

Kilo wriggled feebly in Dekker's grip.

The gun went off and Dekker staggered backward, a red stain spreading across his cammies. She shot him again. Dekker jerked but stayed put, his feet planted, still not letting go of Kilo.

Kilo was barely moving.

Jackie stepped forward, put the gun against Dekker's belly and fired until there were no more bullets. Dekker dropped Kilo to the floor and took the gun from her. He looked tired.

Jackie bent down beside Kilo, saw a hole in his bare chest, a small hole really, an extra nipple with blood spurting out. His eyes were so very wide now, a vast drain down which all the money in the world was spinning, out of reach forever. She covered the hole with her hand, tried to plug the leak. "I didn't mean to," she told him. "Kilo, I didn't."

Kilo's lips moved, but no sound came out.

"Don't die," Jackie pleaded, her hand clamped over his chest. "We're just getting started."

Dekker pulled her up by her hair, threw her onto the bed, moving on top of her before she had even stopped bouncing.

"What did you *do*, Darryl?" said Jackie, trying to see past him. "Look at him. Look!"

"I loved you the first moment I saw you," said Dekker. "I should have died there and then. I would have been happy."

Jackie scratched him. "I would never have had to look at a price tag again, never had to do *anything* I didn't want to."

"You were the one who came to me, you were the one who called," said Dekker, making no effort to defend himself from her, blood gushing out of him, soaking them both. It was like stepping into a warm bath.

"Get *off* me," said Jackie, pounding on his chest.

"We were doing just fine until we met Kilo," said Dekker. "We should have left him there in the hotel room that first night. We should have just walked out on him and his big ideas." He leaned forward, blinking, as though he had lost sight of her. "I *told* you."

"Let me up, Darryl!"

"What was so special about him?" Dekker reached down and caressed her throat. You wouldn't think such a big man could be so gentle, but he was. "That's what I don't understand. What was so special about Kilo?"

"You're *hurting* me. Let me go."

Dekker was crying, eyes rolled back in pain—he coughed and Jackie felt a warm, pink mist drift down onto her face. She had emptied the gun into him, so why wasn't he dead? She didn't even see Kilo get hit and he was dead—what was Dekker doing still alive? She saw Val lying in the corner. He had pulled his hands apart and was working to free his ankles, a ribbon of tape trailing from one wrist.

"You married Kilo." Dekker's eyes were back from wherever they had been. "You married him, but *I* was the best man." He circled her neck with both hands, slowly squeezing, cutting off her air. "I was the best man, but you never noticed, and I was right here all the time."

Jackie struggled, kicking. She could barely see Dekker now. There were so many spots in front of her, red ones and black ones. Too bad she couldn't breathe spots.

Dekker suddenly jerked and his grip loosened slightly, just enough for her to catch a breath. There was something around Dekker's head. A pair of arms. Val was behind Dekker, throttling him with a strip of silver tape, cutting deep into his windpipe. Dekker bent forward, staring at Jackie, filling himself with the sight of her. He made no attempt to fight off Val, to tear at the tape. He kept his hands on Jackie's throat instead.

The spots were back in front of Jackie's eyes. She tried to pull free, but Dekker's fingers kept digging in deeper and deeper. Val was saying something, but she couldn't make it out. First Kilo, now Val—people should learn to talk clearer. It was the least they could do.

Kilo was kissing her, his breath warm and sweet, her loving Kilo, her golden boy. She blinked and saw Val over her. He bent down, kissing her, breathing into her, filling her lungs with fresh air. She tried to kiss him back, but she was so tired. Best just to lie back and let him do all the work. Such nice work too.

Chapter Thirty

Val was sitting on the edge of the bed, pulling on his jeans, when there was a knock on the door and detectives Holguin and Dillinger walked in, still talking to each other, as though the two of them were just strolling down the corridors of Newport Bay Hospital and decided to pay him a visit. At least Holguin averted her eyes.

"Where do you think you're going?" Dillinger said jocularly, just a hint of challenge in his voice. "I figured you'd still be laid out with tubes in your arms. What do you think, Inez? Don't he look worse than last night even, face all swelled up like an eggplant?"

"Last night?" Val hopped around, pulling up his jeans, then reached out to steady himself. He remembered calling 911 after giving Jackie mouth-to-mouth, seeing Dekker's purple fingerprints on her throat. He remembered the bumpy ambulance ride and a gruff doctor yelling at a nurse, but he didn't remember the two detectives. "Did I see you last night?"

"We interviewed you just before midnight—you confessed to everything." Dillinger grinned. "Just kidding."

"Your doctors said you were staying another day for

observation," said Holguin. "You had a severe head trauma—"

"Was Kyle here too?" asked Val, searching the closet. He couldn't find his T-shirt, so he kept on the blue hospital shirt, grabbed shoes and socks. His cell-phone was in a plastic bag on the shelf, along with his wallet and keys. "I thought I heard her voice, but every time I opened my eyes she was gone. I called her apartment, but—"

"The night nurse said you kept asking for her," said Dillinger. "Kept asking for your piece, too. Couldn't make up your mind."

"I need my weapon," said Val. "It's the Glock 9mm— you must have found—"

Dillinger shook his head. "No can do."

"It's licensed, Phil—"

"Under which one of your names?" Dillinger smiled. "Come on, you know how it works." He flopped down on Val's bed, stretching out among the newspapers, joints popping. "You don't mind if I make myself comfy, do you? Hey, what's your hurry?"

"Do you know where Kyle is?" Val asked.

"I'm sorry, no," said Holguin.

Val was having a hard time lacing his hightops. It felt as if he was wearing barbecue mitts. He thought of Kyle leaning over the hibachi on her patio, her hair smelling of smoke and lemons. A good time. Then Kyle had listened to her phone messages and heard Jackie's voice and the whole evening shifted. They still had fun. Kyle told him about the happy sounds made by an eleven-foot newborn gray whale, and Val told her about the cricket chorus undulating across the Everglades at dusk, the males sawing away for a mate. Kyle had made a crack about that and they had both laughed, but she was distracted with the news of her brand-new sister-in-law and the prospect of even more awkward family gatherings. Mrs. Abbott had been murdered that same night. Now there weren't going to be any more family dinners, none with Gwen watching over the table, turning a sharp eye on self-deception, cutting to the core without ever raising her voice. It seemed like a long time ago.

"You okay there, pal?" Dillinger pushed the newspapers off the bed.

Val could see the killings fluttering to the floor. The whole front page of the *Register* was devoted to them: pictures of Jackie and Kilo taken at the tennis tournament, and above the fold, a large photo of Dekker's draped body being carried out of the house. Val thought he had avoided the cameras, but the *Times* had printed a shot of him ducking into the ambulance. One of the nurses had come in with her own copy and asked him to autograph it for her. She said she had Jan Michael Vincent's scrawl too. Val finished his laces, stood up again. "How's Jackie doing? The nurse didn't know and—"

"Released early this morning," said Dillinger. "She's got a bruised larynx, but otherwise she's fine. Maybe better." He fluffed up the pillow, settling his head in. "She's got this husky voice now, reminds me of Marlene Dietrich. I was getting turned on taking her statement."

Holguin rolled her eyes.

Dillinger pressed the button that raised the back of the bed with a flurry of metallic grindings. "Ahhh," he said, folding his hands on his stomach. "These all-nighters are getting to me. I don't know how you do it, Inez—fresh as a daisy no matter what's gone down."

Val felt like going back to bed for a week himself.

Instead he went into the bathroom to splash water on his face. Time to get out of here.

"The docs found a nasty cut on your belly," called Dillinger. "They said you should have got stitches—you wouldn't want to tell us how that happened, would you?"

"I cut myself shaving."

"Yes, officer, I believe Mr. Duran is still a patient," said the old biddy behind the main admissions desk, turning away from her computer screen, her eyes huge and distorted behind thick glasses. Mrs. Fucking Magoo.

Junior folded the police ID, tucked the dead Santa Monica cop's silver shield away. He had covered the cop's picture with his thumb, but he still didn't like flashing it.

Mrs. Magoo leaned forward over the fancy white granite counter. "We've put him in the west wing, tenth floor, away from—" Her bulgy eyes darted to the TV news crew smoking cigarettes outside.

"Thank you kindly, ma'am," said Junior. "Where's the nearest elevator?"

"I saw you limping when you came through the door, detective."

"I wrenched my knee pulling a kid out of a burning building," said Junior. "Got a citation from the mayor."

Mrs. Magoo turned her cocktail ring round and round like she didn't believe him. "I'm simply pointing out that the west wing is a very long walk from here. I would suggest you drive through the security gates to the other side of the building. It's Physicians Only parking, but the guard will pass you right through. Just show your badge."

"I can use the exercise," said Junior. "Now where's the elevator?"

* * *

"You and Jackie got a departmental commendation coming," said Dillinger. "Heck, Old Man Abbott was talking about offering a reward. . . . I don't know if he ever got around to it, but if he did, you and Jackie can split it."

Val looked at Holguin.

"Last night we searched Mr. Dekker's motel room," she said. "There were numerous items from the Abbott estate and the Del Mar residence in his closet."

"Yeah, and Thursday a couple of Newport cops took a report on a Darryl Dekker loitering in a 7-Eleven just across from where Jackie worked. Don't forget that, Inez." Still stretched out on the bed, Dillinger wiggled his toes. "Between the three bullets Jackie put in Dekker and your duct-tape garrote, I'd say the two of you not only earned a reward but saved the taxpayers the cost of a trial. Not to mention the appeal and the retrial and the appeal of the retrial." He winked at Val. "Bottom line, speaking as a representative of your law-enforcement authorities, muchas gracias, amigo."

"Please, Phil, your accent is abominable," said Holguin.

"Sorry I came down so hard on you at the beach," Dillinger said to Val. "I was trying to shake something loose, but I was wrong. Dekker wasn't working for you, he was just love-crazy." He grinned. "If Jackie don't get a stalker-movie-of-the-week deal out of this, I'll kiss your ass." He covered his mouth. "Sorry, Inez."

"Yeah, that sounds right," said Val, his head throbbing from trying to remember everything that had been said in that powder blue Cadillac. "Dekker was pretty hung up on her . . . and he *hated* Kilo."

"Dekker worked for a loan company upstate," Dillinger said, staring at the ceiling. "About a year ago he got sent out to repo Jackie's car and fell hard—couldn't take her wheels. A repo man in love—can you believe it? He started bothering her at work, coming by her apartment—Jackie had to leave town in the middle of the night to get away from him."

"Is that what she told you?"

Dillinger chuckled. "Once a cop, always a cop."

"We're still checking," Holguin assured Val.

"Dekker had a history of violent assaults," said Dillinger. "He beat a man to death at a biker bar couple years ago, but it was ruled justifiable homicide. There were three of them that jumped him. One ended up on a slab and the other two ended up in traction. If it was my call, I would have ruled it justifiable too. 'Taking out the trash,' that's what we call it in the locker room."

"If Dekker was after Jackie, why did he pull that home invasion in Del Mar?" said Val.

Dillinger played with the controls of the bed, raising and lowering first the head, then the foot, riding up and down, the motor whirring. "I got to get me one of these things for my bedroom. The wife will just go nuts."

"We're not sure if he selected the Del Mar house as a trial run for the Abbotts'," Holguin said to Val, "or if he was just trying to raise money, perhaps to impress her."

"That seems like a stretch," said Val. "There had to be easier—"

"Jackie is no cheap date, even I could see that." Dillinger sat up. "Dekker was a war hero—did you know that? Gulf War, but that still counts in my book. Then about three months ago he ups and leaves his collection job, doesn't even pick up his last paycheck, just *goes*. He must have gotten a whiff of where she run off to and—"

"Phil." Inez shook her head.

"What's it going to hurt, Inez?" said Dillinger. "We owe our boy here." His legs swung back and forth over the side of the bed. "The way we figure, Dekker must have broken into the Abbotts' house thinking Jackie would be there with Kilo. Same as he done at the Laguna place last night—better late than never, I guess." He shook his head. "Mrs. Abbott, poor lady, she just picked the wrong time to be home."

"Val, I *am* a little curious why Mr. Dekker chose to kidnap you?" Holguin's expression was impenetrable. "Did he have a reason to be jealous of you, as well as with Kilo?"

"He thought he did," Val admitted.

"There you have it, Inez." Dillinger yawned wide, showing off his fillings. "You must be the luckiest man alive, pal. The M.E. said you should have broke your neck when Dekker shoved you through that picture window, but it turns out the glass wasn't up to code. Ain't that a hoot? It was *supposed* to be reinforced, double-pane, but instead it was single-pane." He shook his head. "What a world— you're alive and kicking because somebody ignored the law and put cheap glass in a two-million-dollar house. Honest workmanship would have killed you."

"Don't sound so disappointed," said Val.

"You're *awake.*" Kyle stood in the doorway. Her hair was limp, her eyes red-rimmed and exhausted, her clothes looking as if she had slept in them. She was beautiful.

Junior watched Armando hurry away while he waited for the elevator. The kid had been even more squirrelly than usual since Val had knocked him around. The bandage across his nose didn't help his disposition either. At least

Armando could walk without people thinking he needed a wheelchair.

This morning Junior had spilled his room-service fresh-squeezed all over himself when he saw Val on TV. Val had been trying to cover his face as he left the house, a redhead hanging on to him, a real knockout too, patting her hair for the cameras. "Ms. Jackie Abbott," according to the newsbabe doing the on-the-scene reporting. The guy Val killed looked like Haystack Calhoun under the sheet. It had taken two attendants to push the gurney across the lawn. Junior had laughed watching them lean into it, one of them slipping on the wet grass, almost dumping the load.

Three nurses walked over to the elevators, yapping about the photographers and asking one another if they had been interviewed. Junior's knee was killing him, puffed up to twice its size. He had taken six aspirin, but his knee still throbbed like a bishop's hard-on. He was tempted to offer the nurses a couple hundred bucks for a dozen Demerol. Here he was, a major player with no prescription downers. Like Val had said, Junior didn't belong in California. The elevator dinged as the doors opened. Junior stepped in front of the nurses, limping worse than ever now.

Val held Kyle tightly. He felt dizzy, held her even tighter to keep from falling. He didn't know how long the two of them stayed there, but when they finally separated, both Holguin and Dillinger were studiously looking away.

"I peeked in on you last night and this morning. . . ." Kyle wiped off tears. "Everything is *such* a mess, I just can't believe that Kilo is dead. . . ." She wiped more tears. "I was so scared when I couldn't find you after the tennis tournament. I didn't know why, but I was. I kept calling your number, and then around midnight, my phone rang and it was Chuck, speaking very slowly, very deliberately, saying everyone around him was dead, everyone he loved, and I couldn't tell who he was talking about and—"

"We have to leave," Val said to her.

"Is your stepfather still being treated?" asked Holguin.

"He's in a room on the fifth floor," said Kyle. "The doctors have him under constant supervision. They're concerned that he might do something . . . foolish. I don't know what to do, Inez. I feel like a basket-case myself."

"Has Jackie been in to see him?" said Holguin. "She was very worried—"

Kyle grimaced. "She tried, but Chuck wouldn't talk to her. He ordered her out of his room, out of his *house,* if you can believe that." She shook her head. "He was *shouting* at Jackie, accusing her of killing his son—"

"It was an accident," said Val. "She was trying to shoot Dekker—"

"Chuck said that if it wasn't for Jackie, Kilo would be alive and so would Gwen," said Kyle. "He blames her for bringing Dekker into our lives. An hour ago he called his attorney trying to get the marriage annulled. It doesn't make any sense, Val, there's nothing for Jackie to inherit. Kilo didn't *have* anything. It doesn't matter to Chuck— he just wants to be rid of her."

"Your stepdaddy sure runs hot and cold, Miss Abbott," Dillinger said. "One minute Jackie's the answer to his prayer, the next she's out on the street and some shyster's trying to take away her name. You must be all broke up about that, too."

Kyle ignored him. "If you're ready to leave, Val, I'll drive you."

Holguin stopped her with an upraised hand. "I may need to contact you if we have any final questions."

Kyle scribbled on a notepad, tore off the top sheet, and handed it to Holguin. "Call me at this number. I bought a cell-phone this morning. I hate those things, but Chuck's doctors want me available at a moment's notice."

Junior banged on the bathroom door, heard a muffled reply, cursed and limped over to the door for the stairs. He sat down on the top step, soaked with sweat. His leg felt like somebody had cut it off at the knee and poured gasoline on the stump. Fucking Val. Junior had taken three different elevators, asking directions from every moron with white shoes. He even had an orderly draw him a map on a paper towel. Junior should have simply commandeered a wheelchair and had Armando push him to Valentine's room.

He straightened out his leg, cursing, then reached into his jacket and pulled out a vial of his personal best. He poured about a gram onto the back of his hand, then hit both nostrils, his head rocking back on his shoulders. Houston, we have ignition. Crack was more cost effective, but there was nothing like uncut flake. He rubbed the last of the coke onto his gums, then stood up, using the banister to pull himself to his feet. His knee was still a bitch, but Junior didn't care so much about the pain anymore.

Kyle was reaching for the door when an elderly balding man opened it and peeked in. "I called your father's room," he said to her, "they told me you were here." He shook her hand with both of his. "I am *so* sorry, Kyle. Your family has had too many tragedies." Val read the man's name tag: Dr. Williamson, Director, Oncology."

"Thank you, Jonathan."

Dr. Williamson nodded to Holguin and Dillinger. "Detectives."

"We were just leaving, Jonathan," said Kyle.

"Ah." Dr. Williamson smiled wanly at her. "I have to make rounds anyway," he said, backing away. "You call me if you need anything. Day or night, I mean that."

"I think that sawbones is sweet on you, Miss Abbott," said Dillinger, as the door closed after him. "Lucky you. After I got done interviewing him last week I asked him to take a gander at this plantar wart on my foot, and you'd have thought I shot his dog."

Val was the only one in the room who laughed. It hurt, but he laughed anyway.

Dillinger looked around. "What did I say?" He sat up. "Before you two lovebirds head out, Val, how about you and me step into the little boy's room for a chat?"

It was a tight squeeze in the stainless-steel bathroom. The two of them were standing so close that Val could see the veins in the bags under Dillinger's eyes—he didn't check out his own reflection in the mirror. Dillinger reached into his jacket and handed Val a crumpled paper bag that smelled of egg salad. A .32 automatic was inside. "That's my drop gun," said Dillinger. "I don't like the idea of a cop walking around naked."

Val checked the magazine.

"You don't trust nobody, do you?" said Dillinger. "That's smart."

"What's this about? And don't hand me that cop-to-cop line."

"I don't know who you are or what's going on with

you and that Miami task force," said Dillinger, his voice low, "but I made a call to a pal in south Florida does favors sometimes for the DEA. My pal says that if you really smoked the Jackson brothers, half the squad wants to buy you a drink; the other half wants to add some names to your hit list."

Val tucked the revolver into his waistband, covering it with the baggy hospital shirt. "I don't know what you're talking about."

Dillinger opened the door. "That's my guy."

"I *told* you, officer—Mr. Duran left about ten minutes ago." The skinny Filipino nurse behind the counter tapped her pencil on her *People* magazine. Bitch had a mole on her chin big enough to channel fucking Ferdy Marcos singing from the grave. "Now, if there's nothing else—"

"I thought Valentine was pretty badly banged up," Junior said. "The hospital could get sued for letting an injured man check out."

"We don't lock our patients up. That's *your* job, officer."

Junior grinned, trying to control his temper. "Sorry, lady, I haven't had my morning sit-down yet, and I'm just a bear until I do."

The nurse grimaced. "Mr. Duran didn't have health insurance. That might explain his eagerness to leave so quickly."

"Did he leave word where he was going? It's life and death important."

"Have you asked the other detective? He should be around somewhere."

"You said he went off with Ms. Abbott," said Junior. "You got an address for her, don't you?"

"I don't, but if you check with Admissions, they should be able to give it to you." The nurse was tapping that pencil again. If she kept it up much longer, Junior was going to shove it through her eye. "Her stepfather is a patient in intensive care, officer. Perhaps she and Mr. Duran went there."

Junior had taken only a couple of steps toward the elevators when the doors opened and the redhead walked out. Mrs. Abbott herself, looking like she was ready to kick some ass and she didn't much care whose it was. Junior smiled.

"That's Jackie Abbott, officer," the nurse said. "Kyle Abbott is her sister-in-law."

"Kyle . . . who's Kyle Abbott?"

"Kyle Abbott is the woman who went off with Mr. Duran," the nurse clucked, exasperated. "Perhaps her sister-in-law might know where they are."

Junior nodded, understanding his mistake.

"Nurse!" Jackie strode down the hall, trailing a black silk scarf. "Nurse," she rasped, her voice hoarse, "I'm looking for my sister-in-law, Kyle Abbott. They said she was here."

"This is officer . . . what was your name again?" the nurse said to Junior.

Junior flipped his ID open and shut. He needn't have bothered. The redhead wasn't interested in looking at another grimy badge. She wasn't interested in looking at anything he had to offer. "Afternoon, miss," said Junior, his eyes on her tits.

"Where's Detective Dillinger?" said Jackie.

"I'm detective J. R. Jones." Junior shook Jackie's hand, and felt her pull back. "Sorry to interrupt your grieving, but we need to talk privately."

Jackie glanced at his seersucker sports coat and light-blue Dockers. "I don't think so." She snapped her fingers at the nurse. "Are you on a break? I *asked* you a question."

The nurse walked over to a row of file cabinets, showing them her back.

"Maybe I can help," Junior said to Jackie. "Your sister-in-law flew the coop with Valentine Duran," he said, taking her elbow. "Do you know where they went?"

"Do I look like Kyle's social secretary?"

"No, ma'am, you most certainly do not," said Junior. "You and I do need to talk, though. It won't take long."

"It had goddamn *better* not," said Jackie. "I've got to get back to my father-in-law in a few minutes. I want to be there when he wakes up."

"You got my word on it," said Junior, leading her toward the elevator.

"Where are we going?"

"You ask a lot of questions." Junior grinned. "Keep it up I'm going to deputize you."

"I don't like your tone—"

"We got a command post set up in the parking lot." Junior stepped into the elevator and held the door open for her. "Come on, ma'am, the sooner we get this over, the sooner you can be done looking at my ugly face."

Jackie strode into the elevator and checked her watch. "You've got fifteen minutes."

A hand reached in as the elevator closed. The doors slid open and Armando walked in carrying three dozen red roses, his face peeking through the blossoms. He was wearing the same outfit he had on when Steffano was whacked—a white sailor suit with gold piping. There was a thick bandage across his nose. The bouquet brushed against Jackie's arm.

Remote and imperious, Jackie pursed her lips.

Junior hit the ground-floor button twice, then once again for good measure. He stuck his face right in the middle of all those flowers and inhaled. "Smells real nice," he said to Armando as the doors slid shut. "Somebody special must be dying."

Chapter Thirty-One

⚬

Kyle clicked off her cell-phone. "The nurse said Chuck is sleeping—I don't blame him for not wanting to wake up. I wish I could sleep."

"When you talk to him again, tell him that Kilo could have gotten away, but he stuck around to confront Dekker. I actually think he was protecting Jackie."

"That's very kind of you, Val."

"I'm serious. I was pretty out of it, but it looked like that's what he was trying to do. Kilo didn't seem afraid of Dekker, not as afraid as I was anyway."

"Fight or flight, the basic mammalian quandary. Wouldn't you know it—the first time in his life Kilo chooses to fight, he picks the absolute worst moment." Kyle bit her lip.

Val put his arm on her shoulder and felt her give way. She had lost weight in the past few weeks, and there were dark circles under her eyes. "I'm so sorry . . . I wish I could have done more to save him, but I was barely conscious. By the time I got free—"

"This man, Dekker, the newspapers said he was crazy from drugs and Gulf War Syndrome."

"I don't think the war had anything to do with what Dekker did. It was beauty killed the beast." Val turned around in the passenger seat of Kyle's Suburban, watching the cars behind them as they drove north on the 405 freeway. "Dekker was strong enough to pull apart an iron fence and toss me around like a Teddy bear, but he had a marshmallow heart when it came to Jackie. She was all he talked about in the car. I almost felt sorry for him." He pointed. "Take Westminster." The Suburban veered over, horns blaring behind them as Kyle exited the freeway. His head throbbed from the sudden movement. He hadn't taken the time to get his prescription filled, but he *had* chewed up the half dozen Midol in Kyle's purse. They hadn't helped. Kyle said they never helped her either. "Pull into the mini-mall."

"Now what?"

"Now we wait." All the signs in the mini-mall were written in wavy Cambodian script. Women in long colorful skirts led small children by the hand into the ice cream shop. Outside the video store, slim Asian boys in wraparound shades smoked cigarettes, holding them between thumb and forefinger. No cars had followed them off the freeway, but Val wanted to wait a few minutes anyway.

"I still don't see why we can't go by your apartment house and pick—"

"I told you, Junior arrived in town a couple of days ago. If he's still here, he knows what happened last night— my name and picture were in all the papers and on TV."

"Then why don't you leave? If Junior knows you're in L.A., why not just leave?"

"Junior has *talked* to you, Kyle. He knows you and I are involved—"

"Then let's *both* leave. We can be in Baja in a few hours—"

"Junior will find us in Baja or anyplace else you have a connection to. You can't disappear; you have responsibilities. Just stay with me until this thing is settled and—"

"*Then* can we go to Baja?"

"Promise." Val saw the teenagers talking to one another as they watched the Suburban. "I was surprised to see the head of Oncology take time to locate you. This Dr. Williamson must have really wanted to pay his respects." One of the Cambodian kids flicked his cigarette toward them.

"Don't credit Jonathan with a bedside manner. He just has a keen sense of the bottom line," said Kyle. "Gwen and Chuck were major contributors to the hospital. For the last few years, they underwrote the shortfall in the children's oncology unit." She nodded at the teenagers. "Shouldn't we be going?"

"After the doctor left my room, Dillinger said that he and Holguin had already interviewed him. Why would they have done that?"

"Does it matter?"

"I don't know. That's why I'm asking you."

Kyle's smile was gone. "A few years ago Jonathan treated my mother for adrenal cancer. She had to have one of her adrenals removed. We thought they excised all the cancer. Evidently they didn't."

Val watched Kyle try to control herself. She stared at the steering wheel. "Inez told me that during the autopsy, the medical examiner discovered that my mother's cancer had returned. It had metastasized into every major organ. They checked her records. Jonathan had been treating her for months, pain management mostly. Aggressive therapy was considered . . . useless."

"Your mother didn't tell you she was dying?"

"She didn't tell anyone." Kyle gripped the steering wheel. "I can understand her not telling Chuck or Kilo. Chuck fell apart the first time she was sick, almost finished off his liver feeling sorry for himself, and Kilo—she wouldn't have wanted to give him the satisfaction. I can understand her hiding her cancer from *them*, but she should have told *me*."

"Maybe she was waiting until things got closer to the end. She knew you were almost finished with your studies—"

"I was her daughter—she should have told me." Kyle started the car.

"Take a right onto Warner and head toward the water. Grace's house isn't too far."

"My mother was a very proud, a very *private* woman," Kyle said bitterly. "The very idea of her medical history being bandied about by family, let alone strangers, would have infuriated her." She raked the back of her hand across her eyes. "Detective Dillinger had the audacity to say that for a dying woman she fought like somebody with a whole life ahead of her." Kyle was speeding. "I think he actually meant it as a compliment."

"I'm sure he did, Kyle." The Suburban rumbled through an amber light as Val gave directions, hanging on. About a half hour later the car bounced up into his grandmother's driveway. Damn. She had put the retread-tire alligators in the front yard. The painted sawtooth gators were an open invitation to anyone driving past, anyone who knew what to look for.

Grace's house was a small flat-roof rambler that backed up to the Bolsa Chica wetlands. It had taken him forever to find it when he first moved them out here. It rented for three thousand dollars a month, but some mornings it almost looked like home. There were egrets nesting in the stunted trees, frogs and sunfish in the soggy marshes, and cattails as high as a man. Two blocks away there were surfers and a Jack-in-the-Box and fire-rings on the state beach, but from her backyard all Grace could see was the wetlands.

The front door opened before Val could knock. "What are you doing out of the hospital?" said his grandmother, hands on her hips, the perennial thin black cigar stuck in the corner of her mouth. "TV said you were in serious condition."

"Serious condition isn't serious. It just means you should take it easy," said Val. "Grace, I'd like you to meet—"

"What do they say when it's *really* serious?"

" 'Critical.' If they said I was in critical condition, that would be serious."

"Damn doctors, they'll do anything to keep people confused." Grace patted his cheek. Her touch was as gentle as her tone was gruff. "I was worried." She was a bright-eyed bird with a high, intelligent forehead and long white hair that floated in the breeze like Spanish moss.

"Kyle, this is Grace, my grandmother. Grace, this is Kyle, the woman I—"

"I know who she is." White, peppery smoke trailing from her nostrils, Grace shifted the twisted cigar to the other side of her mouth without touching it with her hands. "Valentine never brought anybody here before."

Kyle smiled.

Grace took both of her hands. "I'm sorry about your mama, I truly am—and that boy killed last night—he was your relation too, wasn't he?"

"Thank you," Kyle said softly.

"You're not over it by a long shot. I can see that." Grace gave her hand a squeeze. "You should take care of yourself."

"I'm doing my best. Val . . . he's helping too."

"Well, Val and me have had some bad times too—it always hurts, but you learn to live with the pain. You hang on." Grace gave Kyle's hands a last squeeze and ushered Val and Kyle into the living room. The walls were stained with smoke, and the air was thick and heady as port wine. "You really have done it now, haven't you," she said to Val, her voice low, "got your face all over the news. That damn cracker is probably on a plane out of Miami—"

"Junior's already here."

Grace gave a barely perceptible nod toward Kyle.

"I told her about Junior—he knows about *her*, too."

"You *never* could let well enough alone. Well, too late now—might as well go on out to the patio, both of you. I'll bring you something."

"May I help?" asked Kyle.

Grace snorted.

Val settled himself into a chaise longue while Kyle sat in the white wicker rocker, Grace's chair. He thought to say something but decided it would be more interesting to watch the two of them work it out. It was peaceful in the yard, flowers were everywhere, and the grass was so tall it looked as if it had never been cut. As the afternoon sun filtered through the surrounding trees, the two of them watched a white egret settle into the swampy wetlands with a flapping of wings. "Sorry about . . . before," Val said. "Grace is a little rough around the edges."

"That's never bothered me before, has it?"

Grace pushed open the screen door with her foot and came out carrying a tray with peanut butter sandwiches, a glass pitcher, and three tall glasses on it. "You sitting in my chair?" she said to Kyle as she handed a glass to Val. "Don't get up," she ordered, giving Kyle a glass. "My grandchild *let* you sit there. He must have been hoping you and me would have words. Divide and conquer—ain't that just like a man, hoping to gain an advantage over two poor defenseless women?" She watched Kyle take a tentative sip. "You like it?"

"Yes," said Kyle, "what is it?"

Grace laughed. "You musta never had real iced tea before."

"It's very . . . sweet," said Kyle.

"Iced tea is *supposed* to be sweet," said Grace.

"It's very good." Kyle forced down another mouthful. "You'll have to give me the recipe."

"Yeah, I can see you and me trading recipes." Grace pulled up a stool and sat beside Val. "You don't look so bad—I seen you look *lots* worse. Your no-account daddy looked at you when you were born and said it looked like we threw away the baby and kept the afterbirth."

"*Grace—*"

"Valentine used to come home from school all the time tore up," Grace said to Kyle. "He had a mouth on him, that was part of the problem, but he usually gave as good as he got."

"Kyle doesn't really want to hear this," said Val.

"Sure I do."

"I'm just saying, I seen you look worse than now, that's all. I'm trying to give you a compliment, dammit. Shoot, you going to outlive me, boy. I know that much." Grace stroked his forehead. The tip of her cigar glowed brightly. "Course I could drop dead any second, so don't you get too high and mighty. See you buy only ripe bananas, no green ones—I hate to see food go to waste."

Val stirred in his sleep, and Kyle and Grace turned to watch him until his breathing smoothed out. Kyle rarely saw him in repose. His raw, angular features were relaxed now, and his long lashes made him appear almost delicate.

"He's got my cheekbones." Grace finished her iced tea in a long syrupy swallow, smacking her lips. "My husband said I looked like a hawk."

"I love his hands. . . ." Kyle blushed.

Grace twisted the gold band on her ring finger as she watched Val snore, her eyes bright, dark brown face creased with a road map of fine lines and wrinkles. She must have been a raving beauty as a young woman. She stood up and beckoned to Kyle. "I got worms on my tomatoes. You can help if you want."

Kyle followed her to the fenceline, where the tomato plants grew tall and bushy in full sunlight. Grace knelt down and lifted one of the leaves—it was covered with tiny white worms the size of fly larvae. Grace pulled a worm off, pinched it between thumb and forefinger, then went back for another one. Kyle joined in. The two of them worked side by side, sweating in the sunlight, bees buzzing around them. It was messy work, this smearing worms to paste, but the tomato leaves had a clean pungent smell and the tomatoes were fat and red, their ripe sides splitting in the afternoon.

"I like a pretty woman who don't mind squishing bugs," said Grace. "Shows character."

Kyle reached for another worm. "Val said you used to read fortunes."

Grace's seamed fingers moved deftly among the leaves. "Mostly I just threw the bones and told tourists what they wanted to hear—new love, new job, new baby on the way. I can't read the future, nobody can. Sometimes, though, I get feelings about people." She tossed the cigar stub onto the grass, picked a fleck of tobacco off her tongue. "Not that feelings are worth much, but what else we got?"

"Val gave my stepfather a spirit pouch to put in my mother's coffin," said Kyle. "I want to thank you for that. I'm sure you were the—"

"Spirit bag?" Grace cawed. "Val was playing injun on you poor, dumb white folks. Spirit bag." She shook her head. "Girl, next you'll be asking me about the happy hunting ground and if I knew Hiawatha."

Kyle glared in the direction of Val. He stirred in his sleep.

"You got yourself something there, girl." Grace crushed another worm. "You be careful with my grandson."

"I'm not sure what you mean, Grace. Are you worried about him or me?"

"You just be careful."

"I'm not going to stay away from him, if that's what you're asking," Kyle snapped. "I'm not afraid of Junior"—she looked straight at Grace—"or anyone else."

"I guess that puts *me* in my place," said Grace, pulling

apart the clustered tomato leaves. "I was the same way when I met Valentine's grandpa. It was a damn foolish thing for a sixteen-year-old girl to marry a white man—and practically the only white man in Miami without an automobile to boot—but I was like you. I didn't care." She looked off into the wetlands. The egret was jabbing at something in the muddy water. "Lord, how I loved that man." She shook her head. "If I had known . . . known for certain how bad things would turn out, I *still* would have married him."

Kyle wiped her hands on the grass, plucked a cherry tomato, and popped it into her mouth. The seeds exploded in her mouth, the juice warm from the sun.

"You move right in, don't you?" Grace said, watching her chew. "Move in on folks like you belong there. No wonder my boy is crazy about you." She gave Kyle's hair a tug hard enough to make her wince. "I hope you know what you're getting yourself into. My Valentine's got his grampa's eyes, them warm blue eyes that stir up your private parts, but that boy attracts trouble."

"I told you, I'm not afraid."

"That's what you told me."

Kyle dug her fingers into the dirt, breaking up the sandy soil and letting it run across the back of her hands. "I know Val is worried about me. He's worried about you too. He said you had to leave your home because of him."

"I don't approve of so much talk." Grace stood up, sighing with the effort. "Valentine is the same way. I guess he trusts you."

"I trust *him*, Grace."

"I can see that," said Grace, staring at her. "Let me tell you a story. One morning about eight or nine months ago—I was still living in my house off the Tamiami Trail—

one morning I woke up with the feeling that *this* was going to be the last sunrise I saw. The very last one. That afternoon I saw a car drive past, and I knew it was true. I'm an old woman, you'd think I'd be ready to go, but I was *scared*. Understand, it wasn't just the dying that scared me. It was the *way* of it. I could see what the two boys in that car had in store for me."

Kyle had to help Grace over to her rocking chair because her legs were trembling so much. She poured her a glass of iced tea and waited for her to speak.

"I called up Valentine. . . ." Grace held the glass with both hands. "He must have driven like a bat out of Hades he got here so quick." She looked over at Val as he slept, drawing comfort from the steady rise and fall of his breathing. Her face seemed to smooth out, and her grimy hands became supple again. "I raised my kids in that little house, got their birthday grow-marks scratched on the closet wall to prove it, but when Val said to pack my things, I did it quick and never asked why. Didn't need to ask. I knew my grandson." She looked at Kyle. "I know him even better than you do."

"What happened to the two men?"

Grace took another drink of tea, her eyes lidded almost shut. "Why, I expect they were right disappointed finding an empty house when they came for me."

"One of the detectives investigating my mother's murder told me those two men were never seen again." Kyle leaned forward. The air was so still that she could hear bees buzzing around the tomato plants. "She said the police in Miami think Val may have . . . done something to them."

Grace fumbled in her dress and brought out a cigar. "Honey, take it from an old woman, you can't trust the police." She lit a safety match with her thumbnail, and puffed the cigar to life. "I only knew one good cop in my life . . . and he's dead now."

Kyle's cell-phone beeped.

Grace looked at Kyle as she rocked, her seamed face impassive behind a cloud of blue smoke. "I guess that's for you."

Chapter Thirty-Two

"This is a Chanel *original*, asswipe," Jackie hissed at Junior as she folded up her cell-phone. "It cost fourteen thousand dollars. So kindly remove your grubby fingers from my shoulder."

Junior took his hand off her. "Is Val coming with her?"

"Would you *mind* turning up the air conditioning?" said Jackie. "It's roasting in here, and I'm sick of smelling your cheap cologne."

Junior looked at Armando. "I fucking *hate* California."

Armando turned up the air conditioner. The Range Rover was parked at the very rear of the High Five parking lot, its engine idling. Junior and Jackie were in the back, and Armando was behind the wheel, his nose thickly bandaged. The parking lot was dark back here, and the Range Rover's tinted windows kept things way too private. Jackie had tried signaling to a couple of patrons, but there was no response—which obviously meant they couldn't see her.

Jackie tugged her collarless jacket down. It was a

lovely suit—a nubby black silk with pink embroidery down the front and accenting the pockets. It was a perfect ensemble for a widow in mourning, and the pink set off her hair and milky skin. She wished Kilo was here to appreciate her. Her hand went to her throat. She had laid on the mascara and used more makeup than she liked to cover the bruises on her face, but nothing would hide the purple fingerprints on her throat.

"How long do you think it will take for Kyle to get here?" asked Junior.

"What am I—the American Auto Association?" Jackie rasped.

"Keep it up," Junior warned, "I'm in a bad mood already. My leg is killing me."

"Do you have any mineral water?" asked Jackie.

"Where would I get mineral water?" said Junior, carefully straightening his knee.

"We're sitting behind a restaurant, Einstein." Jackie sneered. "Restaurant. Water. See the connection? Send sailor boy inside to get me a bottle."

Junior stared at her.

"May I kill her *now,* Junior?" asked Armando.

"What happened to sailor boy's nose?" asked Jackie. "It looks like he's wearing a Kotex pad on his face."

"Please, Junior?" said Armando. "We no longer need her, and I want to see her bleed all over her fine Chanel suit."

"Not yet."

"Can I get that water sometime this millennium?" Jackie demanded.

"No," said Junior.

"I have a damaged larynx—if I don't keep my vocal cords lubricated, I'm going to lose my voice." Jackie crossed her legs, black spike heels raking the door panel. "What if Kyle calls me back needing directions? If I can't talk what are you going to do then?"

Junior wearily shook his head. "Armando . . ."

"Let the red-headed bitch lose her voice," said Armando. "We would both benefit from her silence."

"Get her the goddamned water."

"Pellegrino," Jackie said. "The bubbles are smaller."

Armando slammed the door and stalked across the parking lot. His white sailor suit looked silvery under the yellow lights. Not speaking, Jackie and Junior sat side by side listening to the air conditioner blow. A Volkswagen slowed, the driver gawking at Armando as he went into the restaurant.

"You think your sister-in-law is going to bring Valentine with her?" asked Junior.

"I doubt it."

"She might though?"

"Kyle is very threatened by me," said Jackie. "Not that she doesn't have reason to be worried. You should see the way Val checks me out. It's almost obscene the way he looks at me."

"Yeah, I bet you get all flustered from the attention."

Jackie tugged at her skirt. "Val does have a certain charm—"

"Don't get your panties in a yank. There ain't going to be nothing usable on Valentine when I'm done with him."

Jackie shrugged. "The world's not running out of men any time soon." She checked her reflection in the window. "My point was that you don't need to waste time with Kyle. If you want to lure Val here, I'm all the bait you need."

"Your sister-in-law is the girlfriend, not you, I already established that." Junior lifted his right leg with both hands, gasping as he changed position.

"What's wrong with your leg?"

"I'm one of Jerry's fucking kids, okay? You send in your pledge yet?"

"Val is much more interested in me than he is in Kyle," said Jackie. "I haven't been available before, that's all. Now my husband is dead, and I'm back on the market. You watch the way Val looks at me, then decide if you want to waste your time with *her.*"

"Just sit back and give your larynx a rest."

"I can't sit back, there's not enough room in this stupid car. Couldn't you have rented a limo, or didn't you have a discount coupon for that in your tourist guidebook?"

"Limos draw attention."

"God, Range Rovers are just *so* not happening." Jackie sneered. "You might as well be driving a mini-van with a couple of brat-seats in back."

"You *ever* quit complaining?" said Junior.

"What do you want with Val?" asked Jackie.

Junior glanced out the window, looking for Armando.

"He must have done something really bad—personally, I wouldn't put anything past him," said Jackie. "Or Kyle either, for that matter. If there's anything I can do—"

"How about shutting up?"

"Some men like a woman with a mouth."

"I like a woman keeps her mouth *shut* until I tell her to put it to good use," said Junior.

"I never do what I'm told," Jackie said, looking him right in the eye, "and I've *never* had a complaint from a man yet."

Junior laughed. "You are really something, you know that?"

"I know that."

Junior put his hand on the back of her neck and gently kneaded her smooth skin. "You ever been to Miami?"

Jackie brushed against Junior's ankle with the tip of her shoes. "Are you going to do something awful to Kyle and Val?"

"Maybe."

"You can tell me," said Jackie. "I follow only three or four of the Ten Commandments."

"That's a pretty good average." Junior watched her legs.

"I know where Val lives, if that helps," said Jackie.

"He's too smart to go back there now," said Junior. "Your sister-in-law is our best chance. Once we get our hands on his girlfriend, Val will come running."

"You may be overestimating his attraction to Kyle," Jackie said coolly.

"Val is going to walk into whatever trap I lay for him, walk in with his eyes wide open," said Junior. "Part cause he wants to save the girl, but mostly because he needs to prove something to himself. The day before yesterday Valentine could have killed me, could have killed Armando too—he *had* us, had us cold, but he couldn't do it. That's going to eat at him. Once I got his girlfriend, he's going to do *anything* to make up for that." Junior chuckled at some private thought, lifted a lock of her hair, twirled it round his fingers. "I bet you're a real redhead, aren't you?"

Armando came sauntering up at that moment, his gold braid flashing. He opened the door on her side and shoved a bottle of Pellegrino at her.

"No glass?" said Jackie. "No *ice?* You just blew your tip."

Armando's narrow face was sharp as the blade of an ax. "Keep talking, chica. Before this day is done, you will beg to die. I will cut you many new mouths, and they will all be screaming."

Jackie took the Pellegrino.

"She looks even better scared, don't she, Armando?" said Junior. "Brings the color to her face."

Armando got behind the wheel.

Jackie sipped from the bottle. Her teeth rattled against the glass rim until she got a grip on herself. Junior was a man—anything was possible.

"Better?" asked Junior. "See, I'm not such a bad guy once you get to know me."

"I just wish sailor boy had brought ice." Jackie stroked the intricate embroidery on her Chanel, regaining her composure. "I can do some fun things with ice cubes."

"Party tricks?" Junior had eyes like a wild boar. "Best turn up the air conditioning another notch, Armando, it's getting pretty steamy back—"

"There she is," Jackie said, pointing as the white Suburban, a big ugly whale of a vehicle, pulled into the parking lot. "That's Kyle's car."

Armando was already out the door. He moved off into the shadows and seemed to disappear, then suddenly reappeared in a row of cars, his arms swinging as he walked.

Junior hit a button and rolled Jackie's window down. "Earn your keep. You fuck up, I'll show you some tricks *I* can do."

Jackie stuck her head out the window, waved to the Suburban, which was parking nearby. "Kyle! Over here!"

The Suburban's car alarm chirped as Kyle got out and started over toward the Range Rover.

"Check out the fashion disaster," Jackie said to Junior, noting Kyle's khaki shorts and expedition shirt. "She looks like she belongs digging for dinosaur bones or chasing butterflies with a net—you still think Val's going to be interested in her when *I'm* here?"

Kyle's steps had slowed as she approached the car— she stopped now, considering the situation, but it was too late.

Since Armando was small, he had to reach up to put his hand at the back of Kyle's neck. Jackie didn't know what he said to her, but Kyle allowed herself to be pushed forward, guided by the little sailor boy. Junior got out and shoved Kyle into the back seat; then he got in after her. Jackie could see a thin trickle of blood running down from Kyle's ear.

"Glad you could make it," Jackie said, scooting against the door so she wouldn't get her Chanel stained.

Chapter Thirty-Three

Val opened his eyes and saw his grandmother leaning over him. "Is everything okay?"

"You tell me, boy."

Val peeled the cool washcloth off his forehead and looked around. "Where's Kyle?"

"She got a phone call a little bit ago from some woman. . . . Jackie, I think it was. Drove off right away to meet her."

Val sat up, then carefully got to his feet. It was nearly six P.M. What was Kyle doing running off to see Jackie? "You should have woke me up, Grace. Did something happen to Kyle's father? Did she say?"

"She didn't say and you needed your rest. You still do."

"Did she leave a number where she could be reached? She just got a cell-phone. . . ."

Grace shook her head, easing herself down into her rocking chair.

"I'm going to find her—"

"Course you are," said Grace. "See you change out

of that hospital shirt first. You don't look *anything* like a doctor, and it makes people think you stole it, like some drug addict walks into the emergency room and grabs whatever. They do that, you know."

Val watched his grandmother, taking her in—the tiny wrinkles and details of her face as she rocked back and forth, the concentration of her movements, the *fineness* of her.

"What's wrong?"

"It's just really good to see you."

"If you like seeing me so much, you could come over to visit more often."

Val smiled. "What did you think of her?"

"Who?"

"Don't tease me, Grace—the newspapers said I've got a head trauma."

Grace rocked back and forth, nodding to herself as though she was waging an argument only she could hear. "Well, she didn't tell me that smoking stogies is going to kill me—that's in her favor—and the two of us picked worms off my tomato plants while you slept, and she got right down in the dirt with me. Still . . ." She tugged at her lower lip—it was the same gesture she had made when Val had told her what had happened to Steffano, her way of struggling to understand a situation. "There's all these people keep dying around her—it's like she was born under a bad sign."

"People keep dying around me, too. Does that mean I was born under a bad sign?"

"I don't know," said Grace. "Maybe it would be better if you was—then you wouldn't be so troubled about the Jackson brothers. Don't deny it. I was there too, Valentine. I seen your face when you came back afterward, clothes soaking wet, hands shaking—"

"I did what I had to."

"I know that and I'm grateful, but *don't* pretend it didn't take something out of you. I couldn't love you like I do if it didn't tear you up inside."

Val watched her rock, remembering that night in the Glades, the darkness sticking to him as he pushed the Firebird into the water, Troy Jackson's new car bubbling its way to the bottom. He had buried his clothes in the swamp, then cleaned out Grace's cedar chest looking for some of his old pants and shirts—Val had to leave the top buttons of his jeans undone to get into them. Grace had rested peacefully against his shoulder as they zigzagged across the country on three different no-frills airlines, but he was miserable, his pants too tight to cross his legs.

"I like a bright girl and Kyle's as bright as they come," said Grace. "Tough too, but not rough—you don't find that too often. I can see why she got you going."

"I'm crazy about her, Grace."

"You told her about Junior," Grace said disapprovingly. "That's not like you at all."

"I *had* to . . . it's a long story."

She waved toward the house. "Go on. I got clothes laid out for you in the sitting room. You'd think I have nothing better to do than wash and iron for you."

Val patted his pockets.

"I took that pistola you had tucked into your belt, if that's what you're looking for." Grace took Dillinger's .32 out of the side pocket of her dress. "This thing goes off you're going to lose something important, and I'm never going to get me a great-grandchild."

Val tucked the automatic into the small of his back. "Do you still have that revolver I gave you?"

Grace patted the other pocket of her dress.

"Keep it handy. I'm not sure what's going on. If I call and tell you to get out of the house, you leave. Understand?"

"Don't you talk to me like I'm addle-brained."

"Sorry, I'm just—" Val caught the keyring she tossed over, anticipating him again.

"It's got most near a full tank," said Grace, and *don't you be changing my radio stations or I'll whup you.*"

Val embraced her and felt her heart flutter against him.

Grace's car was a 1988 green Thunderbird with a devil's head stick shift, a perfect wax job, and talk radio on every button of the radio. The car started on the first turn of the key. Val waited until he was on the freeway before calling J. Edgar's pager. The skateboarder called him back immediately.

"Dude!" erupted J. Edgar. "I read about you in the paper, 'sex and violence with an ocean view,' that's what Fox news slugged it. I call it in-*tense.* Charles Abbott III, that was one of the names I ran for you. Whoa, update the file, that puppy is snuffed. And the Jacqueline chick who was there . . . I ran her too, didn't I? Dude, working with you is like *Mission Impossible.*"

"I'm glad I'm holding your interest."

"Totally."

Val drove with one hand, his foot tapping the brakes as traffic slowed. The battery on his phone was low, and the right light was flashing. "I need you to run another name for me," he said, talking faster.

"Whip it out."

"Dekker," said Val. "First name—"

"Darryl," said J. Edgar. "Darryl Dekker, the other dead guy at the house, the one you wasted. Now you want his history for your scrapbook—lethal cool. You know, if you're into the ghouly stuff, I can get you Phil Hartman's autopsy report or Vince Foster's crime scene photos so you can see the neck wound—"

"How soon can you get me a printout on Dekker?"

"Midnight tonight—there's a twenty-four-hour Kinko's on Grand Avenue in Santa Ana. Same terms as before—"

"I remember," said Val. "There's one more search I want you to run for me."

"You keep this up, dude, you're sure to qualify for the corporate volume discount."

"I'm not sure you can pull up the information I need—"

"I told you, I can get anything. Almost anything." J. Edgar lowered his voice. "I ran your file, man. Practically baked my system."

Val heard a call-waiting beep on his phone. He let it beep.

"I saw the account number you used to run that whack Mickey Mouse infosearch," J. Edgar bragged, "that was my initial entry. Between that phony account and the stuff in the newspaper, I triangulated the data, hacked you clear back to Miami. That's as far as I could get. You got some serious black ice protecting you, man, wheels within wheels."

"I've got another call," said Val. "I'll see you tonight, J. Edgar. We can talk about that other search then." He switched to the waiting call. "Hello?"

"Val?" Kyle sounded out of breath.

"Where *are* you?" Val said. "I was worried."

"Shucks, you don't have to worry about her," said Junior. "She's in good hands."

Val almost drove off the road—finally pulled onto the shoulder of the freeway. His chest was so tight he could hardly breathe.

"I saw on TV you killed somebody last night, bare-handed and everything," said Junior. "I *told* you that you were going to develop a taste for it."

"How's your knee?" Val said, teeth clenched.

"I just got done running some wind sprints," said Junior. "I'm ready for the Olympic tryouts, but Armando, his hooter is *all* messed up. I think he wants to talk with you about that, maybe get an apology."

Val tried to think. A double-wide semi roared past, vibrating the Thunderbird, but Val hardly noticed. "Is Jackie there too?"

"The redhead? That's affirmative, good buddy. What I want to know is how a swamp dog like you manages to surround himself with such class-A, free-range pussy? Where is the justice?"

"In your back pocket."

Junior guffawed. "You're lucky in love. I'm lucky in *law*. Which one of us you think is better off?"

Jackie had somehow lured Kyle to Junior, but how had Junior gotten to Jackie? He was going to have to call Grace and tell her to get out of the house.

"What do I do, Valentine?" asked Junior. "I mean, the redhead is a royal head case, but I just know she's a raunchy ride, and now your girlfriend shows up. Kyle's a little old for my tastes, but she looks tighter than a drum. I can't decide who to bone first. I asked Armando, but he's no help. You're the heartbreaker, Val, which one of them leads off the inning?"

"Don't hurt them, Junior."

"I bet you're kicking yourself now that you didn't pull the trigger back at the hotel."

Val didn't answer.

"You and that conscience of yours—I warned you that it would get you into trouble. Now me and Armando are sitting around with your womenfolk, and you're wondering what you can do about it."

"Let them go. I'll meet you anywhere you want."

"Well, butter my biscuits, and call me Monty Hall. Let's make a deal," said Junior. "Tell me where you are, and me and Armando will pick you up, curb service. I'll let the pussy go as soon as you get into the car, word of honor."

Val laughed. He couldn't help himself, and Junior gave up and laughed along with him.

"I don't blame you for being skeptical," said Junior, "but what choice do you have? You want to hear the women squeal again?"

"You push things too far with them, you've lost any room to negotiate."

"Maybe I say the hell with negotiating and just turn them over to Armando. You and me can go back to playing fox and hounds. That what you want?"

Val sat there with the windows rolled up. Grace's car was shuddering as the traffic roared past.

"You still there?" asked Junior.

"How much time can you afford to spend looking for me?" said Val. "You're not taking care of business back in Miami. You're preoccupied, and people are noticing. You told me Amy Huckebee left with a chunk of your money. Would that have happened six months ago? When the bankers start running out on you, Junior, it's over."

"Let's cut the shit," said Junior. "What say we make

a swap in plain sight? You park your car at one end of the street; we'll park at the other. The girls will get out and start walking the same time you do—"

"I know a spot where we can make the exchange," said Val. "It's a deserted stretch of beach just south of Newport. Kyle knows where it is. Tell her I'll meet her in the Playhouse in a couple of hours."

"The Playhouse?—sounds like a strip club," said Junior. "Let's make it an hour. I wouldn't want you to stay up past your bedtime. Oh, hey partner, before I forget, you wouldn't know where Amy Huckebee is, would you? I sure would like to pay a visit to my money."

"I'm really looking forward to seeing you again, Junior."

"Don't go getting sentimental on me," said Junior. "I've been telling your new girlfriend all about you, Val. She seemed a little surprised by the things you done. I sure hope I haven't spoiled your Boy Scout image."

"Don't worry about it."

"By the way, you bring in the cops, I'll kill them both— that's a redneck promise, Valentine, I'll kill them and I won't spend a day in jail. Not a fucking day. I got too much to trade. I held back my main connection in Bogotá from Bernard, and there's a federal prosecutor interested in what I know about *official* corruption in Miami. These Feds are really something. You could kill a Kennedy and walk if you had the goods to trade to those fellahs."

"No cops," Val agreed. "I want you and Armando all to myself."

"That's my guy."

Val switched off the phone. "That's my guy"—that was exactly what Dillinger had said to him in the hospital.

Chapter Thirty-Four

Val heard cursing and peeked over the boulder. Junior was sliding down the steep path to the beach, holding on to Kyle, grunting with every step. Val smiled, imagining the man's right knee the size of a rotten grapefruit. Then Junior jerked on Kyle's ponytail to maintain his balance, and Val stopped smiling. Jackie followed behind, walking gingerly, barefoot, holding her high heels in one hand while Armando brought up the rear.

It was only fifteen minutes ago that Val had arrived on the beach. The surfers packing their boards up the path eyed him as they passed. He was hiding thirty or forty yards offshore now, braced in the crevice that led to the Playhouse, watching the four of them struggle down the slope. Their faces were edged with red in the last of the sunset, molten figures crossing a molten landscape.

"Valentine?" Junior limped out onto the sand, half-dragging Kyle as he looked around. "Come on out, you ain't fooling anybody!" He released Kyle, pulled a .45 out of his jacket, and scanned the driftwood piled along the tideline. He was searching the shore for any sign of Val, giving only cursory attention to the rocks. It was readily apparent that the path was the only way into or out of the cove, and from the beach the breakwater appeared solid, its honeycomb of tunnels hidden from view. Val had been deceived the first time Kyle brought him here, too.

Armando pushed Jackie and she fell in a tangle of arms and legs, scrambled up, yelling at him. Armando ignored her, looking out to the rocks, then up to the top of the bluff.

Kyle stepped onto the edge of the breakwater, the wind whipping her hair—a storm was coming in, and the rocks were slick with spray. It wasn't cold, but she was shivering. Val hadn't counted on the storm when he told Junior to meet him here.

"Valentine!" Junior shouted. "You don't show yourself, I'm going to start without you."

Val stood up, using an outcropping of rock for protection.

"What are you doing out *there?*" said Junior. "You put yourself in a box, Valentine. China is thataway, but I don't think you want to make that swim."

"I'm cozy out here, but I don't think you would do too well on these wet rocks with that bum knee of yours," said Val. "It's getting dark. If you want me, you let them go."

Kyle stepped farther out onto the breakwater.

Armando walked toward Junior, an apparition of childhood innocence in his snow-white sailor suit, a deadly mirage. Jackie came after him, threw a chunk of driftwood at him, which bounced off his back. He chased her, tripped her onto the soft sand, and she screamed, trying to brush off her dress.

Junior turned around and saw Armando kicking sand on Jackie. "Armando! Quit fooling around!"

"He's not listening, Junior. You better send him back to obedience school," said Val.

"Don't I know it," Junior said wearily. "He ain't been right since you messed his face up. Maybe after he takes care of you, he'll get back to his normal self."

"Normal?" Val laughed. "Let the women go, Junior. When they get halfway up the trail, I'll start walking toward you. Let them go and you can take me alive. That's what you really want, isn't it?"

"Gosh, ain't you the hero." Junior sneered. "Where was you when your buddy Steffano was getting sliced and diced?"

"I was with you, Junior. Just like now."

Kyle was looking frantically up and down the beach. Maybe she thought he had called the police. But there was no one in sight, no one who could do her any good, just Armando and Jackie throwing seaweed at each other, their voices shrill.

Junior tapped the .45 against the side of his head, finally nodded. "Let's do it, Val. This cat-and-mouse shit gets old fast. The girls walk and you get a first-class ride back home on Air Junior. Heck, if you ask him nice, maybe Armando will serve you some of them honey-roasted peanuts." He looked at Kyle and jerked a thumb toward the trail. "Get out of here. Jackie, you can go too. But if you ever want the grand tour of Miami, you give me a call." He grinned. "I *still* want to find out if you're a real redhead."

Armando spit at Jackie, then turned his back on her. Jackie followed him, whacked him across the head with her spike heel, flailing away while Armando tried to protect himself.

"Jackie, *no!*" Val shouted. "Kyle, get out of here!"

Kyle sprinted toward Val, nimbly leaping from stone to stone while he yelled at her to turn back. She slipped once, banged her shoulder, and raced forward.

"Son of a bitch!" said Junior, shooting at Kyle. The shots were echoed by a few more—from Val, who fired back at him. The two of them were blazing away at each other, but the angle was bad for both, and the footing was unstable. Shadows didn't help either. They missed. Val squeezed off another round as Kyle jumped down beside him, wide-eyed.

Jackie ignored the gunshots, advancing on Armando and screaming at him. She lifted her shoe high, ready to drive the heel through his eye, but his hand suddenly flicked out, barely touching her. It looked more like a caress than a blow.

"Why didn't you leave?" Val asked Kyle. He fired again at Junior. The beach was a nest of shadows now. "You could have gotten away. You both could—"

Kyle held on to him, trying to catch her breath.

Val tried to remember how many shots he had taken. Dillinger's .32 had a nine-round clip and one in the chamber.

"I was afraid," said Kyle, her teeth chattering. "The things Junior said he was going to do to us. God, Val, I had . . . no idea. . . ."

"It's okay." Val squinted at the beach. "Do you see Jackie?"

"What do we do now?" said Kyle.

"Jackie?" Val heard a sizzle and ducked as a bright light arced through the air. A highway flare sputtered on the rocks. Junior must have raided the emergency kit of his car. A second flare spun toward them, landed a few feet away, spotlighting them.

"Circle around from that side, Armando!" called Junior. "Dammit, Armando, quit fucking around and *help* me!"

Jackie's neck felt warm where Armando had touched her. Her high-heel pump dropped from her grasp of its own accord—not that it mattered. Armando was racing out onto the rocks toward Junior, not even looking back at her. God, the expression on the little creep's face when she whacked him with her shoe, that was priceless. Well, they were welcome to each other, all of them. Jackie was going to get out of here right now. Right this minute. Her knees wobbled, the strength gushing out of her as she sank onto the moist sand, flinching at the gritty feel of it. Oh well, she could always get the Chanel cleaned. She could buy another one, as many suits as she wanted.

"You must have a plan," said Kyle, still clinging to him. "I *know* you would never give yourself up to those two."

"I was going to wait until you and Jackie were safe, then duck into the tunnels." Val punched 911 on his cellphone, keeping low, the flare giving away their position. "Even if they found the right tunnel, I didn't think they would follow me down there. Junior's claustrophobic." The phone beeped again, useless, the battery dead. He could see a flash of the white sailor suit out of the corner of his eye, but he couldn't get a clear shot. He squinted, shading his eyes from the flare, looking for Jackie.

"We can't hide in the Grottos," said Kyle. "The storm—"

"I can't see Jackie. The beach is too dark . . ."

"The tunnels will be flooded," said Kyle.

"We can't stay here." Val heard Junior scuttling over the rocks, huffing and puffing. He stood up, fired, and ducked back down. Junior yelped, but Val wasn't sure if he had hit him or if it was just his knee going out. He handed Kyle a small flashlight. "Go on, I'll follow you."

Kyle looked at him in the sputtering light from the flare, then gave him a quick kiss and slid down into the crevice. Val was right behind her.

"Where did they go?" Junior called. "Armando, be careful!"

They had gone maybe twenty feet when Val heard someone drop down into the crevice. Kyle switched off the flashlight. The two of them hurried through the darkness.

"Armando! You get back up here now! Armando!"

Armando must have lit a flare. Val heard the hissing behind him as Kyle tugged him along. The tunnels were damper than the last time they had been here, whole sections awash, soaking them as they bellied forward. Armando didn't know the tunnels, but he was smaller than Val, more agile. He could keep up as long as he followed the faint sounds of their movements against the rocks.

"Armando, you get back up here!" Junior tracked the light of the flare shining up between the gaps in the rocks. "You got nothing to prove!"

Val stumbled out of the passageway and into a pool of icy water. The pistol slipped out of his hand. He bent forward, shivering as he felt around for the gun. "Kyle?" A pencil of light shone in his eyes, blinding him.

Kyle pulled him to his feet. "We've got to get *higher*. The tide is coming in—"

"I need my gun," said Val, still feeling around with his hands. A crushed beer can fooled him for an instant. He tossed it aside and kept searching. Her flashlight whipped around the room, and he saw graffiti on the walls and wine bottles canted against the rocks, dripping with colored wax.

"We have to *go*," said Kyle as the incoming waves shook the room, the walls streaming water now. She grabbed Val's hand and led him to an opening high up on one wall.

"It's too *small*," said Val, as she climbed in. "We didn't come that way last time. There must be another—"

"The other passage is already under water." Kyle switched off the light.

In the darkness Val could hear the faint hissing of Armando's highway flare, closer now. Kyle tugged harder on him, and Val followed, scraping against barnacles as he shimmied into the tunnel. The storm was rolling in so fast he could hear the gigantic slabs of rock shift on the seabed grinding against each other. He was about ten feet into the tunnel when a light flashed in the Playhouse and then went out. Val heard Armando splashing around below, waited for him to light another flare, but there was only darkness. He heard Armando cursing as he waded around, bumping into walls, slipping on the mossy floor.

"Junior!" shouted Armando, the sound echoing off the rocks. "Junior!"

Jackie heard Armando screaming, the wind carrying his fear to her. It sounded as if he was calling out from inside a bottle. Jackie smiled. She had tried to stand up

a few minutes ago, but her legs weren't working so well.
She must have cut herself because there was all this blood
leaking down her neck, soaking her beautiful dress. She
was going to ask Kilo to go shopping with her tomorrow.
They'd find the perfect outfit.

Jackie looked up at the sky. She wished there were
some stars out. A star to wish on—that would be just the
thing. Not that she needed any more wishes. She had limos
and private jets on call, sales clerks jumping—Jackie was
an Abbott now. From the moment she walked into that
grand house she knew that she belonged there. Jacqueline
Abbott. She was never going to give that up. Never. She
started crawling. Armando was crying out for Junior again.
Forget it, sailor boy, you're never getting out of the bot-
tle. The wind blew a cool spray across her skin as she
slowly made her way across the sand. It felt like she was
being kissed by the ocean, kissed by the deep, blue sea.

"This is the wrong tunnel," Kyle whispered.

"Junior!" screamed Armando. "I am in *hell*, Junior!"

"This way is blocked," said Kyle. "We have to go
back down."

Val eased himself backward, glad now for the storm
raging around them. Armando wouldn't be able to hear
him coming. He felt his feet dangling in space and gently lowered himself out of the tunnel as Armando thrashed
around nearby. There was a hissing high overhead, and a
faint light seeped into the room from a crevice in the ceiling. Val pressed himself into the shadows.

"Junior!" Armando threw his head up toward the light.
"I am here!"

"Armando!" Junior sounded as desperate as Armando.
"Can you see me?"

"Junior!" Armando looked up to the light, the gold buttons on his sailor suit gleaming. The water was waist-high around him, gushing in through the rocks. He held his hands up to the light, arms outstretched. "Junior, por favor!"

"You get out of there *now*!" Junior yelled. He must have dropped the flare into the crevice because Val heard it clatter down the rocks, sputtering and smoking before it got lodged halfway down. The Playhouse was brighter.

Armando saw Val. He blinked, grateful in that instant to have some company in that little room under the sea, then his relief turned into something else, his eyes red in the glow. He slogged through the water toward Val.

Val stayed where he was, watching Armando getting closer. He had solid footing here. Out of the corner of his eye he saw Kyle work her way out of the tunnel.

"Armando!" called Junior. "I can't stay here much longer!"

"I have him, Junior!"

"Fuck that!" shouted Junior. "Get out!"

"Val," Kyle said quietly, inclining her head to an outcropping of rock near the tunnel they had just left. "The passage we want is over *there*."

"Go ahead," said Val, keeping his eyes on Armando. "Go *on*, I'll be right there."

Armando circled in, the water lapping at his chest.

Kyle slipped and fell back into the water. Val glanced over as she stood up, pushing the hair out of her face. He cried out, scrambled away, clutching at his side. In the few seconds he had been distracted, Armando had stabbed him. Val gingerly touched his ribs, blood clouding the water around him.

"Val, *hurry*," said Kyle.

"Yes, Val," said Armando, closing in, *"hurry."*

Val cocked his fists as he edged closer to Kyle, trying not to slip.

"Do not go, Valentine," teased Armando. "Stay with me."

Val punched Armando in the face as the smaller man lunged at him. Armando moaned, and the pain in his eyes changed to pleasure. Val looked down. There was a long slash in his shirt, a dark stain seeping down his chest. A new wound. He still didn't see what Armando was using to cut him.

Armando rushed in, but Val hit him again, caught him square in the jaw and knocked him backwards. Armando surfaced and shook his head. Val had another new cut, a deep slice in his left shoulder. Armando's eyes were bright in the glow of the hissing flare.

Val's hands were so cold that he couldn't feel his fingers, and his side was aching worse now. He kept turning as Armando circled in. The kid was getting closer all the time, unafraid of Val's fists. Val grabbed a wine bottle, held it by the neck, wax flaking off as he brandished it.

"Thank you for your kind offer, Valentine," cooed Armando, "but I am too young to drink." Val's blood had turned his white jacket pink. The flare sizzled in the rocks above them and went out. The Playhouse was in utter darkness again.

"Val!" called Kyle.

Val backed against the wall, waiting for Armando to rush him in that long night.

"Val! Close your eyes!"

There was a flash of light. Val opened his eyes, saw Armando right in front of him, blinded, caught in the beam of Kyle's flashlight. Val swung the wine bottle down against Armando's head as hard as he could, hitting him again and again, swinging wildly as Armando howled and staggered, the sound of his outcry echoing in that tomb of rock.

"Armando!" Junior bellowed from above them. You would have thought he was the one who had taken the blows.

Kyle grabbed Val on the shoulder, sending a shock of pain through him. She turned the light toward the ceiling and dragged him up toward the opening in the rocks.

"Valentine?" called Armando. There was no challenge in his voice anymore. No bravado.

Kyle flicked off the flashlight as they crawled into the passage, the stone around them sweating, slick with moisture.

Armando splashed around in the darkness, trying to find the entrance. "Valentine!" His voice echoed over the sound of rushing water. He was speaking Spanish now, gasping, speaking too fast for Val to understand everything he said. It sounded as if he was making a confession, but he never used the words yo siento, never said he was sorry. It was more like Armando was trying to explain something to a thick-headed God who didn't understand the ways of the world.

Kyle stopped.

"Please don't say you took the wrong tunnel again," said Val.

Armando shrieked—a long drawn-out wail that stopped abruptly.

Kyle turned on the flashlight—Val couldn't see anything but the corona of light around her body. "The tunnel splits," she said. "I'm deciding which is the right way."

Val felt something brush against his foot and he jerked,

thinking it was Armando. It was worse. It was water. "Kyle, *make* a decision."

Kyle crawled to the left and he followed, the storm drowning out all conversation. Two more times he felt the water lap at his feet as they scrambled on, coral tearing at their hands and knees. Val didn't know how long they were at it—there was no time to think of anything but the water behind them. It seemed like hours when Kyle suddenly disappeared. He heard a roaring and felt the wind on his face. The wind on his face!

Kyle helped him out of the tunnel and onto the rocks. The two of them were soaked, exhausted, stumbling toward the shore. Val's left arm had no feeling in it.

"Where's Armando?" called Junior.

Val took shelter behind the rocks and pulled Kyle down beside him. The wind had blown the clouds away from the moon. He could see Junior sitting on the steps at the very bottom of the path, the .45 loose in his grip.

"Where *is* he, Valentine?"

The height of the storm had passed, but waves still crashed over the breakwater, white foam boiling around their legs. "He's dead," Val said, straining to make himself heard. His lungs felt like they were filled with broken glass.

Junior looked out to sea. "I knew it." He sagged against the steps, shaking his head.

"Put the gun down," said Val.

Junior peered at him. "Armando must have hurt you good before he died. I watched you walking, and you moved like a crab. You couldn't even stand up without that bitch's help."

"What are you doing sitting down, Junior? Can't you move?"

"I bet Armando sliced you like a po-boy sandwich. I bet he cut you to the bone." Junior started coughing. He couldn't seem to stop.

"There's a storm drain at the far end of the cove that leads under the highway," Kyle said to Val. "If Junior is really immobilized, we can escape that way."

Val stepped away from the rocks. Kyle tried to stop him, but he shook her off. "That gun looks heavy, Junior. You should put it down—give yourself a rest."

Junior flicked the gun toward him, then let it drop. "I don't feel so good."

"Me neither."

"What are we doing here, you and me? We should be home." Junior was coughing again. "There's plenty of other folks I'd rather kill than you."

"Thanks."

Junior stared at the tide rolling over the breakwater. "I can't get my mind around the idea that he's really dead. I expect him to show up with some new funny-ass outfit, rings on his fingers, bells on his toes. . . ."

"You're getting sentimental, Junior. I must have shot you in the heart."

Junior spit and wiped his mouth. "Come closer, you can see for yourself." He tried to lift the gun but couldn't keep it up.

"Let's go," Val said to Kyle. They kept low, stayed in the rocks, resting when Val needed to. The wind had slacked off now. He turned around once and saw Junior slowly making his way up the trail. When they were almost to the storm drain, they found Jackie lying in the sand, one arm outstretched, her hair plastered across her face.

Jackie opened her eyes as they knelt beside her.

"Kyle. . . ." She tried to laugh. "I should have known you would get away." Her eyelids fluttered as Kyle smoothed her hair away from her bone-white cheeks. "That feels nice." The sand was black with blood.

"Shhh," said Kyle.

"Such a good touch, . . ." Jackie said softly.

Val took Jackie's hand. His hand was cold, but hers was colder still. "You're going to be all right."

"What do you know?" whispered Jackie.

Epilogue

␣

The roadside altar was made from glass pop-bottles, green and red and yellow, hundreds of bottles fused together with a propane torch. The altar sparkled in the Mexican sun like an exploded rainbow. A battered tinplate image of Our Lady of Guadalupe, her sad face pitted by wind-blown sand, looked down on the guttered candles dotting the bottles, looked down on the slips of paper and coins stuffed inside—prayers for full bellies and healthy children, prayers for love and safe passage, prayers for the dead. Val stood there in silence, heat waves shimmering in the still air, stood there waiting, finally pushed a five-dollar bill into the mouth of a 7Up bottle and got back into the Jeep.

He had spent the last six hours driving north from Cabo San Lucas on Highway 1, a crumbling two-lane blacktop that ran the length of the Baja peninsula, the Pacific on one side, the Gulf of California on the other. The surrounding sea teemed with orcas and whales and black marlin, shrimp and newborn turtles, but the land was a sun-blasted volcanic finger eight hundred miles long, desolate and forlorn—lizard country.

Two kilometers past the altar, Val took an unmarked cutoff, fishtailing across the dusty gravel before gaining control. A half hour later, the Jeep rounded a bend, hit a washed-out arroyo, and went into a skid, the 4 x 4 almost turning over before finally coming to a halt. Dust billowed through the open windows. Val wiped off his sunglasses, took a long drink of water, and got out to make sure he hadn't broken an axle. There were no other dust clouds on the road, not a bird or a cloud in the immense blue sky. He should be close to Kyle's base camp, at least if he was reading her directions accurately. It had been two months since he had last seen her, two months since their game of hide'n'seek in the Grottos. She had called him almost every day when he was in the hospital, but the connection was often erratic, their voices crackling with the distance.

It took another hour for Val to reach the bay where Kyle's camp was located. It was almost dusk now. The Gulf stretching out before him, Val could see five Quonset huts far down the beach and a sleek motor yacht moored offshore. He stayed where he was, resisted heading toward those distant lights for as long as possible, driving on only when the orange-red sun dipped into the Pacific, turning the sea to fire.

The Quonsets were new, their corrugated aluminum still shiny, air conditioners humming in the windows. Somewhere a generator chugged away. Before Val had even turned the motor off, a man walked out of the nearest hut, a stocky Mexican in baggy jeans and a Mickey Mouse T-shirt.

"This area is posted, señor." He kept one hand in his pocket.

"I saw the signs, amigo," said Val, getting out. "I'm expected."

"Val?"

He heard her before he saw her, heard the joy in her voice. Barefoot, Kyle stood in the doorway of the hut, her tan stark against the white shorts and polo shirt, her hair in a loose braid, her smile stretched wide. He was moving toward her before he realized it, drawn to her across the sand, hurrying now. They embraced and she was as warm and clean and sinewy as he remembered but darker now after two months in the sun, darker even than he was.

"I've *missed* you," she said, her breath hot against his throat. Then she turned to the man in the Mickey Mouse T-shirt. "Felix, this is Valentine, the one I told you about." Val and Felix exchanged nods. She waited until Felix went back into the hut before breaking their embrace, leading him to the water's edge. The sun was soft on her face. "This is just so perfect. I'm all caught up with work, so I can take the next couple of days off, and we can get to know each other all over again."

Val kicked off his sandals. "I've already made a start."

Kyle smiled, then cocked her head.

Val indicated the Quonset huts with a sweep of his hand. "This is quite an upgrade from the few tents on the beach you told me about."

"We can camp out, if you prefer?" Kyle teased as they walked along the beach. "How is your grandmother? I've thought about her a great deal."

"Grace is back in Florida. She's living deeper in the Glades now, a long airboat ride from the nearest road. She's as safe there as any place."

"I thought Junior was taken care of," said Kyle. "I gave a deposition—"

Val shook his head. "Junior had too much information to trade, just like he said. He's in a witness protection program, looking at three or four years of trial appearances. Our depositions are just insurance to make sure he cooperates."

Kyle kissed him. "You did what you could." She pulled him toward a small boat halfway on the sand. "Come on, I have to do my evening survey, and I'm not about to let you out of my sight again."

"I was going to clean up first. It was a long drive—"

"I like you a little dirty," said Kyle, her eyes bright. "We can take a bath together when we get back." She dragged the boat into the water before he could respond. The boat needed painting, but the outboard motor was new, a high-tech, damped thirty-horse with minimal sound and vibration. Val sat beside her while she took the wheel—it seemed like she was always driving him someplace. "These past months have been difficult," she said over the hum of the engine, guiding the boat out into the bay. "Chuck made me executor of his estate. I didn't want the distraction, but he's just signed off on life—"

"I've been to see him."

"When was that?"

"Yesterday. Just before I went to the airport. He didn't even recognize me at first. His nurse wouldn't let me stay too long, and I don't blame her."

"He's on antidepressants, but they don't seem to be doing any good," said Kyle. The wind picked up as the boat rode over the swells. She stretched out her long brown legs. "You don't have to go back any time soon, do you? I intend to seduce you totally."

Val held her gaze. "Mission accomplished."

They were silent now, awkward with the intimacy after so many weeks apart. They settled for holding hands as they passed beyond the arms of the bay, the salt spray drifting over them like a veil.

"A pod of gray whales comes in just after sunset to feed—you can sometimes see a circular ripple just before they breach." Kyle scanned the water as she steered. "There's a pair of binoculars in the compartment on your left."

"That's quite a chunk of teak and mahogany," said Val, nodding at the motor yacht anchored offshore. It must have been at least a ninety-footer. "Looks like something God would own if he had the cash flow."

"It's a research vessel. The Baja Marine Institute is leasing it."

"You *are* the Baja Marine Institute."

Kyle turned the boat into the current. "Have you been checking up on me, officer?"

Val didn't answer.

Kyle headed farther out, steering with one hand, the other resting on Val's arm. The water glowed with a faint phosphorescence. Jellyfish floated around them for miles, a sea of stinging tentacles. She plowed right through them, leaving iridescent ripples in their wake.

"It's beautiful out here," said Val.

"I think so too. Not everyone appreciates it," said Kyle, slowing the engine, so they could watch the shimmering jellyfish. "I've waited so long to share this with someone, year after year. You have no idea how lonely I've been. I had almost given up." She smiled. "Then I met you."

"Did you ever take Jackie out here? Did you ever share it with her?"

Kyle looked as if he had slapped her. "I don't . . . understand."

"Sure you do." The wind was picking up, and the jellyfish rolling on the choppy surface were thinning out now. "When we found Jackie on the beach, the way she spoke to you . . . there was such tenderness in her voice. I had never heard her talk like that to anyone, not even Kilo."

"She was *dying*, Val."

"I know."

"I'm afraid you've lost me."

"I asked you once if you knew your mother was dying. You said you didn't. Dr. Williamson wouldn't talk to me, but I know a computer kid, a skateboarder . . . he can pull up almost *anything*. You signed for your mother's prescriptions twice. Tincture of morphine is a class-A narcotic, Kyle. You *must* have known she was very sick."

Kyle shook her head. "My mother is dead, and you're violating her privacy."

"They're all dead—your mother, Kilo, Dekker, Jackie. Only you and Chuck are left."

"And you." Kyle watched the water, the Gulf the color of mulled wine now. "You're still alive, thanks to me. You would have drowned in the Grottos if I hadn't saved you."

"You saved me. I admit it."

"Well, don't you think you owe me the benefit of the doubt?"

"I owe you more than that, but it wasn't enough to stop me once I got started," said Val. "I had the skateboarder run a background check on all of you, but the problem with emptying a database is that you get too much information, too many details. I missed some things the first time through. Cross-checking is the only way to make any sense of it. If I hadn't been stuck in the hospital with nothing else to do, I might never have taken the trouble."

"Most people in the hospital just lie around watching television and waiting for their sponge bath, but not you, Val." Kyle smiled. "You have a very active mind—no wonder I was so attracted to you." She looked peaceful now, eyes half closed as the two of them rocked gently on the tide. He remembered swimming with her off the breakwater, seeing her rising slowly to the surface, remembered the saltiness of her kiss. "Don't look so sad," she said.

"It *is* sad."

"We're together, that's all that matters." Her bare leg brushed against him, and he felt the same electricity he had that first morning on the stairs. Her eyes caught the light. "You *see*, nothing has changed. Not between us."

Val shook his head, startled by the effect she still had on him. He was tempted to keep quiet, to let things be, but he couldn't do it. "Jackie told the cops that she left Bakersfield because Dekker was stalking her, but when she disappeared, he didn't follow her or try to find her. Dekker *stayed* in Bakersfield." He thought he heard Kyle sigh, but her face was turned away from him. "Then, a couple of months before your mother was killed, almost a *year* after Jackie left town, Dekker got a collect call and dropped everything. He didn't even pick up his paycheck."

"This is *so* unnecessary. Look around you, Val, the whole world is right here." She turned to him. "*I'm* here."

Val looked into Kyle's eyes and he saw only himself. "That collect call to Dekker was made from a payphone in Cabo San Lucas. You were checked in at the Hotel Finisterra when that call was made. It's on your Visa card. You were a regular there. Hot showers and cool sheets must have been pretty inviting after a few weeks living in a tent on the beach. I was at the hotel today."

"The Finisterra has the best view in Cabo." Kyle brushed his cheek with her fingers. "We can check in tomorrow if you like, spend the whole week—"

"You and Jackie acted like you met each other for the first time at your mother's birthday party," said Val, "but the manager at the Finisterra remembers seeing you and her together months before that. He said he could never forget Jackie's hair. He called her the fireball."

Kyle turned her face into the wind, loose strands of hair dancing around her calm expression as she watched the water. "The fireball . . . Jackie would have liked that." She pushed back her hair, annoyed. "I told her to wait until she got back to the States to call Dekker. I *told* her, but Jackie, she did what she wanted."

Val felt like he was buried under a mountain of rocks and every word that she spoke added another stone to the pile.

"The first time I saw Jackie, she was in the Finisterra bar and the manager was informing her that the gold card she was using had been reported stolen. He was quite loud, threatening to call the police, but she never flinched. She just kept flirting with him. I intervened—as you said, they know me there. Jackie and I adjourned to the patio and got to talking, and there was an immediacy, a certain . . . rapport." She looked at him. "That happens sometimes, doesn't it?"

"Yeah, it does."

Kyle leaned forward, staring at the surface of the water. "Jackie and I stayed up all night drinking tequila, talking about what it would take to make our lives perfect. It was more of an intellectual exercise for me, at least at the beginning, until Jackie mentioned a man she knew who would do anything for her. A lot of men will tell you they'll do anything for you, but she said Dekker . . . he really meant it." She jabbed a finger at the water. "There, Val!"

Forty yards away the sea burst into a huge plume that became a gray whale, then another and another, the sea erupting with whales, drenching Val and Kyle with spray. Val counted at least eleven or twelve of them breaching, adults and calves cavorting in the twilight. Their boat rocked wildly, water slopping over the sides, while he hung on, too overwhelmed to be frightened. The whales were gone as quickly as they had arrived, the waves returning to their choppy regularity. The night was empty without them.

"They are magnificent, aren't they?" Kyle wiped her face, then wrung out her hair with both hands. "Such a vast and quiet intelligence. They dwarf us in every conceivable way. We're such small and fragile creatures. . . . Our petty concerns are nothing to them."

"Petty concerns?" snapped Val. "You had your mother killed. Move over. I'll steer."

"My mother was dying," Kyle said, exasperated, as Val took the wheel. "This whole situation is Chuck's fault anyway. The first time Gwen had cancer she tried to get him to include me in his will, but all she got was airy promises. Chuck didn't have a backbone; he had a notochord, *except* for when it came to his trust fund. He didn't know how to use a microwave or open the hood of his car, but he could tell you the closing price of a thirty-year T-bill down to three decimal points."

Val made a slow turn, heading back to shore.

"There's no need to go back—we have plenty of time."

Kyle's fingers drummed on the side of the boat. "Without Gwen to fend him off, Kilo would have gone through Chuck's fortune and have *nothing* to show for it. I'm doing important work here, and I saw no reason to allow an accident of birth to destroy it. I have a responsibility to science—"

"First Gwen, then Kilo—what were you going to do about Dekker when he was finished? Or Jackie? Where were you going to stop?"

"Gwen and Kilo would have been quite enough," said Kyle. "I'm the only family Chuck has left now."

"Do you have any idea how you sound?"

"This display of outrage is a bit disingenuous," said Kyle. "Your friend Junior told me all about you. You're the *last* person who should be acting morally superior. You're just angry that you were fooled. It's all right when *you're* deceitful, of course—that's different." She leaned back, pillowed her head in her hands, enjoying the ride. "I don't want to argue. People like us, we're above the restrictions most people live by. Don't try to pretend there's not a part of you that approves of what I've done."

Val gave the engine full throttle now, the boat skipping over the waves.

She took his arm, dug in her nails until he twisted away from her. "That day we were snorkeling and I brought up the sea urchin . . . I saw your face when I scooped out the eggs, Val. You hesitated for a moment—the urchin was still alive—you hesitated, then gobbled my fingers clean. You're *just* like I am."

"I can imagine you and Jackie sitting out on the patio in Cabo, basking in your ruthlessness, your willingness to do whatever it takes. 'Just Do It'—that was Kilo's motto too. I *hate* that phrase—they sell gym shoes with that slogan, Kyle, it's not a philosophy of life." Val could see a glimmer of light ahead. He steered toward it. "Jackie marrying Kilo, I bet *that* never came up out on the patio."

"I had promised Jackie a million dollars for her help. She just had to wait until Kilo was dead. Instead . . . I have to give her credit. That was a bold move." Kyle caressed the back of his neck. "You didn't come all the way to Baja just to talk with a hotel manager. You knew before you got there what he would say. You wanted to see me again."

"I wanted to be wrong."

Kyle kissed the side of his jaw. "Let's save the lies for what we tell the rest of the world. I'm *glad* you know what I did. This little secret of ours—it's brought us closer together."

"Our little secret? Do we get merit badges and a decoder ring, too?"

"Why are you so sad?" She tried to stroke the pain out of his face. "Don't waste your sympathy on the dead. My mother was the only one worthy of grief, and there was nothing anyone could do to save her."

"Why me, Kyle? Why did you get me involved in this?"

"Is that what's really bothering you?" Kyle smiled. "I was attracted to you from the moment I saw you—I never expected to fall in love with you, though."

"Were you worried about Jackie? She had Dekker—"

"I love you, Val."

"I heard you the first time." Val drove the boat up onto the shore, scrambled out. His Jeep was just down the beach.

"Do *not* do this to me," said Kyle, reaching for him. "Do you really think it was all *my* idea? Do you think I could have had my mother killed unless she was part of the decision? Gwen knew she was terminal. Do you think she could have tolerated Kilo getting everything? *Do* you?"

Val slowed his steps in front of the Jeep, uncertain now.

"Cancer is a terrible way to die, slow and painful. My mother died quickly, and she knew she was dying for *me*. It wasn't murder. It was a mercy killing."

"I saw the crime scene. Your mother *fought*. Dekker's blood was all over the—"

"She knew."

"Gwen took the stairs two at a time trying to get away from Dekker," said Val. "She snapped some of the banister spindles in her haste. She didn't want to die, Kyle. You wanted her dead." He stalked down the beach.

"Val! Don't you *dare* walk away from me! If you want to blame someone, blame Kilo," she protested, running to catch up. "None of this would have happened if he hadn't gone along with Jackie, if he hadn't jumped at the chance. He had talked about killing Gwen since he was fourteen. . . ." She put her arms around him, holding him tight, sobbing.

He held on to her now, not resisting, not wanting the moment to end. He knew that once he let go he was never going to hold her again. "I had *so* many plans for us," he whispered, as though someone might overhear. "All the things I thought were out of reach. You'd laugh if I told you what I wanted for us." He inhaled the fragrance of her hair, her skin, wanting to remember her scent, to lock it away in his heart.

"You win." Kyle punched him lightly in the chest. "Look, I'm crying. You broke my heart—are you satisfied? You win, can we stop now?"

Val pulled away from her. "Do I look like a winner to you? Look again. We *all* lost, every one of us. Jackie and Kilo, Dekker . . . no one got what they wanted. Except for you, Kyle. You wanted Chuck's money, and you got it. Congratulations."

"I want you too, Val."

Val threw open the door to the Jeep, almost tore it off the hinges.

"Why are you in such a hurry?" said Kyle. "What are you afraid of?"

Val turned the ignition, revved the engine, trying to drown her out.

"Leaving isn't going to bring anyone back," Kyle shouted. "They're all just as dead, whether you stay or not."

She was right, as usual—the dead *were* past saving and the world was born in blood. Yeah, and he and Kyle loved each other, too, but it wasn't enough. Val shoved the Jeep into gear. He wanted to floor it, race off, but he drove away slowly, lingering, unable to make a clean break. For an instant he glimpsed her in the rearview mirror, her tears running red in the glow of the taillights.

ROBERT FERRIGNO is the author of four previous novels, *The Horse Latitudes*, *The Cheshire Moon*, *Dead Man's Dance*, and *Dead Silent*. He lives in the Pacific northwest.

PRAISE FOR *HEARTBREAKER* AND ROBERT FERRIGNO

"A hard-swinging Southern California writer. . . . Ferrigno has a gift for creating confrontations of high impact, and his dialogue bites hard. . . . Like other inheritors of the Hammett-Chandler-Ross McDonald private-eye tradition, Ferrigno balances the tough doings with a strong sense of moral outrage and compassion."

—*Los Angeles Times Book Review*

"Witty, dark, and enticingly clever. . . . Mr. Ferrigno has captured that unique brand of So-Cal tropical sociopathy."

—*Dallas Morning News*

"His best yet."   —*Seattle Times*

"Ferrigno can make you afraid, he can make you laugh, and he can keep you turning the pages."

—*Washington Post Book World*

"The Southern California atmospherics and razor-sharp dialogue are first-rate. . . . The interplay of comedy and extreme violence keeps HEARTBREAKER humming along."

—*New York Times* Summer Reading Guide

"HEARTBREAKER is Ferrigno's best yet . . . a taut page-turner that is destined for the shelf with the rest of the noir classics." —Michael Connelly, author of *Void Moon*

more . . .